A VAMPIRE FAIRY TALE

Melissa Hansen

iUniverse, Inc.
Bloomington

TOUCH

This is a work of fiction. All of the characters, names, incidents, organizations, and dialogue in this novel are either the products of the author's imagination or are used fictitiously.

iUniverse books may be ordered through booksellers or by contacting:

iUniverse
1663 Liberty Drive
Bloomington, IN 47403
www.iuniverse.com
1-800-Authors (1-800-288-4677)

ISBN: 978-1-4759-9108-6 (sc)
ISBN: 978-1-4759-9110-9 (hc)
ISBN: 978-1-4759-9109-3 (e)

Library of Congress Control Number: 2013908751

Printed in the United States of America

iUniverse rev. date: 6/11/2013

For My Muse
Venilla

And

For My Mother
Gayle

Thank you both for your endless laughter.

May we hold on tight and scream together as
we ride this crazy thing called life…

1. Time

Once upon a time the world was alive. I could remember the feeling of the wind as it tickled my skin and the tender warmth of the Florida sun as it blanketed my body in rays of light. I had nearly forgotten those feelings—except for when I returned to them. Only then did I remember what it was like to live again.

Hiding in the shadows listening to the Perish Key cicadas as they hissed their strange intermittent lullaby invigorated me with a newfound exhilaration. There was nothing quite like the thrill of the hunt; watching and waiting for that one quintessential moment. It was the moment when my instincts dominated my ethics and my darkest desires felt free to emerge.

Beams of sunlight pierced through the verdant canopy above me showering the vegetation in rays of pure light. I could no longer appreciate the splendor of the sun. Ever since I changed—became a vampire, the sun was an insurmountable adversary, its beauty made ugly by its capacity to eradicate me with the blaze of its burn.

"Oh the sun," I sighed shading my eyes from its harsh brightness. It was still difficult getting accustomed to my new self: the keenness of my heightened vision and the absolute vulnerability of my corpse-like skin. But there were many advantages too. I found pleasure in this life's little details; the thrill of the hunt, the heightened speed at which I could move and the ease with which I could use my abilities.

I leapt gingerly through the woods when suddenly I was distracted by a rustling in the distance. I froze. My eyes widened like saucers. This was the moment I had been waiting for. It was her and she was approaching. My skin shivered with an electric excitement. Her tiny footfalls were like the tender sound of rain upon rose petals. I licked my lips and grinned. It was time. I sped through the pines with the swiftness of a rocket in an effort to catch up to her.

And then she stopped. I stopped too—dead in my tracks.

I swept my long blonde hair out of my eyes and over my shoulder. I looked ahead and grinned. "*Today was the greatest day of all*," I sighed to myself. My hungry eyes fixed on the pint-sized profile of her blood filled frame when she started moving again. She was a vision of heaven galloping spryly along her pathway of pebbles. Deeper into the woods she stepped, so incredibly carefree and undeniably alive.

I hid behind the lush plumage of the palmettos to conceal myself from her. My black T-shirt and jeans made me practically imperceptible, and like a shadow I disappeared into the darkness. She was beautiful. And the longer I looked the more I felt my honey colored eyes glimmering like molten gold. *BOOM*. My inhuman heart thumped a solitary strike in my chest. *Her* very presence had seemingly brought me to life again.

She laughed. Its tender tone was sweeter than fairies fluttering their wings. My ears even tickled with the delicateness of the sound. All of a sudden she picked up her pace. I followed behind, right on her heels.

The sweet scent of her young blood hung in the air. *She* was the most indelible picture of perfection: naïve, innocent and pure. I rubbed my tongue against the sharp tip of my fangs and grinned. Life, I contemplated watching the gentle throb of her pulse beneath the surface of her lily-white skin, it was so fragile and fleeting.

Just then she stopped to pick a blossom. She reached out and ruthlessly snapped the tiny flower's neck. She was resolute, cruel even in her vicious assault on the fragile bloom. A quiet laugh escaped my lips when she turned around. "Oh no!" I uttered aghast. *She heard me.* And then it happened. Our eyes met. For one brief implausible moment we were locked in an unbreakable stare.

She gasped, but she wasn't frightened—curious perhaps. I smiled at her unintentionally. Regret rushed through my veins like poison. *BOOM*. My chest thumped with another thunderous strike. My heart, or at least what was left of it, felt as though it was breaking inside me. I turned my back to her and raced through the pines away from the past—*away from myself.*

With a deep exhale I returned to the present again. Moving through time was as easy as breathing. It was quickly becoming one of my favorite indulgences; that and feasting on Christian's blood. *Christian.* He was the object of my affection as a child, the man of my dreams as an adult and the true love of this peculiar afterlife I was living. But he was also my creator; the one who bestowed my immortality. I loved him in a way no words could even begin to describe. He was in essence my reason for living again.

"You went back didn't you?" he asked in his fading English accent. Christian was young and gorgeous and leaning against an old-fashioned push mower by the pool. His sculpted pale body poured out of the tight, white tank top he was barely wearing.

"Why would you say that?" I asked my mind still consumed with my carelessness in the forest. I was getting sloppy with my ability and I was afraid of what that might mean. An eerie chill ran down my spine. I quickly busied my thoughts. I could already feel Christian slipping his way inside my mind. I didn't want him to know about what happened in the forest. I drew upon as many cluttered ideas as I could to try and mask the truth.

"Your thoughts are like fireworks today," he said determined to read what I was thinking. Christian and I had a special connection, a silent connection. At times it was the most beautiful thing in the world. It made our love stronger, but it had drawbacks too: privacy didn't exist and I really never had a moment to myself.

"Get out of my head Christian!"

"No way," he teased moving into the shade. "I've got an inside track into figuring out the woman I love. Do you know how many men would kill to have that skill?"

I laughed and let my eyes linger upon him. His face was sweet like a boy's, but also chiseled and angular like a man's too. His dark hair shimmered like a blackbird's feathers in the dappled sunlight. Christian was beautiful. There was simply no other way to describe him. It definitely didn't take much for him to dominate my thoughts: the tenderness of his touch, the tin-cinnamon scent of his skin and his deeply devoted love for me. I rushed through the trees like an animal toward him. "I missed you," I said shoving him to the ground.

"Hope!" he gasped.

I pressed my soft lips to his in a kiss. It was heaven. His mouth moved in perfect unison with mine. I was helpless in his arms, with his touch, and when his long pale fingers stroked the span of my spine I gave in to him with ease. I felt him roaming the corridors of my mind. He was seeing what I had seen as though he was reliving it for himself when I felt him withdrawing.

"You *did* go back," he said pulling away. His glorious green eyes were angry and electric with hints of silvery iridescence.

"So?"

"Hope," he chastised.

"What?" I flirted. "Is fighting really the only thing you want to do with me right now?" I slipped my hands beneath his tank top and grinned.

He laughed, his pretty face softening.

"We're alone," I said pushing his shirt off of his body. *His body*—it was exquisite: lean yet muscular and incredibly well-defined. I stroked his porcelain skin and smiled. "Why won't you give in to me? We're young, in love and we have forever together."

"Exactly," he uttered. "We have *forever* together. What's the rush? And besides," he cleared his throat, "we don't live alone. We have to be respectful of the others."

"The others? The others aren't out here right now and I certainly don't think Bambi and little Thumper will mind if we—"

"Hope!"

"What?"

"Your grandfather lives with us! I couldn't bear the thought of disappointing him." He planted a kiss on my forehead and rose to his feet.

"Henry wouldn't be disappointed. He'd probably give you a high-five."

"God!" he exclaimed mortified.

"Okay," I said rising to my feet. "Maybe that was out of line, but the truth is we're alone—*finally alone*. You know how hard it is for us to get a second alone together."

He grinned moving from the shade into the sunlight again. "What's gotten into you? You're incredibly feisty today."

"I am?" Christian was a beautiful vampire—the most beautiful I'd ever seen. I watched his fair skin radiate as the sun singed him with the usual subtle burn. I was still fascinated by the casual way he stroked his body in an effort to liberate himself from a dusting of his own ashes. It was so normal and yet so extraordinarily bizarre.

"What are you looking at?"

"I just love how you make suffering seem so sexy." My gaze met with his tattoo. It was an elegant and detailed phoenix inked along the length of his ribcage.

"When can I tattoo you again?" he asked eavesdropping on my thoughts.

My mind returned to the wretched sting of his needles as they carved the delicate filigree wings of the black butterfly on the back of my neck.

"You know," he said moving into the shadows again, "it won't hurt as much this time, now that you're not human anymore." He moved his lips to my skin.

"Christian..." I moaned with the feeling of his mouth on my neck. I wanted him to kiss me, bite me or taste me even; the thrill of the feed brought me to life.

"Hope," he whispered.

"Yes?"

"It scares me how good you are at being a vampire."

"You do know how to ruin the moment," I insisted deflated.

"I wasn't trying—"

"I know. You were just mentoring me again."

"You wanted to know the truth about what you've chosen to become."

"Yes. And I...I've been thinking a lot lately about when I was a little girl."

"Little girl?" he scoffed. "And?"

"And what if you had changed me back then—when I first wanted you to?"

"Hope!" he exploded. "How can you say such a thing? This is all about you going back to the day we met. Isn't it?" He shook his head.

"You're addicted. You spend more time in the past then you do here in the present—with me."

"You're exaggerating."

"Have you ever considered how it makes me feel?"

"Well I wasn't expecting jealous."

He fluttered his long eyelashes and the world around us went silent. Time was little more than a useless convention. There were no birdcalls nor wind songs to distract from the tension between us. Christian could easily slow time to its most infinitesimal measure. The world was frozen, apart from us, and we were alone together in a moment of perpetual eternity being forced to face our feelings.

"What does *he* have that I don't?" he asked frustrated.

"He is you!"

"Not the *real* me."

"Well it was real...once."

"The past is the past for a reason Hope. Can't you keep it that way?"

I pressed myself against him and gingerly inhaled the sweet tin-cinnamon smell of his body. "I try. I really do. But I love seeing us back then...so innocent and virtuous."

"Well that's debatable."

I moved my head to his chest and listened to the nearly inaudible beat of his listless heart. "Hear that?"

"What?"

"I even got your old heart racing again!"

He smiled and tightened his hold on my waist.

"I love you Mr. Livingston, now, then and for always."

He fluttered his eyelashes and suddenly the world came alive again; birds sang, cicadas hissed and the wind resumed its whistle. Christian planted a kiss on my forehead and withdrew from me. He moved toward the old push mover in the sunlight.

"Yeah, yeah," he teased. "I know what you're going to say...just because I'm like two-hundred years old doesn't mean I have to use contraptions from the era."

But I didn't say it. In fact I wasn't even thinking about it. I was far too consumed by the wave of guilt that had overwhelmed me. I needed to tell him about what happened in the forest. I needed to tell him about connecting with *her*.

"She saw me," I blurted.

"Who?" he said halting his stride.

"In the forest, she was picking flowers. *She saw me.*"

"Hope!" he snarled. "This could change everything. It could ruin us!"

"I hardly think I could ruin us by shifting through time a little."

"You know the risks. A small change can alter everything—it's the butterfly effect."

"I know," I insisted. *"Residuals.* It worked when we killed Sakura after her and her crazy vampire boyfriend practically slaughtered us."

"You're smarter than this Hope."

"She was a dangerous bloodsucking bitch and deserved to die. Sometimes the residuals are worth it."

"But this was different. It was *you* making a connection with *yourself.*"

"But it was only me as a little girl.

"It was still you."

I shook my head. "I've gone back dozens of times and I never—"

"Dozens?" His voice was panicked.

I darted from the shadows and into the sunlight. I placed my hand on his cheek and stared into his angry eyes. "I would never do anything to ruin us."

"Then promise me you won't go back anymore."

I started to speak when swiftly a searing surge of pain enveloped me. My skin stung with an insatiable intensity. Subtle tendrils of smoke abruptly rose from my flesh. "The sun!" I howled.

2. Déjà vu

"Move!" Christian shouted thrusting me back into the shadows. We hit the ground. I felt the burn diminish instantly. A covering of fine dust graced the surface of my skin. I sat up and stared at my arms. My eyes were fixed on the dust-like layering that coated my skin. *Ashes*, I thought to myself. *My ashes*. And as I brushed the ashes away I couldn't help but feel a little like Cinderella without the slippers of course.

"Are you okay?" my dark prince inquired.

I ran my palms along my skin.

"Hope," he insisted. "Are you okay?"

"No," I said. "Not really. It's like a continual cremation...like I'm dying over and over again." I looked up at him. "I'll never be able to run in the sun again will I?"

He pulled me into his arms. "Of course you will. In time. You've not yet built a tolerance to the sun. It just takes patience."

"Patience," I groaned. "I was never very good with patience." I buried my face against his chest. The sweet scent of his skin enlivened me again.

"And you're not dead," he said. "We have a heartbeat."

"Slowly living."

"Exactly."

The scent of his body was divine. I nestled my face even harder against him.

"What are you doing?" he asked.

"You smell so good," I said. "Good enough to—"

"Eat?"

"Don't tease me Christian."

He guided my face to his with the gentle sweep of his hand. I looked into his eyes and grinned.

"Are you sure Bambi won't mind?" he whispered mischievously.

I bit my lip. I loved it when let himself act like a teenager instead of the prudent two-century old Englishman that he was.

He ran his lips along my collar bone. "*You* smell good too," he uttered, his voice raging with juvenile enthusiasm.

I giggled and closed my eyes. A moment later I felt him reaching for my hand. He traced the scar in its center with the tips of his fingers. The scar was evidence of a blood pact we made together when I was just a child—a blood pact that seemingly triggered my progression into becoming a vampire.

"Mmm," he purred. I could feel his ancient adolescent hormones working in overdrive. He wrapped his long pale fingers around my hand and brought it to his lips. His sharp teeth grazed my skin. I wanted to gasp, but held it in. He moved his mouth to my wrist. A moment later he sank his sharp incisors into me, the burn of his bite paling in comparison to the sting of the sun. "*Sweet Christian*," I sighed through my thoughts. "*Let me drink with you.*"

"*Do it*," he replied soundlessly.

His tender request instantly erected goose bumps on my skin. I felt my fangs cut through my gums and my eyes ignite like molten gold. I wanted him. I leaned close to his neck, watching as his jugular pulsated ever so unhurriedly beneath his flesh.

"*Drink from me*," he implored.

My body swelled with his words. An animalistic hunger dominated my every sensibility. I drew back my head; fangs exposed, and leaned in to lunge when I was stopped by the crude sound of Christian's name being called in the wind.

"Oh god," a sharp familiar voice interrupted.

Our alone time was abruptly brought to an end. Christian withdrew from my wrist and wiped the blood from his lips. "What do you want Eva?" he snarled.

Eva was the worst of our roommates. She was like the sister I wished

I never had. Everything about her motivated jealousy and fostered insecurity in me. Her face was seductive like an old time Hollywood starlet and her body was curvy like a forties era pin-up. She was beautiful and she knew it too. Eva was a vampire vixen with scarlet colored hair as fiery as her personality.

"You know you're not alone right?" Her tone was surly, like usual.

When my estranged grandmother bequeathed her Victorian-inspired estate Ambrose House to me after she died, she also bestowed her roommates as well. They were a collection of motley vampires including my twenty-five year old blind, therianthropic grandfather Henry, a tattooed Hispanic with physical prowess that would rival the likes of Hercules named Baptiste and his ladylove Eva, the shape shifting shrew.

"What were you two doing exactly?" Eva pried straightening the lace frill on her red blouse.

"None of your business," I snapped.

Her eyes shot over to me. She glared, running her sharp red fingernails along her tattooed arms. "You really have become quite a fireball since you changed."

"Fire ball?" I scoffed.

"I like it," she admitted. "It sure as hell beats the Snow White act you had going as a half-breed."

"What did you call me?"

"Snow White," she said innocently, "or maybe half-breed. I think I called you both actually."

"You really are such a—"

"What do you want Eva?" Christian interrupted.

She placed her hands on her hips and smiled. "Baptiste is not working the graveyard shift anymore."

"Why not?" Christian asked.

"He's tired. We're all tired," she said. "B has worked four nights this week already. I can't have that. I'm...I'm with child." She stroked her perfectly flat stomach.

"You're playing the pregnancy card?" I sneered. "Don't you have like six more years ahead of you to carry that *thing* in your belly?"

"Don't mess with me," she barked. "I'm beyond hormonal."

"Eva," Christian insisted. "Why'd you really come out here?"

"I came out here to threaten you. Wake up Christian! We've barely corked enough blood to survive the next six months. There are five of us to feed now—now that *blondie's* living here."

"Well six," I said, "if you count B's demon spawn in your perfectly toned abdomen."

"That's it!" she raged. She lunged toward me.

"Eva!" Christian shouted stopping her. "We're all on the same side here. No more drama okay?"

"I'm *never* dramatic," she insisted.

A loud laugh escaped my lips.

"Don't test me blondie," she warned, "or I'll show you dramatic."

"Enough with the threats already." Christian's voice was hard.

"It's time to get your ass back to work lover boy. La Fuente is your shop—*your tattoo shop* and you need to run it. Everyone's been asking for you." Eva sighed. "If you two want to survive without having to go all savage like those murdering vamp freaks Maxim and Sakura then you have start pitching in. We've corked a lot since that bitch destroyed our collection, but we're nowhere near where we need to be."

"You racked nearly forty bottles last month," I interjected.

"Forty bottles that *you* had absolutely nothing to do with!" Her eyes bulged as she spoke. "If you want to survive then you have to cork and to cork you have to tattoo."

"Fine," Christian said.

"People have been asking where you've disappeared to. It's been weeks since you've even been to the shop." Eva cleaned some dirt from her fingernails and flicked it at me. "You're like some celebrity now Christian. Ever since that guy wrote that damn article in the magazine the phone's been ringing off the hook. I'm not your secretary."

"Actually you are my secretary Eva."

"Well," she said befuddled. "You know what I mean."

"I'm no celebrity," he assured humbly.

"I know that," Eva insisted. "But the humans don't." She kissed her teeth. "There are humans full of blood out there just begging for a chance to have you give them a tattoo." She shook her head. "I'm tired of making excuses for you. Pull your weight. You and Hope have been living in a fairy tale for weeks now. It's time to get back to reality."

"Okay," he said. "I'll work tonight and tomorrow and—"

"Now that's more like it," she interrupted.

"And tell B to take some time off."

Eva grinned. "That's all I needed to hear."

"So can you go now Eva?" My voice was icy.

"With pleasure," she retorted. She shifted her eyes to Christian again suddenly noticing his naked chest and the dried blood at the corner of his mouth. She grimaced. "Honestly," she uttered. "Why don't you two just do it and get it over with already."

"Eva!" he shouted mortified.

"Put a shirt on Romeo. This isn't Club Med. And you," she said moving her eyes back to me again, "start acting your age. It's revolting watching the way you treat him like your little boy-toy. You're thirty not thirteen."

"Eva!" I shouted.

"Don't," Christian insisted. "She's definitely not worth it."

"Ciao lovebirds," Eva snickered. She turned away and marched across the lawn in her red stilettos.

Christian sighed reclining on the ground. "I hate to admit it," he said. "But she is right you know."

"Yeah," I agreed feeling him inside my thoughts.

"I didn't mean about that!" he said realizing I was focusing on the *just do it and get it over with* part.

"Oh," I uttered deflated. If my cheeks could have flushed they probably would have.

"Hope," he said. "I just think we should move slowly is all." He smiled. "I've waited an eternity to be with you."

"Well in that case Eva isn't right about anything! I'm *not* thirty. I barely made twenty-nine before you took my life."

"*Took your life!*" he said horrified.

"You know what I mean. *Changed* me—whatever." I flopped down on the ground next to him.

"Funny," he said, "how one insidious comment from Eva can tarnish all the beauty of our time together in Hawaii—that sweet night when I breathed new life into you."

Regret consumed me instantly. "Oh Christian," I said, "I didn't mean to trivialize—"

"I know."

"Eva gets my back up. She knows what buttons to push with me. I hate the way she makes me feel—almost like I'm not good enough."

"Not good enough for whom?"

"For any of you."

His face eased. The edges of lips swept up into two perfectly parallel arcs. "Well that *is* ridiculous," he said. "You are better than all of us put together. Your grandmother knew it. Henry knew it. And I," he smirked. "I've always known it—even when you were a dewdrop of a little girl with bouncy golden curls and a pink dress." His eyes glimmered like silvery stars.

I smiled.

"The things you would say back then...you weren't a normal kid. I remember times when I wished," and then he stopped himself mid-sentence.

"Go on," I urged excitedly. "*Please?*"

He shook his head and smiled. "You restored my faith in life, or whatever you want to call this prison of eternity we're trapped in."

"Hardly a prison! Look around. This is paradise!"

Christian went quiet. I tried reading his thoughts, but they were clouded like dirty water and practically impossible to understand.

He heaved a sigh. "Maybe it is time to face reality again."

"But this is reality," I countered. "Isn't it?"

He smiled. "I wish I could spend every moment with you, but you heard Eva. The shop needs me."

"Well I need you more." I grabbed him by the arm and grinned. He was enchanting, like a character from a storybook, so incredibly divine and seeming unreal. "Don't go back to reality," I pleaded. "Let's stay in this fairy tale."

He laughed. "Oh Hope. How is it that even time can find a way of holding eternity hostage?"

"It doesn't have to," I said.

"Is that so?"

"Stop time," I grinned. "Stop it right here in this moment and let us live in it forever."

He pulled me against him and grinned. He fluttered his long, beautiful eyelashes and halted the moment for us alone. The world went silent again. Christian leaned in close and pressed his soft lips to mine in a deep, passionate kiss and there on the forest floor we spent what felt like forever enjoying our fairy tale for just a little bit longer.

3. Blood

Tattoo shops scared me to death until I became a vampire. When Christian first introduced me to his world of ink and flesh I was surprised by how easily it seduced me. I had always loved the way tattoos looked on people and secretly imagined having my own one day, but my fear of the pain and stupid concern with what others would think always stopped me. Christian changed all that. When I fell in love with him I felt freer and more alive than ever before. He awakened a side of me I'd always longed to live.

I let him give me my first tattoo at La Fuente when I was still a human. I practically had to force him to do it. And I was right about the pain—it hurt like hell, but it was all worth it in the end. The black butterfly he embedded on the back of my neck that day marked the moment my true metamorphosis began. I haven't let him tattoo me since. I just don't want to do anything I'll regret. I'm immortal after all and need to be conscientious of such incredibly permanent choices.

The tips of my fingers throbbed. I looked down at my hand. My fingers were covered in blood. I'd cut myself on the razor-sharp edge of the magazine I was holding. Crimson droplets splattered upon the page. "Ha!" I laughed.

"What?" Christian asked wiping down his client's back.

"I just bled on your face!" My voice was playful.

"Beg your pardon?"

"The article," I insisted. "It's another one about you."

He rolled his eyes and finished his work on the whimsical tattoo of Alice sitting on a toadstool.

I licked my finger. *"Hungry for ink?"* I read aloud. *"People are coming in droves to satisfy their craving at the pea-sized shop in Key West known as La Fuente."* I giggled. "Christian this is hilarious!"

"Maybe for you," he garbled.

I cleared my throat.

"The shop's pretty-boy owner Christian Livingston is real up and coming in the tattoo world. With artwork on skin more realistic than old masters on canvas, Livingston's way with the tattoo machine has been compared to Caravaggio's way with the paint brush!"

I laughed.

Christian rolled his eyes. "Not as low profile as I'd like." He started bandaging his client's tattoo.

"Oh come on," I said. "It's only words. And besides it's already drawing in more clients. Which is good because it means more..."

"I guess," he admitted grudgingly.

"Get this," I said reading another passage. "A recent client even went so far as to describe the feeling of being inked by Livingston as serene."

"I'd agree with that," the blonde client with the new Alice in Wonderland tattoo gushed. She handed Christian a wad of bills.

"Thanks," he said slipping the tip in the back pocket of his jeans.

"Thank *you*," she flirted. There was a strange glassy look in her eyes, as though she was awake and asleep simultaneously. She waved goodbye and left the shop—a little more inked and a little more bloodless.

I sighed. Like Briar Rose pricking her finger on a spindle these women welcomed the pierce of Christian's tattoo needles. Once they fell under the veil they'd virtually let him do anything to them.

Veiling really was one of the quintessential perks of being a vampire. Possessing the ability to sedate a human into a temporary hypnosis-like dream state felt masterly. Veiled was that "serene" feeling they talked about in the article; a pleasure induced sensation of euphoria that dominated each and every sensibility. Vampires could veil humans for any number of reasons: to let someone forget something, to force someone to remember something or even with the intention of inserting false information. It was manipulative and dishonest, but it was fun and sometimes even necessary. The only thing we couldn't do was veil each other. That was impossible.

When it came to customers at the shop veiling was common practice and used with the utmost discretion. It was in essence the easiest way to pinch blood without the bother of having to be discreet about it.

"She'll be back," Christian mumbled watching his client leave. "They all come back."

"And why is that Christian?"

He winked at me and grinned. "We really should be keeping a low profile. I just don't understand why are there so many articles being written about me lately?"

"Oh poor you!" I teased. "Are you having a tough time handling your fame?"

"It's not funny."

"It's kind of funny."

He shook his head. "It all started last month when I tattooed that guy from that entertainment magazine."

"The tricky tribal cover-up guy or the last supper sleeve?"

"Last supper sleeve."

"I think I remember him."

"Ever since he wrote that little blurb it hasn't stopped. I've got people from magazines and newspapers leaving all sorts of messages now."

"That's cool Christian."

"It's exactly why I didn't want to face reality. I don't want to be in the spotlight. I *can't* be in the spotlight."

"Veil some of these reporters. It might keep them off your back."

"Maybe," he said, "but only if they came to the shop. I don't think I could veil them over the phone. Truth is I don't want more people probing around in here. It's hard enough having to veil the health and safety inspectors on such a regular basis."

"Humans are pretty gullible though."

"Perhaps, but we can't afford to take that chance. Some humans are more resistant to the veil than others." He shook his head. "Even though our tattooing experience feels the same as an ordinary one—it isn't."

"Yeah, but a reporter isn't an inspector. It's not like they'd be looking for the *bloodsuckers*."

He shrugged. "They wouldn't find them even if they did. The action of the extraction tubes—"

"You mean the *bloodsuckers?*"

He nodded. "They're seamless with the motion of the needles. It would be virtually impossible for anyone to know the difference."

"Sounds like you're giving me an interview answer."

He laughed. "Imagine the title of that article?"

"*Two-Hundred Year Old Vampire Steals Human Blood via Tattooing Machine*." I grinned. "Sounds pretty hot to me."

Christian laughed.

"Imagine how famous you'd be?"

"More *infamous*." He shook his head. "I'm no Lestat. I think we'd better leave the whole rock and roll vampire thing to Anne Rice."

"Yeah," I agreed brashly. "You're not arrogant enough to be Lestat."

"Why the sudden interest in tattooing? You want me to give you another—"

"Not today thanks."

"Just as well. I prefer your blood straight up—not collected through some tube."

I smiled and watched as he started fumbling with his black latex gloves. Droplets of blood sat upon the lengths of the latex. They shimmered like rubies in the dull light of the room. My thoughts immediately recalled the sweet, blonde girl to whom the blood belonged and suddenly I became thirsty. My fangs shot through my gums. My eyes ignited like molten gold. My skin felt barely strong enough to contain the impetuous throbbing that had begun inside of me. I grabbed Christian's fingers and pulled the bloodied latex to my mouth.

"What the hell?" he barked pulling away. He tore the gloves from his hands and tossed them in the trash. "You know better," he chided looking around cagily.

"I'm sorry," I apologized. "I don't know what came over me."

"Still such a babe in the woods." He shook his head and tightly fastened the knot on the trash bag.

"Just when I think I've got these urges under control I realize I don't."

"Yet another reason we must keep a low profile. Look," he said stroking my shoulder. "Don't feel bad. It took me years to conquer the come hither call of the fresh stuff."

"Well why do you wear gloves then? I mean you're clearly able to control yourself around it and it's not like it can infect you or anything."

He laughed. "It's about safety standards and keeping up appearances. We must *always* keep up appearances." His eyes narrowed. "You know that right?"

"Yes Christian. I'm not an idiot." Our entire existence on the Florida Key of Perish relied on our ability to keep up appearances. Christian and the rest of them had been this way for years, centuries even—I was a tenderfoot by comparison and still bursting with uncontrollable urges.

Just then the bell at the front of the shop suddenly rang. Its sharp chime was like the clamor of a penny being shaken in a tin can. A strange chill ran down my spine. Every time I heard that bell it reminded of me of the day that Maxim entered the shop. *Maxim*, I sighed uneasily in my thoughts; he was the nomadic vampire we crossed paths with a few months ago—just before I changed. He and his crazy girlfriend Sakura were on the run like a bloodsucking Bonnie and Clyde. They were desperate to evade the stifling constraints of a bigger vampire society we only recently became aware of. Maxim and Sakura were dangerous. They annihilated our coveted blood-wine collection and nearly destroyed our furtive existence on Perish Key. But comeuppance hit them like a hurricane when we ended them in the wreckage of Christian's sunken ship the HMS Ambrose. Maxim and Sakura were dead, but I couldn't stop myself from wondering if someday, somehow, someone else just like them would come again.

"And if another sets foot on our land—this time we'll be ready. It's been months and nothing's happened. Don't worry."

"I'm not. But change that damn bell okay? It makes me cringe every time I hear it."

He nodded in reply before withdrawing to attend to the customer at the front of the shop.

At times La Fuente felt more like a blood bank than a tattoo shop. Without the slick leather furniture and eclectic portraits on the walls it really was just like any ordinary donation center. Eva was always sure to have a steady supply of orange juice and snacks on hand for the weaker set and the benches, although white vinyl and modern, still looked like rows of hospital gurneys set up in a ward. I never felt bad for the humans. They weren't being killed—they weren't prey. They got what they wanted and so did we.

La Fuente, *the fountain* as it translated from Spanish, really did flow with an unstoppable force. Day or night there was always a steady stream of customers.

I extended my gaze. Christian was talking to a big brawny guy with a dark complexion. I looked closer. His pulse throbbed beneath his skin. He was nervous. Humans fascinated me: the fickle flux of their feelings in constant contrast with the steady machine-like functioning of their bodies. Thump. Thump. Thump. His heart raced like a Ferrari. I licked my lips and felt my body starting to respond again.

"They're customers Hope," Christian whispered, "not cuisine."

"I know that."

Christian dropped a large white sheet of tracing paper over the light board and began sketching a skull. "The urges will pass you know."

"And what about the sun," I said. "Will it ever stop singeing my skin?"

"Eventually, but you have to build a tolerance to the sun. The urge to kill however, that's in your control."

I watched the super-sonic speed at which his pencil fluttered across the paper as he drew.

"You like to watch?" he teased.

"You gotta problem with that?" I smiled. Watching him draw reminded me of when I was a little girl; I loved spending afternoons with him in the forest watching him sketch in seconds what others could only hope to accomplish in hours.

"Ah, flattery," he smirked. "I'll never grow tired of listening to you think about me."

"Can't I ever have a personal thought to myself? Hence the word *personal*!"

He grinned.

I rolled my eyes. "So," I said changing the subject, "what are you drawing? Skull with rose? Skull with snake? Skull with—"

"A sugar skull actually."

"A sugar-what?"

"Dia de los Muertos. The Day of the Dead." The words were ominous as he uttered them.

I shrugged. "Never heard of it."

"You've never heard of Dia de los Muertos?"

"No."

"It's Latin American. It's a holiday when people remember friends and family that have died."

"A holiday about death?"

He grinned.

"I like it."

"They build altars and stuff to remember their deceased. They use flowers like marigolds and calaveras made of sugar—*sugar skulls*."

"Creepy," I uttered, "but cool."

"Do you want to watch me tattoo this one?"

"Yeah," I said. "I'd like that."

"Think you can *behave?*"

I nudged him in the arm, "of course." I grinned, but the thirst was still present deep down inside of me just waiting for a chance to rear its head again.

4. Death Flower

The bigger the human—the bigger my appetite. And Christian's client was big. He walked slow as he approached us giving La Fuente a good once over with his dark eyes as he moved. His pants were baggy and the gold chains around his neck were showy, but I could tell that there was more to this guy than met the eye. He had a nice looking face with good features, a little stubble under his mouth and a baldhead. In all honesty he reminded me a little of Baptiste.

"Hey," he greeted with a low rumble. "I'm Marco."

"Hey," I replied. "I'm Hope." I slipped into the seat next to him. He smelled of spices and limes. *Behave*, I told myself inside my thoughts. *He's a man not a meal.*

Christian glared at me with one of those *"don't do anything stupid,"* looks before turning away again.

"Do you tattoo too?" Marco asked.

"No," I said. "I just like to watch."

He laughed under his breath.

I was mortified. I really had to stop saying that.

"What Hope means is that she wants to apprentice and I'm—"

"It's cool," Marco interrupted.

Low profile, I sighed in my thoughts. *Don't say anything stupid.*

"Here's the sketch I came up with." Christian handed Marco the drawing.

"Nice, but not the marigolds."

"I assumed it was traditional—"

"Yeah," he interrupted, "it is traditional, but I was thinking of something else. You ever heard of the black lisianthus?" His mouth twisted into an ominous grin.

"Flor de muertos," Christian replied.

"What's flor de muertos?" I asked intrigued.

"Flower of the dead," Christian said.

"I'm surprised you've heard of it," Marco laughed. "But then you are Christian Livingston. And you've got skills like Michelangelo."

Christian shook his head embarrassed. "These articles are going to be the death of me," he uttered.

"Naw bro," Marco said. "It's good. Really. I wouldn't have come otherwise."

"See Christian," I said. "I told you it was good for business."

"Look man," Marco uttered. "I ain't one of these jerks looking for a souvenir. My skin is my spirit. And what I put on it tells the world who I am. I don't take this shit lightly."

"I can see that," Christian insisted.

"I ain't even the one bothered by the marigolds. It's my grandmother. She's very old school. She told me that if I was going to get this done it had to have the flower."

Christian's eyes narrowed. "Alright. Let me see what I can do."

Marco nodded.

"C'mon Hope," Christian said standing up.

"Why?"

"I have to get more paper."

"So?"

"I thought you were *apprenticing*."

"Naw," I uttered. "I'm okay."

"Hope," Christian barked.

"I'm fine," I assured. *"I'll behave,"* I said through my thoughts. *"Don't you trust me?"*

Christian heaved a sigh before turning away. Marco's guttural laugh distracted me.

"What's so funny?" I asked brashly.

"Nothing," Marco said.

"Spill it."

"You remind me of my grandmother."

"How's that?" I asked intrigued.

"A strong woman who knows what she wants."

I laughed.

"I mean it as a compliment."

"And I took it as one," I replied.

He nodded.

"Tell me more about that flower," I insisted.

"What do you want to know?"

"Well for starters why does grandma care what kind of flower you have in your tattoo? I mean aren't most flowers pretty much the same?"

"Not this one."

"Why?"

"Because it might not even exist."

My eyes widened. "So it's an imaginary flower?"

"It's a fabled flower—written about in old legends."

At that moment Christian returned with the revised sketch in his hand.

"That was fast!" Marco uttered impressed.

"Well I am the best," Christian joked. He showed him the drawing.

"That's exactly it my brother!"

"Good enough for grandma?" I asked.

Marco laughed. "Probably not, but let's do it anyway."

Christian began preparing his station for the tattoo.

I leaned in close and whispered, "Tell me more about this flower of yours."

"Well," Marco sighed. "They're the blackest flower in nature. Their blooms are long and droopy and hang like a teardrop ready to fall."

"How poetic," I gushed.

Marco grinned. "And people plant them around the graves of the ones they loved."

My eyes widened.

"Can you take off your shirt?" Christian asked. "I'd like to put the stencil on you now."

"Yeah," Marco replied. He moved his hands to his shirt and pulled it off over his head. My eyes inadvertently shifted toward him to watch.

"Wow," I uttered unintentionally. "Hit the gym much?" His body was unbelievable; rock hard and muscular.

Marco laughed. Christian stepped on my foot under the table.

"What?" I said. "It's not like I embarrassed him."

"No," Christian uttered, "but you did embarrass me."

"It's cool," Marco insisted.

"See," I said with petulance.

He rolled his eyes and began plastering the stencil on Marco's huge bicep.

"Tell me more about that flower," I said changing the subject.

"Well," Marco said. "There's an old story about the plant having powerful healing properties."

"Cool."

"It's all about the roots."

"Roots?"

He nodded. "They are said to feed the souls of the dead buried beneath."

"I like that."

"And the more the roots feed the more it is said that they could..."

"What?" I asked keenly.

"Resurrect the dead," Christian interrupted. His voice was hard and edgy.

"Really?" I exclaimed.

"It's just an old myth," Marco replied grinning. "But my grandmother believes in it."

Christian's tattoo machine started buzzing. I sighed inside. I knew the first cut into flesh was coming next.

"Are you ready?" Christian asked.

Marco nodded. I watched him flinch the moment Christian's needles sliced into his skin. Ink spewed and flesh stretched. I wondered if the bloodsuckers were at work; stealing Marco's blood with its stealthy suction.

"You okay?" Christian asked.

"Yeah," he uttered. "Guess I'd forgotten the sensation of a tattoo."

"What?" I teased. "Aren't you feeling *serene*?"

"Sure," Marco said, "if feeling serene means feeling like shit."

I laughed, but wondered why Christian hadn't veiled him already. A big virile customer like Marco could easily get out of hand.

"I tried," Christian said through my thoughts. *"The veil doesn't seem to be affecting him for some reason."*

"Maybe he's a vampire," I teased.

"With swarthy skin like that—I don't think so."

"Nice," Marco said eyeing the outline. "This is gonna be a sweet tattoo. If grandma says I'm to get the *raiz de la vida*, then I guess—"

The buzzing of Christian's machine abruptly came to a stop. "Raiz de la vida?" he said taken aback.

"Yeah," Marco replied.

"You said la flor de muerto."

"Raiz de la vida—flor de muerto. It's all Mayan baloney if you ask me."

Christian's eyes widened. He flashed me a hard stare before pressing his foot on the pedal again; the tattooing machine came alive buzzing with a sound more strident than a dentist's drill.

"What is it?" I asked soundlessly.

"Nothing," he dismissed, but I knew he was lying.

Just then the bell at the front of the shop rang. I cringed with its sound.

"Gabriel," Christian barked. "Can you get that please?"

Gabriel was another tattooer at La Fuente—one of the human tattooers we employed. He was tall and lean, not particularly attractive and yet not especially unattractive either. He had a mess of brown hair that usually hid beneath a hat and a face that, although pierced in places and unkempt with scruff, was undeniably kind.

"Hey Gabe," I said the moment he sauntered past.

"Hey Hope," he greeted. "I haven't seen you in a while." His voice was soft and his demeanor meeker than a mouse.

"Well I'm here now," I said smiling. "What 'cha working on over there?"

"Japanese concubine," he said bashfully.

"Sexy."

He giggled.

"Gabe," Christian snapped. "The customer is waiting."

"Sorry," he apologized. "It was good seeing you Hope. He studied my face with slight apprehension. "You look different."

"Do I?"

"Gabe!" Christian barked.

"Right," he said obediently moving past me. I watched him for a moment. The docile way he held his hands at his waist, the timid posture of his head and the slight hunched over arch in his back.

"You're so mean to him Christian," I said.

"Well I'm the boss," he replied. "It's my job to be mean."

Marco laughed and Christian laughed too. I rolled my eyes at them before turning my attention back to Gabriel again. Gabe was a nice guy, but he was a human. He had to be veiled. There was no other way around it. Working in such close proximity was dangerous. We needed to keep our secret safe and he needed to stay alive. Veiling him was the only way to assure our working environment remained professional. But there was a part of me that felt incredibly sorry for him too; wondering the extent to which we'd damaged him in the process. How many times could a human be veiled before becoming a vegetable?

"Leave it alone," Christian whispered through my thoughts.

"I can't. I feel so bad for him."

"Hope," Christian said aloud. "You don't have to stay here. Why don't you go home?"

Home, I contemplated. The thought of kicking up my feet and downing a big bottle of blood did sound appetizing. It had been a long day and trying to forget about my little slip-up in the woods was literally exhausting. "Yeah," I uttered. "I think I will go."

"Don't wait up," Christian whispered. "Looks like I'll be here for a while." He smiled and kissed me on the arm.

I moved my eyes to Marco. "It was nice meeting you."

"And you as well," he replied.

"Good luck with the tattoo. I know grandma's gonna love it!"

Marco grinned.

"See you at home Christian." I half-smiled before turning to walk away. I was tired yes, but I couldn't help feeling as though he was intentionally trying to get rid of me. *Why?* I sauntered toward the front of the shop when I overheard something—something that definitely wasn't meant for my ears. My supersonic hearing zeroed in on the quiet conversation between Marco and Christian.

"What do you know about the plant?" Christian asked.

"Raiz de la vida?"

"Yeah. Tell me. And don't hold back either."

"Look bro, this ain't the time or place to talk about—"

"You don't need to school me in its history. I know its potential."

"Then what do you want me to tell you?"

"Where to find it." Christian's voice was hard.

Marco sighed. "It'll cost you."

"I can pay."

"I'm sure you can."

"What's the problem then?"

"Abuela," he said. "It's her that knows the old ways. Not me."

"So will *she* help me?"

"No."

"No?" Christian said frustrated.

"But *I* will."

I continued walking pretending as though I hadn't overheard their conversation. My imagination ran wild with their words.

"Bye Hope!" Gabe uttered startling me.

I jumped. "See ya'," I replied reaching for the front door. I swung it open. Ting. Ting. Ting. Chills ran down my spine the moment that damn bell chimed its dreadful ring.

5. Old Friends

My grandfather looked like an Abercrombie model as he sat poolside. He was shirtless and wearing his favorite pair of blue jeans. Henry was attractive and it didn't gross me out to admit it either. I was still getting used to this whole young body—old soul thing that both Henry and Christian had going. Admittedly Henry was my biological grandfather and a vampire no less, but he was also a shape shifter. I'd seen him as a raven, a deer, a butterfly—a shark even. Under the circumstances I supposed it made it easier for me to be objective seeing him in his *real* skin as a man. Sometimes I couldn't help but to think how lucky my grandmother was; being with her spouse her entire life without having to watch him get old. While other women her age were busy tending to their husband's false teeth and sciatica my grandma was still rolling in the hay with the captain of the football team.

"Hope!" Henry shouted sensing my presence. "Come!"

His antique radio was playing music when I arrived. He was singing along to a song and lost in its melody. His mess of blonde hair swayed as he moved. I smiled, impressed by how greatly the music seemed to please him. The song was old and charming, much like he was.

With a pair of dark designer sunglasses covering his eyes, it was easy to forget that Henry was blind. He was quite perceptive and still had his vision when he shape-shifted.

"Sit," he said gesturing to the empty patio chair beside him.

I moved closer and happened to notice the tattoo of my grandmother's name in elegant script written on the inside of his bicep. I'd never noticed it before. It was lovely and somewhat understated.

"I've got you," he sang in time with music, "under my skin."

"Sinatra?"

"Who else?" he grinned turning off the radio.

"Sorry I'm late today," I said slipping into the iron patio chair. I started putting my elbows on the table when I noticed the spread of magazines and newspapers scattered everywhere. "What's all this?" I asked.

"I was waiting for you to read them to me."

"*All* of them?" I said exasperated.

"Oh come on," he teased. "Make an old man happy."

"Alright, so long as it isn't another article about Christian or the shop."

"I know," Henry said. "It's not exactly the low-profile he should be keeping is it?"

"No. It's not. But it was going to happen sooner or later."

"What do you mean?"

"He's an incredibly talented artist. It was only a matter of time before someone noticed."

"I suppose you're right. If you practice something for two-hundred years I guess you would get pretty good at it. I only worry what it could mean for protecting our little secret."

I shrugged. "The world is changing Henry. The unacceptable is much more accepted these days. You can't read a book or watch a movie that doesn't have some kind of brooding immortal in it."

Henry grinned. "You are right about that my dear, but those are fiction. We're a reality."

My heart thumped in my chest. The truth of his words hit me like a slap.

"And if I have to listen to one more of those films about that family of vegetarian vampires I think I'll—"

"Henry!" I exclaimed. "I like those movies. They're romantic and exciting and speak to me on such a personal level." Henry shook his head and sighed, but he didn't respond. I drew my eyes away from him and down toward the mess of magazines on the table. I picked up a geeky looking scientific journal. There was a Team Edward bookmark wedged between two pages. My brow furrowed. "Henry," I said skeptically.

"Yes?"

"Who marked the pages in this nerdy science magazine?"

"Eva," he said. "She was reading to me the other day. The article is fascinating."

Eva, I thought to myself with a chuckle. I ran my fingers along the image and grinned. The attractive pale actor on the bookmark was pretending to be a vampire. He was cute, but he didn't hold a candle to Christian.

"What's funny?" Henry asked.

"Oh nothing. I just figured Eva as more of a Team Jacob fan."

"I don't follow."

"Never mind." I moved the bookmark aside and looked down at the article. "Decoding Cellular Memory," I read aloud. "What are you into now Henry?"

"Just read it."

I cleared my throat.

"After receiving a heart transplant from a 16 year old donor that was killed in a tragic accident, Joe Anderson 61, suddenly began craving junk food and nurturing an unexpected appreciation for the great outdoors. According to his wife, Joe never cared much for sweets prior to his surgery and would hardly qualify as an outdoorsy type."

I stopped reading. "Henry," I said. "What is this drivel?"

"Keep reading," he pleaded.

I shifted my eyes back down to the article again.

When the Anderson's contacted the donor's family they were surprised to learn that the young man whose heart Joe had received was an avid outdoorsman and a lover of junk food.

I looked up at him. "This is stupid," I said.

"C'mon Hope. Give it a chance."

I continued reading. *Do memories have the potential to be stored in individual cells?* I looked up from the magazine. "Do you actually believe this?"

"Why not?"

"Some old guy gets a teenager's heart and suddenly he's all Twizzlers and tents? I hardly think that's scientific proof of anything."

Henry laughed. "Isn't science great? Adam and Eve or evolution?"

"Please don't get all theoretical on me. It's been a long night."

"Yeah, I couldn't help but notice that you're cutting it awfully close today. The sun is nearly up."

"I know," I replied feeling the gentle rays beginning to tingle against my vulnerable skin.

"Where were you?"

"I was at La Fuente with Christian."

"You don't have to keep meeting me here every morning Hope."

"I look forward to this." I insisted. "I like our time together."

"And you must admit the sunrise is pretty neat too."

I grinned. "It's the only time of day that won't kill me!"

He laughed. I knew his sightless eyes were smiling behind his dark sunglasses.

"How'd you get through it?" I asked. "I mean when you first changed."

"Moira and Christian helped me."

I closed my eyes letting the sun cover my skin in a blanket of stings.

"You really are getting there," he assured. "Every day stronger and stronger. And soon you'll be able to walk in the sun again like the rest of us."

"I sure hope so." I opened my eyes. I looked out across the grass beyond the trees. The sun was swiftly rising through the pines. The lawn, the leaves and the sky were beginning to saturate with color.

"We'd better get you inside the house," Henry insisted.

We stood up together. I held onto his arm and we strolled through the garden toward the front door. Ambrose House was Victorian in style with rectangular windows and a huge wrap-around porch. It was named after Christian's old ship the HMS Ambrose since it was actually built from the wood of the wreckage over two hundred years ago. The house stood proudly in the center of the sprawling property like a family tree. It was a continual reminder of our humble beginnings as a family of civilized vampires.

"Read any more of Moira's journals lately?" Henry asked.

"Yes," I said excitedly. "She was incredibly fascinating."

"Yes she was. Did she write anything about me in those journals?"

"Yes," I said playfully.

"And?"

"And I'm not so sure she would have wanted me to share what she wrote about you. It's *very* personal. Very, very—"

"Fine," he interrupted. "Never mind."

I squeezed his arm and smiled. We laughed. I'd never know what it was like to have a family. Richard, my cold-hearted excuse for a father, raised me after my mother died. He made my life miserable. Guilt underscored our relationship more tangibly than sandpaper and no matter how hard I tried to make him love me he continued to make my life a living hell. And when I chose to forego his luxurious human life of privilege for a much simpler afterlife in Perish with Christian, Richard disowned me for good. He knew that Christian was a vampire and that by choosing to be with him meant I was choosing to become one too.

It wasn't until Moira's passing a few months ago and her will that I realized I still had a tie to the estranged maternal side of my family. Henry. He was alive—well as at least as alive as any vampire could be, and he was happy to recommence a relationship with me. I'd spent a lifetime without knowing the feeling of family and now that I had one I wanted to relish in it completely.

"How'd you and Christian end up working the graveyard shift?" Henry asked.

"Eva had a talk with us today and she wasn't very happy."

"That's Eva. She's always got something to say to somebody."

"Isn't that the truth," I giggled. "You know she even had the nerve to tell us to get back to reality."

"Where exactly did she think you'd been?"

"Lost in love, I suppose."

Henry laughed as we ascended the cement steps to the porch.

"Is it so bad?" I asked.

"Is what so bad?"

"Wanting to live in love?"

He sat in the rocking chair on the porch, folded his arms across his chest and smirked. "Hope my dear. No life worth living is without love."

"My thoughts exactly."

At that moment the front door suddenly swung open.

"Baptiste!" I shouted appalled. He was ranting and raving and muttering words in Spanish—swear words I think. His white shirt was slathered in blood and his hands were sopping wet too. "What happened to you?"

"Me?" he said. "Me? You wanna know what happened?" His already enormous chest inflated like a balloon. He was menacing; tattooed from head to toe, big and strong.

"You're covered in blood!" I said.

"And you smell incredible," Henry added.

"I smell good because it *is* good!" he raged.

"But why is it all over you?" I asked.

"Because Esperanza. I'm afraid I've lost my touch. I keep breaking them."

"Them?" I asked confused.

"The damn bottles! I infused the most delectable sprig of biker's bone with spray of blackberry juice. I mixed it with natural redhead, a chocoholic tourist and a dash of black pepper. It was almost identical to a cabernet sauvignon. And I went and dropped it. The whole damn carboy!" He looked down at his blood soaked hands and howled.

"You really have to relax!" I insisted.

"No!" he replied. "I will not sacrifice taste for pace."

And then suddenly, like a ghost, Eva appeared. She was standing in the doorframe, her arms outstretched and her body curved in the most elegant arc. She was wearing a long, silk slip dress. It was cream in color and exquisite. Her hair was down, straightened and looked like red fire against her pale face. She was grasping a small piece of paper in her thin hands. "What in the hell is going on out here?" she shouted. "And why does B look like the demon barber of Fleet Street?"

"I lost another vat," he uttered. His voice was pitiable.

"Oh not again," she said opening her arms to him. He moved toward her, ran his big, bloodied hands around her tiny waist and embraced her. Eva kissed her teeth. "You," she snapped, her eyes flitting over to me. "You did this. I told you he was overworked."

"Don't blame this on me!" I fumed. "I had nothing to do with—"

"Girls," Henry hollered rising to his feet. "Don't fight. We're family."

"Shut up Henry!" Eva and I shouted in unison.

Henry laughed and sat back down in his chair again. I turned to Eva and grinned. She reluctantly grinned back at me.

"What we need around here is something to lighten the mood," Henry said.

"What? Like a party?" Eva suggested.

"A party?" Henry contemplated. "Remember when Moira used to make us have those ridiculous parties?" He giggled. "She'd make us get all dressed up and—"

"She'd make that disgusting Ambrosia salad of hers!" Eva interrupted.

Henry laughed.

"And she'd try to convince us that it was actually food for the gods," Baptiste added.

Henry smiled. "Didn't she always say that it was a recipe handed down from generations in her family lineage?"

Eva laughed. Her eyes glimmered with iridescence. "Maybe what we need *is* a party! We haven't had a party here since...since Madonna was still a virgin!"

"Then I'd say it's about time," Henry agreed.

"I suppose I could blend something special," Baptiste said inspired.

"So what shall we celebrate?" Eva asked. "Preservation? Christian's celebrity status? How cute my new Louboutins look on me?"

"Hope," Henry interjected.

"Hope?" Eva snapped bitterly.

"Me?"

"Yes," Henry grinned. "You are my granddaughter, the new owner of Ambrose House and the most recent addition to this family. You deserve a proper debutant ball."

Eva rolled her eyes disappointed.

"Esperanza should be welcomed into our family the same way I was many years ago," Baptiste added.

"With a stolen buggy and a half-dead courtesan?" Eva's snarled. "Not sure blondie would appreciate it as much as you did."

"Oh Eva," he laughed grabbing her with his big bloodstained hands.

"Then it's settled," Henry said. "We'll begin at dusk."

"Oh, I almost forgot. This came for you." Eva tossed the small piece of paper she was grasping in her hand through the air.

"What is it?" I asked plucking it in mid-flight.

"A postcard."

"Well where did it come from?"

"The mailbox."

I glared at her before looking down at the card. "Are you sure this is for me?"

"Well it has *your* name on it," Eva snapped. "I *do* know how to read you know. And speaking of reading—I read the back. I don't get it." She shrugged. "C'mon B. We have a party to plan." She pulled him into the house with her.

"Privacy really doesn't exist around here does it?" I complained.

Henry laughed. "Eva is the biggest busybody in the world."

"And with Christian in my head all the time listening to my thoughts I really am like an open book." I looked at the postcard. There was a photograph of a white sand beach against an azure ocean. *"Greetings from Mexico,"* I read aloud. "I don't know anyone in Mexico."

"The more important question is who even knows you're here in Perish?" Henry's voice was troubled.

I turned the postcard over. There were only four words written on the back in black ink: *Paradise found. Come now.* I recognized the handwriting straight away. "My god," I said.

"What it is?"

"It's Ryan," I uttered. "This postcard is from her. It has to be."

6. Dusk

Ryan was the best friend I ever had—too bad she was a liar. A few months ago she showed up on the shores of Perish and divulged that our entire friendship had been a sham. I nearly crumbled with the news. She explained in detail how she had been employed by some bigger society of immortals to study my progression as an ageing half-breed. I was dumbfounded. I thought I'd known Ryan since childhood, but in reality it was only a short while. I'd been veiled. At the time I wasn't a full-fledged vampire and so the veil worked like a charm. And when I learned the truth I wanted to hate her. But I couldn't. She confessed that knowing me had changed her existence for the better. She said that watching me inspired her and made her want to learn to live again. She even admitted to lying to her employers in order to protect me. I didn't know what to believe.

I stroked the ornate diamond and ruby pendant on my necklace and sighed. The necklace was gift from Ryan on my last birthday as a human. Apparently it was a family heirloom—from her human family and one of the only possessions that she actually kept from her past. I wanted to believe that this time she was being honest—I think a part of me needed to believe that she was. And when she gave me the necklace I saw it as a request for forgiveness.

I stared into the large, gilded bedroom mirror and grimaced. I was pale, paler than normal and even looking a little transparent. Starvation did make a reflection fade and I was hungry. Our sustenance supply had been very limited for some time now. Baptiste had been working hard to cork as many quality bottles as he could, but it certainly wasn't enough to satisfy everyone's thirsts entirely. I was still new to this life and struggled to control the urges I felt. At times the craving within me clawed like a wild animal and I wanted nothing more than to go all savage and dig my teeth into something with a pulse. Even the filthiest of prey seemed to seduce me. The pitter patter of tiny mouse feet running across the porch at night played on my conscience like a fiddle. But I was civilized and promised the others that I wouldn't resort to such ghastly behavior.

"Oh Ryan," I muttered staring at my waning reflection. "I sure hope you're eating better than I am these days."

Ryan was on the run, but until recently she had been living off of something called a sustenance implant (a nourishment device inserted beneath the skin at the wrist). The implant apparently also served as a tracking device. By the time she'd arrived in Perish she'd already ripped out her implant and was living as a fugitive. I was happy for her and hoped that she was strong enough to survive the urges. She wasn't the first fugitive to step foot on our land. When Maxim and Sakura arrived they too were on the run. Like Ryan they'd also ripped out their implants, but the urges seduced them and won. They were killers. I truly hoped that somehow Ryan managed to find another way.

I straightened the edge of the tiny black dress I'd squeezed myself into and walked to window. I peered through the blinds. The sun was swiftly sinking below the trees in the distance and soon the party would begin. I moved back to the bed and flopped down. I stared up at the ceiling. Eva told me I wasn't to come out of my room until Christian came to get me. Christian wasn't even home from La Fuente yet. Time felt as though it was at a standstill. I needed to do something to occupy myself. I grabbed a couple of my grandmother's journals from beneath the bed. I chose to read the one with the dark blue cover first. I opened it up and eyed the first page. I loved reading her journals. Coupled with Henry's stories I really felt like I was finally getting to know my family.

January 19, 1951.

Not a day goes by when I don't

remember what his warm flesh felt like to hold. I miss my warm Henry— hot-blooded, rosy lipped, touchable Henry.

Would I have chosen otherwise? HEAVENS NO!

Fate is not my mistress!

She holds no power over me!

Even a sightless, cold-bodied Henry is better than none at all...

My eyes widened, awed. I had no idea that my grandmother secretly longed to have Henry as a human again. I knew the intensity of their love for one another and I'd always considered the benefits of Henry being a vampire. I suppose I simply never contemplated that Moira may have felt otherwise. I closed the book and laid it beside me. I grabbed the other journal, opened it up toward the middle of the book, picked a random passage and started reading.

September 8, 1935.

Are the heavens enraged at what I've become?

This dreadful hurricane refuses to retreat. In all my years I've never been so terrified. I fear we shall end up over-the-rainbow once the wrath of this storm finally subsides...if ever.

My eyes widened. What was Moira ranting about? What exactly had *she* become? My grandmother wasn't a vampire. She was just a woman in love with Henry back in 1935. Henry hadn't even become a vampire yet! I was frustrated. Moira's writing was always a little puzzling, but this was outright cryptic! I couldn't help but feel as though I was missing a pertinent piece of information—like the key to unlocking some dark secret that would inevitably allow me to finally make sense of all her writing. I had no key. I sighed inside, knowing full well that my meager brain would have to continue working over-time in an effort to continue decoding Moira's journal entries. I looked back at the words again. "This dreadful hurricane refuses to retreat." I bit my lip. Had there really been a hurricane on Perish Key back in September of 1935 or was this another metaphor for something more profound? My mind flooded with questions. I flipped ahead in the journal, skimming the cream colored papers at super-sonic speed. Big, bold black letters all in capitals immediately caught my attention. I focused on the entry and began reading.

September 20, 1935.

FATE IS A DARK SORCERER!

I pulled my eyes away from the words. *Fate is a dark sorcerer.* What the hell was that supposed to mean? Moira's writing was somehow getting more and more bizarre as I continued reading.

Sorcerer, I contemplated. It was a most peculiar choice of word, underscored and laden with notions of magic. Why was she likening fate to sorcery in the first place—and dark sorcery no less? I was desperate to know. I flipped ahead in the journal, my brows abruptly knitting together in the center of my forehead. The following half-dozen pages that remained in the book were entirely blank. There was nothing more written, no rants about fate nor rambling about metaphorical hurricanes whisking her over the rainbow. There was nothing. My eyes narrowed. The blank pages bothered me. Of all the journals I'd read thus far, Moira never left any of them unfinished. Something didn't feel right. I put the book aside and extracted another from beneath the bed. My eyes widened. I didn't recognize the cover. It was lighter than the others and stained with water marks. I opened it impatiently and began reading.

October, 1958.

Audrey refuses to learn her lessons. If only she would embrace her potential. That girl is so damn stubborn—Fairchild stubborn.

Fairchild? The name hung on my lips like a murky haze. I drew my eyes back down to the words again. *"Audrey refuses to learn her lessons."* What lessons? What possible potential had my mother failed to embrace? I was frustrated. The enigmatic nature of my grandmother's writing was unnerving me. My mind flooded with question when suddenly the bedroom door swung open. "Christian!" I exclaimed. I stashed both journals beneath the bed and leaped toward him. I plastered his face in kisses.

"Wow," he sighed, "I've only been gone a few hours!"

"I know, but they told me I couldn't come out of this room until you came to get me."

"Get you?" he said. "For what?"

"The party."

His eyes widened. "Party? We haven't had a party at Ambrose in over twenty years...ah," he nodded, "that would explain what's going on downstairs."

"What's going on downstairs?"

He winked at me before running his hand around my waist. "You look amazing in that dress."

I grinned. "Let's forget about the party," I said luring him toward the bed. "We can have our own little party up here instead."

Christian laughed. "Tempting, especially in that dress, but not right now. You should see it down there. Looks like they've gone to a lot of trouble."

"Really?" I smiled.

"Really." A moment later he pulled me by the hand and within a split second we zoomed through the hallway and descended the staircase.

My eyes widened like saucers the moment I set my sights on the main floor of the house. It was unbelievable, like an ethereal storybook come to life within the walls of my very own home. Palm fronds and gardenia blooms carpeted the ground while twisted boughs lined every wall and archway. Garlands of fresh greenery adorned the portraits. Thick tufts of Spanish moss hung from the ceiling like streamers and ivory colored roses ornamented furniture in bouquets like balloons. A collection of pastel colored songbirds tenderly enchanted us with their chipper melodies while thousands of tiny fireflies hovered together lighting the interior of the house with a most spectacular glow. It was beautiful; indelible eye candy to say the least.

"What do you think?" Henry asked.

"Beautiful," I replied mesmerized. "How did you—"

"I had to do a little negotiating with the fireflies, but the songbirds were more than willing to help out."

I put my hand over Henry's and smiled. "Thank you," I said. "For everything."

He grinned in reply.

"There you are," Eva said approaching. She was wearing a scarlet colored silk dress that wrapped her body tighter than latex. She was carrying a large gift in her arms. It was rectangular in shape and pristinely wrapped in black paper. A beautiful satin bow sat proudly on the top. It too was black in color and elegant as well. "Here," she said shoving the box in my face.

"Thanks," I said taking it from her.

"You won't like it."

"You didn't have to give me a present."

"Henry said I did."

"Well thanks Eva."

Just then Baptiste entered the living room. He was wearing a maroon shirt and black jeans. He looked fancier than usual. He was holding a green glass bottle in his hand.

"Esperanza," he said eagerly.

"Thanks B," I said. I always thought it was sweet the way Baptiste used my name in Spanish.

"I didn't have time to wrap it for you." He rushed across the room and handed me the bottle. "Here," he said smiling. "Not quite Stromboli, but the closest I've come in years." Stromboli was the perfect blend Baptiste sought to make. It was his name for the first bottle he ever corked and he compared everything to it.

"Can we drink it now?" I asked excitedly.

"Why of course!" Baptiste replied. "This one is a special blend. The blood of a big, Mexican mixed with aged virgin. It's fresh. Christian just brought the Mexican's blood."

My eyes widened. *Marco? Could it be?* Just the thought of downing a sip was enough to get my body to kick into gear. I felt my fangs cut through my gums and my eyes ignite with iridescence. *I'd never actually seen the people we drank. This would be a first.* I brought the bottle to my lips and tore the cork from the neck with my teeth. I spit the cork across the room. Everyone laughed.

"God that smells good," Eva gushed inhaling the succulence of its scent in the air.

I pressed the opening to my lips and let the luscious liquid slip down my throat. I swallowed hard and smiled.

"Good?" Baptiste asked impatiently.

"Unbelievable," I replied swallowing, the last of the taste lingering on my tongue. I passed the bottle to Christian. He downed a swig and grinned before handing the bottle to Henry.

"Hey," Eva complained. "Don't Bogart that bottle Henry." She grabbed it from him the moment he swallowed. She threw back her head and guzzled.

"Eva!" Baptiste shouted. "Relax. I made more."

Her eyes widened. She wiped the spill of blood at the corner of her mouth. "You did?"

Baptiste nodded in reply producing three more bottles from behind him.

"*Now* it's a party," she said excitedly.

"C'mon," Christian said tugging at my hand. He led me to the large, red Victorian couch in the living room. He sat down and yanked on my fingers. The force of his tug was so strong I fell upon his lap.

"Eww! Gross," Eva shouted making her way into the living room too. Her eyes were fixed on us.

"Oh Eva," Christian retorted. "Get over it."

She pulled her face at him as I moved myself from his lap to the empty spot on the couch beside him.

"Now that we're all here," Henry said. "Let's give Hope our gifts."

"Take mine," Eva snarled. "Go on blondie. Rip that present open."

"Okay." I fondled the elegant back bow on top.

"I said *rip it!*"

"Fine." My voice was hard. Eva was incredibly bossy; like the horrible mother-in law I never had.

"We ain't got all night," she continued.

I rolled my eyes and moved my fingernails to the fancy black paper and instantly shred it to bits. Beneath was an old wooden case with a fancy metal hinge.

"Open it," she barked.

"I am," I said annoyed. I unlatched the box and pulled it open. There inside laid an unusual antique wooden board.

"Know what it is?"

"Um..." I stared at the peculiar letters and numbers burned into its surface.

"Ouija board," she said.

"Ouija board." I grinned. The only other time I'd ever seen a Ouija board was back in grade school at a slumber party. That board certainly didn't look like this. It was thin and plastic and probably purchased at Wal-Mart. This Ouija board seemed antique and handmade. It looked like someone traveled to Diagon Alley to buy it.

"It belonged to a friend of mine," Eva said.

"Wow," I insisted surprised. "This is really kind of you."

"I know," she said proudly. "It was collecting dust in my closet. I haven't used it in years. And I read this article about Ouija boards bringing bad luck to people that owned them. Better you than me," she scoffed.

My smile turned hard. "Oh Eva," I grumbled. "Couldn't you have just said you're welcome like a normal person?"

She kissed her teeth and hissed. I rolled my eyes and moved the Ouija board to the side.

"I'd like you to open my present next," Henry said. He handed me a small parcel. "Careful," he insisted.

"Thanks," I uttered taking the present from him. The wrapping was soft and silken. It was mostly black with hints of an iridescent blue patterning. It was lovely to say the least. "This paper is beautiful Henry."

"Is it?" A big smile was plastered on his face.

I reached for the wrapping when suddenly it quivered. My eyes widened bigger than saucers. "What on earth?" I muttered. A moment later the lovely black and iridescent blue wrapping began to flutter. A surge of delight coursed through me. It was literally one of the most beautiful things I'd ever seen. "Butterflies!" I giggled watching the wrapping take flight.

"Well," Henry said. "I'm blind and possess the power to commune with animals. This was easier than struggling with tape and paper."

I reached for his hand. "Thank you." I said touching him.

"You're welcome Hope. Now open your gift!"

"Butterflies?" Eva's voice was surly. "Honestly."

"You're just jealous," Baptiste snarled cheekily.

I grinned at them before turning my attention back to the parcel again. Without the butterflies present it was easy to see the box. It was beige in color and just large enough to fit within the cradle of both my hands. I opened it. "Oh my goodness," I gushed.

"Do you like it?" Henry asked.

My eyes widened as I stared upon the exquisite hand mirror that lay within the box. "It's wonderful," I said extracting it.

"It belonged to your grandmother's grandmother. It's a family heirloom."

I beamed studying the intricate mother of pearl patterning that had been inlaid into the small patch of wood on the back.

"It's been in the maternal side of your family a very long time Hope."

I stroked the mirror with the tips of my fingers and grinned. It was regal and elegant and designed with heavy metal symmetrical flourishing swirls on each end.

"You're its rightful owner. It's time I gave it to you."

"I've never seen anything like it," I said turning it over. I grasped the metal handle and moved the mirror upward until it met with my reflection. "Whoa," I said startled.

Henry grinned. "Your grandmother used to say that there was no other mirror quite like it."

"No kidding." I studied my reflection. "I'm practically invisible."

"You're thirsty," Christian interrupted.

"I guess," I said concerned. "I just didn't think I looked so much like a ghost is all!"

Henry laughed. "The mirror reflects the truth, not necessarily what you see."

"Great!" Eva barked annoyed. "Magic mirror trumps Ouija board. Thanks a lot Henry."

"Well delectable blood blend trumps everything," Baptiste uttered in his thick Latin accent. He uncorked two more bottles with his sharp teeth and grinned.

The succulent smell in the air made my mouth water instantly. I put the mirror back inside the box when Henry touched my hand.

"Do you really like the mirror?" he whispered.

"I love it."

"Good, but be cautious my dear."

I nodded forgetting that Henry was oblivious to my reaction. There was a peculiar expression on his face, like he wanted to tell me something, but intentionally held it back. I looked down at the mirror again. *Magic*, I thought to myself. Was it possible that the mirror possessed some kind of power? I grinned realizing how silly I was for even contemplating such an absurd idea.

"And what about *my* present?" Eva's voice was resentful. "Don't I get a thank you?"

I moved my eyes to Eva. "Thank you," I said. "I've always wanted one of these Ouija boards."

She feigned a smile. "Hey," she said mischievously. "I didn't see lover boy give you anything?" She pointed at Christian.

"I don't have a present," he replied. "I didn't know we were even having a party for Hope. I just got home remember."

"Some excuse," she snorted batting her long lashes.

"Well he did bring home the blood." I put my hand on Christian's knee.

"Maybe you're getting your present later blondie." Eva snickered, her voice dripping with innuendo.

"Eva!" Christian and I shouted in unison.

Everyone laughed—even the songbirds. And to the merry melody of their cheerful tune under a luminescent cloud of fireflies we continued drinking and giggling the night away.

7. Ouija

I couldn't sleep. I was revved up like an engine. There was definitely something unusual about those bottles Baptiste corked. We partied all night and it was great. We never did this; we never took time to be together and have fun as a family. I was glad that Henry forced a party on us. It was good for me—for all of us.

Christian passed out the instant his head hit the pillow. He *didn't* give me a present (like Eva had implied). I couldn't simmer down even a lick. I knew the sun would be up soon and that Christian would be off to La Fuente again. I grabbed his white button-up shirt from the floor, slipped into it and kissed him on the cheek before leaving the bedroom. I tiptoed through the hallway and made my way downstairs. The main floor of the house was dark and surprisingly deficient of decorations. The leafy garlands and twisted boughs had vanished. The perfect blooms and butterflies were nowhere to be seen either. And while a single songbird sat atop the statue of the wooden lady at the foot of the staircase, all of the other creatures had seemingly returned home for the night. Just then the sound of Eva's cackling surprised me.

"Eva!" I called out with a whisper. She didn't reply. I tiptoed across the ragged Persian carpets toward her. As I neared I noticed that she was sitting on the floor, her porcelain-like skin and fiery red hair illuminated by the gentle flickering of a few dozen candles. She was wearing a sheer, cream-colored negligee with a black bullet bra and matching boy shorts underneath. Her delicate hands hovered above the Ouija board—*my* Ouija board. "Eva," I said laying a hand on her shoulder.

"Oh you," she snapped in reply.

"What cha doing?"

"The laundry," she spit back with sarcasm.

I rolled my eyes at her.

"Sit!" she ordered. "I gave you this thing. Don't you wanna know how to use it?"

"I know how to use it," I said sitting on floor across from her. The old wooden board sat upon the table like a chalice.

"Ever summon the dead?"

"Once. I was eleven at a slumber party."

"That doesn't count." Her eyes narrowed. "Summoning the dead with a vampire is serious business."

"What if two vampires summon the dead?" I jeered. "Is that serious *serious* business?"

"Hope don't join me if you can't take this—"

"Seriously?" I interjected with sarcasm. "Look," I said. "As long as you don't put on some lame accent and start pretending you're a gypsy..."

"My people were gypsies!" she snarled. "Way. Way. Way back."

"Oh Eva," I groaned.

"Shh," she said looking around the room. She seemed nervous and Eva never seemed nervous. A moment later she shape-shifted into an inexplicable blackness.

"Eva?" I whispered perplexed. I looked around, but she wasn't there.

"Fuel for the fire," she said rematerializing again. There was a wine bottle cradled in the crook of her arm.

"Where'd you get that?" I asked excitedly.

"I stole it from B's private reserve."

"He'll kill you if he—"

"Like he'd ever kill me," she said tearing the cork from the neck with her sharp teeth. "Besides," she said spitting it across the room, "I corked this particular bottle myself." The sweet smell of blood immediately sailed past my nostrils. I could feel my body coming alive with the divine succulence of its scent. Eva took a swig straight from the bottle before passing it to me.

"*You* corked it?" I asked skeptically. Eva had a bad habit of mixing odd ingredients together.

"It's not gross. But if you don't want to drink—"

I downed a swig and smiled.

"It's good right?"

"Not bad." I grinned surprised. "Not bad at all Eva."

She snatched the bottle away from me and took another mouthful. "Perfection," she purred. "Blood of a college frat boy and mine mixed together in a divine drink for the damned!"

"You really think you're damned?" I asked taking the bottle back. I downed another taste.

"Naw. I'm having too much fun to be damned." Her eyes glimmered with iridescence. "Christian on the other hand, he's..."

"Yeah, I know." I handed the bottle back. "He's all *eternity-is-a-prison* and blah, blah, blah." The drink immediately revived my buzz from earlier.

"It's the devil in the details. God's in the flaws."

"What does that even mean?" I giggled.

"I don't know," she laughed handing me the bottle again.

I took another sip. "Can I ask you something?"

"Not if you want me to answer."

"Eva," I glared.

"I just hate it when people ask if they can ask a question. Just ask the question damn it!"

"Okay. How old were you when you changed?"

She smirked. "How old would guess?"

"Nineteen?" I lied flatteringly.

"Twenty-four."

"Isn't it all the same really?"

"No," she snapped tearing the bottle away from me. "It's not the same." She downed a swig. "When I was human, twenty-four was old. It meant you were supposed to be married and surrounded by a gaggle of nattering children." She swallowed. "And if you weren't—then you were a..."

"What?" I asked taking the bottle.

"Look, in my day women were one of two things."

"A saint or a sinner?" I teased.

"A homemaker or a home wrecker." Her voice was hard.

"And let me guess, you were a—"

"I didn't plan for it," she interrupted. "He promised he'd leave her." She licked her lips and sighed. "Look Pollyanna, you're not the only one who believed in fairy tales...running off into the sunset, getting married and having a family." She shook her fiery, red hair and snatched the bottle away from me again.

"How are you feeling?" I asked changing the subject.

"Me?"

"Yeah you," I said miming a huge, round, pregnant stomach.

"Oh," she smirked. "Fine. Good, I guess. I never imagined it was even possible. And now that it is," she paused, "I guess I'm...glad." Her eyes narrowed. "But if you tell anyone what I just said I'll literally rip you to pieces."

I grinned. "I won't."

"I mean it's not like I'm maternal. The only thing June Cleaver and I have in common is our savvy penchant for pearls."

"You'll be a good mother."

"You think?" Her voice was almost desperate.

"I know! You're definitely bossy enough to be a mother!"

She laughed and took another drink before sliding the bottle in my direction.

I shifted my position on the floor and reached out to take it from her. I took a sip. "Do you feel different? I mean can you feel *it* inside of you?"

"Yeah," she said with a surprising genuineness. "I think I can. I always thought it was indigestion," she laughed, "like a rock in my belly. I remember waking up one morning a few years back and feeling this really bad gut-rot. I thought it was just another hangover from the blood bender we'd been on, but somehow it felt different."

"How? I mean what did if feel like?"

"Like a medieval mace pressing on my bladder."

"Ugh," I replied moving the bottle back toward her.

"I got used to it," she said downing a sip of what was left.

"Are you scared?"

Her eyes hardened, the glimmer sharpened. "Not yet. But I've still got six more years or so to worry about how the hell we're going to get this thing out of me."

I laughed.

"So," she said playfully changing the subject. She slid the nearly empty bottle across the table toward me. "What's with you and the Tin Man? I thought he was the love of your life and you two were all gaga about each other. Why haven't you...you know, sealed the deal?"

"Ask him." My voice was bitter.

Eva took a deep breath. "Christian's not like other guys. He's older than old fashioned!"

"That's for sure." I drank some of what was left in the bottle.

"He vowed to protect you," she said. "It's a big deal to him. And come to think of it I never remember seeing him with a woman since... well since forever really."

My eyes widened. "Has he been saving himself?"

Eva laughed. "It's not like he took a vow of abstinence and wants us to throw him a purity party. Thirty years is like two weeks to vampires." She reached out and took the practically empty bottle back. "He's put you so high up on that damn pedestal he's probably worried you'll be disappointed."

"Or maybe he's worried that I'll disappoint him."

"Well, whatever," she dismissed with her usual insolence. "Now do you want to summon some dead people or what?" She downed the last drops of what remained in the bottle and sighed.

"Hell yeah!" I said.

She took a glass goblet from the table and turned it upside down on the Ouija board. "Here's your pointer," she said tapping her sharp, red fingernail upon the base. "Watch this." She lit a match and then gently blew it out trapping the smoke inside the chamber of the inverted goblet.

"Smoke in a cup? I don't remember doing this at Jenny Smith's eleventh birthday party."

Eva smiled. "That smoke in there is the spirit we've summoned." She winked. "Don't let it out—unless of course it's a nasty spirit."

I half-smiled and forced myself to enjoy the *sort-of-séance* as much as Eva wanted me to.

"You know how to do this right?"

I shrugged. "It's been a long time. Refresh my memory?"

"If I must," she sighed melodramatically. "Look here. The board is divided into three parts: the alphabet to spell out words, the numbers zero through nine to relate numerical messages and of course there's the yes and no bit at the top of the board."

"Okay," I uttered confused.

"Your finger goes on the base of the cup—Hope, are you even listening?"

"I'm listening."

"Don't tip the cup," she ordered. "Or you'll release the spirit. And don't be a smart ass either and push the cup around. It's much more fun if we—

"Okay, I think I remember now."

"Good," she uttered touching the base with her thin index finger. "C'mon," she insisted.

I reached out and gently placed the tip of my finger on the cup as well.

Eva closed her eyes. "Spirit," she chanted, "summon your medium."

I bit my bottom lip to keep from laughing when suddenly the cup began sliding across the board with our fingers at the helm.

"I told you not to push the cup blondie!"

"I'm not," I said. The goblet slid about the board until finally it stopped in front of me.

"Gee what a shock—considering *you* were pushing it."

"Eva," I said rolling my eyes. "I wasn't."

"Never mind, just ask it a question."

"A question?"

"Like whether it has a message for us."

"Okay." I cleared my throat. "Spirit," I said theatrically. "Have you come to bring us a message?"

At that moment the cup slid across the board again moving with swiftness toward the word yes.

"Stop pushing the goblet Hope!"

"I'm not!"

"Your eyes flicker when you lie," she snapped.

"I'm not lying Eva. I told you."

"Whatever. Just ask it another question." Her voice was testy. "Ask whether it's a man or a woman."

"Are you a man or a woman?"

"Not like that!" she exclaimed irritably. "You have to ask: are you a man *or* are you a woman—not both you idiot!"

I shook my head. "I don't want play anymore." I drew my finger away from the goblet.

She grabbed my hand in mid-air, her eyes alive with iridescence. "Don't leave," she pleaded.

"Why not? Will the spirit police track me down and—"

"I don't want to be alone," she interrupted. Her voice was more serious than usual and absent of mockery.

"Eva," I said gently. "How can you feel alone? You have a baby in your belly."

She shook her head and released her grip on my hand. "Ever since I've known about this person—this thing inside of me I've felt more alone than ever."

"But you're not alone. I'm here. I'll help you through it. You know I will." I smiled at her. She smiled back. "But on one condition."

"And what's that?" she asked perking up.

"You need to lighten up a little if I'm going to continue playing this game with you. Okay?"

"Fine," she laughed and we both returned our index fingers back to the base of the invert goblet.

"Where did we leave off?" I muttered.

"Man or woman remember? But forget all that," she said trying to cooperate. "Just ask if we know the spirit."

"Spirit," I said. "Do we know you?"

The goblet whirled around the board, quickly and forcefully with our fingers upon the base until finally it stopped at the word yes.

Eva's eyes widened. "Ask it to give us the first few letters of its name."

"Spirit," I said politely. "Can you please give us the first few letter of your name?"

The goblet slid across the board until meeting with the letter W.

"W," Eva said.

"It's still moving," I insisted.

The goblet moved around again stopping briefly at the letters I, L and O.

"W, I, L, O," Eva uttered.

"Wilo?" I said perplexed.

Eva's eyes locked on mine when suddenly the goblet began moving by itself; our fingers lingered mid-air while the glass slid across the board unaided. Swirling like a whirling dervish the goblet moved until finally flying off of the table entirely. It soared through the air and smashed upon the hardwood floor. Wisp of grey smoke hung suspended, just above our heads, before crystallizing into ashes. Like snowflakes the ashes descended, falling through the air and landing upon the Ouija board.

"My god," I said taken aback.

"Impossible," Eva uttered.

"You can say that again."

"No," she snapped. "I used to call him Wilo. It was my nickname for him. He hated it."

"Who Eva? Who are you talking about?"

"William," she said. Her voice was like ice; cold and sharp.

"William?" I asked confused. "You mean Christian's old friend?"

Eva nodded. "But it's not possible. There is no way that he could be contacting us."

"Why not?"

"The Ouija only contacts *human* spirits." Her eyes glimmered. "William wasn't human. He was a vampire."

8. Postcard

Eva didn't say much after the *semi-séance* with the Ouija. She didn't speak about William and I didn't feel comfortable asking either. I could tell the incident unnerved her in a way I'd never seen her unnerved before. And when she started complaining of a headache I knew it was an excuse to get away from me. A little while later she headed off to bed. I on the other hand was fiery and far too excitable to sleep. I'd only been a vampire for a short while and drinking so much blood made me feel more alive than ever! We shared three bottles at the party and then Eva and I split another bottle over Ouija. I was simmering with vivacity. I simply had to find something to occupy my time until the others awoke.

Much to Christian's dismay I tried amusing myself with my ability for a while; shifting through time, going back to the other day in the forest when he got a little friskier than usual. I liked being a voyeur on my own experiences. It was strangely satisfying; like watching a home movie only much more immersive. But after a while even that got boring. Watching Christian's hands on me wasn't quite the same as actually feeling his hands on me. I needed his touch. I ran my fingers along the collar of my shirt and grinned. It was his shirt actually and still smelled like him. "*Tin-cinnamon*," I sighed with a ginger inhale and suddenly I wanted nothing more than to be with him again. I flew up the stairs faster than a speeding bullet, opened the bedroom door and slipped between the sheets.

"Hope," he sighed feeling me against him.

I snuggled myself within the mountain of ivory colored sheets and grinned. He was more beautiful than an angel as he slept. "Dawn is breaking," I whispered.

"Well then fix it," he teased in reply.

I laughed and stroked his dark hair. "Christian," I said. "You have to wake up soon."

Slices of early morning brightness had already begun shining through the sheets. Christian would leave for La Fuente and I'd become daylight's prisoner again; being forced to keep in the shadows and hide in the slim pockets of darkness.

"It's morning?" he asked. "You should be sleeping." He opened his eyes. They were beautiful and glowing more brilliantly than a pair of perfectly faceted emeralds.

"I can't sleep," I said. "Eva and I were playing Ouija."

"Oh my god," he groaned covering himself back beneath the mountains of sheets again.

"What?" I said fumbling around to find him. I heaved one of the sheets high into the air; its billowy swell bulged like a balloon as it fell. I spotted Christian immediately. He was lying at the foot of the bed. "There you are," I said lunging toward him.

"Hope!" he laughed when swiftly the sheet fell down upon us both. Hidden beneath our snowy white tent I grabbed his hand and pulled him close. The moment out faces met he smiled at me. "You look beautiful this morning," he whispered.

"And so do you," I replied.

A moment later he pressed his tender lips to mine in a kiss. My skin tingled with his touch. It wasn't long before I felt him roaming the length of my body with his hands. I smiled inside; and suddenly I was the farthest thing from a fly on the wall. I grabbed his back and pulled him closer.

"You feel so good," he moaned in my ear.

"So do you."

He drew his lips to my neck and slathered my skin in kisses. A tiny breath escaped my lips while his fingers unbuttoned my shirt faster than the speed of light. He ogled my body eying the practically see-through white tank top and matching panties I was wearing underneath his shirt. He bit his lip and grinned.

"Touch me," I sighed through my thoughts as he pulled the button-up shirt off my shoulders and tossed it to the floor. A moment later I felt his hand upon the small of my back. With a hard tug he pulled me close. My chest heaved against him. His soft, cushiony lips graced my cheek and when he dragged his tongue along the length of my throat I wanted to explode inside. I couldn't hold back any longer. "I want you," I whispered.

Christian stopped; abruptly and completely. He withdrew himself from me and sighed.

"What's wrong?" I asked.

"We're moving too fast."

"No we're not."

"We are." He forced himself out of bed.

I reached for his arm and stroked it. "I'm not human," I insisted. "You won't break me." My voice was seductive.

He grinned.

I pressed the palms of my hands against his sculpted, naked chest. "Don't you want me that way Christian?"

"Of course I do!"

"Then what's stopping you?"

He heaved another sigh.

"What?" I asked sliding inside his thoughts. His mind was filled with me. Visions of me as a girl and images of me as woman underscored each and every one of his elaborately detailed thoughts. I licked my lips and grinned. "Our love has changed so much over the years," I said. I kissed his cheek. "I want to take it to that next level."

"I know you do," he replied easing under my touch.

"Don't get me wrong. It's not like messing around with you isn't fun...biting you," I teased, "tasting you," I giggled, "but I'm ready for more now—more than just your blood."

He laughed.

"When we drink from each other I can barely contain myself."

"Isn't that good enough?" he asked.

"No," I snapped. "I need more. I need all of you." I grinned. "And besides, the more I drink from you the more it's starting to feel as though something is fighting to take over."

"It's called pleasure."

"It's *not* pleasure."

"Paradise then?" His eyes glimmered playfully.

Paradise. "I want to show you something," I said moving from the bed to the antique wooden dresser. I grabbed the postcard from Ryan and handed it to him.

"What is this?" he asked eyeing the picture on the front of the postcard. He turned it over and read the inscription on the back. He drew his eyes away from the card and up to me. "Did Ryan send this to you?"

"That was my guess too."

"Who else knows you're here?"

"Richard."

"Your pathetic excuse for a father?" Christian shook his head. "It's not from him. He cut you off the moment you chose to be with me."

I nodded in agreement. "Do you remember that day when Ryan came here?"

"That day on the beach after we killed Maxim and Sakura?"

"She said something to me before she left. She told me that she wanted to find her own little piece of *paradise*." I swallowed hard. "At first I wasn't certain, but then, while you were sleeping, I went back to that day just to make sure."

"You went back?" he snarled, "even after I told you not to?"

"You told me not to go back to the day we met!"

"Hope," he said crossly.

"I don't remember you saying I couldn't go back at all."

"Why don't you go back and double check it?" he snapped.

"Don't be mad. I was just making sure." I pressed my lips to his shoulder in a kiss. "I'm not trying to ruin us. I'm not stupid."

He ran his fingers through his hair and sighed. He shook his head at me.

"C'mon Christian. Help me," I pleaded.

He thumbed the postcard again. His eyes narrowed. "Why do you think she sent it?"

I shrugged. "It was risky and she would have known that. I can't imagine why she'd take the chance of leading any of those bloodsucking murderers back to us—or even to her for that matter?"

"Maybe it's a trap?"

"Maybe," I said, "but that conversation about finding paradise was private."

"Maybe it's a cry for help," he insisted.

"You mean she *wants* me to find her?"

He stared at the photograph on the postcard again.

"But how would I find her? It's not like she left a return address."

"Well," he said, his eyes still glued to the photograph. "We know she's in Mexico."

"That narrows it down," I scoffed.

"Tulum," he said all of a sudden.

"Tulum?"

"Definitely. Look," he said showing me the photo. There was an image of a ruin atop a hillside. "I know that ruin. It's in Tulum.

I shook my head. "But why would Ryan go to Mexico? The sun is so strong that far south." I stroked the cable chain of my necklace.

"The further south she fled the better her chances were of outrunning anyone that would be searching for her."

I nodded. "So when do we go?"

"Go?"

"Mexico," I said. "When can we leave?"

"Hold on a second. We can't just pick-up and go to Mexico!"

"Why not?"

"I'm supposed to be running the shop. Eva already gave me a lecture about not being there enough."

"I'm sure they can manage for a few days without you."

He shook his head. "I don't know Hope. Travelling out of the country is a huge deal. It requires money and passports and a ton of veiling along the way."

"Christian," I insisted sweetly. "You said it yourself. The only reason Ryan would risk sending this was if she needed to tell me something— needed to tell *us* something." I stroked his chest. "C'mon," I purred. "It could be fun."

He grinned.

"And you know," I teased, "you were the only one who didn't give me a present."

"Ah," he snickered, "a guilt trip."

"Oh Christian," I pleaded. "Please?"

He took a deep breath. "It would be safer for you if we fly out at night."

"Thank you!" I beamed.

"But we can only stay a couple of days at most."

"Fine. Great!" I ran my hands around his neck and plastered his face in kisses.

"You're so gonna owe me for this," he said swiveling me around in his arms and pulling me against him. I pressed my lips to his and we kissed. A moment later we were back on the bed again. My body fell limply upon his and we melted together like sugar in water. Kissing turned to touching and touching quickly turned to something else. *"Taste me,"* he said through my thoughts. My fangs shot through my gums and within an instant I dug my teeth into his neck and started drinking his blood leaving the consummation of our love unrequited yet again.

9. Time Tunnel

I awoke with a shock enveloped in a cold sweat feeling the coercive pull of something fighting to take over. It definitely wasn't pleasure. The defiant draw forced my body into a paralyzed state of inertia. I struggled to resist it, but I was powerless. It was a force so tremendous pushing against me I had no other choice but to surrendered to it. I breathed in deeply, taking air into my lungs with a profound inhale.

A moment later my ability kicked into gear; I felt myself moving through time into the past. But something was different. I wasn't in control. I looked around and caught a glimpse of the bedroom sheets; they were speckled with droplets of blood, *our blood*, and suddenly I couldn't look any longer. I was jolted backward, through the bedroom door, along the hallway and down the stairs.

At the front of the house I found myself on the porch. The sun blazed. My virtually silent heart thumped a single beat in my chest. I was being pulled against my will from the shade covered veranda toward the sun. I tried to exhale; desperate to stop the rewind altogether, but nothing happened. The force of the pull was far beyond anything I'd ever experienced before. A swift jolt heaved me again, tearing me from the shadows and yanking me into the light. I slammed my bare feet on the porch and clenched my toes, digging my nails into the old, wooden planks for traction. It wasn't working. The force continued tugging me along. My heels gouged an unfathomable trail of slivered lumber behind me as I moved. I screamed inside, the sheer pain utterly implausible to vocalize.

The sun. A searing surge singed my skin the moment it touched me, but I didn't burn. There were no tendrils of smoke rising from my flesh. I throbbed lingering in the shower of beams and yet I didn't smolder.

An instant later I began to move at a speed more volatile than I had ever moved before. I was thrust into the driver's seat of Christian's 1969 raven-black Boss and found myself barreling along the road away from Ambrose House, away from everything. And that's when it hit me. I wasn't moving through *my* past, I was in someone else's—Christian's to be precise.

I was speeding through his experiences like a freight train. Within three seconds I had already surpassed the day we first met in the forest and within five seconds more I had taken in the entire twentieth century. I was flying rapidly and fighting against the coercive pull to try and push an exhale from my lungs. I wanted to stop. I needed to stop and an exhale was my only way of halting the rewind. These weren't my memories and I had no place being in the middle of them. Christian was angry enough that I frequented my own past, (constantly reiterating the imminent danger of the butterfly effect), he'd hate that I found a way inside of *his* past too.

Exhale, I told myself fighting against the force of the pull, but it was futile. I was utterly powerless. I couldn't catch my breath. Faster and faster I rushed rearward through the barrage of unfamiliar experiences that belonged to my beloved. And soon I was moving so quickly that it became virtually impossible to discern anything around me. Light and color merged together in a seamless unification while sounds began to blur into a numbing stream of static. Just then everything began to curve. I found myself surrounded by a concave tunnel, a wormhole of Christian's memories, and I was being pulled astern through the very heart of them.

Exhale damn it. I continued struggling to resist, shoving against the force just enough to let a single breath escape my lips. It didn't work. I couldn't breathe and my body began aching inside. I needed to stop the shifting immediately. The physical impact was crushing. I didn't know how much longer my body could take the pressure and I was starting to fear what residuals I was manifesting as well. I had to return to the present. There was simply no other choice. Tears rushed from my eyes and descended down my cheeks like rain. I pushed and pushed with all my might when suddenly, and most unexpectedly, the pressure finally began lessening. Optimism coursed through my veins like fire and as the force waned I exhaled, breathing out in a single overwhelming burst.

Instantly the concave time tunnel collapsed. Like a broken mirror it shattered into millions of miniscule pieces. I watched in awe as the colorful fragmented particles of Christian's past speckled the air. Just then everything went dark and a boom so loud it practically deafened my eardrums cut the silence. I closed my eyes and when I opened them again, when the boom subsided, I couldn't believe what I saw.

It was dark and hazy. Rain pelted my practically naked body as it descended from the dark sky. The planks beneath my feet creaked just the way the porch planks did at Ambrose, but this wasn't my house—I wasn't even on the ground! Just then a huge swell unexpectedly shook the earth. I began falling. I looked around as I tried to steady myself when I realized exactly where I was. "My God," I uttered aghast. This was the Ambrose, but not my house. It was the HMS Ambrose, Christian's ship.

I knew her skeleton like the back of my hand. I'd grown quite familiar with the HMS Ambrose when we defended ourselves against Maxim and Sakura beneath the sea. But that wasn't the only reason. Christian kept a healthy supply of the not-so-fabled treasure of El Dorado still aboard for safe-keeping and from time to time I'd helped him dive for capital.

This was Ambrose in her glory. I'd never her seen her like this before. The cannons, although not coral encrusted, were definitely the same cannons I knew from the bottom of the ocean. And the masts were the same masts upon which Sakura finally met her end when I shoved her over the side of the trawler and impaled her upon their tip. There were ropes and pegs and boards and other identifiable objects that seemed entirely familiar too. And since most of my house was built from the wreckage it seemed as though I was somehow strangely at ease with being aboard.

"Bloody hell!" a gentle male voice in an old-English dialect startled me.

I pivoted around on my heels, brushing my long soppy locks out of my eyes. A young man with straggly strands of wheat colored hair was staring at me. I recognized him immediately—from old photographs. It was William. He was Christian's closest friend in the world, the one with whom he built Ambrose House and founded our little family of vampires. My faced paled as I stared at him.

"Who are you?" he asked spellbound.

I looked at his face and wanted to grin. Willo, I thought to myself. Eva and I had just summoned him on the Ouija board only hours earlier in the present.

"So pale and so...what are you?" he asked mesmerized. His English accent was thick.

I didn't respond. This was Christian's past. I wasn't supposed to be here let alone interacting within it.

"Beautiful," he said with a toothy grin.

I fought the smile that crept its way across my raindrop-studded face. I knew it was against my better judgment to respond, but I wanted to. I'd heard so many stories about William and seen so many photographs I practically felt as though I knew him already.

"Where did you come from?" he asked wide-eyed, his dirty hand inching its way towards my cheek.

I recoiled a little stumbling over my own feet as I moved.

"Careful there," he urged. "Don't be frightened."

The blue of his eyes and the tenderness of his face reminded me of my own. I felt like I was living a dream and yet I knew that I wasn't. This was reality, granted an ancient reality hundreds of years in the past, but still reality.

"So lovely," he said inching closer.

William's realness captivated me: the tattering of his shirt, the rips in his woolen breeches and his smell too. Christian spoke of the ripe rankness once and here I was aboard his ship practically tasting the cloying stench for myself.

"Did you come from the sea?" William's eyes were elated with excitement.

A laugh escaped my lips and yet I managed to abstain from speaking. I tried to absorb all that the moment had to offer. I prepared myself to exhale, ready to speed ahead away from the past and back to the present—*my* present, when all of a sudden I felt a hand upon my wrist. William grabbed me with a tough tug and pulled me into a dark corner of the ship with him.

"Shh," he insisted pressing his grimy finger to my mouth in an effort to silence me.

I trembled in his arms and I listened anxiously to the voices and footfalls that resounded.

"This is hell," an airy male tone insisted. "The entire voyage has been a sham. We should have abandoned ship back in Colombia."

"Perhaps," a sweet, familiar male voice replied. "But we're here now and we have to make the best of it if we want to stay alive."

A chill ran down my spine. My heart thumped in my chest and my body fluttered with delight. It was Christian. The sweet tenor of his voice was irrefutable. I had to see him. He was still human—still seventeen and vigorous with life; his human heart beating seventy-two beats per minute and his unsullied blood coursing through his vulnerable, human body. I moved from the shadows to steal a glance when William grabbed my arm and stopped me.

"It's not safe for you," he insisted.

"It's not safe for you either," I replied unthinkingly. I froze.

"You can speak!" he uttered. "And your voice...your accent." His face paled.

I bit my lip, my body stinging wildly with regret. I knew it was a mistake to speak—it was a mistake to even be here at all. The cold blood in my immortal veins felt as though it was freezing over. I was paralyzed with remorse. It was though I could actually feel the universe suddenly shifting beneath my feet. The butterfly effect was in motion and I knew that somehow the residuals were manifesting in that single moment somewhere ahead in time.

"Who are you?" William asked when suddenly the ship heaved. The immense upsurge moved the ground and I took my chance to escape. I exhaled hard, pushing every last breath of air in my body out through my lips and within a fraction of an instant I was moving again.

There really was no place like home and I wanted to be there more than anything in the world. I didn't belong in my Tin Man's past and I needed to get out of it as quickly as I could. I closed my eyes and wished for a pair of ruby slippers to whisk me back to where I belonged, but knew I'd have to settle on travelling the time tunnel instead.

Faster than any measure I soared ahead into the future toward the present. Light and color blurred together while time and space seemingly didn't exist. And before long I knew I'd be home again. When the flash of white dulled and the deafening boom subsided I opened my eyes. I was shrouded in my satin sheets back in Ambrose House nestled in my bed next to Christian. The sweet tin-cinnamon scent of his body was potent. I opened my eyes and froze. His chest was partly draped with the bed sheet. The satin and his skin were slathered in blood—vermilion in color and dangerously irresistible.

10. Truth

His face was angelic. His body was bloodstained. Hunger mounted in my throat as I stared. I wanted to taste him. I wanted to lick his skin and delight in the succulent tin-cinnamon savor that seeped through his pores, but I didn't. As tempting as it was the immense spill troubled me. I'd never seen this much of his blood out in the open before. Sure we drank with heedlessness to heighten our pleasure, but this was different. We never drank to this degree and we *never* left any of our blood behind.

"Christian," I said in an effort to rouse him. He didn't respond. "Christian," I insisted shaking his arm. He still didn't respond. My god, I thought to myself. Was this the residual—the butterfly effect of my reckless actions? "Wake up damn it!" I slapped him on the bicep.

"Okay," he uttered drowsily.

"Thank god," I sighed relieved.

Christian sat up. Blood leisurely oozed down his torso. He touched himself. "What happened?"

"I don't know."

His brow narrowed. He brought the stained satin sheets to his nose and inhaled. "This is my blood!" he said appalled.

I moved toward him. I ran my fingers up his chest and played with the gooey red pools on his skin.

"Hope," he snapped. "What the hell happened here?"

I shrugged. He smelled delicious and felt so good to touch. The feeling of his blood was divine, like running my fingers through trickles of diamonds. I was mesmerized and felt my body beginning to respond when unexpectedly he withdrew from me. He yanked the sheets with a hard tug. The soiled satin flew though the air, its billowy hollows swelling bulbously in their centers as they floated to the floor. Visions of us together kissing, touching and drinking abruptly flooded my mind. I looked at his neck and then at his wrists. Faint scarring of freshly healed bite marks covered his skin like polka dots.

"I remember drinking from you," I admitted. I stroked the sets of bite marks on his skin. "But I don't remember doing all of this."

"Well I certainly didn't do it to myself," he said withdrawing. He jumped out of bed and threw on his clothes.

"We drank from each other—remember? And then we fell asleep. I was right here beside you. I swear."

"And that's it?"

I nodded.

He shook his head and glared. "Your hair," he said. "Why is your hair dripping with water?"

"My hair?" I said perplexed. I grabbed a few strands. It was wet; drenched with rainwater from over two hundred years ago in the past—*his past*. My heart thumped in my chest. Guilt rotted in the pit of my stomach. I couldn't tell him where I'd been. The truth felt like a sledgehammer to the skull.

"Don't bother lying," he said. "I can read your thoughts."

"Then why even ask me? If you plan on reading my—"

"I ask because I'm a gentleman," he interrupted. "And I'd rather give you the benefit of the doubt. I'd like to think that we trust each other. I'd like to think that you would *want* to tell me the truth."

"I do Christian. I really do."

"Then why aren't you?"

"I...it's complicated."

He shook his head at me. The tension in the room was high. I hated deceiving him, but I knew the truth would infuriate him. Somehow disappointing him seemed easier than hurting him.

"What a mess," he said eyeing the bedroom.

"I'll clean it," I offered.

"I wasn't talking about the room." His voice was hard. "Us," he uttered.

My eyes widened. "We're not a mess Christian. I won't let anything ruin us. I love you."

"Then why is it so hard for you to trust me?"

I turned away from him. I stared at the shafts of sunlight blazing though the blinds. Rays fell upon the bloodied sheet like stained Bordeaux on a tablecloth after a good party.

"What a waste," Christian lamented picking up one of the sheets. "B could have used this to cork. It's such a waste of blood." He heaved a sigh and tossed the sheet to the floor again.

Blood I thought to myself with revelation. It was Christian's blood in my veins that enabled me to travel within his memories. It had to be. I always came alive when I drank from him and this time I drank more than I ever had before.

"Sun's up," he said sitting on the edge of the bed. He started tying the laces on his old, dirty running shoes. He looked like a kid; a teenager with unkempt dark hair and scruffy old runners. "I've got to go," he said standing up, a brilliant beam of sunlight circled his skin in a subtle halo of smoke.

"You look pale," I uttered, "paler than normal."

"You're right," he snapped bitterly. He ran his fingers through his dark hair before liberating his arm of a dusting of his own ashes. "I look pale because I am pale. You nearly bled me dry last night." He turned away and started walking toward the door. "I need to eat...blood or chocolate or candy or something."

And then it hit me. My thoughts abruptly filled with notions from that stupid article in Henry's nerdy science magazine. I remembered Joe, the heart transplant recipient, and his sudden desire for candy and camping after recovery. They were memories—memories from Joe's donor. I stared at Christian again and the blood speckled bedroom from last night. Memories, I thought to myself. If memories had the potential to be stored in individual cells, and blood were cells so to speak, then maybe Christian's blood possessed the possibility of retaining memories too. Maybe the oversaturation of *his* blood in my system gave me the capability to somehow travel into his past on a cellular level.

"Christian!" I called out elatedly.

He stopped walking and turned back around to face me. "Yeah," he said with anticipation.

I looked him in the eyes, my heart breaking as I stared. What was I thinking? I couldn't tell him my revelation. I wasn't ready to divulge that fact that I did it again: time-shifted. It would kill him knowing that I'd not only gone against his wishes, but that I'd potentially made things even worse.

"I'm...I'm sorry," I uttered.

He heaved a heavy sigh. "Me too," he said deflated. "Be ready when I get back. We'll leave at sundown."

"Mexico?" I said hopefully. "You still want to go with me?"

"Of course."

I smiled, but he didn't smile back. He turned around, moved toward the door and left instead. I didn't feel him inside my head. Not even a little. He didn't help himself to the truth and I didn't divulge it either. I knew he preferred hearing my truths to taking them uninvited and he would wait, no matter how long it took, until I was ready to tell him. *When exactly would I be ready?* Divulging the fact that I'd I discovered a portal into the past, a past that wasn't even my own, wasn't simple. There was no way to soften that kind of blow. Christian was going to be angry and I knew for certain that he'd fixate on what could happen instead of what did happen.

I shook my head and tried clearing my mind. I focused my thoughts on Mexico instead. I was glad Christian was still okay with going on our trip. I wanted him there. I needed him there. I'd never traveled anywhere beyond locally since becoming a vampire. I felt like I didn't know how to blend in or how to act normal anymore. He could help me. I moved to the dresser, opened the drawers and took out some clothes.

What to pack? I didn't really know what we'd be doing in Mexico or even how long we'd be staying. I tossed some shirts and socks across the room, whipping them to the bed like snowballs when I hit the antique lamp on my nightstand. I bolted diagonally at a super-sonic speed through the sunlight to catch it before hitting the ground.

"Ah," I sighed cradling it in the palm of my hand. And then I looked ahead. I blinked my lashes a few times to shade my eyes from harsh brightness. *The sun*, I thought to myself. It was shining upon me and yet I wasn't burning. I put the lamp on the floor and raised my hand into the light. I played with the rays, daring myself to expose more and more flesh to it and linger longer. *Why wasn't I burning like before?* The ash was there, but not the pain. I was withstanding the sun! *Why?* I stayed and played for what felt like forever just basking in the rays until finally, creeping out like ghosts from deep within my pores, the smoldering actively returned. The tingles turned to pain and I knew instantly that the continual cremation was imminent. I pulled myself away from the light and back into the safety of the shade again.

I inspected my hands with a peculiar pride and smiled. I was getting stronger. I could feel it. I hid in the shadows. The blood-soaked sheets sat near my feet. Christian's blood was everywhere. I eyed the spill and grinned. I carefully inhaled. *Tin-cinnamon*, I sighed in my thoughts and suddenly my body began responding. My fangs shot through my gums and my eyes glimmered. I dropped to my knees.

"Forgive me," I pleaded. I took the sheets into my hands. I brought the fabric to my mouth and sucked it, imbibing every minuscule morsel of Christian's blood that remained. The addicting savor of his sweetness invigorated me instantly. I felt alive and suddenly I was desperate to go back into his past again—desperate to go back to William.

11. Mates

The gods were most definitely angry on the night that Christian became a vampire. I had never seen so much rain in my entire life. Torrential downpour didn't even begin to describe the seething tempest that scathed the blackened skies. It was dark too. A thick haze of smoke stained the air like a sickness. Even the stars refused to shine; hiding high in the heavens above, keeping a safe distance over the gloomy grimness that plagued the earth below.

Was it wrong to be here? A blaze of guilt surged through my body. I was about to exhale, return to the present again, when the ship moved. The Ambrose heaved like a seesaw beneath my feet and I stumbled, dropping to the wet, wooden planks with a thud. I fell hard and immediately began sliding across the deck. I dug my fingernails into the boards clawing for traction, but my effort was futile. As the ship continued heaving, I continued sliding when all of a sudden something stopped me—someone had caught me!

"You!" William said amazed. He pulled me from the floor. "Where did you go? You were right in front of me and then you—"

"Shh," I whispered.

"*What* are you?"

"It's not important."

At that moment a thunderous howl filled the air with a strange menacing resonance. Was it the beast—the evil monster that I knew would soon turn both Christian and William into vampires? Had he already arrived to desecrate the crew of the Ambrose as Christian had described in our present life?

"Dear god," William uttered. He pulled me by the hand into a nearby enclosure. "You'll be safe here," he said and then he started to leave.

"You're leaving me?" I asked.

"Aye," he said. "I must find Alex."

"Alex?"

"She's on the ship somewhere. I must find—"

"A woman? I didn't think women were allowed on military ships."

"They're not," he said. "But you're here aren't you?"

My eyes widened.

"Keep quiet and you'll be safe." William moved away from me and back out into the storm.

A woman, I thought to myself. Christian never mentioned a woman on the Ambrose. I brought my knees to my chest and wrapped my arms around them. I kept quiet just as William had instructed, but it wasn't without difficulty. The sounds of death drowned out the storm. It was all I could hear. I closed my eyes and tried silencing the noise. Cries and whimpers, wails and sobs, each man's last breath was like a chorus of ghastly harmonies. It was insufferable to make quiet. I couldn't bear it any longer. I opened my eyes and readied myself to exhale just as William returned again. He was dripping with rainwater and grasping what appeared to be a young, slim boy under his arm.

"Batten down the hatches misses," the young fellow said, "it be hell out there." He crouched in the darkened narrow enclosure with me.

"This is Alex." William motioned to the young boy.

"You're a woman?"

"Aye," she replied. "Alexandra was me real name once upon a time."

I nodded captivated by her utterly androgynous appearance. She was dirty and dressed in men's clothes. Her hair was short, blonde and scruffy and her features were both feminine and masculine simultaneously. Beneath the filth she really did look like a young boy, but also a young woman too.

"Thought I'd lost you out there Alex." William's voice was tense. "I nearly couldn't find you."

"It's a good job you did," she replied. "That blasted howling is givin' me a headache."

"It's a demon I tell you." William's voice wavered.

"A demon?" Alex scoffed. "No such thing."

"It isn't human," I uttered inadvertently.

"That be so?" Alex's thick English accent dripped with skepticism.

"And I know it's not a demon either," I said.

Her untidy brows narrowed as she stared at me. "You with that monster is ya'?"

"No!" I snapped. "I just happen to know that he's dangerous."

"And you?" she pressed. "Is you dangerous too?"

"Alex," William defended. "The lass is me mate. She's the one I told you of...from the sea. She ain't dangerous."

"The sea eh?" Alex said. "Is you a mermaid then?"

"No." I snickered.

"She ain't got no tail," William insisted. "She be a siren!"

"A siren," Alex uttered. "Then sing us a song! Us lot could use a tender tune. Go on!"

At that moment another howl echoed through the night air. This time it sounded much closer than before.

"He be nearing," William uttered worriedly.

Alex took a deep breath. "Women really is bad luck aboard a ship." She shook her head. "How's it me and the likes of you happen aboard this ill-fated vessel at the same time eh?"

I shrugged.

"If evil comes our way its 'cause of you misses." Her tone was sharp. "I did me best to play the part. *I* wanted to see the world and they weren't taking women. I took matters into my own hands. Changed me fate. Became a boy."

"And do they know? I mean that you're a-"

"Girl?" she interrupted. "Can't imagine I would have survived the sail with these savages had they'd known."

"But *he* knows," I said pointing to William.

"Aye, but only him. He ain't even told his closest mate."

"Lord," William said. "I need to find Christian. Did you see him out there?"

"Christian!" I exclaimed.

"You know Christian?" William asked taken aback.

"No," I lied. "Forget it. In fact forget me altogether." Just then there was another howl. Louder than thunder, the beast's bawl resonated with ferociousness. The man-sized monster was right upon us just outside when suddenly his arm thrust through the haze inside our enclosure. I spotted his scar immediately; it was large with teeth like a jigsaw and it sat across his forearm just as Christian had described.

"Dear god!" Alex shrieked the moment the monster touched her with his hairy hands. An instant later he grabbed her. He pulled her up, gripping her by the arm and dragged out into the open.

"No!" William roared. He pulled at the hilt of his cutlass.

"Don't!" I ordered apprehending him. "It won't kill him."

Just then the sound of Alexandra's scream shook the deck beneath my feet. The beast had flung her through the air with a hard swing. Her skull thumped like a rock upon the wooden planks as she landed.

"Let me go!" William shouted. "I will not sit by and watch her die!"

"I can't. It's for your own good. Trust me."

"Trust ya'?" His voice was incensed. "How can I trust ya' when I don't even know who ya' are!"

"I'm no one," I replied, "but I really need you to trust me. Don't go out there! He'll only end up killing you too and I know for a fact that you don't die here." Regret surged through my body the instant the words left my lips. What had I done? Why had I said that? I felt the earth suddenly shifting beneath my feet again, only this time it wasn't the boat. *Residuals*, I thought to myself. What terrible consequence had I caused somewhere in time? My body froze. I wanted to dwell upon my mistake, but I knew I still had a chance to fix things. I needed to help William. I needed to protect his destiny.

I grabbed him by the shoulders. I pressed my hand over his mouth. "Shh," I whispered. A moment later the sinister sound of soft tissue being torn cut the silence. William and I looked ahead. The beast had bitten into Alex's warm flesh. He was drinking from her; I could smell the potent essence of her life energy in the air. And then he stopped. He retched with pain and doubled over. He coughed up Alex's blood across the deck in a shower of crimson.

"Wo-man," he roared dragging the word out as he spoke. His voice was dark and so incredibly deep it seemed abysmal. He howled and dropped her limp body like a sack of rocks. The sound of her bones breaking echoed upon impact. "Dir-ty bl-ood," he mumbled spitting the last of her blood upon her broken body. He leaned in close and smelled her skin, his long dreadlocks swept across her face like rows of dangling snakes as he moved. And then he spit on her, secreting with a swift splat. The liquid emerged like venom, brownish in color, before becoming a steamy, vaporous haze that burned holes in her flesh. The holes illuminated with flashes of light when all of a sudden Alexandra vanished altogether.

"Where did she go?" I uttered, panicked. I looked ahead. All that remained was a large wooden sarcophagus in the form of an old fashioned ship's figurehead; a wooden lady with scales like plates of armor and hair the faded tone of gold. "Oh my god," I uttered. It was her—the wooden lady that hung at the base of the staircase in Ambrose House! My hand slipped from William's lips.

"Demon!" he shouted at the top of his lungs.

The beast heard his voice instantly. A split-second later he was upon us. His huge arm furiously fished through our darkened hideaway. William kicked and shoved, but the beast was relentless. I could have left. It would have been easy. I could have forced my time-traveling exhale, but I didn't. The beast's sharp nails clawed at William's skin and with each swipe chunks of his flesh were ripping apart. I couldn't just leave him like that and so I decided to join him instead. I was caught up in the moment. I began fighting for William, but even I couldn't seem to stop him. Just then my arm began to throb. I looked down. Deep fingernail impressions had been scratched into my flesh! The beast had cut *me*! The injury burned like fire! It was so raw and deep. It even appeared to smolder. A crimson spill oozed from the cut and within an instant the beast had already detected the distinct scent of *my* blood in the air! With a guttural howl he forced his immense frame even farther into our little enclosure.

"NO!" William grunted struggling to heave the beast away with all his might. The beast stumbled backward, but the strength of the thrust forced William to fall out into the open.

"No!" I shouted, prepared to retrieve him, when suddenly the beast lunged, attacking William's body as though it was a piece of meat! I watched appalled as the beast dug his sharp fangs into his flesh! The sickening sound of ripping flesh scathed my eardrum. I was horrified by what I'd seen—what I'd caused. Tears fell from my eyes, stinging my cheeks and in a moment of sheer repugnance I exhaled, pushing air from my lungs in a desperate effort to return back to the present again.

Why? Why? Why? There was no righteous answer. I'd done something terrible and I wasn't ready to pay the cost for my actions. Anger, regret, hate and disgust swirled within me. I was frozen in a statue stance as I sped back to the present. A sweeping state of darkness overwhelmed me entirely. My mind was like a sieve and couldn't hold even a single thought. But when the wormhole finally fragmented and the boom subsided I reanimated again. I knew I was home. I could smell it.

12. Vortex

Everything had changed. I felt it in my bones. I rushed from the bedroom and down the stairs to the front of the house. I practically trembled as I reached the first floor. It was her—the wooden lady sitting as she always had by the foot of the staircase. I recognized her timber locks and crimson lumber pout instantly, but there was a sadness in her face I'd never noticed before.

"Alexandra," I whispered to her. My eyes filled with tears again. Droplets instantly caught themselves in my lashes. I blinked, but the tears wouldn't clear. And when I went to wipe them away I realized that they weren't tears at all, but blood in fact. A chill ran down my spine.

I opened the front door of the house and sped across the porch. I stumbled as I moved down to the grass. "The steps?" I said perplexed. "Where the hell are the cement steps?" My eyes bulged. I scrutinized the absence of the crumbling cement steps that normally sat at the foot of the porch. Why weren't they there? The moment my feet hit the grass, I knew that it was because of me. *A residual*; I was changing things.

I turned away from Ambrose House and rushed across the lawn. The sun was shining brightly above me, but I didn't care. I wasn't burning in it. Faster and faster I ran until finally I reached the threshold of the woods. I bolted through the trees like a rocket at super-sonic speed. I didn't know where I was going, but I knew I couldn't stay cooped up in the house all day. The quicker I moved, the better I felt. At one point I was moving so rapidly that even the mist-like air began smudging and bending around me as I soared through it. I felt good, but after a while reality seeped its way back into my thoughts again. I stopped running. Perish was an island and not a very big one at that; my problems were bound to catch up to me sooner or later.

When I reached the beach I headed for the water. The sun was high in the sky and hotter than hell. I walked through the rays and let the radiant beams tingle against my skin. It felt good and almost reminded me of being human again. I looked out at the ocean. A dolphin swam past, just ahead, in the distance. I knew that my grandmother loved dolphins. She wrote about them quite frequently in her journals. I started to smile when all of a sudden I felt myself rushing to the water's edge! I plummeted beneath the sea. An instant later I realized that I was swimming next to the dolphin! I reached out and grabbed its fin. His body was strong and felt like rubber to touch. I closed my eyes, emptied my thoughts and let him sail me along for a while.

I used to fear the water. I used to dream about it pressing in on me and appropriating my last living breaths. I felt differently now. I wasn't afraid of anything! My heart barely beat—I wasn't human anymore. I was practically invincible. I could even stay beneath the water for hours without needing to go up for air.

All of a sudden the dolphin dove down deep! I held on tighter. He was very obliging and even took me on a grand tour of the cemetery at the bottom of the sea. Perish Key was cursed. Everyone knew it. Over the years numerous ships had sunken here, just off shore. I opened my eyes to scrutinize the rows of fallen vessels laid to rest in a crowded graveyard on the seabed floor. I liked it down here—its silence was peaceful despite the rumors that it was haunted by the souls of deceased sailors. And when we neared what remained of the HMS Ambrose I was back on familiar ground again. I let go of my dolphin friend and watched him swim away.

The HMS Ambrose, I sighed in my thoughts. I'd been aboard her in Christian's past only moments ago and yet here I was looking at her shattered skeleton at the bottom of the ocean. I swam closer. Shafts of sunlight cut through the water with beams of brilliance as I moved. The Ambrose looked different to me now—now that I'd been aboard her back in her glory days.

I neared what remained of the deck and swam its length when all of a sudden I saw it: the narrow enclosure. I recognized it instantly. It was the spot where William, Alex and I hid from the beast. My eyes widened as I stared. The enclosure was shattered and badly coral encrusted, but still identifiable. A surge of guilt hit me and then I saw something through the corner of my eye! I pivoted around. Like a shadow in the distance, the strange vision captivated me. *Was it a ghost?* I edged closer to take a better look.

I moved through the kelp with a steady swiftness. The sounds of the ocean throbbed in my ears with a muted haze. And then I saw it again! It was an outline; blurry and translucent and it stood before me as plainly as the seaweed at my feet. Like a man, the inky shadow wobbled with the motion of the water. He was tall and pale with blondish colored hair and blue eyes. He was familiar—*very familiar.* He looked an awful lot like William! My eyes widened! I tried focusing on his face when suddenly he spoke to me!

"Human," he uttered.

I froze when all of a sudden a massive creature grazed me! I fell forward, my ankles tangled in the seaweed. It was the dolphin I'd hitched a ride with earlier! I looked ahead. The ghost, or whatever it was, had disappeared. *Damn it,* I uttered in my thoughts. I returned to untangling myself from the seaweed when I was distracted by the most peculiar thing. It was a bubble and it moved toward me with an undeniable gracefulness. Shaped like a doughnut, this perfect bubble neared, and when I reached out to touch it, it instantly shattered into a multitude of mini bubbles! I widened my gaze again and watched as my dolphin friend swiftly blew two more bubble rings. One daintily floated through the water upward toward the surface, while the other stayed behind. The dolphin played with it for while, carefully nudging and toying with it until it too dispersed into a mass of mini bubbles. And as I watched I knew instantly that these spectacular vortices were much like my ability to shift through time; sooner or later the delicate balance I was toeing would inevitably shatter too.

Moments later the dolphin swam away. I stiffened and set out to find the ghost, or whatever it was again. I swam toward where I'd seen it last. I rounded a huge wall of rotted wood, evidence of where the ship's hull had been. I saw movement within the Ambrose's skeleton, when I ran into something. *SMASH!* I looked up. *Christian?* He was standing before me, shirtless and radiant. He was grasping a gold plate in his hand.

"What are you doing here?" he asked soundlessly through our internal connection.

I shrugged.

He glared, grabbed my hand and pulled me up to the surface. When we reached the beach I flaked out on the sand.

"Hope!" he raged. "Get out of the sun!"

"It's okay," I sighed stealing a breath.

"Okay?"

"Yeah. I'm tolerating it a lot better all of a sudden."

He grimaced. His face was vexed, but pretty as ever. Water droplets hung from the tips of his dark hair like snowflakes.

"Why are you out here?" he asked.

"I was..."

He ran his hands through his hair. He was wet and pale and strong and beautiful. I grinned.

"Hope," he pressed, distracting me.

"I was swimming," I said stupidly, "with dolphins." I cringed instantly at the absurdity of what I'd just uttered.

"Dolphins?"

"It was only one dolphin actually, but yes."

He raised an eyebrow at me.

"It's the truth Christian."

"Swimming with dolphins. That's the truth?"

I nodded.

"If you say so." There was disappointment in his pretty green eyes.

"Why were *you* down there?" I motioned to the treasure in his hand.

"I was making a withdrawal."

"Seems a shame," I lamented. "Having to give up something so beautiful."

He eyed the plate. "Everything has a price I suppose."

"Yeah. I guess it does."

He sat on the sand next to me. "Mexico is a big risk. We'll need the cash for incidentals."

I stroked the golden edge of the pristine artifact. "That should buy some kind of incidentals."

"La Fuente doesn't pay for everything you know."

"I know."

"A trip can be—"

"Expensive."

"Dangerous."

"I know."

"Leaving Perish is like leaving heaven." His eyes hardened. "You realize that right?"

I nodded.

He sighed and put the plate on the sand beside him.

"Christian," I uttered. "Can I ask you something?"

"Yeah."

"Do you come here a lot?"

"The Ambrose?"

I nodded.

He shrugged. "Not often." He licked his lovely lips and grinned. "Why would anyone want to come here—this cemetery beneath the sea," he sighed.

I half-smiled.

"For me it's like revisiting the scene of a crime when I go down there. I'll never forget the faces of the crew."

I nodded uneasily.

"Why do you ask anyway?"

"I don't know."

"Hope," he pressed. "Why do you ask?"

"Have you ever seen anything strange while you were down there?"

He lowered his brows. "The whole thing is strange!"

"Never mind."

"Seen anything," he insisted. "Like what?"

I shrugged. "Like something that shouldn't be there."

"Let me tell you, all of those fallen vessels shouldn't be there, but they are."

I nodded empathetically.

"So many souls of lost sailors," he shook his head.

"It really is a graveyard isn't it?"

"It's worse. It's like a submerged city of the dead down there. I find it nearly impossible to not believe in ghosts."

"Ghosts?" I said intrigued.

"Don't you believe in ghosts Hope?"

"Well yeah."

He turned to me and smirked. I could feel him penetrating my thoughts. "What aren't you telling me?"

"It's nothing," I uttered.

"It's something," he countered. "Tell me."

I shrugged. "I mean it's probably nothing—maybe just my eyes playing tricks on me."

"Your eyes don't play tricks on you Hope." His voice was hard. "Now tell me what happened."

I shrugged. "I was down there in the Ambrose and I thought I saw something."

"Like what?"

"A person."

His expression hardened instantly, concern overwhelmed him.

"I don't think it was a *real* person."

"A *real* person?"

"He was more like a vision."

"*He?*"

"Oh forget it. This is stupid."

He smiled. "It's not stupid." He touched my hand. "What did you see down there? Tell me Hope."

"A man."

"But not a *real* man."

I shrugged.

"What was he then?"

"I don't know. A ghost." I sank my head in my hands. "This sounds so dumb talking about it."

"It's not dumb. What did he look like?"

I peeked up through my fingers. "Well, he was blurry, but I knew that he was tall. Blonde. Fair skin."

Christian nodded.

I pursed my lips.

"What?" he pressed.

"I think it was William."

"William!" he exclaimed.

"Forget it," I quickly retorted. "I...I'm not sure what I saw."

Christian's face was vexed with emotion. He looked into my eyes. "That's not all—is it?"

I knew he could sense my apprehension.

"Tell me Hope. What else happened down there?"

"It spoke to me!"

"It spoke?" His eyes widened. "*William* spoke to you?"

I shrugged. "I don't know. Maybe it was just *you* in my head!"

"It wasn't me." He heaved a sigh. "So what did he say?"

"Only one word. Human. I think."

"Human?"

I nodded.

"Well that's odd, considering that you're *not* even human."

I shrugged and stared into Christian's electric green eyes. He was so incredibly beautiful. He smoldered with attractiveness. After a long moment he leaned into kiss me. The touch of his lips to mine was like heaven. I wrapped my arms around his back and pulled him against me and suddenly I was beneath him on the sand. His body pressed down upon mine. I sighed inside. I twisted my leg over his and forced him even closer.

"Christian," I whispered soundlessly. *"I love you. I don't want to fight with you anymore."* I ran my hands down his back and around to his waist and when my fingers met with the button on his pants I felt him withdrawing from me once more.

"I can't," he said retreating.

"Why?"

"Because. I just can't."

I sat up and glowered.

"Oh Hope," he snarled.

My eyes hardened. "It's not that you can't Christian. It's that you won't."

He smirked, leaned in close and kissed me on the forehead. "I've booked us on an eight-thirty flight."

"Whatever."

"Don't be mad. I thought you didn't want to fight anymore."

I shrugged.

"And besides," he scoffed. "I'm the one who should be mad."

"Why?"

"You won't tell me where you've been going...what you've been doing." He heaved another sighed. "I just want to protect you. Can't you understand that?"

My stomach sank. I cringed with remorse. I didn't want to lie and yet I hated keeping secrets from him. I wanted him to know where I had been—I just didn't want to have to tell him. I tried imposing my thoughts, but his mind was like a wall; hard and impenetrable.

"I told you," he said. "You're gonna have to tell me if you want me to know." He picked up the antique golden plate and rose to his feet. He shook his head at me. "Eight-thirty Hope. We've got to be at the airport a little earlier. So be ready."

"Fine."

"See you at the house," he said. He turned around to leave and within seconds he was gone.

I looked out toward the ocean. It was peaceful and tranquil and nothing like the way I felt inside. I thought of the dolphin again. I recalled the delicate bubble rings he was playing with at the bottom of the sea. I sighed inside. I was on the verge of shattering my own bubble and I didn't even know how to stop it from happening. Shifting through time so often and now moving through Christian's blood on a cellular level into his past, was altogether risky and I knew it.

I flopped further back on the sand and watched as subtle tendrils of smoke started rising from my skin. "This is going to be a long trip," I groaned under my breath feeling the weight of the world suddenly pressing against me.

13. Mexico

November, 1984.

I worry for my daughter Audrey. When will she ever grow up and finally start acting like the woman she's meant to be? Henry says she is not to be pushed, but I disagree. Audrey needs to learn control. She needs to harness her anger—especially now that she is to become a mother herself! I'm drained. I can't parent her alone anymore. I need Henry's support in this.

I flipped ahead a little. I stopped flipping when I reached the page laden with heavy ink. Words were angrily scrawled across the page. I drew my eyes downward and continued reading.

December, 1984.

PERISH HASN'T SEEN THE SUN FOR DAYS!

Henry and the others have been rejoicing in its absence.

FOR ME...

It's become cold and my old bones have grown heavy with doubt.

I look to the sky above and fear that something sinister is brewing...

I had another dream. Last night I dreamt about an accident. A terrible accident. Lives were lost. My heart still hurts when I think about it.

"Hope!" Christian shouted distracting me.

I jumped, startled, pulled my eyes away from the journal and looked up.

"We're here."

I peered out of the tiny airplane window. "*Mexico,*" I sighed. A rush of adrenaline was beginning to surge through my body. I reached inside my purse and pulled out my grandmother's hand mirror. I eyed my reflection.

"You're still the fairest," he whispered cheekily.

I put down the mirror and nudged his arm. Our adventure was about to begin.

Christian and I barely talked on the plane and the cab ride from Cancun was even worse. Our conversations were brief and pointless and driving me crazy. There really was only so much we could keep saying to each other about the weather. I was glad when we stopped in the seaside town of Playa del Carmen to rent a motorbike. There was an unusual, spicy tang in the evening air. It reminded me that we were indeed in a foreign country. I liked travelling. Distant places filled with foreign mysteries intrigued me greatly and now we were in the middle of our own little mystery. I needed to find my friend Ryan. If Christian was right, and he usually was, then Ryan's postcard was a call for help. What the hell had she gotten herself into?

"Where are we going?" I asked. "Did you make a reservation somewhere? I hope you did. You should have let me organize everything."

"Relax," he said. "Don't you trust me?" There was a hint of cynicism in his voice.

"Hum," I said picking up my heavy backpack and slipping it over my shoulders. "Why couldn't we take luggage like normal people?"

"I told you. No checked bags. It's too risky."

"Yeah, I know. It's dangerous. Risky." I rolled my eyes.

"C'mon," he insisted getting on the bike.

"I'm coming," I said hopping on the back, "but I still don't see how a rental car would have been dangerous."

Christian laughed. "It's not."

"Then why didn't you rent one?"

"Because Hope," he said, "where we're going there are no roads."

Just then he revved the engine and within an instant we sped off into the night. I wrapped my arms around him and let the soothing sound of the wind tickle my ears. Mexico was somber at night and I was eager to see its splendor in the day. As we flew through the dark along the empty road I started thinking about finding Ryan again. I wondered why she'd come to Mexico in the first place and worried whether she'd gotten herself into something she couldn't get out of. I was starting to think that finding her would be much more difficult than I even imagined.

Christian unexpectedly veered off the main road. We drove through a thicket of greenery. Verdant leaves brushed against me as we sped along. Christian was right—there were no roads where we were going. The ride got bumpy, but within a few minutes he decelerated and finally killed the engine altogether.

Tropical plumage hugged the surroundings. Only a tall metal gate with an ornate iron lock stood out from the greenery. He jumped off the bike and walked over to the gate.

"Where are we?" I asked.

"Home," he said, "at least temporarily." He turned around, grabbed our backpacks with one hand and helped me off the bike with the other.

"This doesn't look like a hotel."

"It's not," he said dropping my hand to fiddle with the lock.

"No key?" I teased suspiciously.

"Who needs keys when you're a vampire right?" With a crushing grip he broke the lock in two. The gate swung open.

"What are we doing here? Breaking and entering? How is any of this going to help us find Ryan?"

"Already thought of that."

"You did?"

"The festival," he said. The bright moonlight illuminated his pale skin with an incredible pearl-like glow.

"What festival?"

"The one in town. If she's really here then tonight she'll be at the festival."

"How can you know for sure?"

"Because she's a vampire and tonight is a celebration of the dead." He walked through the gate and grinned.

I nearly gasped the moment my eyes met the magnificence of what lay beyond the entranceway. It was the most beautiful villa I'd ever seen. It was two stories tall. It was quaint, yet contemporary. The entranceway was lined with a steep slope of steps. Huge glass windows framed the structure itself. It was without a doubt a modern Cinderella's castle. The front door was surrounded by yuccas and bordered by only the most decadent dahlia blooms. I moved closer. The artfully decorated interior glowed with golden hues and through the large front windows I could actually see the white sand beach on the other side.

"Can vampires go to prison?" I joked enthralled.

"Only the stupid ones." He pushed the front door open.

"Whoa," I said ogling the interior. "This place must have cost you a fortune to rent!"

"That's why I didn't rent it." He flung the backpacks onto the overstuffed couch in the living room. He grabbed me by the waist and pulled me against him. "Sometimes you gotta break a few rules."

I grinned. I liked it when the bad-boy in him came out to play. "Okay rebel," I said flirtatiously. "Tell me this. How can you be sure no one's coming back?"

"The undisturbed cobwebs over the doorframe are a sure clue." He kissed my cheek. "The tire tracks on the road out front are at least a year old." He nestled himself aside my ear. "And if that's not enough," he whispered, "the fact that I veiled the guy at the bike shop into telling me which properties were empty should prove it to you."

I laughed.

"The truth is, I just wanted to be alone with you."

I grinned.

"I owed you a present after all. Will this suffice?" He pulled me by the hand toward the wide glass doors on the far side of the villa. He pushed them open and together we stepped foot outside. The smell of saltwater and sand saturated my senses while the warm wind delighted my skin.

"Wow!" I said impressed. I gazed out at the ocean. The sparkle on the surface of the sea was magnificent. "So beautiful."

"Yeah," he said smiling at me.

I smiled and let myself go limp to his touch. A moment later he pulled me to a wide hammock hanging between two perfect palm trees on our spread of private, white sand beach. We reclined together within the breadth of its arms.

"Where you've been going Hope," he asked me again. He stroked the recently healed scar on my arm.

"Read my thoughts. Please Christian."

"No."

"Why?"

"Because I want you to tell me."

"Stop being so damn virtuous!" I shouted leaping from the hammock.

"I can't," he snapped. "Not when it comes to you anyway."

"Honestly!" I complained running my hands along my arm.

"Just tell me," he pleaded.

"I can't."

"Just use your voice and tell me!"

"No."

"C'mon Hope. Why can't you be honest with me?"

"You don't understand. You won't like it."

"Why? Because you've gone against my wishes—even though I asked you to stop going back into your past? In fact I think I insisted upon it."

"I didn't go into *my* past."

"Yeah right."

"I didn't! I swear it."

"Well then where the hell have you been going?"

"Into yours."

"Mine?" His face dropped. "As if you could—"

"It's true. I went farther than I've ever gone before. It started the other night, when I drank from you."

He sprung from the hammock and stood on the sand next to me. "What did you do?" he asked dejectedly.

"I blacked out on your blood and somehow it let me inside of you—inside of your past. I shifted through time and when I finally stopped moving I was..."

"Where Hope?" he barked. "Where were you?"

"On the Ambrose and William was there and I—"

"What?" he interjected, his eyes glimmering fiercely.

"I didn't know I was capable of such—"

"An atrocity," he snapped.

"I know you're mad, but try and understand what this could mean for us."

"What? What could it possibly mean for us?"

I turned toward him and grabbed his arms. "I can know you in a way no one ever gets to know the person they love. Think about it. We'll have no more secrets between us. Oh Christian," I said elatedly, "if you were only there—if you could have felt what it was like inside your past, what it felt like to interact—"

"I have," he said. "It's my past. I've already lived it once." His voice was sharp. "I never gave you permission to experience my past."

"You let me drink your blood. That was your permission."

He ran his hands through his hair and sighed.

"What was I supposed to do?" I stroked his arm. "I can't fight against it forever. It's a part of me. It's what I'm capable of."

"And so is killing, but you're managing to control that."

"Barely," I uttered.

"Oh god Hope."

"I love you." I looked into his eyes and smiled. "Look," I said. "I know all about residuals. I'm quite conscious of the fact that I've probably screwed up a bunch of stuff because of what I've done. I mean I've even started crying tears of blood for some reason."

"Blood?"

I nodded. "Don't be mad."

He ran his fingers through his hair again, each shiny strand falling tenderly in front of his eyes as they moved back into place. "You really went to the Ambrose?"

"Yes."

"What did she look like?"

"She looked like the wreck…and the house too." I grinned.

He smiled and then his face hardened. "You met William?"

I nodded. "But I didn't talk to *you*," I quickly added. "I heard your voice, but I didn't even look at you. I worried about the effect it would have—the residual in the future."

"I'd rather you'd talked to me," he snarled.

"But I thought I was being careful."

"But you talked to William."

"It was an accident," I avowed. "I had no intention of interacting with anyone!"

"But you talked to William."

"Yeah. I talked to William. Why do you keep saying that Christian?"

He stiffened his spine.

"What?" I demanded.

"He's…"

"He's what? Tell me!"

"He's your father Hope."

"My father?" The words sat heavily on my lips.

"Your biological father."

My listless heart nearly exploded in my chest. My blood raced through my veins with an icy numbness, stinging as it surged. I was about to collapse. My feet gave way and I began falling, gracefully descending to the ground beneath me, when suddenly I was weightless. The world was silent again and I was suspended and dangling in mid-air sheltered in the strong arms of my savior!

14. Daddy Issues

Vampires didn't faint—at least I didn't think they did. When I opened my eyes the dark velvet sky above filled my vision.

"You okay?" Christian asked.

I was lying in the hammock and he was standing over me, watching me. I tried sitting up, but quickly fell back down again.

"Easy," he whispered.

"What have I done?" I lamented rubbing my temple.

"Nothing other than destroy the whole time-space continuum."

"Oh god," I uttered appalled.

"Hey," he said soothingly. "I'm not mad. I'm just worried is all."

"Well I'm mad. Why didn't you tell me that William was my father? You've known all along!"

Christian sighed and sat next me in the hammock. "Would you have believed me?"

I shrugged.

"I didn't even know for sure, until of course your friend Ryan happened to mention that even *we* can procreate. I put two and two together and..." He smiled, tracing my face with the tips of his fingers. "Same big blue eyes. Same tenaciousness."

My graceless heart thumped in my chest.

"A half-breed," as they say, "born unto a human mother and a vampire father."

"So it wasn't you then?" I uttered. "You weren't the one who started the change in me?"

Christian shook his head.

"Our silly blood pact when I was a child had nothing to do with me becoming a vampire? And yet you've spent years feeling guilty, living with the shame of thinking that you were somehow responsible for starting the progression in me?"

"And the truth shall set you free," he muttered.

"Funny," I replied. "I don't feel so free. Do you?"

He laughed. I laughed too. The cool night air swaddled us within its embrace. I pressed my head against Christian's chest. "Why don't I remember him?" I asked. "When you restored my memories I—"

"You were veiled." His voice was emotionless. "William did it to you when you were just an infant. The bond between biological relatives must be strong—even stronger than the one you and I share. I couldn't undo it even if I wanted to."

"You were there?" I looked up at him.

He grinned. "From the moment you came into this world."

"But I thought we met in the forest...when you saved me from falling into the estuary." And then I read his thoughts. I finally knew the truth: that my reality was yet again shrouded by the simple insertion of another veil.

"There's nothing I can ever say that will make up for all the deceit. But you must understand that your life was far too precious to be subjected to the horrors we were harboring." He kissed my forehead and sighed, his broad chest heaving with the weight of his breath. "You were our beautiful ray of hope and we took it upon ourselves to try and look after you in the only way we knew how."

"By lying?"

"By protecting you," he defended.

"We didn't want you to live in Perish." He grabbed my hand. "You deserved to have a chance at a real life—a normal life."

"And that's why my mother left, even though Henry and Moira didn't want her to?"

He nodded.

I bit my lip and snuggled myself against him again. "Were you really there?" I asked, "the day I was born?"

"It was the moment of all moments," he smiled. "My life changed. And when I held you in my arms for the first time—"

"Held me?! *You* held me?" I withdrew from his arms; the same arms that cradled me as a baby.

He pulled me close again. "Yes. I held you." He kissed my lips. "And I knew instantly that my life had purpose."

"This is a lot to process Christian. I don't know how I'm supposed to feel."

"Feel loved," he said. "Your life has been full of love."

I half-smiled in reply.

"I'd seen sadness beyond what any eyes should have seen and death... plenty of death. And then that stormy night when your mother gave birth to you on the red velvet couch in Ambrose House I saw life for the first time ever. I realized how precious life really was. How precious *you* really were." He wrapped his arms around me. "You gave us hope. That's what I told your mother and that's what she decided to name you."

My eyes welled with tears. "She named me Hope because of you?"

He grinned.

"I don't remember any of this."

"No one remembers being born."

"I mean *any* of it." A flood of crimson tears fell from my eyes.

"Veiling you was the right thing to do—even Richard agreed."

"Richard?" My eyes bulged. "That useless excuse for a father? But Richard's not a vampire and I wasn't even his daughter."

Christian wiped the blood from my cheek with his hand. "He wanted to believe you were his daughter. He loved your mother. He wanted nothing more than for all of you to leave Perish for good." He licked his fingers and tasted my blood.

"But I wasn't his."

"No. The Richard-Audrey-William love triangle seemed neverending. It went on for years and almost destroyed us. Well," he hesitated, "it did destroy your mother and William in the end." He groaned. "Perish wasn't the place for a child and everyone decided it would be safer if you left—everyone but William of course."

"Why not William?

"He loved you more than anything. You were his daughter Hope. He was desperate and needed to do something to stop you from leaving."

"What did he do exactly?"

"He inserted one more veil before you left. He forced you to believe you had an aversion to water. He thought that if you feared water then maybe, just maybe, you'd be too frightened to leave."

"Because Perish is an island."

"When you told me how much you hated water I remembered instantly what William had done to you."

"So the fear of water wasn't real?"

"No."

I shrugged. "Anything else you wanna come clean about?"

"No," he smirked. "The veil didn't work. You left with Richard and your mother anyway.

"But I lived with a fear of water for the better part of my life."

Christian grabbed my hand. "He didn't know what else to do."

"Why are you telling me this now?"

"Because you met William—and because I'm afraid that if I don't tell you it may change forever." He swallowed nervously. "You made contact with your own father over two hundred years ago. What if the residuals—"

"I know," I interrupted. "Don't think I haven't contemplated the consequences of what I've done."

"Then promise me you won't do it again. *Please.* Stop now before something terrible happens."

I shook my head in agreement.

"Hope?" he said tenderly.

"I don't want to ruin us Christian."

He wrapped his arms around my waist. "I know. And you won't, just as long as you stay here in the present where you belong."

I looked up at him and grinned. "If only I could have seen you back then. Just a peak at you as a human."

He smirked. "I'm much hotter now."

"Sure you are," I teased in reply and at that moment the boom of our unhurried hearts echoed through our chests like thunder. The time for talking was over. Christian stared into my eyes before kissing my lips. A moment later he swept me off my feet and carried me inside the villa. At the speed of light he tore up the wooden staircase to the second floor. He flew through the long hallway until he reached the huge master bedroom. I sighed as he gently laid me upon the elegant, white bedspread. I didn't bother trying to read his thoughts—his body spoke volumes.

He tore off his shirt and tossed it to the floor. I thrust my hands upon his chest and moved my lips to his skin. "*Tin-cinnamon*," I sighed soundlessly. He slipped my shirt over my head and threw it to the cold tile floor and then I felt his fingers unbuttoning my jeans. He slid them off in a single sweep. I giggled, impressed with his talent for undressing me. He ogled at my panties and grinned. They were tiny, black and lace and a good choice considering I almost wore my comfy cottons.

"The cottons would have been good too," he said reading my thoughts.

I laughed, embarrassed, as he brought me back to his lips. And then he kissed me again. I reveled in the sweet heaven of his touch.

"I love you," he whispered tracing the span of my spine.

"I love you too," I replied arching my back in his arms.

And when he drew his lips from mine and ran them along my body I trembled. It wasn't about blood this time—the taste of it coursing through our veins. It was about love—the touch of our bodies finally coming together.

He grabbed me under the knee and wrapped his fingers around my leg. I fell back upon the bed. He leaned in close and pressed his lips to my hip before drawing his mouth down even further. And when his mouth met with the tender skin at which my thigh joined my abdomen I stifled a scream. He'd never gone this far before. Paradise was finally just within reach; that most tender, of tumultuous moments when we would finally be together. And then suddenly everything changed. Paradise turned to perdition. His fangs cut through his gums. His touch turned hard and he bit down into me. His sharp canines pierced the artery at the bend in my thigh. I winced in his arms!

No, I howled in my thoughts, a spill of crimson streaming from my eyes! Why wasn't it enough to just want me for me?

A moment later I pushed him away. If he was going to indulge, then I was going to indulge too. I dug my fingernails into his shoulder blades, tilted back my head and bit down into his jugular. I sucked hard, with bitterness, and continued drinking until the pain of being unwanted dissipated and I was in a complete and utter state of unconsciousness.

15. Goodbye

I awoke in shock! I scanned the bloodied bedroom. Crimson stained the sheets and the tiled floor too. It was happening all over again only this time we weren't in Perish; we were in Mexico! Christian was passed out at the bottom of the bed. He was covered with blood and I couldn't see his face! Instantly I started moving, speeding though his recent experiences until I was back inside of the time tunnel again.

I zipped through days and decades at a speed even more volatile than before! After a while I caught my breath and forced an exhale from my lungs. The tunnel collapsed. Everything stopped. Christian's past shattered into millions of tiny pieces speckling the air like fireworks. There was a loud boom and when the sound subsided I knew I was back again—aboard the HMS Ambrose.

It was dark and hazy. Rain pelted my practically naked body as it descended from the sky. A dirtied linen shirt sat on the deck. I grabbed it and quickly pulled it over my head. It reeked with perspiration, but I put it on anyway. A moment later I heard a voice.

"Where'd ya' go?"

It was William. His wheat colored hair and big blue eyes were much more meaningful to me now—now that I knew he was my biological father.

"You was right in front me," he said, "and then ya'—"

"William," I interrupted. What was I doing here? This was my father and he was still human. I shouldn't have drunk from Christian again. I promised him that I wouldn't return and yet here I was smack dab in the middle of a mess. It was incredibly dangerous—perhaps even perpetual suicide! If I altered this reality too much—if I stopped William from becoming a vampire it was quite possible that I would never exist in the future; William would never meet my mother and I would never be born.

"You," he continued. "Where'd you go?"

"I can't help you," I said. "I can't save you. I shouldn't even be talking to you."

"Save me?" he said perplexed.

"You're a brave man William." I smiled and touched his shoulder. "I wish I could have known you." I wrapped my arms around him in an embrace. "Don't veil me," I whispered. "Please. Don't do it." And then I withdrew.

He was silent, rapt with speechlessness and I was glad. The less we communicated within this ancient reality the better. I smiled at my father one last time before disappearing into the smoky haze again. I readied myself to inhale and return to the present when I felt a hand grabbing my shoulder. I spun around and I froze. "Christian," I said by mistake.

"Yes," he replied astounded.

It was him and he was beautiful. He was tall and strong and different. His hair was long, his cheeks were flush and his lips were more blush than the petals of a rose. As I stared into his lovely green eyes a chill ran down my spine! He was alive—so incredibly alive.

"Who are you?" he asked in a whisper.

I didn't answer. I smiled instead. I took his hand from my shoulder and touched it to my chest—over my heart. It beat with a single unhurried strike beneath his unscarred palm.

"Beautiful..." he muttered incoherently.

I smiled again. His hand was warm, clammy even and I'd never know Christian to be clammy. I leaned in close, swept his long, dark hair off of his shoulder and pressed my lips to his ear. "I love you," I whispered with a kiss and then I inhaled, filling my lungs with a deep breath of his scent—his human scent and suddenly I began moving again.

As I moved away from the past through the concave time tunnel of his memories that brought me here, I reveled in the strange absence of tin and cinnamon on my breath. My senses were saturated instead with a divine foreign succulence—the headiness of his sweat and his skin; his natural human scent. I exhaled back to the present and when the flash of white diminished and the sonic boom subsided I opened my eyes.

The bloodied sheets were gone. The crimson covered tiled floor had been wiped clean too. "Christian," I called out, but he didn't answer. He wasn't there. I panicked! What had I done? Had my wrongful meeting with my beloved over two-centuries in the past obliterated him from my present altogether? I had to find him. I had to hold him in my arms, touch his skin and know for sure that everything was still okay.

I hurried through the villa, down the stairs and to the living room to find him. "Christian," I hollered, but still no answer. It was day outside and the world was alive with the splendor of the sun. I shaded my sensitive eyes from the glare and stared beyond the glass toward the beach. The sand was white like snow and the ocean more dazzling than a sapphire. And then I noticed the large bonfire ablaze just ahead. I pushed the door open and set foot on the sand. "Christian," I shouted nearing.

He turned around. "You're back," he greeted stoically.

I eyed the fire. Our bloodied bedroom sheets smoldered in a flaming pile on the sand. "Burning the evidence," I said.

He nodded and stoked the fire with a stick. "Where'd you go this time?"

"The Ambrose."

"Why aren't you wearing any clothes? And you're wet..."

"I had to see him again."

Christian shook his head and tossed the stick into the fire.

"Don't be mad," I pleaded. "I didn't do it intentionally. What we did last night together made it happen."

He heaved a sigh. "So what did Will have to say for himself?"

I shrugged. "I just wanted to say goodbye."

He ran his hands through his hair.

"He's my father Christian. I just wanted to know him—even if only for a split-second." At that moment I felt the earth suddenly shifting beneath my feet. "What's happening?" I uttered feeling myself falling into oblivion again. Montages of memories abruptly realigned in their place in my consciousness. I felt faint and started collapsing. Christian caught me in his arms an instant before hitting the sand.

"Hope?" he said. "Are you alright?"

I opened my eyes and nodded. "I remember." I said. "I think I remember everything."

He set me down on the sand and stroked my hair.

"I remember William now. I remember him and my mother together. I even remember Richard there too. There was a fight, a terrible fight." I looked into Christian's eyes. "My god," I said appalled. "I know how they died."

"There, there," Christian consoled. "Just relax."

"Relax? He killed them! Richard killed both of them. It's true—isn't it?"

He nodded. "There was a chunk of wood Richard was wielding. He was drunk—more drunk than usual. He was aiming at William. He wasn't expecting your mother to step in front."

"My god," I said horrified.

"A sharp wooden object to the chest would kill anything—human or vampire. And it did." He swallowed hard. "I wasn't aware you even knew?"

"I didn't."

"Then how do you?"

"I don't know," I interrupted. "I think it's a new memory."

"What!" Christian raged.

I felt tears of blood welling in my eyes again.

"Hope," he said. "Did you talk to William when you were on the Ambrose?"

I nodded reluctantly.

"What did you say? Tell me exactly."

"I asked him not to veil me. But I didn't believe he'd actually do it—practically two centuries later."

"Did anything else happen?"

"No."

"Did you interact with anyone else?"

"No." But I was lying. I'd seen him on the ship too. I touched him and let him touch me back. I even had the audacity to profess my love for him with a kiss.

"We should go inside," he said. He smothered what remained of fire and sighed.

"Are you mad?"

He kicked the hot cinders with his sneakers. "No." he said. "It's my fault this happened. If I hadn't drunk from you—"

"Shh," I interrupted running my hands up his arms. "It's done now. Whatever the residuals are it doesn't matter."

He shook his head clearly trying to avoid saying something else. "Are you hungry?" he asked changing the subject.

"Yeah," I replied. "I think I am." We were vampires yes, but we had a pulse and a little life that still inhabited our bodies. Sometimes we craved something other than blood; the odd feeling of food against our tongues and the touch of it to our teeth.

"Is steak okay?"

I smiled. "Yeah. Steak, rare, would be good."

"You'll need your strength for tonight," he said pulling me by the hand toward the villa.

"What's tonight?"

"The festival," he uttered. "And if Ryan's in this city then that's where she'll be."

16. Festival

We drove into town. I loved the feeling of the wind rushing against my face as we sped through the night. The stars shone like coins in a velvet sky overhead. I wrapped my arms around Christian as we neared the city. Empty roads suddenly filled with people and the faint sounds of mariachi music began to resonate. The festivities were well under way. The air was warm against my cool skin and the night was alive. Death was the theme of the evening and we fit in just perfectly.

"C'mon," he uttered helping me off the bike.

"Were do we start?" I asked. "I mean she could be anywhere—if she's even here at all."

"Over there," he said confidently. He grabbed me by the hand and pulled me toward a crowded street. My eyes widened as we neared. A parade was already in progress. Oversized vibrant colored floats lined the roadway. Huge paper mache skulls drifted down the street. It was a macabre Mardi Gras and it was spectacular. There were skeleton-faced stilt walkers waddling alongside the floats. Men were wearing suits and sombreros and women were dressed in long evening gowns with wide hats and feathers.

"What is this exactly?" I asked intrigued.

"Looks like some kind of celebration of the dead," he uttered.

I smiled gingerly inhaling the atmosphere. The soft tang of spice and the sweetness of chocolate infused the air. Little children dressed as brides, skeletons and devils darted through the crowd. Cups of cocoa were cradled in their hands. "It's like Halloween," I smiled.

Christian laughed. "C'mon," he insisted pulling me through the people.

"Where are you taking us?" I shouted just louder than the sounds of the crowd.

"This way." He looked around purposefully.

"Are you looking for Ryan?" I asked.

He scanned the crowd. "Yeah," he uttered unconvincingly. He tugged my hand harder. I moved like a ragdoll as he pulled me through the people when finally he stopped. "Stay here," he instructed.

"Why?"

"I'm gonna ask around a little."

"Don't leave me alone!"

"You'll be fine." He smirked. "It's a party. I won't go far." He winked and then walked away.

"Christian," I shouted, but it was already too late. He was headed toward a row of vendors selling food and souvenirs. He spoke to a man wearing a skeleton mask. I watched for a moment trying to listen, but the sound of the parade drowned out their conversation—even with my super-sonic hearing. I relied on my eyes instead. I watched Christian hand the vendor a stack of bills. The vendor pushed his skeleton mask atop his forehead and started counting the money.

"Hola!" a loud voice said startling me.

I whipped around and found myself face to face with a beautiful woman. She was dressed in an old-fashioned evening gown and wearing a huge, fancy hat. Her face was painted like a skeleton—a beautiful, elegant skeleton. She placed a sunny marigold in my hair.

"Cempazúchitl," she said.

I grimaced. "No hablo Espanol."

"Flor de muerto," she said pointing to the marigold. "Mexican death flower."

Flor de muerto. My eyes widened. This flower wasn't the Mexican death flower. I recalled the strange black bloom that Christian tattooed on the guy at La Fuente. "No," I said fervently. "Not flor de muerto." I pointed to the cheery yellow flower. "This is a *marigold.*"

"Si," she replied nervously.

I drew my eyes away from her and fumbled to find where she'd stuck the flower in my hair, but when I looked up again the woman was gone. I turned my attention back to Christian. He was still conversing with the vendor only now an elderly woman had also joined them. She was dark skinned and wrinkly. She was grasping a little blue piece of paper in her hand. She handed the paper to Christian. He nodded and grinned. I blinked and suddenly he was by my side again.

"Nice flower," he said instantly eyeing my hair. He was beaming. I hadn't seen him this happy in a long time. He handed me a bottle.

"Tequila?" I said reading the label.

"When in Rome."

"But we're not in Rome," I joked. I tried reading his thoughts, but I couldn't get in.

"Lighten up a little," he said snatching the bottle out of my hand. He unscrewed the lid, downed a swig, a very large swig, nearly emptying half the tequila in one sip.

"Do I get a taste?"

"Of course." He handed the bottle back.

I pressed the glass to my lips and drank. The alcohol burned as it slipped down my throat. "Peppery," I said after swallowing.

"Is it? I wouldn't know."

Seemingly all of us lost something fundamental when we changed. When Christian became a vampire he lost his sense of taste. Since then there were only two things that he was ever really sure about: the savor of cinnamon and the sweetness of *my* blood.

I took another drink and said, "Definitely peppery."

Just then the loud sound of an argument distracted us. We turned around and noticed a man and woman standing in the alleyway just behind us. They were engaged in a heated quarrel.

"That's the woman that gave me the flower," I said.

"And him?" Christian asked.

"I don't know him." He was short, but beefy. His black hair was slicked tight to his head and his immaculately manicured beard was creatively carved into flourishing peaks. He definitely stood out from the crowd. An oversized image of the Virgin of Guadalupe was printed on his shirt and an animal claw protruded from the huge gold ring on his index finger. All of a sudden he grabbed the woman by the arms and started shaking her! She let out a scream! He then punched her in the ribs!

"That's it," Christian said speeding toward them.

The man spotted Christian immediately. He drew his eyes upward, to the roof of the building across the alley, and just as Christian went to reach for him he vanished disappearing like a snuffed-out flame.

"My god," I uttered taken aback.

I turned my attention to Christian again watching him catch the woman just as she was about to fall. I rushed over to help.

"Who was that man?" Christian asked.

"I don't know," I replied alarmed by what I'd seen.

"Vena," the woman whispered her eyes glimmering with iridescence as she spoke.

"Her eyes Christian," I said through my thoughts. *"She's a vampire. Maybe she can lead us to Ryan."*

Christian nodded.

"Cuál es tu nombre?" Christian asked.

"Maria," she uttered.

"Do you speak English?" I asked.

"Some." She replied. "You must go. He will return." She freed herself from Christian. She pushed past us and started walking toward the festivities.

"Wait!" I hollered. "We're looking for someone...*someone like us.*"

She stopped mid-stride and turned around, her pretty skeleton make-up immediately smudged by the incident.

"Her name is Ryan," I said. "She's slim with short black hair and eyes like star-sapphires. My name is Hope. I'm her friend and I've come for her."

Maria cut through the crowd like a blur of color toward me. "Hope?" she said.

"Yes."

"Paradise," she said her eyes glimmering wildly.

"Yes!" I answered. "Paradise! Do you know where I can find Ryan?"

Maria touched my hair and extracted the marigold. "Si," she said. "But very dangerous." She pointed at Christian. "For him."

"Me?" he asked perplexed.

She nodded. "The Vena don't play good with other men."

My eyes widened. "Vena?"

Maria stroked the side of my face and grinned. "You so pretty," she said and then she nodded. "Okay. I help you." She grabbed my hand and pulled me through the crowd of people. Christian followed closely behind. We walked and walked until finally we met the end of the festivities. The road ahead was dark and barren.

"What are we doing?" I asked concerned.

"Take you to your friend," she replied.

A moment later a blood red Lamborghini Diablo screeched along the road from out of the darkness. It swerved to a squealing stop, practically running us over, as it stopped to let us in.

"Get in," Maria insisted. "I take you to Ryan."

I looked inside the car. A skinny girl with pale skin and wavy blonde hair was at the wheel. Her eyes glimmered as she glared at me. "We can't all fit," I said.

Maria shouted something to the girl in Spanish before kicking her out of the car. She slipped into the driver's seat and said, "Hurry. No time."

Christian started getting in when Maria kissed her teeth at him. "You sure?" she asked.

"Where Hope goes. I go," he replied sitting down.

"I warned you." She shook her head, yanked off her big hat and tossed it out the window. Her long auburn colored hair fell against her shoulder like a waterfall as it moved. "Hope," she said. "Vamos!"

I slid inside the car and sat on Christian's lap. The door shut and like a bullet we were off.

Maria drove fast, even faster than Christian as we flew along the road into the darkness. Everything about this didn't feel right, but I had no sense of fear anymore and I was drawn, more than ever, to the thrill of new experiences.

"I recognize you," Maria said looking over at Christian. "From picture in magazine."

"So much for a low-profile," I said nudging him in the arm.

"I not read English well, but when I ask other girl what it say you sound like us—*vampiro*." She grinned. "When I saw you at festival I know yes—is true."

"Christian's becoming quite the international celebrity," I said through gritted teeth.

"You make tattoo?" she asked.

"Yeah," he said, "something like that."

"Maybe you make tattoo on me." She pushed back her sleeve and showed us the scar on her wrist from where she'd extracted her implant.

"Yeah," Christian said. "I could do that."

She grinned and pulled her arm away.

"Maria," I asked changing the subject. "Who was that man with you at the festival—the one in the alley?"

"Dangerous."

"We saw him hit you," Christian said.

She didn't reply.

"Vena?" I asked. "Is that his name?"

"No. Means veins. In body," she said, "veins carry blood to heart." Her English was broken and yet still clear enough to understand. "The Vena is same thing. They bring to El Corazon."

"El Corazon?" Christian pried.

"The Heart." She bit her skeleton painted lip. "I not say more. We here now."

At that moment we slowed down. We pulled off the rickety road and parked in a driveway. Maria got out of the car first. "Come," she said waving us on.

I looked ahead and there, past the driveway, were the remains of a rundown hotel. It had an old, electric sign out front with white bulbs that hummed like a horde of mosquitoes. The sign read one word and one word alone: *Paradise*.

"This is Paradise?" I muttered.

"Si," Maria answered.

Christian's eyes scanned the surroundings. It was though he was gathering intel; making sense of everything and anything that we could use in our defense if the need arose—and somehow I felt like it would.

Maria looked around. "They not here. Come." She motioned for us to follow her.

We followed behind, past the hotel and along what seemed to

be a little stone pathway up a hill. When we reached the top I froze. "Paradise," I said, my eyes glued to the view. It looked exactly like the picture on the postcard! There was a beautiful beach below and the ocean rolling in over it and in the distance, perched high atop a cliff stood the ruins.

"Tulum," Christian whispered grabbing my hand.

I laced my fingers with his and nodded. *This doesn't feel right,* I said through my thoughts.

"I know," he replied soundlessly.

We turned away from one another and continued following Maria down the hill toward the beach. There was a group of people sitting together laughing in the distance. "They're all women," I said perplexed.

"Si," Maria replied. She tore across the sand toward them. She rushed over and threw her arms around some of the girls.

"Hope?" I suddenly heard a familiar voice calling.

I turned around. "Ryan?"

"Well I'll be damned!" she said rushing toward me, enveloping me in her arms. She didn't feel cold anymore! She felt like me!

"What are you doing here?" I asked elatedly.

"Moonbathing," she teased. "My god I thought I'd never see you again."

"I got your postcard," I said withdrawing. She looked practically the same as I remembered her despite the fact that her face was painted like a pretty skeleton.

"I knew you'd figure it out," she said grinning. "You smell different. You've *changed* haven't you?"

"Yeah." I smiled.

"Guess you don't have to worry about tan lines anymore!"

I laughed.

"I knew Christian would come to his senses and do the right thing."

"He's here," I said motioning toward him.

Ryan looked up. "My god," she said uneasily. "You brought him with you?"

"Of course."

Panic glimmered in her eyes. "This isn't Perish," she said.

"Yeah, I'm starting to gather that."

"Most of these people are renegades like me, but some of them," she hesitated, "some of them aren't." Her voice was guarded.

"What exactly have you gotten yourself into?" I asked.

She looked around, her dark eyes sparkling. "Beggars can't be choosers. I was hungry and they were willing to take me in." She bit her lip. "They don't kill humans, but their arrangement, well, it isn't..."

"What kind of trouble are you in?" Christian asked.

Ryan shrugged. "I was looking for Paradise and I found this place instead. I thought it was a sign—I was wrong."

"Can't you just leave?"

Ryan shook her head. "None of us can."

"Maria mentioned something about the Vena," Christian muttered, "and El Corazon."

"El Corazon is the devil as far as I'm concerned—the heart of this bullshit freedom operation promising a new life to refugees, but once you sign away your soul it's all over."

"Sign away your soul? What are you talking about?" I asked.

"The Blood-Trade," she whispered. "The Vena, they find migrant vampire women like me and use us to lure in the human men for their blood. The men pay good money to come to us and the Vena force us to purge the blood in favor of El Corazon."

"*Purge?*" I exclaimed aghast.

She nodded. "We vomit the blood we imbibe." She groaned. "And then it is collected and given to El Corazon as an offering."

"Ryan!" I snapped. "We are getting you the hell out of here!"

"Then you'll have to help get the others out too. I can't leave them behind."

Christian shook his head.

"I never should have sent you that postcard. This isn't your problem. I just didn't have anyone else to turn to."

I touched her shoulder. "It's okay. We're gonna get you out of this—all of you. You did the right thing. Here," I said unfastening my necklace and sliding into the palm of my hand. "This belongs to you," I said giving it back.

"Hope, I gave you that necklace because you needed it."

"And now you need it more." I put it around her neck and fastened the clasp.

"No!" Ryan uttered looking up the beach. "It's too late...they're here."

Christian and I looked ahead.

"Who is that?" I asked.

"The Vena," she replied nervously. "And now that they've seen you, they're out for blood."

17. Ballgame

The bright moonlight that graced the white sand beach abruptly dulled as the Vena neared. There were three of them: a stout bald guy, a lanky guy with a scar on the side of his face and the beefy guy with the slicked black hair from the alley in town. It was the ring on the beefy guy's index finger that caught my eye. I'd first noticed it when he was manhandling Maria. There was something creepy about that ring and the way he constantly spun it around his finger as though it was a roulette wheel.

"Well, well. What do we have here?" he said spinning the ring again.

"Nothing Lobo," Ryan replied. "They were lost and I was trying to—"

"Enough!" he snapped. He grabbed Ryan by the arms and held her from behind "Lies. You know what El Corazon does to liars?" He ran the golden claw on his ring down the side of her face, smudging her skeleton make-up in a single streak.

"Si Lobo," Ryan whimpered.

"Let her go," Christian ordered.

Lobo's eyes glimmered. He pushed Ryan to the sand and glared at Christian. "I know you," he said moving closer.

Christian's eyes narrowed.

"Why are you here?" he asked spinning his ring again; it whirled like a spindle.

"We don't want any trouble. We just came for our friend." I pulled Ryan from the sand. "And now that we've found her we're leaving."

"No!" he ordered. He grabbed Ryan by her hair and pulled her toward him.

"Hope!" Ryan shrieked.

"What do you want for her?" Christian asked.

Lobo licked his lips. He ran the golden claw along Ryan's arms. "This one is smart," he said continuing to move his ring down her body. "Real smart. Not like the others. She's a prize. So we play for her."

"Don't," Ryan pleaded. "Christian I'm not worth it."

"You must," I said soundlessly. *"Please."* Tears of blood were beginning to well in my eyes.

"I accept," he said fearlessly. "And when it's over you let her leave with us."

"If you win," Lobo laughed. His men laughed too.

"And what if we lose?" I shouted. "What then?"

Lobo smirked. "Then you become ours. And him," he glared at Christian, "he dies!"

"NO!" Ryan begged. "Please don't do this. Just let them kill me. This is all my fault!"

"Christian," I said through my thoughts. *"What do we do?"*

"We have no choice." His eyes were hard.

"Come," Lobo ordered.

We turned our backs to the moon and followed Lobo and his men along the beach to a secluded area tucked within the walls of the cliffside.

"Christian," Ryan whispered grabbing his shoulder. "I'm sorry."

He nodded.

"I've never known a man like you. Why would you do this for me?"

He heaved a sigh. "You're like family to Hope and that makes you like family to me."

Her eyes filled with tears. She was breathless. "Thank you," she uttered. "I'm forever in your debt."

At that moment Lobo stopped walking. His men edged closer from behind and started breathing down our necks.

"The court," Lobo said with a spin of his ring.

I looked around. There was nothing but sand and rock.

"Up," Christian said without a sound, *"The ruins are above us."*

I shifted my gaze upward and spotted the tip of the large ruins overhead. I looked down again and noticed a peculiar stone hoop protruding from the rock a few feet above us.

"A secret court," Lobo declared. He moved his gaze aloft, to the top of the cliff and then he said, "Where the gods can watch from above." He laughed.

This was the court? There was nothing but a huge stone wall with a jutting hoop on one side and the dilapidated remains of second wall on the other. It was kind of like something I'd seen in a brochure advertising a tour to Chichen Itza, but this was much smaller. "What is this game?" I asked concerned.

"It's an ancient ballgame," Ryan explained.

"How is it played?"

"To the death," she uttered teary-eyed. "It's dangerous. I've seen them, the Vena...I've seen them playing it with some of the human men that come to us. There's blood—a lot of blood."

"If that was your idea of a pep talk," Christian interrupted, "it didn't help."

"I'm sorry," she replied.

"Come," Lobo hollered. "Let's begin."

"A really heavy rubber ball about the size of a soccer ball is passed between teams," Ryan explained quickly. "Points are gained if the ball hits the opposite end and points are lost if the ball hits the ground. Look Christian if you pass the ball through that small stone hoop up there the game is immediately over and you win."

"So try and get the ball through the hoop," Christian said. "Shouldn't be too difficult."

I turned my attention to Lobo and his men watching as they began emptying their pockets. Wads of money, knives and guns hit the sand like rocks. A chill ran down my spine.

"The ball must be kept in the air," Ryan continued. "And you can't use your hands or feet."

"What?" I exclaimed.

"When I was in Columbia I remembered learning something about the Aztec version of this game," Christian added. He looked at Ryan. "Hips, forearms and thighs."

"Right," Ryan nodded. "But they don't play fair Christian." She sighed. "It's not too late. If you and Hope make a run for it I can—"

"It's too late," I said eyeing the sudden appearance of the game-ball. A tall red-head carried the ball in her hands. It looked like a human skull that had been wrapped with rubber strips—and it probably was. Lobo planted a sloppy kiss on the red-head's mouth. She pretended to like it. I wanted to be sick. An instant later he snatched the ball from her and suddenly the game began.

"El Corazon!" he shouted thrusting the ball high above his head in the air. Everyone started cheering, even the group of women.

I grabbed Christian's arm. "Be smart. Be fast. I love you."

He smirked and kissed my cheek before making his way toward the court.

"You know the rules?" Lobo asked.

Christian nodded.

"Good, because there are no rules!" He laughed and spun his ring again, the golden claw glistening as it whirled in the moonlight. His men laughed too. Lobo slipped his hand into the skull-ball. "Hey," he hollered.

"What?" Christian replied.

"No tricks. It would be too easy." He grinned.

"Fine," Christian said.

And thus the game began. Lobo and his men retreated to their side of the court and Christian to his when I realized that Christian was on his own.

"That's crazy," I criticized. "There are three of them. They'll slaughter him!"

"I told you," Ryan said. "They don't play fair."

I moved toward the court. I wasn't afraid to play.

"Don't," Ryan said stopping me. "Women aren't allowed."

"Says who?"

"Them," she replied.

"But he won't win without me."

"He won't win with you either."

Just then Lobo tossed the ball high into the air. When it fell he hit it across the court with his forearm. The ball bounced off the cliff toward Christian. I watched eagerly as Christian dashed across the sand to receive it, knocking it back with a firm whip off his leg.

"He can do this," I said feeling encouraged.

"I sure hope so," Ryan replied.

At that moment the short bald guy intercepted the ball with his forearm. He whacked it back. It flew through the air across the court smashing into Christian's shoulder with a colossal crash. Even though I could hear his bones breaking inside of him, he fought to hit the ball back with his hip. It bounced against the cliff just a few inches shy of the protruding stone hoop.

"My god," I said watching him stumble on the sand. I wanted nothing more than to help. I should have been out there with him. I hated being forced to white-knuckle it from the sidelines.

Lobo rushed in to receive the ball. He hit it with his thigh. The ball flew across the court with the force of a freight train. It struck Christian in the knee. The shrill sound my Tin Man's bones breaking split the silence, but in that same instant he somehow managed to whip the ball back at them with his forearm.

"No!" Lobo howled. He rushed the court and slammed the ball aiming it straight for Christian's skull. The ball flew through the air like a missile and just as it was about to strike Christian reached out and caught it with his hand.

Lobo wailed with rage. An instant later he vanished like ink in water reappearing at the other end of the court. He was standing by Christian's side mere inches away from his face.

"Penalty," he whispered. "No hands," and then he pummeled Christian's jaw with the stone skull.

I gasped, sucking in air by mistake and suddenly everything slowed to a near stop. I watched as Christian took the punch, his pretty face wobbling languidly with the immense force of the blow. Blood spewed from his lips. Crimson beads speckled the sand. I exhaled immediately and the world began running at normal speed again.

"C'mon hombre," Lobo chastised. "Game's not over yet."

Christian pulled himself up just as the short bald guy chucked the ball at him. It struck him in the face at the jaw. Christian groaned and fell back to the sand again, blood spurted from his mouth.

"Stop!" I shouted.

Lobo and his men laughed.

"You need a woman to do your fighting?" Lobo laughed even louder before kicking sand in Christian's face.

Before the spray subsided Christian jumped to his feet. He whipped the ball across the court with his shoulder. It headed straight for Lobo's face this time. Everything went silent. Lobo stopped laughing. He reached out and caught the ball with his hand. Christian fluttered his eyelashes and within a blink he was suddenly standing at the other end of the court next to Lobo.

"Penalty," Christian sneered before slamming him in the face with his fist. He vanished again.

Lobo howled like an animal. He whipped the ball against the cliffside. A huge chunk of rock fell to the sand. "Finish him!" he shouted.

Christian heaved the ball back with a hard thrust of his side. It hit the wall mere inches from the stone hoop.

"Close!" I shouted.

"Close doesn't count," Ryan whispered.

Lobo whipped the ball back with his leg. It flew across the sand practically striking Christian in the chest when swiftly he smacked it back with his forearm. The ball hit the cliffside again.

"You've almost got it!" I said through my thoughts.

Lobo belted the ball back. Christian took the hit and thrust it off his leg. Just then the ball slammed against the rock face and slid straight through the hoop!

"He won!" I shouted. "My god! He did it!" Just then I felt my hands being restrained. I peered over my shoulder. It was the tall guy with the scar on his face. "Let go!" I yelled struggling to get free.

"Hope!" Christian hollered.

I looked ahead to the ball court, but Christian wasn't there. Lobo and the short bald guy were standing in the sand arming themselves with guns. An instant later they aimed their weapons at us.

I gasped and suddenly time slowed to a virtual near stop again. Everything reduced to slow motion. I peered over my shoulder. Christian had come to help me. He grabbed the tall guy's wrist, twisted him around and flipped him upside down and all of a sudden I was free. I fell to the sand in a slow descent watching as Christian managed to position the tall guy in front of us. A slow second later a spray of bullets showered the sky. Droplets of blood stippled the air like crimson snowflakes. Christian pivoted the tall guy's body like a shield protecting us from the spray. And when the firing finally stopped, I pushed a little air from my lungs and time abruptly resumed normal speed again.

Screams smothered all other sounds. I looked to my right. Ryan was hovering over the women. The sand was covered with blood and I knew instantly that the women had been caught in the crossfire.

The thud of the tall guy's body being dropped to the ground distracted me. I turned to look when instantly his corpse burst into flames.

"Hope, are you okay?" Christian asked.

I turned around to answer when instantly Lobo appeared, inking through the air like a puff of smoke. He lunged at Christian in what seemed like hyper-speed and they engaged in a ferocious brawl. Streaks of color stained the night as Lobo and Christian kept appearing and disappearing. The flash fighting was fast, much too fast for me to perceive fully and so I inhaled a little, holding in a breath of air, to take a closer look.

Time abruptly slowed to a near stop again. I saw the fighting as though it was happening in slow-motion once more. I watched Lobo charge Christian, moving with an eerie rage. He tried pummeling him in the face with his claw ring, but Christian was agile and far too quick for Lobo's meek attack. He grabbed Lobo's arm and twisted it backward nearly breaking it when suddenly Lobo started disappearing! I watched his body dematerializing into speckles of color until nothing remained but his right hand. Christian reached out and snapped that right hand at the wrist when Lobo reappeared again! Blood poured from the fleshy stump on his arm. He howled! I accidently released the breath from my lips and time abruptly started moving at normal speed again.

"You will die!" Lobo barked peering through the darkness in a determined effort to find Christian.

And then I spotted him. He was grasping Lobo's severed hand in his palm and sneaking up behind him. I watched on tenterhooks as he slowly brought the hand close to Lobo's neck. With a swift slice slit Lobo's throat using his own precious claw ring. Lobo dropped instantly.

His body burst into flames and soon the flames became little more than a pile of cinder on the sand.

Up the beach the short bald guy was trying to get away. I moved to catch him, but I felt Christian stop me.

"Let him go," he said. "He's not worth it."

I turned to him and nodded. I wrapped my arms around him and squeezed.

"Ouch," he said.

I withdrew immediately. "What's the matter?" I asked noticing the blood on his shirt. I pulled it up to reveal his chest. "My god!" I uttered eyeing the hole in his flesh. "Christian you've been shot!"

18. Escape

We rushed through the sand, along the beach and up the hill back to Paradise.

"C'mon," I shouted dragging Christian by my side. He was weak and bleeding profusely.

"We're trying," Ryan uttered struggling to rally the women into escaping before more Vena arrived.

When we reached the hotel I remembered the red Lamborghini parked in the driveway. I dragged Christian to the car and put him in the passenger seat. "Ryan!" I shouted. "C'mon."

"Just go!" she hollered. "There's no time."

I shut the peculiar vertical passenger side door and rushed over to her. She was standing near the hotel trying to comfort some of the women.

"I never should have brought you into this in the first place," she said. "I'm sorry Hope. So sorry."

"We're not leaving without you."

"You must," she insisted. "I thought leaving was what I wanted, but now," she put her arm around one of the young, wounded women, "helping is what I want. These women need me. I see now that they'll never get their lives back without someone like me helping them. It might not be paradise, but it's what I have to do."

I grabbed her hand and squeezed. "Are you sure?"

"I've done too much wrong in my life to not make this right."

I smiled, tears welling in my eyes.

"Go," she said. "Take that prince charming of yours and find your fairy tale ending. You deserve it."

I laughed, a single crimson tear sliding down my cheek.

"See ya', ciao, adios, until we meet again. Now get the hell out of here!"

I wiped the tear of blood away with the back of my hand and waved goodbye. I rushed toward the Lamborghini, jumped in the driver's seat and let the upright door shut. I turned the key. The engine roared like a lion. I slammed my foot on the gas pedal and we sped off with a deafening screech back into the night again.

I drove through the darkness, like a bat out of hell. I didn't know where I was going, but I knew it had to be as far away from Paradise as possible.

"Thank you," Christian whispered.

"Thank me?" I said. "It's you I should be thanking." I looked over at him. His wounds were almost healed, but his pain endured. "Healing is the easy part, right? The pain's the bitch."

Christian tried to laugh, but winced instead. A moment later I looked over again. I noticed that he'd raised his shirt a little when all of a sudden a tiny, shiny, flat-headed bullet abruptly emerged from the puncture wound in his ribcage. He caught the bullet in his hand just as the wound finished healing over.

"Souvenir?" I teased.

"Don't Hope," he pleaded, "don't make me laugh."

"You did great out there," I continued.

"Yeah great," he replied with sarcasm.

"You kicked there asses Christian!"

"I nearly died, we didn't get Ryan to leave with us and we slaughtered some pretty bad Mexican vampires."

"Well if you put it like that—"

"Here," he said reaching into the front pocket of his jeans. "Take this." He pulled out a little blue slip of paper and handed it to me.

"What's this?" I asked. I recognized the paper immediately from when the old woman at the festival gave it to him.

"Drive here," he said.

I looked down. There was an address written on it. "What's here?" I asked.

"Just do it. Please."

I uncrumpled the paper and held it in the palm of my hand. "Can't we just get out of here Christian? Let's go back to the villa...or home even?"

"Not yet."

"C'mon," I said. "I admit it. This trip was a mistake. We never should have come. Although I wish there was more we could have done for Ryan."

He put his hand on my thigh.

"I'd feel better if we headed straight for the airport!"

"I know you would." He patted my leg. "I just need to make a quick stop and then we'll go. Okay?"

"Fine. Tell me how to get there."

"Take that dirt road," he instructed.

I turned off the main road and onto a not-so-well-travelled path. It was dark and dense with vegetation. "Think the Lambo can take it?"

"It's a Lamborghini Hope. It can do anything."

"Then why is my mind filled with images of us stuck in the mud, standing beside a stolen hundred-thousand dollar car?"

Christian laughed. "Ouch...keep driving."

"Do you really know where we're going?"

"I got...directions."

"From that old lady?"

He smirked. "You were watching me?"

"I'm always watching you."

"Stop here," he said hastily.

I slammed on the bakes and looked around. "Here?"

"We can walk the rest of the way."

"Walk? I don't want to walk. I just want to get the hell out of this country!"

He leaned close and kissed me on the cheek. "Soon—I promise."

I shook my head and reluctantly killed the engine. We got out of the Lamborghini.

"Smells like incense out here," I said breathing in the reek of smoky pine in the air.

"Its copal tree resin. It burns like incense." He grabbed my hand and pulled me along the little dirt road with him. He certainly was a fast healer!

I looked around. The area was abundant with vegetation. The sound of an old dog howling in the distance was making me anxious. I sighed. "Why couldn't we be going somewhere that has sombreros and margaritas?"

He laughed, brought my hand to his lips and kissed it. "Shh," he whispered. "We're almost there?"

"Where exactly?" The heels of my black leather boots crushed the dirt with fierce footfalls. We walked toward what looked like a big, dark park at the top of a hill. I spotted an old, rusted sign in the distance. "Cementerio," I said reading the faded black script.

"Cemetery," he said.

"What the hell are we doing in a cemetery?"

He smirked.

"Don't give me that look. I've had enough action for one night."

"C'mon," he whispered lacing his fingers with mine. "It won't be so bad." He tugged at my hand and pulled me toward the gate.

"Won't be so bad?" I shook my head. "It's a cemetery Christian, not dinner theatre!"

There was a peculiar stillness in the air. It was hot and a little muggy too. The bright moonlight radiated against my pale skin. I'd never felt so much like a vampire as I did at that moment; being led by my immortal betrothed deep into the heart of an ancient cemetery under the moonlight. It was funny in a way, but not quite funny enough to make me outright laugh about it.

"C'mon Hope," Christian pestered tightening his grip on my hand.

"I'm coming," I uttered captivated by the eerie ambiance. Straggly trees and long leafy vines tickled my skin as I walked. Pairs of eyes glowing in the night seemed to watch us as we sauntered. And with my gaze aloft, I couldn't help but notice the rows of tall white crosses that bordered the hills above. They sat like sentinels overlooking the little graveyard below. I felt a little like Snow White wandering through the haunted forest. Just then a colony of winged rats descended from a tree and swooped overhead. I ducked and practically gasped.

"It's only bats," Christian insisted.

"Vampire bats..." I uttered squeezing his hand.

"Hope," he scoffed. "You're not frightened are you?"

"No," I snarled. "I'm not afraid of anything anymore—I just don't like bats is all."

He smirked.

"Don't smirk. Have you ever had a bat fly into your hair?"

"No," he said. "Have you?"

"Well no, but I imagine it's awful." I cleared my throat. "Can we just get to the cemetery already?"

"Yeah," he said with a grin.

We rounded the corner and my eyes widened. "Wow," I said taken aback. Twinkling candlelight illuminated the graves with warm golden glows; their flames flickered like stars in the sky above. Tombstones were decorated with vibrant streamers and painted in vivid colors. Flowers were everywhere; bountiful bushels of marigolds adorned the cemetery in a blanket of honey colored hues. "This is...beautiful," I uttered. My head swelled with the robust scent of incense. And as we treaded between plots the sounds of prayers filled the air with an unexpected serenity. "Who are they?" I asked eying the group of women gathered around one of the smaller graves.

"Don't stare," Christian whispered.

"Why?" I asked watching them place candies and toys next to the marble cherub upon the headstone. "What are they doing?"

"Shh," he urged whisking me into the shadows with him.

I giggled, elated with the sudden intrigue of the situation. We crouched behind a grave with a large, stone angel perched at the summit. I stared at Christian, deep into his eyes, watching the way they practically glowed in the moonlight. "Christian," I whispered. "Why are we here?"

"All Saints Day," he said, "a time for remembering angelitos."

"Angelitos?"

"The little angels. The children that have passed away."

An icy chill ran down my spine. I peeked around the side of the tombstone toward the women and instantly the small toys and candies made sense to me.

"They're ofrendas," he uttered, "offerings for the dead one." He started moving away. I grabbed his arm stopping him. Everything slowed with a flicker. The world was like a dream; slowly easing into the static tableau of an oil painting. I could actually hear the delicate sound of Christian fluttering his eyelashes.

"What are we doing here?" I asked finally feeling the world at a standstill.

"What do you mean Hope?" His voice was guarded. He fluttered his eyelashes reanimating the world around us. The cemetery came alive again; candles flickered fiercely and the wind suddenly howled like a banshee. Life continued living—even in this place of death and inevitability.

"Christian," I said. "What are we—"

He pointed toward the women.

"Them?" I asked. "We're here for them?"

"No," he said, "not them—*them*." The rhythmic tickle of his breath graced my cheek as he spoke.

I returned my eyes to the women again when suddenly the truth hit me like a slap. Bushels of black flowers hung in the women's hands. *The death flower*, I sighed in my thoughts. And there beside the statue of the angel, over a grave and under the brilliant moonlight, I knew exactly why we had come.

19. Angelitos

Clusters of the black blooms were everywhere. They hung atop tombstones, drooped over fences and climbed along crucifixes. They were tiny and dark and barely visible against the vivid colorful decorations that ornamented the cemetery. There were so many of them it was almost frightening; like a disease ready to spread.

Christian's tattoo client at La Fuente said that the flower possessed the power of resurrection. Why was Christian so interested? Who did he want to resurrect? My mind flooded with questions.

"See those women?" he said startling me.

"Yeah," I replied awaiting the truth about the flower.

"Listen to them. Close your eyes. Listen to how they speak."

My stomach sank. I thought he was finally going to come clean about his secret reason for wanting that damn flower. I was wrong.

"Hope," he said. "Close your eyes."

"Fine," I replied grudgingly. I closed my eyes and focused on the women's voices. "What are they saying?" I asked.

"It's something like the Lord's Prayer."

I listened harder. There was a definite rhythm to their words, but the longer I listened the less it sounded like a prayer. I opened my eyes. "The Lord's Prayer huh? Sounds more like a witch's chant to me." I shook my head. "What are we doing here?"

"Shh," he insisted. "You should watch this."

I sighed frustrated. Why was he so captivated by these women? I started shifting my gaze toward them again and then I froze. The moon broke through a cloud swiftly illuminating Christian in a sublime sheen of pure radiance. He was stunning like a sculpture carved in stone. I couldn't take my eyes off of him. I'd always known he was beautiful, but for some reason under the Mexican moon he was even more beautiful. His pale skin was radiant like a soft blanket of freshly fallen snow and his dark hair shimmered like the feathers of a raven. He was crouched on the grass next to me. A pair of stone wings belonging to the angel on the gravestone behind him peeked out from behind his shoulders, looking as though they belonged to him. Christian really was my angel. He saved me from myself and gave me a life beyond anything I could have ever imagined. He believed in me, trusted me and was ready to risk his life for me at any given moment—*so why didn't he want to tell me about the flower?*

"Hope," he said. "Watch the way these women move. It's like they're in a trance...they're not conscious anymore."

"Yeah," I uttered, "a trance." My eyes were still fixed on him. I had no interest in the women—it was him I wanted. I knew it was time to take our love to the next level. I was more than ready. I tugged on his shirt and pulled him close. His body smacked mine like a rock forcing me against the tombstone.

"Hope," he uttered shocked.

"Shh," I whispered. The tickle of his breath excited me. I carefully inhaled his smell and grinned.

"What are you doing?" he asked.

"Trying to love you."

"This is hardly the place."

"I don't care."

"But—"

"But nothing. Kiss me damn it." I dug my nails into his back and forced him closer. He moved his lips to my throat just as a loud crack filled the air.

"Hope," he said withdrawing.

"Shh," I insisted forcing him back.

"Don't you want to watch the ritual?"

"I'd much rather do this."

He laughed and kissed me on the neck, but I could feel his eyes shifting back to the women again when all of a sudden another loud crack resonated.

"What was that?" I whispered.

"That was the sound of the women removing the planks that cover the grave." He stroked my arm with the tips of his fingers. He moved his mouth to my shoulder and kissed my skin. I sighed inside with the tenderness of his touch.

Bang. The sound of the planks being tossed aside startled me. I peered up, my interest in the women peaking slightly. "Why are there wooden planks on the graves?" My voice was breathy.

"They believe the graves are doorways and they've just opened one." He grinned and slid his lips up my neck.

"Doorways? Doorways to what?"

"Death," he replied easing his hand up my spine. "Tonight the curtain between us and them is at its thinnest."

I widened my eyes and pulled him against me. The force of my tug tore his shirt right off of his body!

"Hope!" he said.

"Shh," I replied eyeing the curvature of his chest. I moved my hands to his skin and traced the newly healed gunshot wound on his ribcage. He melted with my touch. And as my eyes met with his I remembered the simplicity of what it felt like to love him for him— without the hunger, without the cravings, without the blood. "I want you," I whispered.

He laughed.

"I'm serious." I licked my lips. "When you were playing that game with those men tonight...I couldn't bear it. The thought of loosing you—"

"Shh," he interrupted.

"Don't do that to me again." My eyes welled with crimson sorrow.

"I never want to hurt you. I love you." His voice was soft and his body radiant in the moonlight. "I love you more than..." and then he stopped himself.

"What?" I asked.

He shook his head. "Words just aren't enough anymore—are they?"

"I wish they were Christian." I wiped a red stream of tears from my cheek.

"Oh Hope," he uttered, his chest inflating with the heaviness of his breath. "This isn't how I wanted it for us. This isn't perfect."

"Perfect? I don't want perfect."

"But it's what you deserve."

"You've already given me perfection on the night you changed me."

"Yes but—"

"I don't want fireworks. I don't even want sunset anymore." I stroked his arms. "I just want you."

"But why..." he grinned. "Why here?"

"Because *you're* here."

His face hardened. "This isn't like being changed."

"I know."

"No. You don't know." He heaved once more. "When you were human and looked up at the sky what did you see?"

The sky? Why was he talking about the sky, when I was vulnerable in his arms, inviting him to love me?

"Hope," he urged. "Tell me what you saw when you were human."

I shrugged. "I don't know...stars."

"Stars," he said running his hand aside my jaw. He edged my chin upward. "And now? Tell me what you see now that you've changed."

Why was he making me do this? I didn't want to look into the damn sky—*I wanted him to kiss me!*

"Hope," he insisted.

"Fine," I replied reluctantly. I widened my gaze and looked above. The heavens were alive with vigor. Stars sparkled like diamonds. Meteors showered the atmosphere. And when I listened closely I could hear the faint orbiting of distant planets too. The universe seemed just at reach. It was spectacular. Our world moved under my feet and I felt as though we were sweeping through space on some grand celestial carousel.

"You see," he said listening to my thoughts. "Everything is much more profound for us. We don't just feel things—we apperceive our existence."

I nodded and shifted my eyes to look at him.

"And to finally be with you," he grinned, "that will be the—"

"I know," I interrupted smiling.

"Once we do this Hope there's no going back."

"I know."

"We only get one first together."

I nodded.

"And you're ready—right now, here in this place of death—"

I grabbed him by the shoulders and pulled him toward me. His body again hit mine like a rock and I smacked into the tomb for a second time.

"Are you okay?"

"Better now," I replied bringing him to my lips. And when we kissed I knew for certain I really was ready. Christian was exactly what I wanted. It didn't matter where we were as long as we were together.

"And you're sure?" he sighed soundlessly, his lips still fixed with mine.

"Yes! Yes! I want you!" This time with my soundless plea he didn't hesitate. His hands circled my wrists and he pinned me against the headstone. The touch of his mouth and the taste of his tongue made me tremble inside. He tightened his grip and kissed me harder—deeper. His usual gentleness seemed replace by a more confident manliness I'd never seen before. *"Mmm,"* I murmured surprising myself. His confidence delighted me tremendously. Then when he released my wrists and moved his hands to my legs I knew we were headed for uncharted territory.

Every bone in my body rattled. I was charged up and raring to go. Patience wasn't my strong suit; I couldn't wait any longer. *I want this. I need this. I love you.* My thoughts screamed like a megaphone in my mind.

"Relax," he whispered like my secret conscience.

Relax? How could I? This was it! This was the moment I'd so eagerly anticipated. Relaxing was literally the last thing on my mind.

"You're tense."

Of course I was tense! We were about to change the rules of our relationship. We were finally about to take it to the next level.

"Your heart Hope. It's practically pounding. Calm down."

Christian was right. Hot and bothered wasn't the way I wanted to be feeling. I stole a breath, gingerly filling my lungs with air. I didn't want to inadvertently shift through time. This was the only moment I wanted to be in and nowhere else.

"Relax. Just relax."

I focused on the feeling of his lips against mine and soon the rhythm of our kiss lulled me entirely.

"Good," he assured.

I smiled inside and let the sweet sound of his inner-voice seduce me. I was finally easing and settling into our gentle tempo when suddenly I felt his fingers slip beneath my skirt. My eyes widened. My body stiffened once more.

"I thought you were trying to relax?" he teased inside my head.

Relax? How on earth was I supposed to relax when every nerve ending in my body wanted to explode!

"Shh," he purred soundlessly. *"Let me please you."*

His request turned me to mush. I may have even gasped a little before settling into a long drawn out sigh of bliss.

"Where can I touch you," he uttered, *"to make you feel—"*

I withdrew from his mouth and brought his hand to my chest. "My heart," I said. "You've touched it in a way no one ever has."

He smiled and slid inside my thoughts. I closed my eyes and slid inside his too and for once neither of us was thinking about blood.

The sweet mélange of his tin-cinnamon scent overwhelmed me and I weakened in his arms. *"Kiss me,"* I urged. A moment later I felt his lips within reach. His kiss was deep and ardent and instantly made every hair on my body stand on end. I moved my hands to his jeans and hesitantly drew down the zipper.

"Do it," he uttered soundlessly.

My eyes flew open. "You mean it?" I asked. "Are you sure *you're* ready?"

Christian smiled and moved in close again. He pressed his lips to my neck and whispered three words I wasn't expecting: "I want you."

I beamed. I knew instantly that everything was about to change forever. I tilted my head back against the tombstone and stared up at the world around us. The night spun overhead like time-lapse photography. I was lost in the moment—lost in my incredible ability to apperceive my experience when it happened! He pressed his body even closer and suddenly I felt him inside me, not his blood this time, just him and it was without a doubt the preeminent sensory experience of my entire existence. I closed my eyes and let the wholeness of his love fill me completely.

My skin simmered with a steady pulse. My mind swirled with an easy current. I was relaxed—utterly and completely relaxed in his arms. And as our bodies coalesced into one I felt myself beginning to melt inside. Christian tightened his arms around me. The measured tempo of our love quickened. As we ascended together to that most transcendent crest of heaven I couldn't contain the breath in my lungs any longer! I exhaled with a hushed moan of release. My heart thumped in my chest.

An instant later I heard the unmistakable sound of a baby crying. I peered over the edge of the tombstone. There at the foot of the small grave surrounded by the women was the lucent likeness of an infant swaddled in a bouquet of droopy, black blossoms.

20. The Morning After

If heaven existed then I definitely found it in the cemetery that night in Mexico. I was in love, a love so big my indolent heart could barely keep from exploding. My Tin Man, my beautiful stranger, my sweet Christian—he was everything I imagined and more.

I pressed my cheek against my hand and watched the artful way he finished tattooing a beautiful Japanese peony on a tough guy's bicep. It felt like forever since our time together in Mexico, but we'd barely been home a week. Life in Perish was easy to slip back into and practically made our trip feel as though it never even happened.

But the truth was it did.

The attraction between us that night in the cemetery was off the charts. Neither of us could deny it, but the next day was different. Reality sank in deeper than a shovel in wet sand. We rushed to the airport, hopped on our plane and headed home. We didn't talk about what happened between us. We didn't talk about the women, their chanting, the black flowers or even the baby crying for that matter. The only thing we did discuss was Ryan, the Blood-Trade and the Vena. The thought of upsetting Henry, Eva and B with the truth just didn't feel right. They didn't need to know that there were others out there like Maxim and Sakura—refugee vampires maybe even more dangerous than we imagined. We knew we needed to protect our family and so we decided that lying was the lesser of two evils.

When we got home we told them that the postcard was a wild goose chase and that finding Ryan was like looking for a needle in a haystack. Eva was beyond angry. She was mad at us for leaving and actually stooped to throwing a tantrum when she learned that we hadn't even found Ryan! She dubbed our trip, *the hedonistic honeymoon*, and threw it in our faces as though we'd somehow deliberately planned the entire getaway. *Ha!* We hadn't planned anything, although Eva was right about the honeymoon part! The others were just relieved that we had returned. B was thankful that Christian was back to help with the shop and Henry was simply glad that we had returned home safely. I smiled to myself recalling our sweet time together in Mexico…

"What are you smiling about?" Christian asked wiping down the tattoo he was working on. I could tell he was pleased with his art even if he was only doing it to pinch blood from unsuspecting humans.

I grinned bigger. "I'm smiling because of you."

"Me?"

I nodded. "You're really good." I eyed his canvas.

Christian shot me an eye roll.

"What?" I said. "It's a compliment!"

He turned away from me and walked his client to the front of the shop. I could tell the client had been veiled. He was a big man and tough, but he had that faraway, serene look in his eyes as he stumbled to leave. The fact that he handed Christian a huge stack of bills was also quite telling. Veiled customers liked tipping big and this guy was no exception. Christian's face lit up like a Christmas tree as he stuffed the money into the front pocket of his jeans. He thanked his client before returning back to me again.

"You're proud of that one, aren't you?" I said.

He grinned and sat down across from me.

"It's okay," I uttered. "You're allowed to be proud of your artwork."

"I guess."

"What's on your mind? You seem…distracted."

"Nothing."

"Not that new article?"

Christian was the focus of yet another printed piece in a local paper while we were away. His sudden rise to fame was beginning to supersede his ability to keep a low-profile on our supernatural lifestyle.

"Hey," I whispered playfully. "I can take your mind off things." I kicked off my flip-flops, stretched my legs toward him beneath the table and ran my foot up his leg.

"Hope," he said bashfully.

I ascended his jeans until my toes met with the hug bulge in his lap. "Christian!" I giggled.

"Stop!" he said pushing my foot away.

"Can I touch it?"

He laughed loudly. Everyone in La Fuente stopped to stare at us. He grabbed me by the hand and pulled me over to the other side of the table. He kissed me and said, "You taste like cinnamon."

I opened my mouth and stuck out my tongue flaunting the tiny heart shaped candy I'd been sucking on. He kissed me again. "You took my candy," I complained withdrawing.

He smirked, his high cheekbones on full display as he sucked on my candy. "C'mon," he said standing up.

"Are we going somewhere?"

He nodded.

I slipped my flip-flops back on my feet.

"Hurry up," he said pulling me by the hand.

"Are you guys leaving?" Gabriel asked as we walked to the front door.

"Yeah," Christian replied. "And don't forget to lock the backdoor tonight."

Gabe nodded pausing briefly to peer up from the tramp stamp he was tattooing on a tanned, blonde girl's lower back. "Oh and don't forget about that camera crew coming in tomorrow."

Christian stopped walking. "What?" he snarled.

Gabe shrugged. His face paled. "Didn't Eva tell you?" His voice cracked as he spoke.

"No. Eva did not tell me."

He swallowed nervously. "I think it's some local station."

"Christian," I said grabbing his arm. I could feel his body tensing under my touch. "Don't do anything you might regret. C'mon," I urged. "Let's just get out of here."

He glared at Gabriel and reluctantly pushed the front door open.

The door swung with a hard heave. I noticed the absence of tiny bells immediately!

"You got rid of the bells," I said pleased. "Thanks." I kissed his cheek. I grabbed his hand harder and we left the shop together.

It was well after midnight, but the moon was bright and radiant. The tender tang of salt in the air graced my mouth. I licked my lips and jumped on the back of Christian's motorcycle. I wrapped my arms around him. A moment later he revved the engine and we were off.

When we reached the beach near Ambrose House I knew exactly what Christian had in mind. Sometimes he brought me here when he needed to clear his head. Watching the water always managed to sooth his ancient soul. We'd hold hands and stare out into the horizon and somehow, after a while, everything made sense to him again.

He parked his bike near the pines and hopped off when suddenly, faster than the speed of light, he was up the beach standing at the water's edge.

"Christian!" I called out tearing after him.

"I never asked for any of this," he complained as I neared. "I've been so careful for so long. I hid in the shadows. I worked in the darkness. I lived in obscurity. Why is this happening?"

"Because you're talented," I said stroking his arm. "Maybe if you hadn't had over two-hundred years to hone your craft..." I smiled. "It'll be fine."

"Its television," he said. "It won't be fine. Nothing good ever came from the invention of that damn box!"

"Hey. I resent that! *Buffy the Vampire Slayer* was a really good show."

"Yeah," he snarled, "a real classic."

"Oh Christian," I said sliding my hands around his neck. "I won't let anything happen to us."

"It's beyond our control now. There are just too many articles. Too many stories. And now television—I've let this get way out of hand."

"Then stop it."

"How? We can't veil the world Hope."

"We can try." I smirked. "Like hypnosis. Do it televised. It will be perfect!"

He shook his head at me.

"Look," I said reaching into my back pocket. "Forget about tomorrow. Let's just focus on right now instead." I pulled out a flask.

He grinned. "Where did you get that?"

"I siphoned it from B's private reserve."

"B has a private reserve?"

"Yeah," I said unscrewing the cap. "Totally unfair right? Eva stole us a couple bottles when we bonded over Ouija the other night." I downed a swig and then passed the flask to Christian.

He took a drink. "Jesus. It tastes like moonshine."

"Yeah, it's got quite a bite. Don't drink it if you—"

"Oh I'll drink it," he said downing another swig. "It's just a lot stronger than B usually mixes."

I smiled. "Finish it then. Seems like you need it more than I do." I released my hands from his neck and unbuttoned my jeans.

"What are you doing?" he asked wide-eyed watching me.

"Going for a swim." I unzipped my fly and slid out of my pants. I tossed them to the sand and rushed toward the water. "You coming?" I asked diving in. "Crap!" I shouted. "It's cold!"

He downed what was left in the flask and bolted toward the water. Within a fraction of an instant he was already by my side. "I can't warm you up," he said, "but I can definitely try." Bright moonlight illuminated the beads of water that dripped down his face. He pulled me against him and kissed me. I closed my eyes and let the feeling of his mouth enliven me. "My sweet siren of the sea," he whispered pulling away.

"What?" I asked taken aback.

"Siren of the sea."

"Why did you call me that?"

"Because," he said wrapping his strong, wet arms around me, "that's what you are to me."

"Since when?"

"I don't know," he laughed, "since the first time I met you."

"And that was…"

"On the Ambrose."

My heart thumped in my chest. The Ambrose I thought to myself. That wasn't the first time we met. A chill ran down my spine. *This was a residual*—the butterfly effect of my actions in his past. I grabbed my face and held it in the palm of my hands.

"Hope?" he said. "What's wrong?"

"Nothing," I lied when in fact I wanted to say *everything*. What had I done? Had I changed the past so definitively that our brief encounter on the HMS Ambrose was now permanently fixed within Christian's accumulation of memories?

He drew my hands away from my face and held them within his own. He looked into my eyes and smiled. "This beautiful woman calls my name, takes my hand to her heart and tells me that she loves me." He smirked. "A man doesn't forget that sort of thing."

My heart sank in my chest. Regret seeped through my veins like venom.

"Your face," he said gently. "It's been with me for over two-hundred years." He stroked my cheek. "I loved you before I even knew it was you." He kissed my lips and said, "You the siren and I the sailor."

"Siren and sailor," I said taken aback. "You told me that story...on our first date, the night you took me to Mallory Square."

He nodded. "I told you *our* story," he said grinning.

"That story is us?"

"Every night at sunset when I stared out into the horizon I knew we'd be together again."

"It was you?" I said aghast. "You were the one staring into the sunset waiting to see her kiss?"

"*Your* kiss," he said smiling. "I waited and waited hoping to catch a glimpse of the green flash."

"Green flash..."

He nodded. "I see it every time you shift and the high pitch sound too."

"What?"

"The siren's song," he laughed. "I guess I might have romanticized it a little over the years..."

I couldn't believe what I was hearing. I felt sick inside.

"Hey," he said grasping my hands. "We were destined to be together. It was written in the stars."

I felt faint.

"You don't look so good," he said.

"I don't feel so good."

He took me in his arms and carried me from the water back to the beach. My body trembled in the wind.

"You're soaked," he said setting me down in the sand. "And shivering. I've got an extra shirt back at the bike. Let me go—"

"I'll get it," I interrupted. "The walk might do me some good."

"I'll go with you."

"No," I insisted. "I'll only be a second."

I moved with the swiftness of a bullet across the beach toward the pines. I saw the bike and yet I didn't stop I continued running instead. Faster and faster I fled into the forest until finally I stopped running altogether. I dropped to the ground. Tears of blood fell from my eyes. I couldn't outrun my problems. I couldn't escape the truth of what I'd done. I needed to face Christian. I had to tell him about this residual.

I turned around and sped through the trees until I reached his bike again. I saw his small backpack hanging from the rear of the bike. I unzipped it and extracted his dry extra shirt when a tiny glass container fell out with it. I picked up the container and studied its contents. It was filled with roots—a collection of tiny, black, droopy blossoms and a snarl of roots. My eyes widened.

"Hope?" I heard him shouting from the beach. "What's taking you so long?"

"Nothing," I replied. "I'm coming." I stashed the vial back inside his bag and slipped into Christian's dry white t-shirt.

"There you are," he said spotting me on the sand. "I was getting worried."

Just then a sharp pain swiftly tore through my abdomen. I doubled over and dropped to the ground. The pain was bad, like a briar thorn pushing on my bladder when all of a sudden a rush of liquid rose in my throat. Blood spewed from my lips covering the sand in a crimson splatter.

"My god!" he said alarmed.

I wiped the excess blood from the corners of my mouth and cleared my throat. "I'm fine," I said. "I just felt a little sick that's all."

"This is not fine." His voice was distressed. "We should let Henry examine you. He's the closest thing we have to a doctor."

"Forget it. Besides, Henry's my grandfather. It would be weird."

"You can't keep shifting," he insisted. "You've got to promise me that you won't go back in time anymore—it's destroying you! First you started having tears of blood and now this?"

"I know," I said rising to my feet.

"Let's get you home."

"Yeah," I agreed when again I felt the pain in my abdomen. I grabbed my stomach and winced.

"You okay?" he asked concerned.

"Yeah," I lied trying to suppress both the guilt I was feeling and the rock-like pain in my belly.

21. The Beach

I swallowed hard forcing the sickness to rescind and soon I felt fine again.

The night was quiet, almost too quiet. We walked up the beach back to the bike when I spotted something in the distance. "Christian," I said concerned.

He looked ahead. "What is that?"

"I think it's a boat."

"Will you be okay for a minute if I—"

"Go," I insisted. "I'll be fine." I nodded at him and suddenly he was gone.

The boat was fairly small. It looked like a dilapidated rowboat. I trudged through the sand at a steady pace and as I neared I noticed Christian helping a woman out of it. She was tall and slim with white skin and spirals of dark curls that fell aside her shoulders. She was beautiful, like a goddess and wearing only the frayed remains of a tiny cream colored dress. I watched her slip her thin hand inside of Christian's. They shook hands and smiled at one another. My heart dropped.

"Who's this?" I snarled approaching.

"Reina," Christian said still grasping her hand.

She smiled at me, her full lips parting to reveal her perfect white teeth. She had a straight nose, high-cheekbones and a pair of thin black eyebrows that arched severely, but what struck me most was the ethereal quality of her skin; it was lustrous and delicately fair in the moonlight.

"Hello Reina," I said nudging Christian in the arm. He released her hand instantly.

"And this is Hope," he introduced.

"Charmed," she uttered icily before turning her attention back to Christian again. "I don't know what we would have done without you," she said. "We've been lost for days."

"We?" I asked.

"Yes. The child and I."

"You have a child?"

"Yes. I mean no."

My face furrowed. "Well which is it?"

"I'm not sure."

"Where is this child?" Christian asked compassionately.

"In there," she said pointing toward the boat.

I gingerly inhaled. I smelled the night, the saltwater and even a hint of something indistinct, but I didn't smell a child. I peered inside the boat. It was dark and there were soiled tarpaulins covering two rather large lumps. I stole another careful breath. *Death.* Its sharp stench filled my lungs. The last time I breathed in such darkness was when Maxim ran his face against me. A chill ran down my spine.

"Hope!" Christian said startling me. "Do you remember seeing anyone out on the water today?"

"No. There is never anyone near Perish." I returned my attention back to the rowboat again. I took another wary breath. There was blood in the air and when I smelled a little deeper I identified the reek of rotting flesh too. *Was the child dead I wondered?* I ran my fingertips along the tarpaulin's edge and with a swift tug I pulled it back. I practically gasped! Death stared me in face with vacant eyes, but it wasn't the body of a child I saw. It was the ravaged corpse of a human man. He was pale and drained of life. Blood and bite wounds covered his neck. I pulled back the other tarpaulin too. A dead woman lay beneath it and like the man she too was ravaged with wounds. "Christian!" I shouted.

"What?"

"Get over here."

"But Reina and I were just—"

"Now!" I insisted.

My eyes widened when I spotted a mess of shiny, dark hair nestled within the cradle of the dead woman's arms. And then it moved. It was her, the little girl, and she was hissing at me like an animal! "Easy there," I uttered when unexpectedly her eyes started to glimmer! *"My god!"* I said in silence. *"She's a vampire!"*

Christian was at my side instantly.

"What took you so long?"

"Reina was—"

"Never mind."

He focused his eyes upon the child and gasped too!

"Yeah," I said watching the way her tiny body contorted around the dead woman. There was an undeniable resemblance between the two of them. Both had auburn curls, petite features and similar skin tones. *"I think that's her mother."*

"Well if that's her mother then who is Reina?"

I turned to him and shrugged.

"Everything okay?" Reina asked approaching.

"No," I snapped. "Who the hell are you?"

"I..."

"Spit it out," I demanded threateningly.

"I don't know."

"Well do you know what you've got in your boat?" My voice was testy.

She nodded. "You mean the bodies?"

"For starters."

"Two days ago I woke up in the boat. We were at sea. Those people were already dead. I don't know what happened to them. I swear. I don't even know who they are."

"I don't believe her," I said through my thoughts.

"Don't judge her so quickly," he replied. *"Maybe she's telling the truth."*

I rolled my eyes.

"Who is the child?" Christian asked.

"I don't know. But she terrifies me."

"So you honestly don't remember anything past two days ago?" My voice was terse.

"I don't."

"Are you saying you have amnesia?"

She shrugged.

"What about the girl?" I pressed. "Does she remember anything?"

"Go ahead and ask her. She won't speak to me. I can't seem to get a word out of her."

At that moment the little girl peeked out from within the boat. She was tiny, only about five or six years old and she was hissing and showing off her sharp, little fangs.

"Maddy!" Reina shouted. "Enough!" The child ignored her order and continued threatening us with her hissing.

"*Maddy?*" I said. "How do you know her name?"

"I don't. The child is crazy—she's incredibly mad so I just started calling her Maddy."

Christian smiled.

"*What are you smiling about Christian?*"

His face instantly hardened. "So Reina," he said. "How is it that you remember your name?"

"Reina isn't my name. At least I don't think it is. Here," she said lowering the neckline on her dress.

Christian's eyes widened like saucers as he stared.

"The name Reina is tattooed over my heart."

"Can I take a closer look?" Christian asked.

I nudged him in the arm, harder than usual this time. "I don't think that will be necessary."

"Hope," he said. "I just want to assess the work."

"Yeah right," I groaned.

"May I?" he asked politely, his hands hovering just above Reina's chest.

"By all means," she said eagerly.

Christian touched her. I wanted to vomit.

"The tattoo isn't old," he said upon inspection. "The lines are good and the ink is quite dark. Whoever gave you this tattoo was no amateur." He moved even closer, his face practically buried in her bosom.

"Whoa' there!" I chided. "How close do you really need to get Christian?"

"I'm looking at the pigment," he defended. "Hum. It's unusual...not like any *I've* ever used before."

"What do you mean?" Reina asked.

"The tone," he continued. "It's darker than most blacks—if that's even possible." He pulled his hands away.

"Well thank you for looking," she said straightening her dress. It was then that I noticed the scar, about an inch long, on the inside of his wrist.

"Stop," I shouted. "Your arm. Turn it over."

"My arm?"

"Yeah. Turn it over."

She turned her arm around and revealed the scar. "Isn't this thing atrocious?"

"She has a scar from an implant!" I said through my thoughts. Like Ryan and the others that had fled the notorious northern vampire society, it seemed as though Reina too was also a defector. The scar on her wrist was proof that she'd once had a sustenance implant. *"She's a refugee Christian. We shouldn't trust her."*

"You know what this is?" Reina asked elatedly. She went to reach for me. I backed away instantly. "Please," she pleaded. "Tell me anything. I'd be so grateful."

"But I don't know anything," I lied continuing to withdraw. "In fact maybe you should consider contacting the local authorities."

"Hope!" Christian raged soundlessly. *"What the hell are you doing? There are two dead humans in that boat over there and that kid is a vampire!"*

"Do you really think the police could help me?" she asked naively.

"No," Christian insisted.

I shot him a glare. *"Why are you protecting her?"*

"I'm not, but we don't have another choice. We can't risk having the police involved."

At that moment Maddy jumped out of the boat. Her eyes were fixed on Christian and me. She prowled across the sand like a spider stalking its prey.

"Oh Christ," Reina uttered. "She's on the loose."

"She's just a child," I defended.

"Well I've never seen a child like that before." Reina took a deep breath and hid behind Christian for protection.

"Hello Maddy," I said extending my hand to her. I wasn't afraid of her—I wasn't afraid of anything. Her amber hued eyes followed me like a hawk. She leaned forward a little. I reached out even further when suddenly she bit me! Her tiny, razor sharp teeth pierced the tip of my index finger. "Jesus!" I shouted, the prickly pain burning my hand like a horde of bee stings.

"Stop taunting her," Christian insisted.

"I'm not taunting her." I replied. *"You on the other hand,"* I continued soundlessly, *"stop flirting with the enemy!"*

"She's not an enemy."

"Well she's not friendly. I don't trust her Christian."

"Am I missing something?" Reina asked perplexed.

"No," Christian said. "In fact we'd like to help you."

"We would?" I raged.

"Yes," he smiled. "Invite them back to Ambrose Hope."

"Are you crazy?" I seethed soundlessly. *"I will not!"*

"The child will be safer in our protection."

"Thank you," Reina gushed. "Thank you so much."

"Do it Hope. Don't fight me on this."

"You've lost your mind Christian."

Reina ran her hands through her jet-black locks and grinned. "I appreciate this tremendously. Just the thought of getting out of these clothes thrills me!"

"I'm sure it does," I said derisively.

"Hope," Christian insisted. *"Invite them."*

"Of all the beaches," I lamented, *"why'd they end up on ours? Another set of wayward vampires just happen to land in Perish? C'mon Christian, admit it, something's not right!"*

"You're overreacting. Now invite them into the damn house!"

My eyes widened. Christian never spoke to me like that. What the hell was going on with him?

"Hope," he shouted aloud. "Don't you have something to say to Reina?"

I glowered. "You and Maddy can come to my house," I uttered through gritted teeth.

"Wonderful," Reina gushed. She fluffed her dark hair. There was a peculiar twinkle in her eyes as she smiled at me. I didn't like the twinkle. *I didn't like her!*

"Let me call B," Christian said grabbing his phone. "I'll get him to bring the car."

"Forget it," I insisted. "I'll take your bike back to the house. It'll be faster."

"Are you sure?"

"Yeah," I replied. "Stay here. I won't be long." I turned away and rushed up the beach. *"Oh Christian,"* I sighed through my thoughts. *"I hope you know what the hell you're doing."*

22. Warning

As soon as I reached the road I jumped on Christian's bike and took off. Dawn was breaking just beyond the trees. I was used to racing against the sun; up until a week ago I was still weak in the daylight. I flew along the highway back to Ambrose. I needed to get to the others before Christian did. I needed to warn them about Reina and Maddy. If they were just another set of hungry nomadic vampires out for blood the way Maxim and Sakura were, then we needed to be prepared.

Henry was sitting outside on the front porch when I arrived.

"Henry!" I shouted killing the engine.

"Is that you Hope?"

"I need your help." I rushed toward him.

"What's wrong? Is Christian—"

"He's fine—we'll he's not fine. That's the problem."

"What do you mean?"

I opened the front door and stuck my head inside. "Eva!" I shouted. "B! Get out here!"

An instant later Eva appeared on the front porch. "What the hell?" she said. "What are you shouting at the top of your lungs for?"

"Where's B?" I asked.

"He's corking."

"Get him. Now. Do it Eva!"

"What's going on?" she asked panicked.

"Eva. Get B. Please!"

"Fine," she said, "don't get your panties in a bunch." She disappeared back into the house. A moment later she returned with Baptiste by her side.

"What's going on Esperanza?" Baptiste asked. "Where's Christian?"

"He's still at the beach."

"Why didn't he come back with you?" Henry probed.

"Something happened."

"What?" Eva snapped panicked.

"There was a boat."

"Was anyone in it?" Henry asked.

I nodded. "Two dead humans."

"My god," Eva uttered.

"And two vampires."

Eva erupted with laughter. "You're kidding. She's kidding right?"

"I'm not kidding. This isn't a joke." My face hardened. "One of the vampires is only a child."

Eva gasped.

"They're waiting for me to return with the car so they can come back to the house."

"*Our house?*" Henry snarled.

"I didn't want them here, but Christian made me invite them."

"Why?" Eva said. "That doesn't sound like something Christian would do."

"I know," I admitted. "He said that we could better protect the child if we brought her here, but..."

"What?" Eva asked.

"I don't think that's the real reason."

"What do you mean Esperanza?" Baptiste inquired.

I shook my head. "This woman...there's something about her...I don't trust."

"And you're sure they're vampires?" Henry asked.

"The woman showed me the scar on her wrist. It was the same scar Maxim, Sakura and Ryan had...like she'd removed a sustenance implant."

"And the girl?" Henry asked. "Did she have a scar too?"

"I didn't notice."

"I don't get it. Why were they sailing with dead humans?" Eva asked.

I shrugged. "The woman says she can't remember anything past waking up in the boat two days ago."

"Amnesia?" Eva scoffed. "And you believed her? Honey, that's literally the oldest con in the book!"

My face hardened. "Christian doesn't think it's a con."

"Well Christian's an idiot!"

"Well I'd rather him an idiot than a dead man. Look," I said to all of them. "I need your help. Tell me what to do."

"Go back to the beach," Henry advised. "Pick them up and bring them here."

"But that's like asking for a massacre!" I shook my head. "What if this is Maxim and Sakura all over again?"

"Hope's right—although it pains me to admit it." Eva sighed. "B and I ain't starting from scratch again. Do you know how hard we've had to work to try and replenish what those bastards destroyed?"

"I know," Henry said. "But Christian has already made Hope invite them into our house. They can come and go as they please now."

"Oh god," I admitted. "What have I done?"

"The pretense of welcoming them in will force them to let their guard down." He grinned. "Go to the beach and bring them back to the house."

"C'mon," Baptiste insisted. He pulled me to the grass.

"Where do you think you're going?" Eva hollered.

"To the beach."

We marched toward the huge, black truck in the driveway.

"Baptiste Alejandro Morel!" Eva shouted. She slammed her hands on her hips. "You get back here. We have enough of our own problems to deal with." She pointed at her belly. "We don't need to get mixed up in all this!"

He stopped walking and turned around. "Christian is out there and Hope needs our help. We're already mixed up in this." He turned away from her and continued walking. He opened the door and slid inside behind the wheel.

"Ah!" she groaned. "We never had any trouble for years here—not until you came along Hope!"

"Yeah Eva," I scoffed. " It's all because of me."

Eva gasped. "How dare you be sarcastic with me blondie. You haven't earned that right yet!"

I rolled my eyes at her, opened the door to the truck and sat in the passenger seat next to Baptiste. He revved the engine. It roared like lion as we idled in the driveway. I leaned out the window. "Eva," I shouted. "Do me a favor?"

"What?" she snapped.

"When I get back..."

"Yeah."

"Be sure to welcome the woman with your special brand of charm—okay?"

Baptiste tried to stop himself from laughing, but it was next to impossible. A grin usurped his face. He pressed his foot on the gas pedal and in warp speed we were off. I stared into the rearview mirror and watched as a halo of dust encircled Eva's fiery red hair. I smiled before turning my attention to the road ahead.

When we got to the beach the sun was nearly up. We jumped out of the truck and headed to the water.

"Hey," Baptiste said as we trudged through the sand. "Are you sure you're okay in the sun?"

"Yeah. It seems I've built my tolerance to it."

"Well that was fast. It took me years."

"I know. I don't understand..." And then I froze.

"What's the matter?"

"Them." I pointed up the beach. Christian and Reina were playing together in the water.

"Is that Christian?" B grumbled.

"Yeah. With *her*."

He sucked his teeth. "Looks like they're on a date."

"Thanks B," I said swatting him in the stomach.

"Esperanza," he uttered, "a girl like you doesn't get jealous. She gets mad."

I shot him a half-smile before soaring up the beach toward them.

"B!" Christian shouted quickly rushing from the water. His wet shirt clung to his body like a second skin. He was positively radiant in the early morning light. "What took you so long?" he said. "Reina and I were getting worried."

"Reina and I?" I scoffed heatedly.

"Christian has been so welcoming," Reina interrupted.

"Oh stop," he gushed like a giddy schoolboy.

"No," she teased smiling. "It's the truth."

"Baptiste," Christian continued. "I'd like to introduce you to my new friend."

"Friend?" I snapped perplexed.

"Hello," Reina said extending her hand to Baptiste.

He eyed her dark damp locks and sheer crème colored dress and nodded.

"Good to meet you," she continued, her hand still extended.

"Yeah," he replied icily, his hands firmly planted inside the front pockets of his jeans.

"So where's Maddy?" I asked looking around.

"Maddy...I don't know," Christian laughed. "Reina and I were so lost in conversation we must have forgotten about her."

"You forgot about her? She's a child Christian. A vampire child! And she's not exactly easy to forget."

"It's my fault," Reina volunteered. She brushed her hair over her shoulders. "Christian was showing me his tattoo—"

"His tattoo!" I snarled. "The one on his ribs?"

"Hope," Christian said. "I was only—"

"Save it," I insisted.

Reina's eyes widened, her brows curved even more severely. "Don't be mad Hope." Her voice was angelic. "Christian's been nothing but a perfect gentleman."

"Oh I'm sure," I scoffed shooting them a sinister glare.

"Christian," Baptiste interjected. "You take Reina and go find the kid."

He nodded.

"When you find her meet Hope and I at the truck. Okay?"

"Okay," he agreed.

I stormed off. Baptiste followed behind me. I could hear him laughing.

"What's so funny?" I snarled.

"I've never seen you so jealous before!"

"Rub it in."

"Hope," he said grabbing me. I stopped walking and turned around.

"Don't B," I said. "Don't say anything you'll regret."

"I'm gonna say it because you need to hear it. You are the best thing that ever happened to Christian."

I rolled my eyes.

"Don't roll those blue eyes at me." He smiled. "I ain't never seen a man love a woman the way he loves you chica."

"Well apparently he's forgotten."

"Because of her."

"Exactly," I sighed. "I can't compete. She looks like a Grecian goddess in that naked dress and she can make him laugh." I sank my face in my hands. "Oh my god."

"Esperanza. That ain't what I mean."

"What then?" I said looking up.

"She's done something to him."

"Done something? Like what?"

He shrugged. "I don't' know. But this ain't Christian."

Just then I spotted them heading up the beach toward us. Reina pulled Maddy by the hand, squeezing her tiny palm with ridiculous force. The poor child hissed and thrashed through the sand like an animal.

"Jesus," Baptiste groaned. "She's gonna break that kid's arm off."

"I don't think she'd care even if she did."

"What's wrong with this woman?"

"I don't know, but we're definitely gonna find out."

"You think she killed the humans?" Baptiste asked.

"I'm sure she did. And I think she turned that child into a vampire too."

Baptiste's eyes widened. "What kind of sick freak could do that to a kid?"

I swallowed and said, "The one about to get into your truck and come home with us."

23. BFF

"Well look at what the cat dragged in," Eva hissed the moment we neared. She was standing on the front porch. A sheer white negligee draped her slim frame. The silhouette of her body was practically impossible to ignore. She was gorgeous, like an old-time Hollywood starlet.

"Eva," Baptiste grunted. "Go put some clothes on." He got out of the truck and slammed the door shut.

"These are clothes you fashionless brute!"

Reina grinned listening to their banter before moving from the truck. She swept her long legs over the cross step and down to the grass with the elegance of a ballerina. She was willowy and graceful and provoked me insatiably with her every move. Christian followed right behind her like a shadow and that infuriated me immensely.

"And who do we have here?" Eva asked as they approached. There was a sudden southern accent in her voice. I wanted to laugh, but I knew she was putting it on for dramatic effect.

"Hello. I'm Reina." She extended her hand.

"Enchante," Eva replied moving closer.

Reina ascended the wooden steps at the base of the porch and slipped her hand in Eva's. They shook.

I stared at them when suddenly I froze. "Wooden steps," I said taken aback. "Since when do we have wooden steps?"

"Since I built them," Christian insisted pushing past.

"What happened to the cement steps?"

"What cement steps?"

Crumbling cement steps sat below the porch at Ambrose House for as long as I could remember. My heart thumped in my chest. The word *residual* burned on the tip of my tongue.

"You okay," Baptiste whispered, approaching.

"No," I said. "I don't think so, but I haven't got time to sort that out right now." I turned to him instantly realizing that he was carrying Maddy. She was tucked under his arm like a football; protected and secured. I grinned. "How on earth did you get her to stop hissing?"

He shrugged. "Kids like me."

"B," I said. "I wasn't born yesterday."

He smiled. "I slipped her a little something in the car."

"What?"

"My parents used to do it all the time. A little whisky for a toothache, a little vino for a tummy ache."

I grinned and stared at the child. She had a faraway look in her juvenile eyes. She was quiet, contented and relaxed—nothing like she was on the beach. "You really are good with kids," I uttered impressed.

"I'm a regular Tony Danza."

I grinned before forcing myself back to reality again. When I drew my eyes up to the porch I was surprised to see Reina and Eva actually getting along! The chipper tempo of their banter was vomit inspiring. I felt like I was listening to a pair of tweens gossiping about their classmates.

"Is that so?" Eva said girlishly.

"Completely," Reina replied. "Although I have to confess I really don't remember because of the amnesia."

They giggled together in unison.

"Eva," Baptise interrupted. "Can you help me?"

"My god B!" she said stunned. "That's a child in your arms!"

"Yeah. And we need to get her inside before she wakes up."

"Alright," she said excitedly. She clapped her hands together. "This is so much fun! It'll be great practice for me."

"You're pregnant?" Reina asked.

"Six years," she uttered stroking her flat abdomen.

"Six years?" Reina said perplexed. "You look amazing. Your body is perfect."

"I know," Eva gloated. "Now c'mon," she said, "let's go inside. We can look through my closet and find you something to wear."

My body iced up. I couldn't believe my ears. *Eva offering to share her clothes with a total stranger?* Now I knew for sure that something was awry. She never shared her stuff. Eva wasn't generous about anything especially her precious couture. "Eva," I shouted. "Can I borrow your red Manolos?"

"God no," she sputtered. "Not even if hell freezes over and I've been reduce to a pile of rubble."

I smiled inside. B and I were right. Reina had definitely done something—first to Christian and now to Eva. Were the rest of us next? I just needed to figure out precisely what it was and then find a way of stopping it altogether.

I started toward the house and spotted the wooden steps below the porch again. The very sight of them sent a tickle of shivers down my spine. *How did I make this happen? Why was the butterfly effect of my actions somewhere in the past manifesting in such a peculiar way?*

Questions swamped my thoughts, but none more than who was Reina and why had she arrived on our shores? The disappearance of my cement steps was no coincidence. I, more than anyone knew that coincidence didn't exist. Reality was like putty; it could be molded and shaped with the flick of a finger. The sudden appearance of a row boat hauling two dead humans, a child vampire and a refugee with no implant harboring a convenient case of amnesia was no coincidence. I needed to get to the bottom of it and quickly. I rushed up the new steps, pushed the front door open and entered the house.

"There you are," Christian said. "Can you make up the guest room?"

"No!"

"Why not?"

"Because I'm not your maid and I don't want her anywhere near me when I'm sleeping!"

"She's right Christian," Reina insisted. "None of you need to go out of your way to help me. I'll be fine on the couch."

"You're damn right you will," I snarled.

Christian shook his head. "The couch is no place for a woman like you."

My eyes bulged. *A woman like her?* Excuse me.

"Take our room," he offered.

"What?" I raged.

"I insist. You've been cooped up in that tiny boat for days. You deserve a bed."

"Christian!" I shouted.

"Esperanza," Baptiste said from the living room. "Keep it down. The kid is sleeping over here."

"Eva will take you upstairs," Christian said. "She'll show you to your room."

"Are you sure?"

"C'mon," Eva said grabbing Reina's hand and escorting her up the stairs to the second floor.

The moment they were out of sight I erupted like a volcano—*a quiet volcano.* "What the hell is wrong with you Christian?"

"Me?" He ran his fingers through his hair. "I'm not the one being a bad host."

"Host? We're not running a bed and breakfast here! She's a vampire Christian. A refugee. She's on the run. She killed two humans already— and brought them with her!" I shook my head. "And I swear she changed that child herself."

"Whoa! You are completely overreacting."

"And you're completely under-reacting! In fact you're not acting like you at all."

"Right," he snickered. "Well then who am I acting like?"

"An insensitive ass!"

He stared into my eyes and started grinning.

"Why are you smiling?"

"Because," he said. "I get it now."

"What?"

"You're jealous!"

"I'm not."

"You are."

"Forget it," I snapped. "I can't talk to you. Where's Henry?" I asked changing the subject.

"Taking a walk."

"A walk?" I said suspiciously. "He's probably at the beach searching the rowboat for clues."

"Clues?" Christian mocked. "This isn't an episode of CSI, Nancy Drew."

"Have you forgotten what happened when Maxim and Sakura came here?"

"*Maxim and Sakura*. Everything is always about Maxim and Sakura. It's over Hope. We killed them. They're dead. Stop talking about them. Please."

My brow furrowed. I was speechless for once.

"Why don't you just give Reina a chance? Spend some time talking to her. You'll see."

I felt my heart breaking inside my chest. Christian smiled at me before rushing up the stairs to the second floor to be with her again. I groaned aloud as Henry walked through the front door. "Thank god you're here!" I said pulling him into the living room.

"What's wrong?" he asked as we sat on the couch opposite Baptiste and Maddy.

"Everything, but more importantly tell me about the beach."

"How'd you know I went to the beach? I only said I was going for a walk."

"I know you Henry. You're my grandfather. We think alike."

He grinned.

"Did you find anything?"

"I shifted into an animal and searched everything. The boat was clean, well other than the corpses of course."

"There was nothing else?"

"No."

"How were they killed?" Baptiste asked "The humans—did they struggle?"

Henry shook his head. "There were no signs of a struggle. However I did notice something a little odd."

"Odd?" I shot back.

"The expressions on their faces."

"What do you mean?"

"They looked peaceful. Almost as if they were smiling when they died."

"Smiling?" I said perplexed.

"I know it sounds strange, but believe me that's what I saw.

"Had they been killed by a vampire?" Baptiste asked.

Henry nodded. "They were drained. Teeth marks all around the jugulars...but no adult did it."

"What are you saying?" Baptiste asked.

"The child killed them."

Baptiste looked down at the child in his lap and tightened his expression. "Impossible."

"Not impossible," Henry maintained.

"But weren't they her parents?" I asked.

"I'm sure they were," Henry continued. "Which would explain the expressions on their faces. If they felt they died to somehow help their own child—they would have died peacefully, don't you think?"

Baptiste sighed. "I just can't believe *she* could kill...and her own family."

"It's all because of Reina," I said. "She forced the child to do it. I know it."

"That woman is barbaric." Baptiste insisted. "To even change a child—"

"Either of you ever hear of Occam's razor?" Henry interrupted.

"The slasher movie?" Baptiste asked.

"No. It's a principle that suggests all things being equal the simplest explanation tends to be the correct one."

"What do mean Henry?" My voice was hard.

"Maybe Hope is right. Maybe the truth is right in front of us."

"So let me get this straight," Baptiste insisted. "This Batman's razor—"

"Occam's razor," he corrected.

"Occam's razor suggests that Reina is the brains behind this operation?"

"A rowboat arrives in Perish carrying the corpses of two humans, a vampire child and a refugee with no memory—just coincidence?" Henry shook his head. "Not likely."

"What does she want?" I questioned. "Could it be retribution for what we did to Maxim and Sakura?"

"Maxim and Sakura were savages," Henry said. "They wanted bloodshed and that's what we gave them. This," he sighed, "this is different. Something tells me killing games aren't exactly what she's after."

"Well what then?" I asked.

"I simply don't know Hope."

"We have to find out," I insisted.

"Yes," Henry agreed.

Baptiste snorted. "Well Christian and Eva can't help. They're both acting crazy."

"Then we'll have to do it ourselves," Henry added.

I nodded. Baptiste nodded too. Just then Eva returned.

"That woman has taste!" she giggled falling to the couch. "It warms my heart." She fanned herself out next to Baptiste.

"That's it," he said slipping out from beneath Maddy. "You're coming with me." He stood up, leaned over and picked Eva up at the waist.

"Put me down!" she hollered.

He threw her over his shoulder like a sack of flour and carried her toward the front door. "I can't take it anymore. That woman did something to you."

"Don't be ridiculous!" she shouted.

"You ain't you Eva! You're being nice and saying nice stuff."

"So?" she snapped.

"So you're a bitch! And I like you that way." Baptiste struggled to open the front door with Eva in tow. "Hope, Henry. I've got to go. I've got to get her outta here. I'm sorry." He left the house in a hurry.

I turned to Henry. "I guess it's just you and me now."

"I guess so."

Just then the sound of Christian's voice hollering my name echoed through Ambrose House.

"Go on Hope," Henry urged. "Here's our chance."

"What should I do?"

"Be aggressive without being confrontational. Talk to her. Learn as much about her as you can."

24. Alone

The early morning light swept through the house as I ascended the staircase to the second floor. I ran my hand over the wooden lady's timber hair. I contemplated how I could get through to Reina. I knew the task would be much more difficult than it seemed. With her feigned case of amnesia, I had to find an ingenious way of gathering information. Simply asking questions wouldn't suffice—I had to be crafty and resourceful.

When I reached the landing I heard laughter coming from behind my bedroom door. It was them: Christian and Reina. I felt sick inside, but I pushed the door opened anyway.

"Don't you knock?" Christian snarled.

"It's my room," I shot back. They were sitting on *my* bed together!

"Well it's Reina's room now."

"I thought I told you—" and then I stopped myself. This wasn't the time to bicker with Christian. I needed to focus on Reina. I needed to find out who she was and what she was doing to my Tin Man.

"Thank you Hope," Reina smiled, "for giving up your room."

I forced a grin. "Christian," I said. "Don't you have that interview this morning at La Fuente?"

His face paled. Anger raged in his eyes.

"Interview?" Reina giggled. "Sounds impressive."

"Oh it is," I bragged. "Christian's famous!"

"Famous? Really?"

"I'm hardly famous," he said running his fingers through his hair as usual.

"Don't be so modest." My voice was chipper. "Magazines from all over the world are taking an interest in your art."

Reina smiled. Her perfect white teeth glowed in the light of the room.

"And," I continued, "he has a television interview today, this morning actually. Isn't that right Christian?"

He glared at me.

"You better get going," Reina said. "Don't let me keep you."

"Yeah Christian. You better get going." I smiled.

"Hope you said you'd come with me."

"I know I did, but the situation has changed. B and Eva left and I don't know where they are. And Henry, well, no one ever knows where he is. So basically I'm the only one who can see to it that our guests are being looked after." I smiled again.

"Oh I don't need any looking after," Reina said. "I'll be fine."

I leaned closer and whispered, "You really want to be alone with that child downstairs?"

A surge of panic pierced her expression.

"You're in my house and it would be my pleasure to help you while you're here."

She grinned hesitantly. "Thank you."

"Hope," Christian said. "Can I speak with you for a moment?"

"Sure."

He grabbed my arm and pulled me aside. "Why are you suddenly acting so strange?"

"Me?"

"You don't like Reina. I can tell. Why would you want to stay here with her?"

"You're right. I don't like her, but I don't trust her more. This is my house Christian. I'm not leaving her alone in it."

He rubbed his face. "That's it. I'm cancelling the TV interview—"

"God no! You deserve the attention you're getting. Don't mess it up just because of *her.*"

"But I don't even want to do this interview."

"You have to," I insisted. "It's good for your career."

"I don't care about my career."

"Then what exactly do you care about?"

He didn't reply. This certainly was *not* my Christian.

"You'll only be gone a few hours. It will be fine." I smiled before moving back to Reina again. I sat on the bed beside her.

"I won't be long. And I'm coming back the moment I'm done."

"Bye Christian. Best of luck!" Reina wished with a wave.

"Break a leg!" I said waving too.

"Hope," he insisted sternly. "Don't do anything stupid while I'm..."

"Go on Christian." I grinned at him through gritted teeth. "Get out of here. Leave us girls to do girl things!"

His brow was furrowed tighter than a knot as he turned to leave. The moment he was gone I swallowed hard. I knew it was time to get serious. I needed to start my investigation.

"I didn't realize Christian was famous," Reina gushed.

"Yeah well..."

"Do you have any of the articles? I'd really like to see them."

"Umm," I got up from the bed and fumbled through a stack of books and papers. "Maybe in here somewhere."

Reina picked up one of my grandmother's journals and opened it. "What's this?" she asked.

"Stop!" I insisted. I tried to snatch it away from her. "Don't read that!" I shouted, but she started reading anyhow.

> The legacy I pray to endow is the knowledge of truth.
>
> If I had one wish it would be to honor those that have come before us. Age reveals truth and life inspires knowledge. I fear that Henry and the others may never find this inner peace. Today I write as an ambassador of goodwill. I can only hope that one day my daughter and my daughter's daughter and those thereafter will

*finally realize their own truths and
thus the power of their birthright...*

"My god! What is this?" she exclaimed.

"Its private," I snarled grabbing the book and tucking it under my arm.

"Well it sounds exciting! Did you write it?"

"No," I said. "It's not a work of fiction. It's a journal."

"That's one hell of a journal! Who does it belong to?"

I extracted the book from my arm and eyed the cover. There was a pencil doodle of a star in the upper left corner. I didn't recognize this journal—I would have remembered the star. I grimaced. I'd never heard my grandmother write with such wisdom and intent before. Sure her ramblings were always intriguing and sometimes even cryptic, but never this moralizing.

"Hope?" Reina barked. "Who does it belong to?"

I jumped, startled at her tone. "No one," I replied tucking the book inside a nearby drawer. "It belongs to no one." I sighed inside. Now wasn't the time to get emotional. I needed to focus on the task at hand: getting information from Reina. I stiffened my spine. "Oh Reina," I said emotively. "It's not fair."

"What's not fair?"

"You."

"Me?" she said confused.

I nodded. "Why do you get to ask all the questions?"

"Because I have amnesia!" she laughed.

"C'mon Reina," I teased. "You must remember something?"

She shook her head. "Nada."

"Nada?" I exclaimed. "You speak Spanish?"

She thought about it for a second. I watched as she muttered something to herself. "Yeah, I think maybe I do!" She sat back down on the edge of the bed again. There was an excitement in her eyes I'd never seen until now.

"See there you go! We're learning things already." I sat down beside her.

"Do more," she insisted giddily. "Ask me more. Anything!"

"Okay. Do you prefer steak or chicken?"

She thought about it for a second. "Steak," she said. "I love steak. Rare." She smiled. "Definitely rare."

I smiled back. I was ready to hit her up with something a little harder. "And alcohol," I said. "Do you drink?"

She licked her pretty pout and grinned. "Bloody Mary. Best drink of all time. Wouldn't you agree?"

I grinned. I was ready. This one was gonna hurt, but I was running out of time and hardly learning anything real about her. "Do you prefer it from the bottle or the vein?"

"What exactly?"

"Blood."

Her face hardened. Her pretty eyes narrowed and then she glared at me. "I know what you're doing?"

"What?" I said anxiously.

"You're trying to see if I drained those humans aren't you?"

"Um..." I was suddenly speechless.

"Well the answer is no. I didn't. When I woke up they were already dead. Believe me, I checked. If they'd had even a drop left I would have sucked it."

"So the vein then."

"The what?" Her face paled.

"You prefer the vein to the bottle."

She laughed. "Yeah. I suppose I would. But please don't tell Christian. He seemed so happy to share a drink from one of your bottles with me. I just wouldn't want to hurt him."

My body trembled with rage. I wanted to rip her eyes out. Why was she sharing bottles with *my* Christian? I feigned a smile. "It will be our little secret," I whispered. I didn't like Reina. And I definitely didn't trust her. Everything she said sounded like a lie. I needed to pry deeper.

"Hope," she said. "Can I ask you something?"

My skin shivered with her words. Was she going to ask me about Christian? Was she going to hurt me? I stiffened and said, "Go ahead Reina. Ask me anything."

"Tell me what you know about us—about our kind."

I sighed inside. I was glad her question wasn't about Christian specifically. "Well," I said. "I don't know much. I've only recently become—"

"But you're so confident and so strong. I just assumed that you'd been this way for years!"

I smiled, flattered, and brushed my hair away from my face.

"What's that?" she asked noticing the scar in the center of my palm.

"That?" I said pointing to the scar that Christian and I made together. "It's nothing. Just a silly blood pact I made with someone when I was a kid."

She nodded. I felt her eyes moving up my arm. She noticed the trail of bite marks etched into my flesh just above my wrist. "And those," she said. "What are those from?"

"Those were a sacrifice."

"A sacrifice?" Her eyes sparkled in the easy light of the room.

"Yeah. It was a sacrifice for a friend."

"Must have been a special friend."

"He was." My thoughts filled with Christian again.

"*Was?*"

"I mean is. Or rather will be again." I cleared my throat and struggled to focus my thoughts.

"Scars are funny aren't they?" Reina laughed.

"How so?"

"Lies exist because we can't see them. Scars prove the truths we fail to tell."

"Very philosophical of you Reina." I nodded impressed.

"Well I figured I had to say something important if I wanted to compete with that journal entry of yours!"

I grinned. "And what about you?"

"Me?"

"*Your* scars. Do you have any?"

She turned her arm over and showed me the scar on her wrist. "I already showed you this one." Her eyes widened. "I know you know what this is Hope."

I nodded reluctantly.

"Tell me?"

"It's from an implant."

"An implant?" she said confused. "What kind of implant?"

"A sustenance implant."

Her face paled.

"A device that was inserted into your body to feed you…honestly Reina I don't know much—"

"Show me yours?" she interrupted.

I turned my arm over. "I don't have one."

"Why not?"

"Because I wasn't," and then I hesitated, "I wasn't *born* in captivity."

"Captivity?" There was a faraway look in her eyes.

"I told you, I'm not much help. I don't really know anything beyond Perish and my family. I'm new to this life."

She ran her fingers through her dark locks and sighed. I watched as her shirt crept up her arm revealing a large scar on the underside of her bicep.

"Wait a second," I said. "What's that?" I pointed to the scar.

She raised her sleeve a little and struggled to take a look. "I—I don't know. I can't really see it."

"Unbutton your shirt," I insisted. "Maybe we can get a better look."

She quickly unbuttoned her blouse and tossed it to the floor. She was wearing one of Eva's flashy and trashy bras. It was black and lacy, low cut and pushing up her already ample chest to the point that she was virtually spilling over the top of the cup! I felt awkward. I wasn't used to being around other women in their underwear. I didn't grow up with sisters or even a mother for that matter. Living with Eva was probably the first time in my life I'd been subjected to such openness, but for some reason this felt different. Reina's almost nakedness was making me uncomfortable.

"Can you see the scar?" she asked. "How big is it?"

I shifted my eyes away from her boobs and back to her arm again. "It's pretty bad," I said. "Looks like you were nearly someone's meal."

"Me a meal?" she laughed.

"Seriously. You have hundreds of bite scars on your back." I looked a little closer. "And what's this?" I said scrutinizing the small circular scar at the side of her body.

"What is it Hope?"

I recognized it instantly. "A bullet hole," I said recalling the similar scar on Christian's ribs.

"A bullet hole!" Reina shouted. "I've been shot?"

"Guess you've seen a lot of action in your time."

"Well none that I can remember." There was disappointment in her voice. She sighed. "Thanks Hope."

I nodded.

"I mean it."

I nodded again.

"You let me into your home, clothe me, and feed me. I know this can't be easy."

"It's no big deal."

"It is." Her voice was instantly more serious. "And Christian..." she grinned.

"Yes?" My tone was suspicious.

"It must be killing you," she said. "Watching the way he smiles at me."

I wanted to punch her.

"The way he makes me laugh..."

"Naw," I lied. "It doesn't bother me. He's like that with everyone."

She smirked, leaned in close and brushed a strand of my hair away from my face. "Well," she whispered. "I wouldn't let you out of my sight if you were mine."

My body froze. I wasn't expecting her to say that. I opened my lips to respond, but nothing came out.

"You're so beautiful," she uttered.

I was petrified, literally speechless.

"Christian doesn't know how lucky he is." She was close; her breath tickled my cheek as she spoke.

I bit my lip, my tongue still tied.

"I wish there was something I could do...to thank you for your kindness." Her words were like velvet as they flowed from her pink lips.

"No," I uttered awkwardly. "Believe me your thanks is good enough."

She giggled. "Oh Hope my thanks is just the beginning." She leaned close and placed her hand on my arm. Her touch was electric, like a sting from a bumblebee numbing me with a wave of tremors. Tingles soared through every part of my body. Even my bones vibrated. I closed my eyes and surrendered to the feeling of her hand against my skin and when I opened them again I felt transformed; as though my cynicism had abruptly shifted into an overwhelming optimism. I stared into Reina's eyes and finally saw what Christian had seen all along. *She really was beautiful.* I reached for her hand just as Christian burst into the bedroom. His sweet tin-cinnamon scent jolted me back to reality.

"What the hell?" he shouted.

Reina grabbed her blouse from the floor and slipped it around her shoulders. I got up from the bed and bolted from the room altogether. I pushed past Christian and straight through the doorway. I soared along the landing, down the staircase and out of the house hell bent on getting as far away from what happened as possible.

25. Neverland

Day turned to dusk like a hummingbird's flutter and then it was night again. I ran through the woods desperate to lose myself among the pines, but somehow ended up back at Ambrose House.

"Hope," Christian called from the porch.

"Go away," I said.

"No," he replied coming closer.

"I don't want to talk to you." I fiddled with my hair and looked away.

"Please."

"No." I started braiding my hair into a long plait down the side of my head.

"Okay."

"Okay?" I said folding the last strands into place.

"If you don't want to talk to me, I can't make you."

I looked into his eyes. They were green and electric. He really was beautiful under the twilight sky. I couldn't stay angry at him. "How was the interview?" I uttered quietly.

"Okay I think." His face lit up with my willingness to speak.

"Were you nervous?"

"Hell yeah!"

I smiled. "What did they ask you?"

"Stupid stuff mostly. What influenced me? Who my inspiration is…"

"And who did you say?"

"Guess you'll just have to watch to find out!" He smirked and tugged at my waist.

"Christian!" I giggled falling against him.

He stroked the side of my face. "What happened to you?"

"Nothing. Why?"

"You ran out of the house Hope."

"Oh that."

"You wanna talk about it?"

"No."

"Did something happen between you and Reina?"

"No!" I snarled, edgily.

"Okay. Don't get upset."

"Why?" I asked warily. "Did something happen between *you* and Reina?"

"No," he said wrapping his arms around me.

I melted against him.

"I love you silly girl." He kissed the top of my head. "I'd never do anything to hurt you."

"Then why did you?"

"When?"

"Ever since Reina arrived."

"I have?" His face tensed. "I didn't mean it. When I'm with her...it's like I can't remember anything else."

"Gee thanks." I pulled away.

"Hey," he said pulling me back. "I'm sorry." His face softened. "C'mere." He pressed his lips to mine in a kiss. My body weakened from within. Christian's kiss was exactly what I craved. I closed my eyes and surrendered to his touch. The feeling of his lips against mine was ecstatic and suddenly I couldn't remember why I'd been mad at him in the first place. He tightened his grip and swept me off my feet yet again. We soared through the house together, ascended the staircase and flew into the bedroom. He laid me on the bed and eased himself on top of me. I beamed inside just before there was a knock on the door.

"I'm not interrupting am I?" It was Reina.

"Reina!" I shouted tearing away from Christian. She was standing in the doorframe watching us.

"I'm sorry," she said. "I can come back."

"No," I smiled. "We were just..."

"It's okay," Christian uttered. "Come in." He moved from the bed to the wall.

A wide grin stretched across her porcelain face. "I just wanted to thank Hope, for helping me today.

"You helped Reina?" Christian's eyes practically bulged from their sockets. He folded his arms across his chest.

"She helped me discover some things about myself." She moved closer.

"Well I'm glad I was able to help." Flashes of the last time I was alone with Reina flooded my thoughts. My stomach started trembling.

She sat down on the bed beside me. I shifted uneasily, brought my knees to my chest and hugged them. Reina made me tense. Her closeness flustered me in a way I couldn't understand. And when she touched my knee I felt every last drop of blood in my body surging to the surface of my skin. *Was I flushing?*

"I brought this for you." She handed me a green glass wine bottle.

"Where'd you get it?"

"The hallway. Under the counter actually." She grinned. "It looked like it had been stashed there. Maybe I shouldn't have—"

"No," Christian interjected. "B's hidden them everywhere. He'll never know its missing." He grabbed the bottle from Reina's hand, ripped the cork from the neck with his teeth in typical thirsty vampire style and spat it across the bedroom. The ambrosial aroma of the drink abruptly filled the air. Reina stood up and turned to leave. I grabbed her hand stopping her.

"Aren't you going to share it with us?" I asked. *Why did I just say that?*

"You want me to?"

I nodded almost as though I wasn't fully in control of my own behavior. *I didn't want Reina sharing this bottle with Christian and me—did I?*

"Thank you Hope," she said tightening her grip on my hand. She moved back to the bed and sat down again.

I smiled in reply and stared at the bold red lipstick that stained her pretty pout.

"What are you staring at?" she asked self-consciously.

"Your lips."

She stroked her mouth. "I borrowed it from Eva. I think it's called Underage Red."

I laughed. Reina was beautiful, enchanting even, and looked as though she'd just leapt from the pages of some fairytale. I'd never seen a woman with such striking features before: the whiteness of her skin against the blackness of her hair, the fierce arch of her shapely brows, the gentle curve of her lips and the compelling twinkle in her eyes. She was visionary.

"Here," Christian said offering the bottle.

"Thanks," I replied taking it. I released my hand from Reina's to drink.

"We shouldn't even be here," Christian said. "This is Reina's room now."

She laughed, a full-on grin filling her face.

"Christian's right," I added. "We shouldn't—"

"I would have been fine on the couch." She leaned closer and touched the end of my braid. "I didn't need you to give up your room for me."

I smiled nervously. I handed her the bottle.

"Thanks," she said dramatically raising her brows. She drew her fingers away from my hair and took a drink. I watched the way she licked her soft lips with the tip of her tongue before swallowing. She sighed and passed the bottle back to me again.

I downed another swig.

"Hope," she whispered, "think you can help me again?"

"Sure. How?"

She grasped my arm. My body tingled under her incredible touch.

"Just like before," she muttered.

"Before?" I uttered awkwardly. Visions of her blouse on the floor attacked my thoughts. *What the hell? Why was I thinking of her blouse?*

"Why don't we make it a game?" Christian suggested. He took the bottle from my hands and downed a mouthful.

"A game?" Reina queried. "Well only if Hope wants to play." She moved her hand to my braid again and prodded the golden folds of my hair. "Will you play Hope?" Her voice was soft.

"Um," I purred mesmerized, my abdomen fluttering from within.

Would I play? No. Yes. Sort of. It was an easy questions and worthy of a simple answer, but apparently I just couldn't give one.

"What about *I've never*," Christian suggested.

"*I've never?*" Reina grinned. "Sounds like fun."

Christian smirked. "It might even help her remember a few things."

"Hope," she murmured softly. "Are you in?"

I looked into her eyes, curiously captivated by her radiance. I wanted to help her. "Yeah," I uttered much to my own surprise. "I'm in."

Christian smiled and sat beside me on the bed. My heart thumped in my chest. Now I was in the middle, sitting between the two of them. I trembled uneasily. I felt like a guest in my own flesh. *Why?* It was only Christian and Reina. *Why the hell was I so nervous?*

"You start by saying, *I've never*," Christian clarified. "Then you say something that you've never done. Anyone who *has* done what you said takes a drink."

"I can't play this," Reina snarled.

"Because of the amnesia?" I asked.

She nodded.

"You can try," I said softly.

She smiled.

"Think of something you've never done. Search your heart." My voice was easy.

Her eyes locked with mine. "I've never...I've never been in love."

Christian downed a swig. I opened my hand and waited for him to pass the bottle to me. I took a drink.

"You've been in love Hope?" Reina's voice was gentle.

"Yeah," I said swallowing hard. The blood was good; like an effervescent jolt of liquid courage against my tongue. I licked my lips. "How do you know you've never been in love?"

"I can feel it. Like an empty hole inside my chest." There was a sad faraway look in her eyes. Her voice was pitiable.

"But what about..." And then I reached my hand across her chest and pulled down her top a little. I stroked the word Reina tattooed across her heart.

"It doesn't feel like love," she said.

I released my fingers from her shirt instantly. *Why did I do that?*

Why did I touch her? It wasn't like me to cross boundaries—and with a woman. I nestled my hand back in my lap and tightened my grip on the bottle.

"Your turn Hope," Christian said readily.

"Yeah," I replied anxiously. "I've never..." *Think of something good, something non-threatening.* "I've never had an implant."

Reina laughed. I laughed too. The air between us was much lighter. I felt at ease.

"Good one," she said and then she slid the bottle from between my legs. I shuddered. The awkward tension returned instantly.

"My turn," Christian insisted stoically. "I've never had amnesia."

Reina smiled and downed another swig.

I held out my hand to her.

"You've never had amnesia," Christian snarled.

"Well it wasn't amnesia exactly, but I was veiled for over twenty years. I'm pretty sure that entitles me to a drink."

"What's veiled?" Reina asked handing me the bottle.

"It's like mind control. I'm sure you can do it if you tried."

"Me?"

"Yeah."

"Will you show me?"

"Um..."

"Please," she pleaded.

Don't do it. Don't show her anything damn it! Just then she moved her hand to my leg.

"Please Hope. I'd be so grateful."

"Um...sure," I uttered unwillingly. I shifted my leg. She released her hand. "Look into my eyes," I said.

Reina turned to face me.

"Use all of your concentration and focus on one thought and one thought alone. Do you have that thought?"

"Yes."

"Okay, now take it and move it from your thoughts to mine."

"But—"

"Just concentrate. Are you doing it?"

"Yes."

"Now move your thought to me." I closed my eyes, but there was nothing. I opened my eyes again and smiled.

"What?" Reina asked. "Did I do it? Why are you smiling?"

"She's playing with you," Christian insisted.

"What do you mean?"

"Vampires can't veil other vampires."

"What?" Her face hardened. Her pretty features mirrored malevolence.

"Reina," I said regretfully. "I was just—"

"Why did you do that?"

Her tone unnerved me. "I was just making sure."

"Making sure of what exactly?"

"That you really are a vampire."

She pursed her lips and glared. Her eyes were dark and angry. "I don't like being tested," she scolded.

"Okay," I said ruefully. "I won't do it again." Reina smiled, but it was clear that she didn't like being made a fool of. A moment later her expression eased. Her pretty features were back to being beautiful again. It was incredibly Jekyll and Hyde of her and made me nervous.

Christian laughed. "Are you two done?" He ran his fingers through his hair as he often did when uncomfortable. "Are we still playing?"

"Definitely," Reina smiled.

I smiled back, but I still felt a little wary. *Why did she reprimand me like that?*

"Seems like Hope here wants to play hardball," Reina's voice was teasing. "Do you Hope? Do you want to play hardball?" She put her hand on my arm and stroked it.

I looked down at her touching me. "Hardball," I uttered senselessly.

"Great!" Reina cheered and like that the game had resumed.

"Whose turn is it?" Christian asked.

"Mine," Reina beamed. She closed her eyes for a moment. When she opened them again she smirked. "I've never met a woman like Hope before."

"Neither have I," Christian laughed.

"Me neither," I added grinning.

None of us took a drink. The laughter was good and eased the tension instantly.

"Now you," Reina said. Her tone was slightly more serious.

"Sure," I uttered. Just then she moved her hand to my shoulder. I trembled under her touch.

"Go on," she urged gently tracing circles on my skin.

The tension was back. The easiness I'd felt only instants earlier had abruptly faded. I opened my mouth to speak, but no words came out. I was paralyzed; the feeling of her fingers upon my skin seemingly stupefied me.

"Hope," Reina whispered, "tell us."

Tell us what exactly? My thoughts surged with a zillion things I'd never done, but none more than, *I'd never had a woman touch me the way you do.* I opened my mouth. "I...I've never..." She moved her fingers to my collarbone. My lips quivered. "Um..." I uttered distracted. "I've never...been impulsive." *Impulsive—where did that come from?*

Christian took the bottle and drank.

"Pass it over," Reina said withdrawing her hand from my neck. She reached across me. Her arm graced my chest. I shuddered again as she grazed me. *Oh my god. Had she done it purposefully?*

"Reina," Christian asked. "How do you know you've been impulsive?"

"I don't. But being here, with the two of you, this is me being impulsive."

Her words flustered me, both affecting and embarrassing me simultaneously. I felt blood rushing to the surface of my skin again as though I was flushing.

"My turn," Christian uttered startling me. He ran his long fingers through his hair once more. He stared at Reina and me sitting together on the bed. He smirked and said, "I've never felt as good as I do right now."

Good? How could Christian possibly say he felt good about this? My body tensed. I tore the bottle from Reina's hand and gulped.

"My turn," Reina whispered wiping the spill of blood that lingered near my lips.

I froze, speechless yet again.

"You really are fascinating," she uttered tracing the line of my jaw with her fingertips. She outlined the sweep of my lips and grinned. "I've never known such beauty until knowing Hope."

My skin tingled. I drank.

"Now you," she whispered beguilingly. She moved her fingers to my hair. She stroked the folds of my braid before releasing the strands. My hair fell wildly against my shoulders and instantly I was paralyzed again.

"Hope," Christian murmured. "It's your turn." *He* moved his hand to my thigh.

I swallowed hard washing away what little saliva lingered in my mouth. *Why were they touching me—both of them?* My cold body felt as though it was about to liquefy. His hand on my thigh and her fingers in my hair were virtually unbearable. *Did I like this? No. No. No. Then why wasn't I stopping it?* Emotions whirled within me like a storm. *Be impulsive. Be utterly and completely impulsive.* I opened my mouth to speak. This time words came to my lips. "I've never," I said, my eyes shifting between them. "I've never felt this way before," I admitted vulnerably.

At that moment everything changed. I knew instantly that the game was over. Christian's lips reached for mine. I closed my eyes and surrendered. The magic of his kiss obliterated Reina's very existence. I grabbed his strong shoulder and edged him closer. The sweet delight of my Tin Man roused me in a way that only he knew how. I stiffened my spine and extended my neck.

"Kiss my skin," I implored soundlessly. He pressed his mouth to my neck when suddenly I felt another set of lips against me! My body froze with a guarded gasp. *Oh my god!* These lips were much gentler and moving upon my mouth like soft clouds from heaven above. I opened my eyes. *It was her!* She was kissing me. What's more I was kissing back! Every bone in my body told me to push her away, and yet I couldn't. My mind was entranced in some insensible state of euphoria. I *wanted* her touch. I *craved* her softness. *But why? What the hell had I done?* The forbidden fruit had been placed before me and I bit into it—hard! My eyes widened to a sudden surge of resonating screams, nearly shattering my eardrums with the sound.

26. Butterfly Princess

We fled the bedroom in a flash. Reina was right behind us. We rushed down the stairs and through the front door. The sultry night air jolted me back to reality the moment I stepped outside.

"C'mon," Christian urged grabbing my hand. I kicked into gear and rushed along with him. "I think it's Maddy!" he said.

Her screams were loud, but not far away. I figured she must have been by the forest.

"Look," Reina said spotting her.

I extended my gaze. Maddy was nestled at the foot of the banyan tree, crouched down low, her tiny body writhing on the ground.

"Maddy!" Christian yelled. He reached out his hand.

"I wouldn't do that," Henry said stopping him.

I looked around. "Henry?" I couldn't see him anywhere.

"I'm here." He was standing on the other side of the tree, his body masked behind the thick roots. "Don't touch her," he warned.

I shifted my gaze downward and practically gasped. Thousands of insects covered every visible part of her tiny body. Even the fair skin on her face was masked with wriggling creatures. Their long bodies swathed her like a shroud. "My god!" I uttered. "What's happening to her?"

"She's molting," Henry stated. "She's shedding her humanness and becoming in touch with the insects."

The spindly legs of the insects tickled her eyelashes as they crawled across her face. Their large veined wings vibrated as they moved.

"They're cicadas," Christian said. "They won't hurt her."

"It doesn't matter what they are. We should help her!" I edged closer.

At that moment a rather large bodied cicada slipped between her lips. The insect moved deep inside her mouth. Her screams began to soften. A moment later she opened her mouth again. A strange hiss replaced her screams.

"Ah," Henry said grinning.

"What?" I asked concerned.

"Now she controls them."

Reina gasped. The color, what little there was, drained from her face.

"Are you okay?" I soothed.

Reina shook her head. "I...don't understand."

"What don't you understand?"

"Her." She pointed toward Maddy. "Why is she like this?"

At that moment Maddy rose to her feet. Cicadas still covered her like a second skin; their hard shells, like plates of armor, protecting her tiny body. She looked as though she was in defense mode. She moved forward.

"My god," Reina uttered. "She's moving toward me!"

"Maddy!" I said trying to distract her. "You're alright." My voice was calming, but she continued moving forward anyway. "You're safe here. No one will hurt you." I edged closer. She stopped. "Good girl," I encouraged. I extended my hand just as her hissing increased, resonating like metallic thunder from deep within.

"Lord!" Reina shouted backing away.

"It's okay," I assured.

The cicadas began moving! Reacting like an army to an order the insects abruptly fled Maddy's little body in small troops. Shifting like a dark cloud, they filled the grass at her feet before finally dispersing back into their natural environment. And when the last cicada disappeared, the child was herself again. I rushed toward her, grabbed her and swept her up in my arms just as she collapsed.

"Is she okay?" Christian asked concerned.

"No," Henry snarled. "There's nothing okay about her. She's a child vampire with tremendous abilities."

"She's an abomination!" Reina snarled.

"She's a child," I countered.

"Well she's needs restraint!"

"What she needs is training," Henry exclaimed.

Reina glared. "What the hell kind of training—"

At that moment Henry transformed into a large raven with iridescent black feathers. He cawed loudly before taking flight into the pines.

"Dios mio!" Reina muttered. She looked at the ground, at the pile of clothes that Henry had left behind and gasped.

"He's a shifter," Christian said. "He can morph into animals."

Reina's brow furrowed.

"He's like the child."

"Maddy's not like Henry." My voice was stern. "She doesn't seem to *become* them the way he does. I think that maybe she controls them." I stared down at Maddy in my arms and smiled. Her tiny features shone in the moonlight. "Hard to imagine something so innocent possessing such incredible power."

Reina raised a brow at me. "Power," she uttered icily. "What do you know about power?"

I shrugged. "The only thing I know about power is that having it makes you dangerous."

I looked down at Maddy again. Her wild mane gleamed with flecks of auburn. I stroked her cheek with the tips of my fingers. She felt good to touch; her skin was soft. Just then I felt the rock in my belly again. I winced.

"Are you okay?" Christian asked, concerned.

"Yeah," I lied.

"Are you going to be sick?" He put his hand on my shoulder.

"No. I'm fine." The pain subsided as quickly as it appeared. I eased Maddy off my lap and laid her upon the tree roots beside me.

"What's wrong with you Hope?" Reina's voice was smooth.

"Nothing."

"Are you ill?"

"No."

"Do you vomit?"

I shrugged. "Sometimes, but—"

"Is it blood?"

"No. Yes. Look, forget about me." I rose to my feet. "Weren't we talking about power?"

Reina's eyes glimmered. "Yes. So," she said, "do you have power Hope?" She touched my arm. I tingled inside.

"We all do," Christian divulged.

"All of you?" Her face lit up.

I nodded. Christian nodded too.

"What kind of power?"

I smirked. "They're abilities really."

"Show me," she pleaded.

"No!" I chuckled.

"I'll show you," Christian said grabbing Reina and me by the hand. He fluttered his long eyelashes and instantly the world slowed to a stop. Everything was motionless except for us.

"Oh my god!" Reina said looking around. "What is this?"

"It's an instant, a second." I smiled. "It's what a moment looks like."

Reina's eyes widened again. "Christian, you can control time?"

"Naw. I can only stretch it, but Hope," he smirked, "she can—"

And then suddenly I felt the world reanimating around us. Time was running at normal speed. Baptiste was hollering my name at a tone so loud it practically cracked the earth. I spun around on my heels toward him.

"Esperanza! Stop!" His face was rigid and his eyes glimmered as he marched across the grass toward me. "What are you doing?" he shouted.

"Nothing," I replied. "Christian and I were just telling Reina about our abilities."

"Jesus!" Baptiste growled grabbing my hand. He lifted me off the ground and threw me over his shoulder just as he'd done with Eva.

"Put me down!" I demanded.

"No."

"Put her down!" Christian shouted.

"No." Baptiste turned around and strode across the lawn back toward the house.

"What do you think you're doing?" My voice was livid.

"Saving you."

"Saving me? From what?"

"From yourself chica!"

Myself? I had no idea what Baptiste was talking about. I didn't need saving—especially not from myself.

"Trust me Esperanza," he uttered. "One day you'll thank me for this."

One day, I contemplated in my thoughts—but certainly *not* today. Grudgingly I decided to surrender to him. Fighting wasn't an option; Baptiste was built like an ox and I didn't stand a chance against him. I shut my mouth and let him continue rescuing me. I lifted my head and saw Christian and Reina in the distance. They were lost in conversation. They didn't even seem bothered by the fact that I wasn't there anymore. Confusion welled within of me. The farther Baptiste carried me away from them the more bemused I became. I shifted my eyes to Maddy instead. She was fast asleep at the foot of the banyan tree nestled beneath a blanket of Monarch butterflies.

27. Incantation

I was Belle in the arms of the beast as Baptiste set me down on the stairs in the hallway.

"Esperanza," he lamented. "What's come over you?"

"What the hell B? Why did you carry me away from them?"

"You weren't acting like you. I thought you didn't trust her."

"I don't."

He shook his head at me. "Her and her fledgling—they've done something to all of you."

"Don't be ridiculous."

He kissed his teeth. "I'm not the one sharing secrets...sharing blood."

"What happened?" He laid his tattooed hand on the wooden lady and sighed.

"Nothing happened."

"Then why don't you remember how angry you were when they came here? How jealous you were of the way she was with Christian." He rubbed his baldhead before putting his hand back against the wooden lady again. "It's like you're under a spell or something."

I froze. My eyes inadvertently shifted to his hand. *The wooden lady.* Maybe Baptiste was right. The beast that created Christian possessed the power to enchant—why couldn't other vampires too? On the HMS Ambrose the beast cursed Alex with some kind of magic to entomb her in this wooden shell. *Could Reina have been doing something similar to us?*

"B!" I gushed elatedly. "You're a genius!" I rushed toward him and kissed him on the cheek.

"Genius," he muttered. "About what exactly?"

"About Reina! Don't you see?"

He shook his head.

"I think it's a curse."

"A curse?"

"When I'm in her presence I can't seem to think of anything other than her. Christian said the same thing. It's like she's brainwashed us." I licked my lips. "But now, here with you, I feel...confused. It's like a part of me remembers the things you're talking about even though I can't feel them anymore."

He nodded. "So how did she do it?"

I shrugged. "I don't know."

"You have to find out."

"But how?"

"Your ability," he said. "Go back and see when exactly your feelings changed."

I grimaced. "It's dangerous. I don't think I should. And I promised Christian that I wouldn't go back anymore."

"Esperanza," he uttered softly. "This time it would be different. It would be because you were trying to protect us. I don't think Christian would mind."

"Oh B," I said undecidedly. "I just don't know."

"You do know."

My eyes narrowed.

"What other choice do we have?"

"Kill her," I said.

He smirked. "Don't get me wrong chica. I would, but I ain't a monster."

"Beat it out of her then."

He smiled. "No more violence. Not unless we have to."

"Fine," I said reluctantly. "But I can't promise—"

"You don't have to promise. You just have to try."

He stared into my eyes and smiled. I nodded. A moment later I filled my lungs with air and as my chest inflated everything began moving in reverse.

Shifting through time was much more controlled for me since becoming a fully changed vampire. I knew how to separate myself from my experiences and I could watch events like a voyeur rather than relive them as I'd done when I was a mere half-breed.

I watched as Baptiste picked me up and carried me through the front door and across the grass. I saw Reina and Christian talking by the tree. And then I saw Maddy cuddled beneath her gently heaving blanket of Monarchs. I sped up a little reversing through time until I was inside the house again—back in my bedroom. A small breath of air escaped my lips. I slowed down for a second. *I simply had too.* It was the unequivocal moment when reality seemed more like fantasy. And there it was—the strange and seductive second when Reina's lips met with mine. It was only a kiss and yet it seemed like so much more. My eyes roamed the union of our mouths when suddenly I gasped triggering the reversal again.

Events blurred like smudges of color as I sped back through time.

I watched Reina smirk, lean in close and brush a strand of my hair away from my face.

"Well," she whispered. "I wouldn't let you out of my sight if you were mine."

I watched a little more.

She giggled. "Oh Hope my thanks is just the beginning." She leaned close and placed her hand on my arm.

A jolt of electricity shot through me numbing me with a wave of tremors. An instant later Christian burst into the bedroom. His sweet tin-cinnamon scent propelled me back to reality, a wave of freedom suddenly washed over me.

I exhaled. The rewind stopped. My sluggish pulse thumped. My emotions crashed like a head-on collision; love and hate whirled within me. I knew the delight of knowing Reina and yet I also knew the distrust and jealousy I felt for her too. *How was it that I could feel in love and indifferent simultaneously?* I needed to know. And so I inhaled once more.

I shifted again to the moment when my feelings transformed.

"Oh Hope my thanks is just the beginning." She leaned close and placed her hand on my arm. Her touch was electric, like a sting from a bumblebee numbing me followed by a wave of tremors.

My eyes widened. The room was quiet except for the tendrils of breath that left my lips. Gently I exhaled a little more and there I was beside her on the bed again.

"Oh Hope my thanks is just the beginning." She leaned close and placed her hand on my arm.

I froze. *It was her touch!*

Inhale. I shifted back to instants earlier. *Exhale.* The jolt of electricity hit me the moment she touched my arm. *Inhale.* I moved back to the moment before the touch again, anger and jealousy seared inside me. *Exhale.* I watched her touch me, a sudden swell of bliss overwhelming my better judgment entirely.

Stop! I screamed inside my thoughts.

I closed my eyes and tried not breathing at all. I didn't want to feel anything at that moment. And as I suffocated inside I realized that the truth was irrefutable: we really were under her spell.

Boom. My heart thumped in my chest. I opened my eyes again and glared at Reina. I felt violated and used, as images of her lips against mine unnerved me. *Why us? Why was she doing this to us?* Was this retribution for killing Maxim and Sakura? And if it was, then why wasn't she woman enough to just fight?

Reina was a killer, psychotic enough to change a child into a vampire and then use her power to profess her innocence. I cringed. She possessed the power to turn hatred and suspicion into some naive euphoria with the simple touch of her hand—she was the most dangerous vampire we'd ever encountered! I had to stop her before she managed to annihilate our integrity altogether. But I still didn't know how.

If I returned to the present my feelings would remain jaded by her power; I would have forgotten the way I felt before her touch. The solution, if there was one, had to be in the past. I needed to find a way of changing things long before Reina and Maddy even arrived on Perish Key.

I exhaled hard and returned back to the present again. Baptiste was still standing at the foot of the staircase awaiting my return.

"Well?" he asked eagerly.

I nodded, turned my eyes toward the wooden lady and grinned. I felt a connection to her now. Her curse was no different than the spell I was under and the only way to free us both was to find someone that could reverse our conditions—someone who possessed the power to annul the work of a vampire, someone like a witch.

My thoughts immediately shot back to Mexico and that night in the cemetery (and oh what a glorious night it was!). I recalled the women with their death flowers. I remembered the way they chanted and how certain I was that they had resurrected a baby that night.

"Brujas," I uttered under my breath.

"Witches?" Baptiste said perplexed.

I nodded.

"She's a witch?" he asked.

"No. But I need a witch to stop her." I pursed my lips. Where was I going to find a witch? Mexico was much too far geographically. Even if I did travel back to that night in the cemetery, how was I to connect with those particular women and somehow have them help me here in Perish? I needed to find someone a little closer.

I rubbed my hands together and it hit me! I pulled my hands apart and turned them over. I stared at the scar in the center of my palm. I ran my index finger across it and grinned.

"Two separate life lines worthy of being read." My body swelled with elation as I gazed at the way my scar divided my life-line into two distinctly different sections. I remembered the moment I first noticed it and I remembered the old woman who pointed it out to me. I needed a witch and I knew exactly where to find one.

I stroked the wooden lady's hair and smiled. "I'll fix this. I'll fix this for both of us." And then I inhaled as deeply as I could.

28. Fortuneteller

With an exhale I stopped the rewind. The sky was alive with color. The sun was on the verge of setting. Droves of tourist in their Hawaiian shirts and flip flops eagerly anticipated the sun's farewell performance. Local eccentrics peppered the surroundings too. It was Mallory Square. I remembered this moment fondly. A smile inadvertently overwhelmed me. I recalled the feeling of Christian's icy hands upon my waist for the first time and the sweet sound of his voice when he uttered, *"If you could live in a moment of happiness with your true love—would you?"*

It seemed like a distant dream. But I knew that it wasn't. This was reality—albeit a reality I'd already lived, but still reality that belonged to me. I momentarily contemplated the effect of my presence here; wondering what residuals I'd be leaving behind when I spotted her. *The fortuneteller.* She was exactly as I remembered: an old woman with wrinkly skin dressed in loose fitting gypsy clothing. She was working the boardwalk offering palm readings.

"Screw the butterfly effect," I muttered pushing through the crowd. "Excuse me," I said putting my hand on her shoulder. "I need to speak to you. It's an emergency."

"No!" she spit back.

I looked closer. It was then that I noticed she was engaged in a palm reading. "Look," I whispered. "I only need advice and I don't have much time before—"

"Hey," a young blonde tourist interjected. "Get in line sister. I'm in the middle of having my fortune told!"

I grabbed the blonde's hand away from the old woman. I examined her palm. "Good strong life line," I uttered. "You'll have two children and meet the man of your dreams here in Key West."

"Really?" the girl said gleefully.

"Really." I smiled. "Now go and find that dream man!"

The girl rushed away with her friends giggling.

"Not bad," the fortune-teller said. "Not true, but not bad."

I laughed.

"Why you do that?"

"Because," I uttered. "I need your advice and I don't have a lot of time."

The fortuneteller shook her head at me and turned to walk away.

I stuck my hand in my pocket and pulled out a stack of bills. I waved them at her. "I didn't say I wanted *free* advice."

She stopped walking, snatched the money out of my hand and stuffed it into her blouse. She tugged on my shirt. I leaned down to her level. She inhaled the scent of my skin.

"I know what you are," she said quietly.

My heart froze.

"It's okay. I can tell you aren't a savage." She grabbed my hand and eyed my palm. She studied the scar in the centre. She pointed to it with her sharp nail. "What happened?"

"It's from childhood. I did a blood-pact with a—"

"Mmm," she sighed. She freed my hand and turned away.

"Well I know what you are too," I shouted audaciously.

"Oh really," she replied turning back to me. "You mean my fortune-telling didn't give it away?"

"I need a bruja, not a fortuneteller."

Her old eyes darkened. "Why?"

"I need some help with something, something that's beyond this realm if you know what I mean. Look you already took my money."

"I don't do voodoo dolls anymore. You women and your broken hearts." She turned away. "You don't need magic to fix—"

"Look, I have a two-hundred year old human trapped in a wooden masthead sitting in my living room."

The fortuneteller stopped. She turned around again. "Cursed?"

"Yes."

She nodded.

"And I'm under a spell too."

She pursed her thin, wrinkly lips. "What kind?"

I shrugged.

"You want advice—you tell details."

"But I don't know the details."

"Then I don't know how to help." She turned around again.

"Wait!" I cried out.

She turned back; the amber burn of the setting sun illuminated her coffee colored skin.

"After *she* touched my hand my emotions changed. It was like some inexplicable euphoria took over."

"Who *she*?"

"This woman—she's worse than a witch!"

The fortuneteller laughed.

"Sorry," I apologized looking away for a moment, watching the sun decline toward the horizon when all of a sudden I saw myself and Christian! We were standing together on the dock. I froze, instantly regretting my decision to return here. I knew time was running out. I had to get this old woman to agree to help me and fast.

"Your euphoria," the fortuneteller said. "How you know it not real?"

"Because," I replied, my eyes shifting between her and Christian and me.

"Oh child," she snapped curtly. "What distracts you so?"

I shrugged.

"What?" she snarled peering over her broad shoulder.

"Me," I answered. "I'm distracted by myself—okay?"

"*You* distract *you*?" She laughed.

"Look," I said pointing to myself in the distance.

The old woman broadened her gaze. She gasped instantly and muttered something to herself in Spanish.

"I'm not from now," I admitted. "This is my past. That's why I know I was under a spell. And it's not just me. There are others."

"Others?"

"A little girl too. They arrived on our beach. We found her parents in the boat with them. This woman...she changed that child into one of us...she has to be stopped!"

"Okay," the fortuneteller said. "What you want me to do?"

"Make me forget. Free me from her spell!"

"I can't."

"Why not?"

"Today," she explained, "here in this reality you are not under the spell. I can't free you from a spell which you aren't even under yet." Her eyes hardened. "I can only warn you."

"Fine," I said with disappointment. "Then please warn me. Just do whatever you can."

"Give me your name child."

"Hope. My name is Hope."

She reached into her satchel and pulled out a notebook and pencil. "When you come from?" she asked handing me the book.

I wasn't good with time ever since I started living with so many vampires. I had utterly forgotten how to comprehend time! Days felt like minutes and hours like months. I was lost in that strange phenomenon—the vampire vortex; that funny thing that happened when we were around each other that at least made immortality seem bearable.

"Don't you know what time you from?" the fortuneteller asked.

I took the pencil and notebook from her. "Los angelitos just passed... and maybe a week more."

Her old eyes widened. "Dia de los Muertos?"

I nodded.

The old woman turned around again and stared at Christian and me in the distance. "Hum," she said. "Still some human in you in this reality."

"*Some* human?"

"Mala suerte," she lamented turning back around. "Okay. I look at you there and I look at you here. Almost same." She smiled. "I say you not seen a year in this new form." She grabbed the book and pencil away from me and scribbled something down. Her writing was virtually illegible.

"So you will help me then?"

She nodded. "But I can only warn you."

"Fine. Anything."

She turned her attention back to Christian and me. "He loves you very much," she said watching the way we flirted in the sunset.

"And I love him too." I smiled.

The old woman smiled back before waddling away.

"Hey," I said. "You believe me right? I mean everything I told you..."

She halted her stride and turned around. "It don't matter what I believe. You pay me and I do what you ask."

I bit my lip in frustration. The fortuneteller turned away. I watched her stride toward Christian and me and wondered whether she'd keep her word.

The sun was almost gone and I knew I had to get back to the present again. I stared out at the sea and smiled. I thought of the siren and her sailor, the green flash and her shrill song and then I remembered the disturbing mix of beautiful violence that surrounded me in the moment Christian returned my memories. *This was that very moment.*

I moved a little closer, through the crowd toward myself. I watched Christian lean in as though he was about to kiss me. And when his tender lips parted a stream of wispy vapor transferred from his mouth to mine. These were my memories—all of my missing memories. When the last fragmented breath of a memory was restored I knew that he was about to stretch the moment; his long eyelashes were set to flutter like the soft wings of a moth. I looked ahead realizing that the sun was nearly beneath the water. It was sunset and time for me to leave. I smiled and stared at the real siren and her sailor and then I inhaled.

29. The Promise

Exhale. I collapsed upon arrival. It was a long way home, but I was glad to be back. I opened my eyes and looked around. Baptiste was still standing next to me in the hallway. My head bobbed like a slinky as I struggled to focus.

"Hope?" he said.

"Reina."

"No, it's me Baptiste."

I stared up at him, into his rugged, pale face and nodded. "It's Reina. She cursed us."

"A curse," he uttered.

I nodded. "I think it's through her touch."

"Her touch?"

"You never touched her did you B? You never shook her hand or—"

"No. I didn't."

"And that's why you're not under her spell the way we are."

Baptiste nodded. "Did you find the witch you needed?"

"Yes," I replied when suddenly there was a loud knocking at the door. Baptiste moved to answer it.

"Stop!" I ordered. "It could be her, Reina."

"She wouldn't knock. She'd just barge in."

"Don't take the chance. If she touches you—"

"Fine," he agreed.

I nodded, sprang from the stairs and edged toward the door. I pulled it open. There was man standing in the threshold. He was tall and broad, his complexion swarthy and his face extremely familiar. "Hello?" I uttered just as he extended his hand to my face and blew a cloud of dust at me! A burst of gray debris instantly blurred my vision. I practically suffocated with the concentration of the spray. I gasped for air, but I couldn't breathe—no inhale, no exhale, nothing. Unconsciousness pulled me under and I surrendered to it. An instant later I fell to the floor.

When I finally woke I was in an unfamiliar room, reclined in a hard bed, swaddled neatly beneath a colorful serape. The blanket was rough against my skin and smelled of patchouli. I tore it from my body and tossed it to the floor. I sprang to a sitting position when swiftly a sharp pain shot through my skull. I fell back into the bed again instantly. I grabbed my forehead

"Wicked dust hangover," I complained. Just then I sensed that someone was approaching.

"Well hello," a recognizable voice greeted.

I opened my heavy eyelids and turned toward the sound. *It was him*: the guy from Ambrose House, the creep that blew that crap in my face.

"You!" I snapped staggering to a sitting position again.

"I apologize for the headache," he said nearing me. "Here." He handed me a pottery teacup.

I recoiled.

"C'mon," he continued. "It's not poison."

"Right," I said. "And I'm supposed to believe you?"

"Drink it. It will make you feel better."

Tendrils of steam swirled from the dark brew. I peered inside the cup.

"It will help. I promise."

"And why should I trust you?"

"Because," he said practically shoving the cup in my face. "It's what you paid for."

My brow furrowed.

"Abuela said you might not remember."

"Abuela?"

"My grandmother."

My head was spinning and no bells were ringing.

"Drink it," he urged grinning. "I can tell you want to."

I grabbed the teacup and gulped. "Hot!" I said the instant the fiery liquid touched my tongue.

He laughed.

"What is this?"

"Something like the hair of the dog."

I looked at the drink again and took a wary whiff. "Smells like apples."

"Among other things."

"It's pretty good."

He nodded pleased.

"Did you make it?"

"Yes," he admitted proudly. "It's an old family recipe."

I took another sip and stared at my new friend. "Why do I recognize you?" I asked.

He sat on the edge of the bed. I recoiled with his sudden nearness.

"Relax," he insisted. "You are beautiful yes, but I know you're spoken for."

I half-smiled. His words didn't comfort me any. Just then he started unbuttoning his shirt.

"Wait a second!" I exclaimed.

He laughed again. "I just want to show you something."

"Oh I bet you do."

He smirked before taking off his shirt. His body was muscular, but that wasn't what caught my eye. It was the beautiful tattoo of a sugar skull on his bicep that intrigued me.

"Remember this?" he asked.

"Oh my god!" I uttered elatedly. "Flor de muerto. You're the guy!"

He grinned.

"But why did you do this to me? Why did you blow that dirt in my face?"

"It wasn't dirt." He put his shirt back on.

"What was it?"

"Do you really want to know?"

I nodded.

"Bone dust."

"What kind of bone dust?"

"Does it make a difference?"

My eyes hardened. "Who are you?"

"I'm Beliarosa's grandson."

I plunked the empty cup on the bedside table. "Who's Beliarosa?"

"My grandmother. You paid her to warn you."

My thoughts churned like a tub of muddy water.

"On the docks...Mallory Square...a while back."

"The fortuneteller!" I said with revelation. "That's your grandmother?"

"Yes! Beliarosa. And I'm Marco."

"Marco," I said remembering. My eyes scanned the surroundings. The room was small, modest and sparsely decorated with religious relics. "Where am I?"

"Over the rainbow," he teased.

"Then where are the munchkins?" I scoffed with sarcasm.

"They're in the other room. C'mon." He motioned for me to follow him.

I stood up. The hangover was gone. I smiled.

"You feel better don't you?"

"Yeah," I admitted. "I really do."

"It's the tea I tell you."

"If you say so." I started walking. I stayed tight to Marco's heels.

"She told me to bring you to her when you woke."

"Who?"

"The Wicked Witch of the West," he teased.

I glared. I wasn't in the mood for humor.

"Abuela," he uttered. "Who else? C'mon. She won't bite."

"But I might."

"Oh we know," he replied. "But you don't frighten me."

"I don't?" My voice was disappointed.

"I believe that you and I are more alike than we care to admit. Abuela on the other hand...her thinking isn't quite as open-minded as mine. She has some..." he hesitated, "history with your kind."

"Vampires?"

"No. *Your kind*. The Fairchilds."

"The Fairchilds?" My mind drew a blank.

"Your family—Moira *Fairchild*, Henry *Fairchild*...forget I even said anything." He walked faster. The house was extensive, not particularly posh, but large and intricately designed with many passageways and corridors.

"Where are we going?" I asked, concerned and feeling as though I was getting lost in the labyrinth of narrow wooden hallways.

"Just a little further." He cleared his throat. "I should probably mention Abuela's stubbornness."

"Is that what you call it, 'cause they way she treated me on the dock," I snickered, "I was more inclined to say she was just being a bitc—"

"Yeah," he uttered. "She can be difficult sometimes."

"*Difficult?* Man she's got you wrapped around her finger doesn't she?"

Marco stopped walking. He turned around startling me; the rustic iron wall sconce lit up his face with a ghostly glow. "My grandmother is very old," he said. "She's seen and done things you can't even imagine. If I were you Hope, I wouldn't question her ways."

"Yeah, but—"

"Trust me. She's very powerful."

"Well thanks for the advice."

"It's not advice—it's an order." He turned around and started walking again. "C'mon," he urged. "They're waiting."

"*They?*" I said hurrying to keep up. "Who exactly?"

Marco didn't answer. We rounded the corner and entered what looked like a kitchen. It was somewhat modern and lofty in appearance. I was impressed by the use of exposed wooden beams everywhere. Despite its openness, there was a pleasant warmth to the room and as I looked around I suddenly noticed Beliarosa and Baptiste sitting at a long wooden table together. A dozen or so mismatched cups sat beside a huge pottery teapot in the center of the table.

"Esperanza!" Baptiste greeted.

"B?" I said surprised. "What are you doing here?"

"Drinking tea," he replied, a wide Cheshire cat grin spreading across his rough looking face.

It was a mad tea party indeed and I felt like Alice again smack dab in the centre of the hellish Wonderland.

"After you fainted," Baptiste continued, "Marco told me what you'd done. How you paid Rosa to warn you about the spell."

I nodded. "Where are we? And don't say over the rainbow or Wonderland or—"

"Rosa's house. Marco thought it would be best if we got you out of Ambrose—away from Reina. I carried you to the truck and we drove here."

I looked around. The kitchen was relatively normal—*relatively*. There was a fridge, stove, sink and microwave, but there was also a bunch of strange witchy stuff too. Hundreds of tiny glass jars filled with herbs and other things lined the shelves, while melted candles and burned incense sticks adorned every visible surface. A rack of antique daggers hung on the wall next to a weird plastic cat clock and strange animal feathers dangled from a long wire that stretched the length of the room. The air reeked of rotten apples. I grimaced, the smell virtually sickening me with its stink. I grabbed my mouth and tried sucking back the blood-vomit that started regurgitating in my mouth.

"You okay?" Baptiste asked in a concerned voice.

"Yeah. It's just that smell...the apples."

"From the tea," Marco said grinning.

"Disgusting," I snorted.

"You should be thanking Marco," Baptiste insisted.

"For what?"

"That bone dust concoction he blew in your face released you from Reina's spell. You're free now—even if she touches you again."

"Really?"

"Can't you feel it?" Marco prodded.

I thought about Reina and tried to assess my feelings, but surges of rage, resentment and bitterness swelled within me. I grinned. "I hate her," I said.

"Good," Baptiste uttered.

"So it's done then," I smiled. "We're all free. We can finally be ourselves again!"

Rosa shook her head, her long dark hair swayed as she moved.

"Why are you shaking your head at me?"

"*You* are free," Marco explained. "Not the others."

"Well blow some more bone dust—"

"No," he replied. "It's far more complicated than that."

"Well do a spell or something. You know witchcraft. Isn't that what you people do?"

"Well yes," Marco admitted, "but it's not that simple Hope."

"So what then? How do we release them?"

Marco sighed. "There are many things we can try." He looked over at Beliarosa for a moment. They exchanged a strange glance.

"Great. Let's try."

Marco shook his head. "You didn't let me finish. There are many things we can *try*, but only one that will assure their freedom."

Baptiste scratched his head.

"B," I said eagerly. "What's going on? What aren't they telling me?"

He took a deep breath and let his tongue run over his dry lips.

"Baptiste," I insisted. "Just say it!

"Fine!" he snapped. "You have to rip her heart out!"

The room went silent, but the ticking of the plastic cat clock on the wall resounded like thunder.

"So do it," I said breaking the silence. "Reina is no match for you."

"Not me Esperanza." His dark eyes narrowed. "*YOU.*"

"Me?" I froze. "Why me?"

"Only you can go back in time," Rosa said.

I knew I'd already upset the balance so much and the thought of creating even more residuals revolted me. There simply had to be another way. "You said there were other things you could try right?"

"Well yes," Marco replied.

"Then let's try," I insisted.

Rosa shook her head. "The longer you waste looking for another way, the more she is corrupting your friends...the man you love."

I shook my head. "If I do go back, what exactly am I supposed to do?"

"End her," Rosa said.

"That's it?"

She nodded.

"Easy."

"End her when she's still human," Marco added uneasily.

My stomach sank. "What?!" I exclaimed.

"Find her as a human and then take her heart."

"But I can't. I can only go back to the things I've experienced. I wasn't there when Reina was human."

"You lie!" Rosa shouted. "When you slept I look at your hand—I read your cards. I know you been into a different past, a past that's not your own."

"Esperanza," Baptiste warned. "I wouldn't screw with these brujos if I were you."

"I'm not screwing with them." My voice was hard.

"How did you go into the past of another person before?" Marco asked.

"Well," I said grudgingly. "When I drank from Christian it was like a wormhole opened up and I just sort of slipped inside of his past."

"Then this will be easy for you," Rosa uttered.

"No," I snapped. "I'd need Reina's blood to get inside her past. How do you expect me to get her blood?"

"Drink it," Rosa replied coolly.

"Forget it!"

"Then your friends will stay under the spell."

"Oh come on," I groaned.

"You're a pretty girl," Rosa flattered. "You're smart, strong—no fear. Take this woman. Seduce her. Make her believe you are still under the power of her spell and then bite into her and drink!"

"God no!" I barked.

"Because she's a woman?" Marco asked.

"Because she's a bitch!" I raged. "She *used* me and Christian and Eva..."

"Then do it for them," Baptiste interjected. "Put a stop to her while you still can."

Rosa got up from her chair and moved toward the sink. She turned on the tap. A sputtering of brown tinged water flowed from the spout. She took a small glass vial from the shelf above, uncorked the lid and filled it with the water. She mumbled something in Spanish before spitting into the vial. Her saliva fused with the brownish liquid instantly and the concoction turned black.

"Take this." She shoved the cork back into the opening and passed me the vial. "It only work once."

"What is it?"

"Magic potion," she scoffed.

"I mean what will it do?"

Rosa sighed. "Where she took life this will return it. Where she destroyed life this will repair it. You understand?"

"No."

"Hope," Marco insisted. "You must use the potion on her to free your friends."

"Okay," I nodded.

Rosa patted my arm. "When the potion is within her human body you end her. Only then will you break the spell."

"And that's it?" I asked shoving the vial into my front pocket.

"That's it," she said.

"No catch?"

"Like what?" Rosa asked.

"Do it before the clock strikes twelve or she'll turn into a pumpkin or..."

"No child," Rosa scoffed. "Now go."

"I'll show you out," Marco insisted.

Baptiste stood up prepared to leave. "Aren't you coming Hope?"

"In a minute," I replied. "I'll meet you outside."

He nodded. A moment later Batiste and Marco were out of sight.

Rosa groaned. "What more do you want from me?"

"I want to know when you'll free my friend, the one in the mast-head?"

"When you return."

"Will it be as complicated as this is?"

She put her hand on mine. "One dilemma at a time Esperanza." I could feel the steady throb of her pulse pounding through her aging veins. "Magic is not like other things. It is not something we become; it is who we are born to be. It is in everything and around us always." She looked into my eyes. "You must feel this. Don't you?"

I shrugged. "I don't know anything about magic. I have my own power problems."

Rosa's dark eyes widened. There was a strange inexplicable expression on her face. "Oh Fairchild," she sighed. "What have they done to you?"

"Look," I said frustrated. "Just promise me you'll undo her curse when I return—okay?"

Rosa nodded, but that curious expression still hung heavily on her face. I turned away and left the kitchen. Just as I rounded the corner to the living room, I unexpectedly bumped into Marco.

"Hope," he whispered pulling me aside. "I wanted to talk to you in private."

"What about?"

"Tell Christian I'm almost done with his roots."

"Roots?" I said suspiciously.

"Raiz de la vida."

"Yes, of course," I lied. I had no idea that Christian was working with a witch.

"It's almost ready," he whispered.

"What's almost ready?"

Marco scanned the surroundings. "Shh," he uttered. "You'd better go." It was obvious that he didn't want his grandmother overhearing our conversation.

I left the house, but my curiosity was peaking with interest. I wanted to know more about what Marco was doing with Christian's roots.

"Hope," Baptiste beckoned startling me.

I widened my eyes. Clearly the root intrigue would have to wait—I needed to settle the score with Reina first. I rushed across the lawn toward Baptiste's truck. I jumped into the passenger seat and slammed the door shut.

"You ready?" he asked.

"I'm not sure, but let's get the hell outta here anyway."

He laughed. He pressed on the gas. The engine roared as we peeled away.

30. No Place Like Home

Vampires, witches and curses oh my! I was living the plot of some prime-time paranormal melodrama. How on earth did boring old me get mixed up in all this?

Ever since returning to Perish, reacquainting with Christian and learning the truth about my past, reality as I knew it had changed. Yet somehow being physically turned into a vampire seemed the least of my adjustments. Overusing my power and worrying about the residuals was destroying me—not to mention the fact that we were being forced to deal with freaky immortal refugees on a regular basis. This afterlife I was living was crazy by every measure. My only concern was whether or not I was woman enough to continue dealing with it.

When we reached Ambrose House I was fuming. The ride from Rosa's place roused my anger. I loathed the fact that undoing Reina's curse relied on me alone. The power to shift through time came at a dangerous price and I wasn't so sure I wanted to pay it this time. Things were changing; small stuff like the cement steps and bigger stuff like the fact I was suddenly crying tears of blood. I knew I was treading on dangerous ground and I worried that my actions were leading up to some ultimate devastation. What if I actually did ruin Christian and me for good?

"Esperanza," Baptiste uttered. "You know what you gotta do right?" The truck came to a stop. He killed the engine.

"I know what I gotta do. I just don't really think I want to do it"

"If I could help you, you know I would."

I turned to him and smiled.

"You afraid?"

I shook my head. "I'm not afraid of anything anymore."

"Then what is it?"

"Residuals," I admitted. "I'm concerned with what Christian will say."

"Ah," he growled. "That's Christian in your head. You can't worry about it. Sometimes you gotta think of the greater good."

"I guess," I replied, but his words weren't convincing me any.

"Look," he continued. "Did I ever tell you how I felt just after William changed *me*?"

I shook my head, my interest sparking.

"I wasn't like I am now."

"You weren't?"

"I didn't believe I was smart enough, strong enough...you get the idea."

"Strong enough or smart enough for what?"

"For them."

My eyes narrowed.

"Will and Christian made it seem so easy. They practically had the world wrapped around their fingers. I, on the other hand, couldn't let go."

"Let go of what B?"

"The human in me."

My gaze intensified.

"My emotions dominated my nature. I felt like I had to justify my behavior every second. Truth was I didn't." He looked over at me. "And you don't have to either. See Esperanza, you aren't human anymore. You are stronger, smarter, better now. You have the power to squeeze life by the balls and bend it to your will!"

I grinned.

"You don't have to justify what you're capable of. It's who you are. What you're meant to do."

I nodded. Maybe Baptiste was right. Maybe a part of me was still clinging to the whispers of humanness that still lingered within me.

"I've seen you do some strange shit Esperanza. Believe me; you're stronger than you think."

I laughed, my face unavoidably easing. Baptiste was like the older brother I never had and to know that William, my biological father, created him really did make him feel like family more than ever before.

"You've got to free Christian and Eva. Don't over-think it. It's what you're meant to do. So do it!" He opened his door and started getting out. "Ready?"

"No," I scoffed, "but I'll do it anyway."

Baptiste grinned. A moment later we left the truck.

The sweet smell of jasmine imbued my senses the instant I stepped outside. The air was heavy, muggy even and the grass was studded with dew droplets. I looked ahead. Day was breaking through the pines.

"Sunrise," he uttered. "Let's get you inside."

"Don't worry. I'm fine."

Batiste sighed. "Just focus on what you've got to do. You got that potion Rosa gave you?"

"The tap-water spit?"

He grinned.

"Right here." I patted my pocket.

"Good."

I walked up the wooden steps to the front porch when I realized that Baptiste wasn't following behind me. "Aren't you coming in?"

"You've got this."

"But I need you."

"You don't."

"I can't do this without you. You're like my...I don't know, you're like my Jiminy Cricket," I blurted stupidly.

"Esperanza," he laughed. "I've been called a lot of things, but never once has anyone called me Jiminy Cricket!"

"Please B. Don't leave."

"You're fine," he insisted, his dark eyes glimmering. He smirked. "Just let your conscience be your guide."

"Not funny," I replied, unimpressed.

"I really need to get back to Eva."

"Where is she anyway?"

"I've handcuffed her to a pipe in the boathouse."

"Oh," I grinned, almost regretting I'd asked.

"Esperanza," he said. "It's time to forget the human part of you and find a way to connect to the killer in you again."

My heart thumped in my chest. I nodded in reply. I watched Baptiste turn away and head for the woods. I turned around, swallowed hard and walked to the front door. And with determination driving me forward, I turned the handle and went inside.

"There you are," Christian greeted the moment I entered. He hurried over, wrapped his arms around me and planted a kiss on my forehead.

"Christian," I sighed. He felt so good to hold. Crimson tears brimmed in my eyes and I knew instantly that Baptiste was right. I really did need to do whatever I could—at any cost to free him.

"We wondered where Baptiste took you."

"Well you know B," I said playfully, "so overprotective." I stole a careful breath of Christian's sweet tin-cinnamon fragrance. His succulence danced on my senses. "Mmm..." I sighed, a flood of pleasure enveloping me and suddenly my tears dried up.

"What's on your mind?" I could feel him helping himself to my thoughts.

"You," I said looking into his eyes. They were faraway and distracted. I couldn't bear seeing him as this brainwashed puppet any longer. "Where's Reina?" I asked unwaveringly.

"Upstairs."

"Good."

"You know," he said running his hand up my spine, "Reina says we should stick together. She told me I was a fool to let Baptiste take you away from me."

"She did?"

"Reina also told me how lucky I was."

"Oh?"

"She said that you were the most beautiful woman she'd ever seen."

"Easy to admit when you have amnesia I suppose."

"Hope," he sneered. "It was a compliment."

"Fine."

"Reina really likes you."

"Oh yeah. I get that."

"She'll be so happy you're back."

"Perhaps," I muttered.

"Aren't you happy to be back?"

"Um...sure." I grinned. "I'm happy to see you." I kissed his cheek. "Will you take me to her?"

"Of course," he said eagerly.

At the foot of the staircase I looked at the wooden lady. There was a moment when I was certain her eyes were following me as I moved. I tightened my muscles and let my thoughts grow angry. I tried connecting to the killer in me. I needed to do this.

When we reached the second floor, butterflies wrestled in the pit of my stomach. Christian pushed the bedroom door open. A blaze of sunlight filled the hallway. The interior of the room was aglow with a cheery, yellow sheen. I moved inside.

"Reina," Christian uttered. "Look who I found downstairs!"

She was draped across my bed, nose deep in one of my grandmother's journals.

"Hope!" she shouted excitedly. She sprung up on her knees and smiled.

I froze. She was wearing *my* clothes! Her curvaceous body was stuffed into my purple slip dress—I hadn't even worn that dress yet! My blood flamed in my veins. "What are you wearing?" I snarled.

"I'm so sorry," she said laying the journal down on the bed. "Christian didn't think you'd mind." She ran her thin, pale fingers down the spaghetti straps and grinned. "I can take it off if you—"

"No!" I interrupted. Thoughts of Rein's naked body made me cringe. "Keep it," I said. "It looks much better on you anyhow."

"Don't be silly Hope. I think it would look amazing on you. You've got that perfect build for dresses like these. I'm so curvy it's a wonder I even fit into it!" she smiled, ran her hands down her silhouette and laughed. The sheer fabric pulled against her curves flaunting every contour of her frame.

Christian cleared his throat. His eyes were fixed on Reina's body. I squirmed edgily, jealousy rearing its evil head again. My lips moved; my mouth on the verge of saying something regrettable. But I was smarter than that. I knew I had to make Reina believe that I was still under her spell. I bit my tongue and smiled.

"I'm glad you're here," she said sitting back down on the bed.

"Me too," I lied.

"Where've you been?"

"With B."

"Where'd you go?"

"Nowhere."

"That's a long time to go nowhere," she teased.

"What have you been doing?" My eyes locked in on the journal beside her—*my grandmother's journal.* She was reading them again even after I told her not to.

"Nothing," she uttered trying to push the book under a pillow.

"Is that my journal?" I sputtered accidently.

Reina's pretty face paled.

"I thought I told you not to read it Reina."

"I'm sorry Hope. Don't be mad." She smiled, picked it up and handed it back to me.

I reached out to take it from her when all of a sudden I panicked. Doubt flooded my thoughts. *Had Marco's bone dust concoction really worked? Was I actually impervious the power of her touch?* Reina shoved the journal against me, her hand purposefully contacting my arm. Her touch was anything but gentle. I was petrified just waiting for something to happen—a shock, numbing, euphoria, but there was nothing! *Nothing happened.* I beamed inside.

"I didn't mean to read it," she insisted, "but I couldn't resist. And after I started reading I couldn't stop! I'm sorry Hope."

I was angry, *very angry*, but needed to continue with the charade. I swallowed my rage and smiled pleasantly.

"You forgive me right?"

"Of course," I lied.

Reina smiled, her pretty face widening with the enormity of her grin.

"What's mine is yours," I insisted perhaps going a little overboard.

Reina giggled. "I'm so glad to hear you say that Hope." She was elated. She leaned close. "I had no idea about your family. *The Fairchild family*—fascinating." She stroked my arm. "I knew you were special."

Her breath tickled my cheek. "From the first moment I saw you," she whispered. "I knew you were different."

I grinned uneasily and started withdrawing when I spotted the antique hand mirror that Henry had given me. It was lying on the bed beneath the edge of the sheet. "Reina!" I snapped. "Is that my—"

She followed my eyes toward the mirror. "Damn that thing!" she shouted grabbing it by the handle and heaving it across the room.

"Reina!" I barked watching it smack into the wall before falling to the floor.

"Why did you do that?" Christian asked rushing to retrieve it.

"I hate that thing!"

I moved toward Christian, leaned down and picked up the mirror. Its ornate frame was still intact, but the mirror itself had cracked. The glass had shattered somewhat significantly radiating like a spider's web across the width. I held it up and studied my fractured reflection. I wasn't pale and ghostly like before. I looked vibrant, strong and powerful.

"And don't forget beautiful..." Christian whispered soundlessly. He was in my head again listening to my thoughts. I turned to him and smiled.

"Did I crack it?" Reina barked.

The tone of her voice enraged me. I tightened my grasp on the mirror's handle, stood up and moved across the room toward her. "Reina," I snapped. "Just look at what you've done!" I held the mirror up to her when suddenly I froze. Her reflection was ghastly! Her face was haggard and old. Her chin was protruded and pointed. Her nose was hooked and studded with blemishes while her eyes bulged and were encircled with darkness. I dropped the mirror instantly. It descended to the bed, falling with a graceful plummet. "My god!" I uttered aghast.

"Damn that thing!" Reina retorted. "Keep it away from me!" She scurried off the bed and into Christian's arms. She pressed her body against him. "Oh Christian," she sighed. "Get me out of here please."

"Of course," he replied automatically. He wrapped his arms around her and started toward the door.

"Wait!" I said. "I want to come too." I eyed the mirror one last time before leaving the bedroom with them.

"Oh Hope," Reina said reaching for my hand. "That was dreadful. Why do you possess something so evil?"

"I don't know," I shrugged. "Someone gave it to me."

"Get rid of it immediately!"

"Of course," I said continuing with the charade.

Reina smiled and tightened her grip on my hand. As we descended the stairs my head swelled with questions, but none more than the obvious: Why was her reflection so appalling?

31. Fairest Of Them All

Reina was a liar with incredible supernatural prowess. She could manipulate anyone on a whim with the influence of her touch. When Henry gave me the mirror he explained that it reflected the truth and not necessarily what we see. Maybe Reina really was the dreadful hag reflected in the mirror. Maybe that was the truth and this, the enchanted reality we were living, was all a lie. A chill ran down my spine.

"Hope," Reina said stepping foot outside. "Are you feeling okay?" Her voice was sympathetic, yet laced with innuendo.

I smiled at her. I guess I wasn't doing a very good job of keeping up the charade. "I'm fine," I said. "Why do you ask?"

"You seem a little distracted."

"I do?"

"Yes."

Hum, I contemplated, I have plans to drink your blood, travel inside your past and rip your heart out—distracted would be an understatement! But I couldn't say that.

"*Hope!*" Christian shouted via our silent connection. "*What the hell is wrong with you? I can hear what you're thinking!*"

My face paled. I was speechless.

"Hope?" Reina asked worried. "Are you alright?"

I nodded.

"What's distracting you?"

"Nothing," I fibbed. "I'm not distracted. Maybe a little concerned, but definitely not distracted."

She bit her lip. "Well then tell me what you're concerned about."

I hesitated.

"You know you can trust me right?" Her lips curved into a wicked grin. "I want you to feel like you can tell me anything."

"Anything?"

"Anything."

I swallowed hard. "It's you actually."

"Me?" she said taken aback. "That's ridiculous!"

"Forget it."

"No," she insisted snappily. "Tell me what it is that concerns you so much."

"I said forget it."

Reina's eyes narrowed fiercely. Her face paled whiter than snow as she glared at me. It was clear she wasn't about to let it go.

"Fine," I said. "It's about the mirror."

She gasped. "I don't ever want to talk about that mirror!" She leapt onto the grass and rushed away from me.

"I saw you. I saw your reflection—"

"Leave it alone Hope." Christian's voice was sharp. He rushed off after her.

My shoulders sank in frustration. I was alone and clearly not very good at keeping my feelings concealed. I looked around. The yard was quiet. Only the sweet sounds of the songbirds prevailed. "Where's Maddy?" I shouted concerned.

"In the forest," Christian said nodding toward the mossy threshold.

"You let her go in there?"

"Why not?"

"It's huge. She could lose her way or fall or—"

"She's a vampire," he snarled. "I'm pretty sure she can handle herself."

"She's a child," I retorted. I jumped off the porch and onto the lawn. The spongy grass felt soft beneath my shoes.

"She's not alone," he added. "Henry went with her."

"Thank god," I said relieved.

"The trees are good protection from the sun." His eyes narrowed. "Speaking of which, I can't believe how easily you've adapted."

"You know me," I replied approaching. "I hate it when things get in my way." I shifted my eyes to Reina. She swallowed uneasily and reached toward me. She touched me deliberately.

"Are you sure you're alright Hope?"

"I'm fine."

She stared me in the eyes and half-smiled. "Well I think we deserve to have some fun today." She grabbed Christian's hand. He smirked boyishly with her touch. "What about you Hope?"

"What about me?"

"Are you in the mood for some fun?"

I shrugged.

She tugged on my hand and pulled me close. "Oh come on. The sun is brilliant. The air is warm and we, my friends, are young and beautiful!"

The sickly sweet tone of her voice made me nauseous. I swallowed hard and struggled to bury the sensation back down within me. I plastered on a silly grin instead.

"What do you think the three of us could do together Hope?" She batted her long, dark lashes at me and smirked.

"I...um..."

"C'mon Hope," she urged flirtatiously. "You're a creative woman. I'm sure you can think of something." Her dark eyes twinkled as she spoke. She was enchanting; skin the color of freshly fallen snow, lips like pillows and hair darker than a starless night.

"Indulge Reina," Christian insisted. His face was hard.

I grimaced. I wanted nothing more than to say how I really felt and yet I knew I needed to continue playing along as though I was still under the spell. It was purgatory; a hell worse than death.

"Sweet Hope," Reina sighed. "Christian and I are all yours for the day. Haven't you got any idea—"

"Maybe we could revisit what we started up in my bedroom." My voice wavered as I spoke.

Reina grinned wildly. Her eyes were glued to my every move. She leaned in close, brushed my hair behind my ears and whispered, "Are you serious?" The heavy stink of seduction hung between us like a fog. It was suffocating, but I knew it was my only way inside her past.

"Yeah," I replied softly. "I'm totally serious."

She bit her lip excitedly. I thought I would die. I was standing between my true love and a traitor, and yet I was obligated to seduce them both equally. I looked around. I needed a safe place where I could drink from her without interference. The garden was far too exposed and the woods were too concealed if she tried to run. *The pool,* I contemplated. It seemed the perfect place to perform the endeavor. I could trap her beneath the water and keep her there until I was finished.

"Should we go inside?" she asked.

"No. I've got a better idea." I motioned toward the pool.

"The water?" Christian said. "But you hate water."

"I don't. Hating water was only an artifice—a veil to keep me from leaving Perish." I moved my eyes to Reina and continued surrendering to the charade I was playing. "I think the pool is the perfect place." I smiled.

A moment later I felt Christian rummaging through my thoughts. I knew he was desperate to decipher what the hell I was up to. I busied my mind instantly—he didn't need to know.

I turned toward the pool. The water was incredibly clear. It was blue and beautiful and reminded me of the ocean. Memories of the day we defeated Maxim and Sakura instantly haunted me, but this wasn't that day. This was the day I would destroy an enemy from within! There would be no battle. Reina's death would be swift and confined to the four walls of my pool.

I straightened my shoulders, kicked off my shoes and walked to the water's edge.

"Hope!" Christian shouted.

I didn't respond. I closed my eyes and jumped instead.

Splash! I slid through the water with ease, feeling as though I had somehow entered into another world—a lovelier world where sounds were like secrets and movements were like a dance. All of a sudden I felt someone grabbing my waist. *"Christian,"* I muttered soundlessly. He pulled me close and kissed me beneath the glassy water. With our lips locked in an unbreakable union, and only a trickle of breath between us, we broke through the surface together.

"Some splash!" Reina taunted from above.

"Think you can do better?" I teased.

She kicked off her shoes and jumped in. Water erupted like a volcano as she hit the surface when everything began to slow, moving with a blurry flicker. My eyes shot over to Christian. His long lashes lingered idly in the process of freezing the moment.

"Reina," I said grabbing her hand. She laced her fingers with mine and smiled. Trickles of water indolently dripped down her pretty face when suddenly the world stopped. Silence prevailed and stillness reigned. Everything was motionless except for us. Encircled within the cylinder of Reina's splash the three of us were concealed and protected from everything—even time.

My eyes flitted over to Christian. His wet shirt clung tightly to his well-sculpted physique. He was beautiful. I wanted to kiss him, but I felt Reina tugging on my hand.

"C'mere," she whispered. She drew me near. I fell against her chest. She was wet. The vivid purple of her dress had deepened to a dark violet in color. It was soaked and molded tightly to the curves of her body. I reclined on her. The stiff points of her breasts pressed against my back. I trembled once more with her touch; unnerved and appalled, but not enchanted like before. A second later I felt Christian tugging at my waist. He pulled me back into the safe circle of his arms.

"Oh Hope," he whispered moving his lips to my ear.

I smiled, relaxed, and then I felt Reina demanding me back to her again! She ran her hand around my hair twisting tightly. She tugged on my long locks and drew me near until finally I succumbed to her persistence. And like a yo-yo I drifted between the two of them; from the genuine affection I felt for Christian to the performance I was playing for Reina.

All of a sudden everything changed! I felt them both upon me at once! I shuddered and struggled to bury the gasp that was begging to escape my lips. My body simmered with an unfamiliar intensity. Being touched simultaneously exhilarated me with an unexpected elation! I felt quivers in places deep down inside me. Blood rushed to the surface of my skin and my heart thumped like an earthquake inside my chest.

I was vulnerable in their arms. Dormant muscles I'd never felt before abruptly came alive from within. I was aroused and provoked in just the right way.

"Ah," I moaned, a careful breath escaping my mouth. And then it happened! I felt lips at my neck and other lips at my wrist. My eyes flew open! The sting of Christian's sharp teeth deep within my throat surprised me, but before I could stop him I felt the ache of being penetrated a second time! *Reina.* I looked down the length of my body and saw her pretty pout fixed on my wrist. Her teeth were much sharper than Christian's and her suction more intense. Shockwaves vibrated through my veins. I closed my eyes and practically died inside. The force of their consumption was relentless, far greater than when Christian drank from me alone, and I could feel myself starting to lose consciousness.

"Christian," I sighed soundlessly. *"Stop!"*

He didn't reply. I moved my eyes to Reina, watching the undeniable grace with which she held my hand within her own. Reina was no amateur. It was clear she was skilled in art of live feeding. I needed to put an end to it. I needed to stop her before she drank me dry and left me for dead.

"Christian," I insisted. *"Please stop! You're under a spell—Reina's spell."* He still didn't respond. I slipped inside his thoughts, but they were overwrought with bloodlust. *"Christian,"* I begged, my inner voice weakening with every passing moment. *"Why are you sharing me with someone else? This isn't like you. You would never want this..."* My eyes grew heavy and my limbs suddenly numb. *"Please..."*

A moment later the weight of his mouth abated. He withdrew from my neck; his pretty lips smothered in my blood. He looked down toward my wrist and watched Reina sucking from my skin. Shock overwhelmed him. His face froze aghast.

"It's okay," I assured via our silent connection. *"I'll fix it. I promise. Trust me."*

I slid away from him and back into Reina's embrace. Our eyes stayed locked in an unbreakable connection as I moved. Christian was stunned; confused and bewildered by the events unfolding before him. He was still under Reina's spell and incapable of comprehending the truth. But I knew our bond was stronger than her power alone. Even if he couldn't understand what I was doing he'd support it anyway because he truly loved me. I nodded at him one last time before slipping away, yielding to Reina's touch.

Reina welcomed me. I fell comfortably between her arms against her chest. I elongated my wrist. She moaned, delighted with my willingness to please her. I closed my eyes and surrendered to the charade again. I needed her to believe that I was still under her power—my family's freedom depended upon it.

Just then I felt Christian against me too. His long fingers stroked my arms. I melted with the feeling of *his* hands on me. I slipped inside his thoughts. His head was clouded with visions of Reina, but then I saw something else. It was small and slight and barely even readable, hiding in the farthest corner of his mind. *It was me*! I smiled inside knowing for certain that even though he was under Reina's spell there was still a part of him that hadn't been affected. And it was that shred of hope that confirmed his trust in me. This was him helping me—by believing in me.

I closed my eyes again and surrendered to Reina's touch once more. Now that I knew I had Christian's compliance everything was falling right into place.

A moment later things got even more intense. Reina's sucking intensified. I worried how much of my blood she could drink before I would lose consciousness completely. My veins burned, incensed, as I readied myself to finally take that bite into her flesh. Suddenly she moved her free hand to my stomach. She pressed down hard. I wanted to scream! The abrupt force of her hand pushed the breath from my lungs up into my throat! Reina was strong, much stronger than she seemed and apparently not afraid to demonstrate it.

I hung vulnerably in her arms, with her lips latched to my wrist and her hand pressed to my body. And when she slipped her fingers beneath my shirt I shuddered uneasily. Her hand against my skin was hard and purposeful. She moved her fingers with a patterned stroke and continued tonguing my blood with a steady rhythm. When she dipped her thin index finger inside my navel I nearly jumped out of my skin. *My god*, I thought to myself. She was seducing me and it was working—I wasn't even under her spell for shit sake!

I widened my eyes and mustered what strength I had left. *This* was my moment; I needed her blood and I needed it now.

I leaned my head against her shoulder and eased my lips to her neck. I licked her skin; fangs exposed, tilted my head back and lunged. I dug my razor sharp canines into her jugular with a swift slice. Blood spewed from the crudeness of my penetration, but I didn't falter. Even when I felt her flinch beneath me I refused to stop.

"Hope!" she shrieked withdrawing from my wrist. "Stop!"

I ignored her entirely and sucked from her as though everything that meant anything to me depended upon it. And as I struggled to swallow I couldn't help but notice her vile flavor. She was foul and flagrant and reminiscent of the scent of Maxim's blood; he drank humans to the death and his blood reeked of its stench—Reina's blood seemed much the same. She too was a killer. Blood didn't lie. I could taste it in her.

My eyes welled with sorrow and my stomach fluttered with the rotten stink of her blood within me. Nausea was nearing. I was a breath away from vomiting just as everything began to change. The coercive pull of my ability began taking over! The defiant draw forced me into a sudden state of paralysis. I surrendered willingly and so began my descent into Reina's past.

32. Queen of Hearts

I flared my nostrils, taking air into my lungs and with a profound inhale everything started moving in reverse. No longer was I drinking from her blood—I was traveling within it.

Actions zoomed by at lightning speed. I zipped through the events by the banyan tree and inside Ambrose House before swiftly passing our first introduction on the beach. I was moving quickly and curious about how far back I'd have to go. Images flashed like a story being told backward when suddenly something caught my eye. I forced an exhale from my lungs. The shifting stopped.

I looked around. It was night. The moon was bright and the air was muggy. I was standing on a beach, a beautiful sandy beach, but it wasn't Perish. Then unexpectedly a rich, chocolate infused, wood-like aroma imbued the air. I inhaled cautiously. It was the robust smell of a cigar. *Was this Cuba*, I contemplated? I broadened my gaze. A small, old rowboat floated at the shore in the distance. I recognized it immediately. It was the same boat that Reina and Maddy arrived on in Perish. I moved toward it when suddenly *they* appeared! I hid in a dark shadow.

"Gracias," said the vaguely familiar looking man. He was smoking a cigar and smiling.

A moment later Reina came into view. She was moving along the beach holding hands with Maddy. *Maddy*, I thought to myself. She looked the same, but somehow very different. And then I realized it: *she was still human.* Reina hadn't changed her yet.

I looked closer and noticed another woman holding Maddy's other hand. It was her mother. I'd seen her corpse beneath the tarp on the boat in Perish. I recognized her immediately.

At that moment the man flicked his cigar across the sand. He smiled and jumped inside the tiny rowboat. Reina picked up Maddy and put her in the boat too. She sat beside her father. I watched as he put his arm around her tiny shoulders and grinned. Just then Reina escorted Maddy's mother into the boat. The happy family sat together. My heart sank in my chest. I had to do something. I had to try to save them. Their lives were at stake.

I stepped across the sand. My footfalls were hard. I noticed the cigar on the ground. It still smoldered. I reached down and grabbed it. A moment later I spotted Reina. She was just ahead ready to jump into the boat. I rushed toward her at supersonic speed and jammed the lit end of the cigar against the side of her neck. She howled with pain while I slipped back into the shadows again.

With no time to waste I jumped inside the boat in an audacious effort to save Maddy and her parents. The family shrieked instantly.

"Shh," I insisted. "I'm here to help you."

"Demonio!" the father barked. He wrapped his arms around his wife and daughter in an effort to protect them from me.

"No," I said. "I help you. Protect you." But my eyes were glimmering with their strange iridescent glow and my mouth I suspected was smeared with a covering of Reina's blood.

I tugged on Maddy's shoulders and fought to extract her from her parent's determined grasp when all of a sudden Reina appeared. Her pale face and dark eyes peered ominously over the edge of the boat.

"Shit!" I muttered. I hid my face from her as she leapt aboard, her sharp teeth shimmering like razors in the moonlight.

The charred flesh on her neck smoldered. "Who are you?" she fumed.

I didn't reply. I continued concealing my identity and trying to extract Maddy from her horrifying fate.

"Speak!" Reina raged, her voice much angrier.

I still didn't respond. She sprang forward, across the boat toward me! The force of her lunge knocking me overboard! An inadvertent gasp escaped my lips as I collapsed into the dark water below.

Splash! As my body hit the ocean I felt time starting to shift again. Moving rearward, the world put itself back together before my very eyes. I sped through Reina's experiences at an incredible velocity when suddenly something caught my eye. I exhaled to take a closer look.

Reina was lying in a claw footed bathtub. She was surrounded by bubbles. The room was dimly lit with candles, and I could barely see what she was doing. I looked a little closer.

"I tell you," she shouted to someone on the other side of the bathroom door. "This will make them trust me."

She was grasping a shiny razor blade between her fingers and carving a deep gash into her arm at her wrist. Blood poured from the cuts and dripped down the side of the white tub onto the tiled floor.

"Now they'll think I'm just like one of them." She cut herself even deeper.

My eyes widened. Was she actually faking the scar from an implant removal? *Why?* I gasped accidently triggering the shifting again. Almost immediately light and color merged in a seamless fusion, while sounds began streaming into static. I was surrounded by the concave time tunnel and being pulled astern through the very heart of her memories.

Faster and faster I sped; regret unhurriedly rushing through my veins. *Why had I tried to save Maddy and her parents?* It was incredibly foolish and frustratingly disappointing. I made a mess; I didn't save anyone, I didn't kill Reina and I risked facing perilous residuals as a result of my actions. It was downright stupid of me to think that I could change the inevitable. I slid my hands inside the front pocket of my jeans when my fingers felt the vial from Rosa. The reason for entering Reina's memories in the first place abruptly filled my thoughts. I needed to find the moment before she became a vampire, serve her the contents of the vial and then rip her heart out. Easy! I pushed a breath of air from my lungs.

Exhale.

Like the shattering of a mirror the time tunnel collapsed, exploding into millions of miniscule pieces. The colorful fragmented particles of Reina's past speckled the air like a rainbow of ashes. Everything went dark and a boom so loud it practically deafened my eardrums cut the silence. I closed my eyes and when I opened them again, when the boom subsided, I couldn't believe what I was looking at!

The air was hot. The moon was bright. Lush, tropical foliage surrounded me. The scent of blood hung in the air. *Paradise?* I rubbed my eyes and tired to focus. I was in Mexico standing at the foot of the Paradise Hotel, but why? Reina was a defector from the north—one of Maxim and Sakura's comrades-in-arms, or so I thought.

I scanned the surroundings. A muggy wind clung to my skin. Although it was night the moon illuminated the immediate area in a sublime brilliance. I shifted my gaze a little further. I froze! My eyes locked on the pale woman reclined in the rusty lawn chair at the foot of the hotel. *Ryan!* Her skin was like ivory. Her hair was cropped short and dark like coal and she was wearing red string bikini. *Why the hell was she in Reina' past?*

At that moment a red Lamborghini peeled up the driveway. It squealed to a stop. I hid deeper behind the palm fronds. The passenger door flew open. It was her—*Reina*! She was wearing an expensive looking pant suit. It was form fitted and lavender in color. The jacket was short and when I looked closer, at her waist I noticed the silhouette of a pearl handled pistol sticking out of the top of her pants. My eyes widened.

"Bonito," Reina greeted in a thick Spanish accent.

"El Corazon," Ryan said perking up.

El Corazon, I thought to myself watching Reina swagger from the car toward Ryan.

"You're new," she said approaching.

Ryan nodded, her dark eyes sparkling like star sapphires.

"You can call me Reina," she ordered harshly. There was an arrogance about her I'd never seen before; a confidence in her voice that flaunted her command.

"But I thought you were El—"

"Si," Reina interrupted. She pressed her hand on Ryan's knee and slid it all the way up to her hipbone. "Believe me," she whispered. "I am the heart of this whole operation, but you my sweet," she grinned. "You must call me Reina." She grabbed Ryan's arm.

"Reina," Ryan replied, seduce by the power of her touch.

"You work for me now." She inhaled the scent of Ryan's hair. "You drink in my honor," she said kissing her jaw, "and purge in my honor because I am your Queen!" She withdrew and grinned.

My brows furrowed. My own memories overwhelmed my thoughts. El Corazon? Reina was El Corazon—the scheming leader of the blood trade operation that Ryan was involved with. *My god!* I remembered being in Mexico with Christian, the brutal ballgame he played with the Vena and the gunshot wound he acquired as we fled the ruins. Reina was their leader! *She* was the one enslaving the women and not some machismo Mexican man as I had so foolishly assumed.

Suddenly I was distracted by the sound of another fancy sports car squealing to a stop in the driveway. It was a bright yellow Ferrari and when its doors opened Lobo got out! My jaw dropped instantly. Lobo was alive in Reina's memories and looked exactly as I remembered; the scowl on his face, his slick back hair and the god-awful golden claw ring he wore on his index finger. He was Reina's lead Vena! My heart thumped in my chest.

I watched Lobo spin the golden claw on his ring and as it whorled I remembered the last time I'd laid eyes upon him. It was here in Mexico after the ballgame when Christian slit his throat with that same ring. It was the first time I'd ever witnessed a *real* vampire death. I remembered watching as he burst into flames...

All of a sudden a gusty breeze soared past, rustling the foliage. The unruly shimmy revealed my hiding spot! Lobo turned in my direction, noticed me and started moving closer. I had to get out of there and fast. I inhaled deeply and began shifting through time again.

I felt sick inside, stupid and so downright naïve. I was wrong about Reina. Never once did I consider that she was connected to what happened in Mexico. After Christian and I decided to put it out of our heads I guess the thought didn't even occur to me. I was a fool. Reina didn't come to Perish seeking retribution for what we did to Maxim and Sakura—she came looking to avenge what Christian and I had done to Lobo and the other Vena in Mexico! Her vengeance was personal and very specific.

Her operation was incredibly demoralizing. The way she was manipulating refugee vampire women to her benefit sickened me; taking them under her wing and using them for their ability to seduce blood from paying customers. It was more than likely that Reina had persuaded Ryan into writing the postcard to lure me to Mexico to join in her blood trade too. *Ugh!* The thought nauseated me. At least Christian's operation at La Fuente wasn't bastardizing anyone. Sure we were using humans for their blood like Reina was, but at least we didn't solicit pitiful refugees in search of the promise of a better afterlife.

My eyed hardened. I had to stop her. I had put an end to her before she even had the chance to know us in the first place. I needed to rewrite history.

I continued soaring. Light and color merged together and sounds began streaming into static. I was moving fast, probably too fast, and so I exhaled a little. The concave time tunnel shattered and a deafening boom assaulted my eardrums, but when the chaos subsided and the air finally cleared, my eyes could barely process what fell within their scope.

"Run!" a panicked male voice bellowed the moment I arrived.

I felt a hand against my back pushing me forward. My feet kicked into gear and I started running. This man, *this stranger*, he grabbed my fingers and pulled me even faster. I looked around. We were in a city. It was dark, raining and cold. *Where the hell was I now?!*

"Hold on," he said and like smudges of color we started vaulting along the sidewalks through the streets. Towering skyscrapers lined our path confining us within the jungle of stone and cold gray. A moment later we had run out of road.

"We're trapped," I exclaimed perplexed.

"Not for long." My new friend yanked me down a dingy alleyway toward a door.

I followed willingly still taken aback by where I was and how I'd suddenly gotten here.

"This way," he uttered brushing back his long onyx colored hair. He was mesmerizing, like a renaissance cowboy; his look was a peculiar mixture of the past and the present equally.

"Where are we going?" I asked. I couldn't take my eyes off of him. He was tall and lean and remarkably attractive. His face was pale and covered in a dusting of stubble while a pair of tiny, metal spectacles hugged his eyes. "Where are we? And who the hell are you?" I asked brashly.

He smiled and ran his gloved hands through his dark hair. He was fascinating. His clothes were both dingy and decadent simultaneously. While his pants were tattered, his flowing velvet coat was remarkably elegant.

"C'mon," he urged tugging at my hand again. He pulled me into a doorframe with him and wrapped his long, brown coat around us both. A bright light, like a searchlight, suddenly filled the alleyway. "Stay still," he insisted.

I nodded and froze like a statue. Once the light disappeared the stranger freed me from his coat.

"Pathfinders," he said. "They must be on to us. We need to move."

"Pathfinders?"

He grabbed my hand again. We vaulted away like vapor through the labyrinth of urban alleyways. The stone gray of the city smeared like a blur past my eyes.

"What's your name?" he asked.

"Me?"

We slowed to a stop. He set me down on the ground and grinned. "I said what's your name?"

"My name?"

"Yeah. You gotta name right?"

"It's Hope," I uttered looking around. "Where's Reina?"

"Who's Reina?"

I grimaced. "I was in Mexico and then suddenly I was here—with you." I instantly regretted opening my mouth and divulging so much information.

"Well," he smirked, "this definitely isn't Mexico." His tone was condescending, but his lips were lovely as they curved up into a grin.

"I don't get it," I lamented, puzzled.

"Maybe our lines got crossed."

"Our lines?"

"Yeah. You know our *paths*."

I looked at him wide-eyed. I had no idea what he was talking about.

"I'm Eradan."

"Eradan," I muttered. It was an unusual name, but a lovely one that somehow suited him perfectly.

"What legion have you fled?"

Legion. The only other time I'd ever heard that word was when Maxim uttered it. My blood boiled instantly.

"The twelve," he inquired with a boyish smirk, "or maybe the five? I bet you're from the five. Look." He flashed me his wrist showing the bloody site of his freshly extracted implant.

"You're one of *them*," I sputtered.

"*Them?*" he said saucily.

"I mean you're from the north."

"We'll where else?" he replied rudely.

I glowered.

"Pulling that sucker out was real bitch wasn't it? I used my teeth. How 'bout you?"

"I—I..."

Just then we spotted the searchlight again. It was ahead in the distance and approaching swiftly.

"Damn it," he uttered. He tugged on my hand and suddenly we were leaping along the streets once more. He led me through another web of alleyways until we reached a foggy passage.

"Who are you?" I asked again.

He set me down. "I told you. I'm Eradan."

"Eradan." His name was like music to my mouth. I grinned, lost in his radiance. And as I stared, I unavoidably became enamored with him.

33. Bad Apple

I was a rag doll in his hands as he pulled me down the alley. My eyes couldn't take in enough of him. He was strangely ethereal, almost like an angel. I grinned.

"This is it," he said moving toward a wide green door. He rolled up the sleeves of his velvet coat and meticulously fingered the doorframe. I couldn't help but notice the detailed tattoo that encircled his wrist. "Halo of swallows," he uttered as though somehow privy to my thoughts. He turned around. "My tattoo," he said grinning. "You were wondering what it was."

"I...um," I uttered surprised.

"Do you have any tattoos?"

"Only one."

"Only one?" He snickered.

"That's funny to you?"

His face hardened. "And what is it?" he asked.

"A black butterfly."

"Cute," he uttered.

"Cute?" I scoffed, insulted.

"What's wrong with cute?"

"A black butterfly isn't cute—it's sexy...elegant. Not cute!"

He cringed. "Not sexy."

"Excuse me?"

"Oh Hope," he sighed. He turned his back to me and fiddled with the door again. "Ah," he mumbled, pleased with himself. He pushed on the upper, left edge. The door opened instantly.

"How'd you do that?"

He shrugged urging me inside. "Get in. Quick!"

The interior was dark. I couldn't see a thing.

"Close your eyes," he said, "and count to five. When you open them again they'll be adjusted to the dimness."

I closed my eyes. *One. Two. Three. Four. Five.* I opened them. "Well I'll be damned," I uttered impressed. "How'd you learn to do that?"

"It's common knowledge," he scoffed.

I scowled, but it was too dark for him to see. He was infuriating and undeniably arrogant.

"Get moving," he ordered.

I grabbed the iron handrail at my side and started descending the long flight of stairs in front me. The cave-like walls were dark and damp with moisture. "What is this place?" I asked.

"The catacombs," he sneered, "to the Emerald City."

"Catacombs...Emerald City?"

"Have you been living under a rock?!" His tone was uncouth.

"No," I defended.

"The catacombs are the trail to freedom. You're from the five and yet you've never heard of the Emerald City?"

I shook my head.

He laughed. "There are hundreds of passages like this below the city...they're the only way to freedom."

"Freedom?"

"Yeah," he sneered, "freedom. You know, where the sun is hot, the air is clean, the clouds are white and the ground is carpeted in the most beautiful green you've ever seen—the *Emerald City.*"

"Sounds beautiful."

"It is."

"You've been there?"

"Only in my dreams." He snickered. "Well it has to be better than New York."

"We're in New York?"

"Come on!" he ridiculed. "Where'd you think we were?"

"Well I *was* in Mexico until—" and then all of a sudden I almost missed the step in front of me.

"Careful," he warned.

"I've got it."

He snickered. "It really is the city that never sleeps. New York." He sighed. "But the big apple's been poisoned for a while now. It's probably why so many of us are on the run."

"There are others?"

"Yeah, from all over the north."

"Like how many?"

"I don't know." His voice was boorish.

"Hey," I said stopping. I peered over my shoulder to look at him. "What's with your tone?"

"I don't have a tone?"

"Yeah right," I snickered.

"What?" he asked defensively.

"You say a cutting remark after everything I say."

"No I don't," he dismissed. "Now turn around and get walking." He laid his hand on my cheek and eased my face forward again.

I turned grudgingly and started descending the stairs. "So how many defectors did you say there were leaving the north?"

"Defectors?" His tone was back again.

I stopped, peered over my shoulder and glared at him. He moved my face forward again.

"Hundreds," he answered bitterly. "I don't know, maybe thousands... what's the difference? It's a lot."

"Okay," I replied.

"One thing I do know is that they're all bloodthirsty." He heaved a sigh. "If only there was a way to mobilize them...now that would be a force to reckon with."

At that moment my foot actually did slip. I lost my balance and began tumbling down the stairs. I inadvertently inhaled and triggered the reversal. I started shifting through time.

"Eradan!" I exclaimed, but he disappeared and before long my pace quickened. Light and sound abruptly merged together in a seamless unification. Soon I was surrounded by the concave time tunnel. I was back on track; being drawn rearward once again through Reina's past.

My head swirled like a pinwheel, thoughts of Eradan principal in my mind. *Who was he? What did he mean about our lines being crossed?* I closed my eyes and stole a breath. Oxygen filled my lungs like fuel. I needed to focus. I needed to put Eradan aside for now and concentrate on Reina instead. *She* was the reason I was risking yet another unorthodox trip through time after all.

I pursed my lips and pressed on when suddenly I started moving even faster. The time tunnel vibrated fiercely and pieces began breaking apart. Slits sliced the lining and bright light flooded my vision. Sound streamed with a sonic intensity and I was deafened with the strength of its blare. I trembled like a leaf; my power surprisingly diminished! I couldn't move! I was paralyzed. I shut my eyes, mustered every ounce of strength within me and forced an exhale from my lungs.

Everything stopped. The only audible noise I could decipher was the unmistakable clicking of a metrical beat. When I finally opened my eyes sunlight practically blinded me. I shaded my vision and looked around. I was surrounded by a crowd of primitive-looking people and apparently no one had noticed my abrupt arrival. I hid behind the edge of a stone building.

Boom!

The bang of my heartbeat synchronized with the pound of a drum being struck. The sound ricocheted like thunder. Everyone silenced and looked ahead. I drew my gaze forward too and noticed the familiar stone building perched at the summit of the bluff overlooking the ocean. I recognized it instantly—it was the Castillo at Tulum, but somehow it seemed different. The stonework was immaculate, as though freshly masoned and the atmosphere thrived with ancient inhabitants instead of tourists. *This was Tulum the ancient city!* It wasn't the ruins left behind and I was standing in its center square among its people.

The drum pounded again. I looked to my left. A group of scantily clad young women were huddled together. And then I noticed her— *Reina!* She was the same, but different too. Her skin wasn't pale; it was golden bronze in color and flush with life. Her hair was more brown than black and her eyes were ocher and lackluster. I watched her for a moment, eying the way her pulse throbbed beneath her skin. *Ba-boom. Ba-boom.* Her heart pounded with vigor inside her chest. I inhaled cautiously. The sweet scent of her blood was blissful and made me salivate instantly. My fangs cut through my gums. I grinned. Reina was human!

I edged closer. I was like an animal stalking its prey just as a deep voice startled me! My eyes shot up to the Castillo, toward the voice, to the two people standing atop the temple. I watched for a moment before shifting my eyes back down again. Reina was gone.

My blood boiled. Panic briefly petrified me. I needed to find her again. I widened my gaze and slipped through the throng of sweat-soaked natives. The reek of such raw, human perspiration nauseated me. Blood rose in my throat. I wanted to heave. I pressed my hand to my lips and sucked it back. I broadened my scope. I moved through the village at supersonic speed. I didn't care who saw me—I simply knew I needed to find Reina before it was too late.

Boom!

The drum beat again. I stopped running and surveyed the crowd. My eyes widened. *Reina.* She was standing by the edge of the temple. I moved a little closer when suddenly I realized that I wasn't the only one who'd take an interest her. There was a man—a vampire and he was standing behind her. He was shirtless with pale bronze skin and his sharp canines were perched eagerly against his lips. *Crap,* I thought to myself. He was about to attack her. He was literally instants from changing her into a vampire. Time was of the essence.

I hid behind a group of women across the way and waited for the right moment to advance. The drum thumped again. All eyes focused on the Castillo in the distance—all eyes except for mine and the other vampire.

Boom! The drum thumped a second time. I began my approach, steady and stealthy as I neared them from behind. *Boom!* Just over Reina's shoulder I could see the events at the top of the temple unfolding; it was a ceremony, a ritual. *Boom!* The crowd cheered. I inched forward. *Boom...boom...boom!* The drumming persisted. I strode in rhythm to its beat.

There was no time for apprehension and no room for error. I knew the other vampire was seconds away from closing in. The sweet smell of Reina's human blood invigorated me. I ran my tongue over my teeth and quickened my approach. The steady pulsation of her jugular throbbed in perfect time to the rhythm of the drumbeat. *Do it,* I told myself inside my thoughts when suddenly the drumming stopped. Reina gasped. The crowd silenced and I was briefly distracted by the sudden stillness in the air.

I looked up to the Castillo. There was an elaborately dressed man wielding a very sharp dagger in his hand. He was about to cut another man—like a sacrifice; the spill of blood that was about to ensue enlivened me with vigor!

I drew my eyes back down toward Reina again, but my view was blocked. I couldn't get a clear path to her. The brawny vampire was standing between us. *Crap*, I thought to myself. I needed him out of the way. I needed to get to her. *But how?* It would be difficult to make my way through the crowd and yet if I tried distracting the other vampire from behind, I risked causing a scene. This wasn't the time for an intricate assault. I needed to do something straightforward and merciless.

I pulled the vial from my pocket and removed the lid. I poured the potion into the palm of my hand and worked it into my skin. Getting Reina to drink it wasn't an option anymore, but I had another idea instead.

The ceremony at the top of the Castillo was well underway. I listened and although I didn't understand what they were saying, I let the fervor drive me forward. I edged closer, delighted by the fact that Reina's finality and my family's freedom was just within reach. I ran my fingers together, feeling the moisture of Rosa's potion still wet on my skin.

Boom! Boom! Boom! Boom!

The drum thumped out its strident rhythm again. The crowd began chanting too. The ancient Mayan air simmered with intensity. My eyes came alive with glimmer. My mouth began salivating with the taste of justice teasing my tongue. I edged closer just as the sound of the sacrifice resonated; the noise of the knife piercing the flesh of the man atop the Castillo abruptly rang in my ears. The crowd cheered. I quickened my step. The smell of fresh blood infused my senses. I grinned inside. A moment later I heard the knife again, ripping through flesh. The crowd frenzied! Now was my chance. Masked by their sounds, I rammed my sharp fingernails through the vampire's back! He winced noiselessly as I drove my fist straight through his body, but I didn't stop there. I thrust further until I felt my hand deep within Reina's chest cavity too! Tissue tore at my fingertips and bones splinted with ease as I impaled them both on my arm! My veins burned elatedly as I held their deaths in my hand, but I wasn't done yet. There was only one way to assure Reina's finality. I closed my eyes. I wrapped my fingers around her heart and rapidly ripped it from her body. With a swift tug I extracted my arm from her torso tearing a deep hole through the other vampire too!

The vampire burst into flames. Death rattled around in Reina's body before releasing itself through her mouth. Blood oozed from the hollow in her chest. I tightened my grasp on her heart in my hand when suddenly a colossal shock wave overcame the city. I struggled to steady myself. The earth shook with vigor while the natives dropped to the ground. *What have I done*, I contemplated before quickly forcing an exhale from my lungs.

34. Rebirth

Home. When I opened my eyes again a whiplash of water smacked against me. I looked ahead. Christian's beautiful face filled my vision. I smiled. He didn't smile back. His face was stern. I looked around. The pool was stained scarlet; water undulated like red ink against me. I looked down at my hands. Reina's heart was still sitting in the center of my palm.

"My god Hope!" Christian uttered. "What the hell have you done?"

I looked to my right, to Reina, watching as she suddenly started fading away. Her body, her face, her everything began disintegrating right before my eyes; her very being abruptly reduced to its most rudimentary, molecular state. A moment later her heart vanished from my hands and there was nothing left of her at all. Reina was gone and Christian was free!

Splash!

I shifted my eyes over to Christian again. An upsurge of red water speckled me as I watched him collapse into the pool. "Christian!" I screamed panicked. I dove beneath the surface and pried him up from the bottom. I tucked him under my arm and hurled him onto the pool deck. "Christian damn it!" I shouted desperate to rouse him. "Wake up." His wet face was paler than usual and his lips were almost bluish in color. I sliced my wrist with my teeth and let my curative blood fall into his mouth. A moment later his lips began moving. I kissed him overjoyed and stroked his dark, wet hair with my hand.

He opened his eyes. "What happened?" he asked bemused.

"You blacked out."

"I did?"

"Yeah. Are you okay?"

He nodded and brought himself up to a sitting position.

"You scared the crap out of me!"

"I'm sorry." His voice was still perplexed.

I smiled and kissed him again. I widened my eyes. "Are you—you?" I asked anxiously.

"Of course I'm me! Who else would I be?"

"I mean are you yourself again?"

"Yeah." He was defensive.

"What do you remember?"

"Being in the pool with you and..."

"Reina," I added.

"Who?"

"Reina," I said. "You know, gorgeous vampire, curves everywhere and legs for days, but manipulative as hell..."

His brows knit together. "She sounds...amazing."

I shot him an eye roll. "You really don't remember her?"

"A woman like that seems hard to forget." He shook his head. "No. I don't remember her."

I smiled relieved. *It worked*, I thought to myself proudly.

"But," he said. "I've got this feeling..."

"What feeling?"

"Like I remember we weren't alone. Does that make any sense?"

"Yeah," I said. "It makes more sense than you'll ever know." I kissed him on the mouth and grinned. "I'm just glad you're back."

"Me too, I think." We kissed again and it was wonderful. The feeling of my Tin Man's lips against me filled me with bliss. The sweet taste of his tin-cinnamon savor on my tongue sent a jolt of verve through my body. I knew instantly that enduring the trip through Reina's past and killing her was definitely worth it. I smiled to myself and reveled in the pleasure of preserving our love when all of a sudden the sound of screaming crudely interrupted us.

"My god!" Christian uttered.

"Oh no," I added looking ahead.

Our eyes were fixed on the forest. Henry was approaching. He was carrying Maddy in his arms. She was screaming and writhing and making it nearly impossible for him to hold on to her.

"Help!" Henry hollered with desperation.

Christian and I rushed toward them at supersonic speed.

"What happened?" I asked. I reached out and took Maddy away from him. I pulled her to my chest and stroked her arm when she collapsed. Her tiny body went limp in my arms.

"The child," Christian said. "She's unconscious."

"My god," I uttered. "I think she's stopped breathing!"

Henry pressed his hand to her tiny chest. "Her heart isn't beating."

"Maddy!" I panicked. "Wake up!"

"Maddy?" Henry said confused.

"Of course. Her name is Maddy," I said.

"Maddy," Henry uttered. "I almost remember..."

"She needs blood," I insisted. "Give her blood—now!"

Christian promptly bit his wrist. His blood flowed instantly. He pressed his arm over the child's insipid lips. I watched on tenterhooks as the crimson fluid dripped between her lips.

"C'mon," I urged impatiently, "drink it." But she didn't respond. Maddy's lips never even twitched. I touched her check. Her skin was cold. "Call Rosa," I said anxiously. "Call her now!"

"Who?" Christian asked.

"Rosa," I repeated.

"How do *you* know Rose?" Henry interjected.

"Don't ask." I shifted my eyes back to Christian again and glared. I knew he and Rosa's grandson Marco had secretly been working with the roots from Mexico. "Christian," I insisted. "Get Rosa. Now!"

"Okay," he agreed and with the blink of an eye he was gone. Just then Baptiste and Eva emerged from within the woods.

"We heard the screaming," Eva shouted rushing across the lawn. "B and I were in the boat house and..." Eva looked at the child in my arms. Her jaw dropped. "It's that kid! The one from the boat."

"Maddy," I said, "and she's not breathing."

Eva leaned closer. She poked Maddy's cheek with her finger. "Can't you help her Hope?"

"I'm trying."

"Esperanza," Baptiste said approaching. "You did it—you saved..." He stopped mid-sentence, his eyes fixed on Maddy's little, lifeless body resting in my arms. "Dios mio!"

"Is she dead?" Eva inquired apprehensively.

"I don't think so."

"She has no heartbeat."

"I know, but she didn't burst into flames either," I admitted.

"Flames?" Eva snorted.

"I've seen vampires die before. They burst into flames and disperse like ash."

"Where the hell did you ever see a vampire die?" Eva's voice was curt.

"Mexico."

"Mexico?" She slammed her hand on her hip and grimaced. "You never mentioned anything about finding vampires in Mexico."

"I guess we just—"

"What, forgot?"

"No..." At that moment Christian appeared. He was moving across the grass with Marco and Rosa in tow.

"Blondie," Eva barked. "This conversation isn't over. I want an answer."

"For crying out loud Eva!" My eyes glimmered. "Are you really this heartless? We've got a nearly-dead child on our hands to deal with. Can't we talk about Mexico later?"

"Fine," she shot back. "But we *will* talk about it." She kissed her teeth and drew her eyes toward the others. "Oh you're full of surprises today Hope." Her eyes narrowed as she stared.

"It's Rosa," Baptiste insisted.

Eva's eyes widened. "Rosa? As in *Beliarosa?*"

"Yeah," I said. "Why, you gotta problem with her too?"

Eva's expression furrowed. She scrutinized the old woman's wrinkly face. "Well I'll be damned," she uttered. "What happened to you Rosie?"

"Watch it Eva," she retorted. "I silenced you once and I can do it again."

"So this what sixty years does to a good witch?" She studied her face as though it were an artifact in a museum.

"Don't stare," Baptiste barked.

"God," Eva snarled. "Even science invented Botox. Couldn't you have whipped up a little something to help yourself?"

"Eva!" Baptiste scolded.

"What? She's old! Like a hag."

Rosa kissed her yellowed teeth before approaching the child in my arms. She reached out and ran her fingers along the sides of Maddy's face.

"You and Eva know each other?" I asked confused.

"Regrettably," Rosa replied.

"Don't make it sound so bad." Eva smirked. "We used to be quite a pair back in the day—like Lucy and Ethel...Ginger and Mary Ann." She paused to grimace. "But now we're more like beauty and the beast."

Baptiste nudged Eva in the arm.

"So Hope," Rosa whispered huskily. "I see you've returned."

"Yeah," I replied. "But look," I said laying Maddy on the ground. "She's not breathing."

"So this is the child you spoke of."

I nodded.

"Marco," Rosa ordered. "Come here." He hurried to his grandmother's side. "Take hold of the child's feet," she instructed. He slipped off Maddy's sneakers and held the soles of her feet in the palm of his hands. "What do you feel?" she asked.

Marco closed his eyes and concentrated. He tightened his grasp. "There's movement," he said. "She's changing." He opened his eyes again.

"Dying?" I interrupted.

"No," he grinned, "being reborn!"

At that moment Maddy's tiny toes started twitching. "My god! Did you just see that?"

Christian nodded.

"Resurrection," Marco said. He released his hands from Maddy's feet and stood up. "She's becoming human again."

"Impossible," Eva insisted.

"Not when you have a time shifter around," Marco retorted.

"You mean Hope?" Her voice was unimpressed.

"Hope," Baptiste interjected. "She changed the past for us—for you too Eva. She saved you and Christian...and this little girl too."

"Is it true?" Christian asked.

I nodded.

"I think I heard you call them residuals," Marco added.

"*Residuals*," Christian mumbled edgily.

"Don't get mad," I pleaded. "I was only trying to help."

He glared at me.

"Is this the ripple?" Henry asked leaning down to place his hands over Maddy's chest.

"Si," Rosa said. "This is the residual of Hope's actions manifesting before us. What she changed in the past, changes the future."

"God, Hope," Christian snarled.

"Its how I freed you from the spell."

"What spell?" he asked.

"The one that Reina put you under."

"And who's Reina?" he pressed. At that moment I felt Christian helping himself to my memories. He saw me in Reina's past, in Mexico with Lobo and in the ancient city of Tulum when I ripped out her heart. He also saw the way I got inside Reina's past too; how I drank her blood and let her seduce me.

"Be glad Hope did what she did," Baptiste interjected. He put his hand on Christian's shoulder. "She didn't want to do it. Believe me. But she did—because of you."

Christian rolled his eyes.

"Her heart!" Henry suddenly exclaimed. "The child's heart beats...a lot!"

I grinned elatedly. "Her eyes," I said. "They're opening!"

A huge gasp of air escaped her tiny body. She rose to a sitting position and coughed. I rushed toward her and held her tightly against me.

"Shit!" Eva gushed. "That kid is alive!" Her face brightened. "How the hell did you do that Rosie?"

"Not me," she replied. "It's Hope."

I turned to Rosa and smiled before looking back at Maddy again. I watched in awe as the insipid tones of her skin swelled with color. Her eyes flickered with iridescence before settling into a lovely deep brown shade and her lips reddened like the petals of a rose. Her cheeks flushed like tiny red apples and I knew for certain that she really was becoming human again.

35. Reunion

It was Maddy's birthday, or perhaps more aptly her re-birthday. She quivered like a leaf in my arms as blood began pumping through her tiny veins. Her cold limbs warmed with life and soon her entire body felt human to touch.

Nothing surprised me anymore. If I possessed the potential to change something as grand as history, then why couldn't it be possible for other supernatural beings to harness the powers of life and death?

As I watched Maddy's angelic face flush I started wondering what dark magic was in play to perfect something as serious as resurrection. This wasn't my first rebirth after all; I'd witness something very similar in the Mexican cemetery when those strange women reawakened a baby. This felt a little different though. For starters, Maddy was a vampire. She wasn't a dead human and this wasn't Dia de los Angelitos. It was an ordinary day. Moreover, I merely paid Rosa to warn me about Reina's spell. I didn't pay her for any resurrection so why was she bringing Maddy back to life at all?

"You happy now?" Rosa asked startling me.

"Yeah," I shrugged suddenly sensing a strange low humming sound in the distance. "My family is free from the spell and even the child has been reborn."

Rosa nodded. "Efecto," she uttered.

"Well thank you for what you did."

"Me?" She shook her head. "You killed this Reina before she became a vampire. *Efecto.*"

My face furrowed, the sound of the hum grew louder.

"By ending her life in the past, you made it so she never existed in her future."

"What about that potion you game me? Surely it—"

"Placebo," she uttered.

I froze. "What do you mean placebo?"

"It did nada. I gave it you like talisman. So you feel directed."

"Rosa!" I exclaimed.

"No matter? You did what you needed to do. You end a life that never got lived. *Efecto.*"

At that moment the humming sound neared. It rumbled as a low drone.

"What about residuals?" I asked.

"Of course there are residuals."

"Like what?"

"Like life," she replied, her old eyes wide as she spoke. "Don't you see child? They all live because she died."

"Rose," Henry interjected. "What did you do?"

She grinned reluctantly.

"Did you enchant the talisman?"

"I...um..."

"Oh Rose," Henry muttered. "How could you?"

"Wait a second," I interrupted. "The tap water spit wasn't a placebo?"

Rosa shrugged, the low drone was getting even louder. "The spit-water was only placebo. The vial...I may have enchanted with protection spell."

"What kind of spell exactly?" Henry pressed.

"Basic spell to protect life—even in face of death."

"Rosa," I said heatedly. "Are you saying that everything Reina did throughout her life was just suddenly annulled the very moment I ended her?"

Marco cleared his throat. "My grandmother's enchantment protected *all life* through Reina's bloodline. Those she turned and those she killed are human now."

Rosa nodded. "Where there was death, now there is life."

"My god," I uttered aghast. "You mean people are actually crawling out of their graves?"

"Some," Marco agreed. "Others are merely changing from vampire to human again."

My eyes widened when all of a sudden the immense humming sound boomed with a thunderous resonance.

Smash! Bang! Crash! The ground shook uncontrollably! I struggled to steady myself. "What's happening?" I shouted.

"*Life,*" Rosa replied. She grasped Marco arm and held on.

The sound subsided, the ground steadied itself and at that moment a feeling of grand transformation usurped us all like some supernatural tidal wave.

"Holy shit!" Eva shouted. "What the hell was that?"

"Residuals," Marco said.

"Awfully big residuals," I muttered, concerned.

Christian stared daggers at me.

"Esperanza," Baptiste interjected. "What did you do with the others?" His voice was low.

"What others?" I asked naively.

He motioned toward Maddy. "Her parents."

My jaw dropped. I'd nearly forgotten about Maddy's mother and father altogether.

"Could they be alive?" Baptiste asked.

"Si," Rosa said. "Where are they Hope?"

I shrugged.

Her old eyes narrowed. "Did you bury them?"

"Yes, they were buried, but *I* didn't do it."

"Who did?"

"Henry did." All eyes were on Henry. "Do you remember where?" I asked.

His face furrowed. He started unbuttoning his shirt.

My eyes widened. "What are you doing?"

"Proving that even science can pale in the face of magic." He dropped his shirt to the ground and grinned. A moment later he shifted into a black raven and flew away.

"Magnifico," Rosa gasped blushing girlishly.

"The torch still burns eh Rosie?" Eva snickered.

"Shut it," Baptiste snarled.

"I'm just saying her wrinkly face lit up like some kind of bonfire the moment she got a glimpse at Henry's chest."

"Enough," Baptiste insisted.

"Clearly the old broad still has a thing for Henry and now that Moira's outta the way—"

"Eva!" Baptiste barked. "How will you ever be a mother to our child if this is how you act?"

"Mother?" Rosa said perking up. "You're pregnant Eva?"

"So?"

"You don't look pregnant."

"Thank you," she replied flattered.

"How do you even know?" Rosa pressed suspiciously.

"Someone told me."

Rosa laughed.

"Is that funny?" Eva's voice was curt.

Rosa shook her head. "You're not pregnant. It's impossible."

"God Rosie, its birds and bees. It's not impossible." Eva was defensive.

"Birds and bees I get, but you are not birds and bees."

Eva glowered. "I *am* pregnant."

Rosa pressed her hand to Eva's stomach.

"Stop!" Eva snapped pushing her away. Rosa stumbled, withdrawing.

"Abuela!" Marco shouted. He hurried to assist his grandmother.

"I'm fine Marco."

"Well I'm not," Eva snapped. "How dare you touch me?"

"Oh Evelyn," Rosa sneered. "No act so foolish."

"Don't call me that! Nobody calls me that anymore."

She rolled her eyes and pressed her hand to Eva's flat stomach again. Eva reluctantly allowed her this time.

"Ah," Rosa smirked.

"What?" Eva asked edgily.

"Ah."

"You already said that Rosie. Now get your hands off of me old lady!"

"I feel it."

"Feel what?"

"Your baby Eva."

A wash of happiness abruptly rushed over her. She smiled brighter than the sun. I'd never seen Eva so happy before—it was infectious. I started smiling too.

"I can't take it anymore," Christian muttered storming off.

"Christian!" I called out. "Wait." But he didn't stop. "Rosa," I said. "Can you watch Maddy for me?"

"Si," she agreed. "Where are you going?"

I slid Maddy from my arms into Rosa's arms. "I'm going to get Christian," I said.

"And the child's parents?"

"I'll find them. I promise."

Rosa nodded.

"Hey," I added. "What about the promise you made to me...my friend, you know, the one in the—"

"Si," she said, "attend to the safety of the child's parents first."

I nodded, turned away and sped off into the woods after Christian.

"Hope!" he snarled sensing my approach. "You didn't have to come with me."

"Why'd you run off like that?"

He shrugged.

"Did something happen?"

"No. But listening to all that baby malarkey is a waste of my time."

"A waste?"

He rolled his eyes. "You didn't have to leave. You could have stayed and gushed with the other girls."

"I hardly think Marco and Baptiste count as girls."

"Marco does whatever his grandma tells him to do and B, well it's his baby so he has to gush."

"Why are you being so bitter?"

"Me?"

"Yeah."

"I'm not." He walked harder.

"Then what is it?"

"Nothing."

"Christian," I pressed. "What is it?"

"You want the truth?"

"Always."

"It's you. I told you not to go back anymore. I warned you—"

"Oh my god! You're mad at me over residuals? Again!"

He nodded.

"I saved your ass Christian."

"I know. I read your thoughts."

"Then you know I had no other choice."

He shook his head frustrated. "Doesn't it bother you knowing that all over the world right now Reina's bloodline is being resurrected?"

"Well...um..."

He stopped walking. I stopped too.

"How can you rationalize re-writing history like that?"

"*Re-writing history?* I hardly think—"

"You caused an epidemic Hope. You did this to save two or three people you love. There is no justification for what you've done." He shook his head. "I would have rather lived a lie than—"

"Christian," I scoffed. My heart beat in my chest and suddenly vomit rose once more in my throat. This time I couldn't stop it. I opened my mouth and released a stream of blood from my lips. I fell to the ground and I retched again.

"God Hope!" he soothed holding back my hair.

More blood spewed from my lips. "I'm sorry," I said wiping my mouth. "I didn't do any of this to upset you."

He heaved a sigh. "It's killing you."

"It's saving *them* Christian."

He held his face in his hands and shook his head.

"Sometimes you have to think of the greater good." I rose to my feet and put my hand on his arm. "Don't hate me," I pleaded.

He moved his hands from his face to stare at me. I smiled. He smiled back and pulled me into the circle of his arms. I melted against him.

"Oh Hope," he uttered. "What am I going to do with you?" His voice had eased to its usual, lovely tone.

I grinned. "You really think I caused an epidemic?"

"Yeah," he sighed nervously. "I really do. C'mon," he said tugging at my hand.

"Where are we going?"

"To help Henry find the girl's parents." He tightened his grasp and within the blink of an eye we were gone.

36. Memorial

We flew through the forest like the wind. I wanted to hold Christian forever. Reina's touch may have had the power to charm me, but Christian's touch had the power to enliven me. Love swelled in my very being. I closed my eyes and within an instant I sensed that we were already decelerating to a stop. I opened my eyes again. The place was beautiful. I didn't recognize it—and I thought I'd seen all of Perish.

"Where are we?" I asked.

"This is where Henry would have come."

"I don't know this place."

"That's because you've never been here before."

It was beautiful. Moss carpeted the ground with supple softness while insects flitted through the air in rhythmic waves. Songbirds hummed in harmony while tall trees loomed overhead like storybook giants.

Christian grinned. "We're very deep in the woods."

I extended my gaze. There was a small clearing up ahead. The sun showered its golden light through the sinewy branches. There was a set of jagged rocks jutting up from the ground in the distance.

"What's that over there?" I asked curiously.

"Let me show you." The softness of his long fingers interlocked with mine. "Come on," he whispered.

"Where are you taking me?"

"To visit your family."

"*My family?*"

"These are memorial grounds Hope."

My expression tightened. A jolt of uneasiness surged through my body. I wasn't upset; I simply didn't realize that we had memorial grounds on Perish.

"It's okay," he assured pulling me closer.

As we neared the stone slabs, my eyes focused in on the elegant scripted initials that had been intricately carved into each of them. I eyed the farthest stone first.

"W?" I asked.

"William," Christian replied. "We buried him here after he..."

"William," I sighed recalling the sweetness of his smile, the kindness in eyes and the valiant way he fought to protect me against the beast on the HMS Ambrose. My eyes welled with tears.

"Hey," Christian uttered. He swept my hair behind my ear. "You okay with all this?"

"Yeah," I nodded sniveling. I turned my attention toward the middle slab. "A?" I asked perplexed.

"Audrey."

"Audrey. It can't be."

"It is. This is where your mother is buried."

"But my mother was buried in the city. Richard put her in a big fancy cemetery. She's in the family plot with a huge headstone. We had a funeral and people were there and—"

"*His* people were there. Your mother belonged here in Perish with us—with her people. Even Richard knew that."

My brows knit together in the centre of my forehead. I was utterly confounded by yet another revelation.

"Hope. I'm sorry I didn't mention it—"

"Then who did we bury that day in the city cemetery?" I interrupted.

"I don't know," he shrugged. "Probably no one. I imagine it was an empty coffin." He moved in close. He held my chin in the palm of his hands. "Saving face was more important to Richard than having to explain the truth."

A flood of red tears streamed from my eyes.

"Don't cry." He wiped the crimson smear away with his fingers and grinned. "It's good news. Your mother is here, with you, with all of us."

I smiled, desperately trying to suck back fresh tears.

"Oh Hope." He wrapped his arms around me.

"I guess I wasn't expecting to learn anymore truths is all." I withdrew. "After you released me from the veil I just assumed there'd be no more secrets."

"Supernaturals are full of secrets." He brushed my hair out of my eyes and grinned. "Our entire existence relies on keeping one very big secret after all."

"Or at least it did," I teased, "until I started an epidemic!"

He smirked ruefully.

I smiled at him before turning toward the stones again. A carved letter M had been newly scribed into the rock face on the end slab.

"Moira," Christian said.

"This is my grandmother's grave?"

He nodded. "It was only fitting that we put her here—beside her daughter."

I started to smile when suddenly I heard a rustling in the bushes! I pivoted around and eyed the woods ahead.

"Hear that?" Christian asked silently.

"Yeah."

"It's coming from over there."

"We're not alone."

Christian nodded. *"Stay here. I'll go check it out."* He bolted through trees in a smudge of color. A split-second later he returned with Henry by his side.

"Henry!" I exclaimed. He was totally naked.

"Hope!" he shouted hiding his crotch with his hands. "I didn't mean to scare you. I just didn't realize that anyone else was out here."

I turned away instantly. I couldn't bear the thought of having a conversation with my hunky, naked grandfather even if he was blind and concealing his privates!

"Did you find the girl's parents?" Christian asked.

"I did."

"That's great," I said still turned away.

"Ahead, about a mile or so there's a small clearing. The earth is upturned from recent digging."

"Can you take us?" Christian asked.

"Of course. Can you loan me a shirt?"

"It's not going to help. What you need are pants."

"Great," Henry uttered bitterly. "Can I borrow yours?"

"No!"

There was a long silence and then suddenly I could hear Christian laughing.

"Hope," he said. "You can turn around now."

"I can? But what about the pants?"

"Henry's taken care of that."

Slowly, I turned around. I smiled, relieved. A pretty deer with big brown eyes was standing by Christian's side.

"Like I said," Christian uttered. "He took care of it."

I grinned just as the deer ran away.

"C'mon. He wants us to follow him." Christian reached for my hand and we sped off too.

We zoomed through the forest, my feet moving so quickly I could barely feel them beneath me.

"Over there," I insisted decelerating to a stop.

Henry was standing beside a large patch of roughed up ground. He bowed his slight face at us before speeding off deeper into the woods.

"The earth is fresh alright." Christian picked up some dirt. "Now what do we do?"

"We wait."

"Wait?"

"You got a better idea?"

"We could dig them out?"

"Eww! No thanks." I picked up a handful of dirt for myself. "The soil is fresh, but it hasn't been moved."

"What does that mean?"

"It means they haven't come up yet."

"*Haven't come up yet?*" Christian laughed. "They're not seedlings Hope. They're people."

I tightened my grip on the dirt in my hand before tossing it at him.

"You didn't!" he shouted grabbing me by the waist and thrusting me against him.

I laughed excitedly and fought to escape his clutches.

"Ever considered that maybe they're not coming back?"

"Of course they're coming back."

He set me down on the ground and released me. "You know, Rosa really isn't as powerful a witch as she pretends to be."

"Why do you hate her so much?"

"I don't hate her."

"You don't like her."

He laughed.

"Tell me."

"There's not much to tell."

I moved close to him again and ran my hands up his chest. "Try me," I pleaded.

He smirked. "For a while Rosa was a regular fixture at Ambrose House."

"She and Eva were close, right?"

"Inseparable."

"Really? I can't imagine them together."

"They were the best of friends. They got into all kinds of trouble together."

"Like what?"

He shrugged. "In the old days people were much more gullible. It was a lot easier to play games and pull pranks."

"Why?" I asked with interest.

"No internet! People weren't as savvy and skeptical as they are today."

I laughed.

"They were quite a tag team. Eva would morph and Rosa would do her magic," he laughed. "But then..."

"What? What happened to them?"

"Love happened, a love triangle to be precise."

"Rosa had a thing for Baptiste?"

"No! Not Baptiste. It was Henry."

"Henry?" I said surprised. *"My grandfather?"*

"He never cheated on Moira," Christian assured. "He loved your grandmother with all his heart."

"Well apparently not *all* his heart."

"You know, they say it *is* possible to love more than one person at a time."

I grimaced.

"I'm not saying I could do it," he quickly defended. "But apparently it is possible."

"And that's why you don't like Rosa? Because she fell in love with Henry?"

He shrugged. "Not completely."

"What else?"

"She's stubborn! Damn stubborn. And before you came along I had no reason to endure eternity."

"I don't understand?"

He combed his long fingers through his dark hair. "I wanted her to do a spell for me and she refused."

"That's it? That's why you hate her?"

He ran his hand up my back.

"She wouldn't do the spell." He moved his lips to my earlobe and kissed it. I sighed, easily succumbing to the feeling of his lips against me.

"Maybe you didn't pay her enough," I teased. "That woman doesn't work for free. I would know!"

Christian grinned. He moved his mouth to my neck. "It wasn't about money," he uttered, his breath tickling my skin as he spoke.

"What kind of spell was it?" I asked breathlessly.

"A death spell.

"Death spell!" My eyes widened.

"Rosa won't do black magic. Shh," he purred easing me down to the ground.

"Christian," I whispered elatedly. I moved my hands to his shoulders and surrendered to him. I moaned feeling the gentle pressure of his body falling against me.

He laughed and brushed his lips along my cheek. He inhaled. "You smell different."

"Like blood-vomit probably."

"No. Not bad different. You smell like you only much stronger—like more of you. I like it." He inhaled again. "In fact, I love it."

I pulled him on top of me and pressed my mouth to his in a kiss. He moaned. I slipped my tongue between his lips and smiled inside. His sweet tin-cinnamon savor excited me instantly. *"I want you,"* I uttered soundlessly.

"Here?"

I moaned in his mouth.

"What's with you and cemeteries?"

I laughed out loud.

"C'mere," he uttered pulling me back.

I smiled and moved my lips to his again. A moment later I felt his long fingers running up the sides of my body. He kissed me deeper and pressed himself even harder against me. I slid my hands to my sides and let them relax on the ground. I was weak beneath him—powerless, vulnerable and loving it.

I felt his hand within reach. I stretched out and grabbed it. I laced my fingers with his and tightened my hold when suddenly he tightened his too. *"Oh Christian,"* I sighed without a sound. A moment later I felt the divine heaven of his fingers gently stroking my skin—*all ten of his fingers*. My eyes flew open. I withdrew instantly.

"What?" he asked concerned.

"Your hands! Show me your hands!"

He moved to a sitting position and held up his hands.

"Oh my god!"

"What Hope?"

I shook my head and unwillingly peering toward my hand—toward my fingers laced in a tight embrace with the dirtied human hand that had suddenly sprouted up from the ground beside me!

37. Shallow Grave

"Let go!" Christian hollered.

"I can't!" I replied. I sprung to my feet.

"Pull it off!"

"I told you I can't."

"Here," he said moving close. "Let me help." He wrapped his hand around mine and yanked hard. The force of his pull was good and within an instant we had extracted the top of a human head from the ground.

"It's happening Christian!"

"Yeah," he insisted, keep pulling."

And with our hands together we continued extracting the corpse.

"The head is crowning the dirt!" I shouted.

"Pull!"

The shoulders and torso emerged next and before long we had drawn the entire body of a dark-haired man from the ground.

"Is he breathing?" Christian asked.

"I don't know." I pressed my ear to the man's chest. "I don't hear a heartbeat." I started pulling away, his grasp on my hand tightened again. "No!" I shouted. "He won't let go of me."

One by one Christian pried the man's dirtied fingers off of me. "There," he said. "You're free."

"Christian," I uttered. "He's turning blue! What's wrong with him?"

"He's suffocating. Help me move him."

We propped him up to a sitting position. Christian slapped him on the back. The man started choking instantly.

"Look at his face." I said. "It's filling with color."

"Where's his wife?"

"Look!" I said noticing the collection of fingertips budding from the earth.

"Let's get her out."

I nodded and rushed toward her. Christian arduously dug around her fingers until her wrist became visible. He grabbed hold and pulled, striving fearlessly to extract her from the ground. I wrapped my hand around his and pulled too. A moment later we slid her from her grave.

"She's turning blue now," I uttered.

"Help me put her beside the husband." Christian's voice was direct.

I nodded and grabbed the woman's ankles. We carried her to the clearing next to her husband.

"Put her here," Christian said. "Let's prop her up."

I nodded in reply and helped set her down. "She's really blue Christian."

He nodded before slapping her in the back too. She opened her eyes and exhaled instantly. Dirt speckled the air like a blast of coal colored snowflakes. Her breathing resumed instantaneously.

"Oh my god," I uttered stunned.

Christian's eyes narrowed. "I don't think God has anything to do with this."

I turned to him and grimaced.

"Don't give me that look," he retorted. "This is the reality of your actions Hope." He shook his head in disgust.

All of a sudden there was a loud rustling in the bushes.

"Shh," Christian whispered. He rose to his feet and skulked into the trees. A moment later a deer suddenly burst through the greenery.

"Henry!" Christian howled horrified.

His brown fur was slathered in blood.

"No!" I shouted watching as he shifted back into his human form. He collapsed to the ground; deep red blood oozed the length of his naked body.

"Henry!" Christian panicked rushing to his side.

"Is he breathing?" I asked concerned. "Is his heart beating?"

Christian pressed his head to Henry's chest and nodded. "Henry," he said. "What happened?"

"I went back to the house," Henry said wearily. "No one was there."

"Not even Maddy?" I pried.

"No. None of them."

"Why are you covered in blood?" Christian asked.

"I was in a fight."

"A fight?" I said confused.

Christian ran his fingers along Henry's skin and collected a thick smearing of blood. He brought the smearing to his nose and then tasted it. "It's not human," he uttered, concerned.

"No. It's not," Henry replied fearfully. "It's vampire, but not like any we've ever met before."

"There was a vampire in our house again?" Christian's voice was irate.

Henry nodded. "It was more of a monster than a man."

"Without an invitation?" I asked.

Henry shrugged.

"Who?" Christian barked. "Who the hell was in our house?"

"Who else," Henry snapped. "The beast. *Your* beast Christian!"

Silence resonated. My mind swelled with visions of the last time I laid eyes upon the beast. It was aboard the HMS Ambrose.

"Shit," I uttered under my breath. "Did I do this too?" My voice was panicked.

"More than likely," Christian snarled.

I sank my face in my hands and hid in my palms. Karma was finally catching up to me.

"Damn it!" Christian shouted kicking a boulder. The boulder shattered with the force of his hit. "I've waited over two centuries for that thing to return and it hasn't. Why would it come now?"

"I don't know," Henry expressed. "But I'm certain it was him. He's exactly like you described. The scar, the long locks of hair...I just can't figure how he got in our house without an invitation?"

"He wouldn't need one," Christian said. "The house is still somewhat the ship and as we well know he's already been aboard the ship."

"Where are the others?" I asked sheepishly. "Eva, B and Maddy?"

"Probably eaten by now," Christian scoffed crudely.

A chill ran down my spine. If it was a residual that brought the beast here, then all of this was my fault. I had to do something to fix it and fast. "Do you really think he found the others?"

"No," he replied. "When I reached the house the smell of fear was still very redolent."

"You can smell fear?" I asked, intrigued.

"Of course I can smell fear. I shift into animals."

"How do you know he doesn't have them?" Christian pressed.

"The little girl," Henry said. "She was frightened by the beast and the residue of her fear lingered long after they left the house." He shook his head. "He didn't have them then."

"But he could have them now," I uttered. "We have to find them."

"We have to stop the beast," Christian maintained.

I looked ahead, toward Maddy's parents watching as they writhed somewhat agonizingly against the trees. It was though they were discovering themselves for the first time; the tightening of their muscles, the stretching of their skin and the unfamiliar sound of their own voices.

"What about them?" I uttered. "We can just leave them out here."

"I'll stay here with them," Henry suggested. "It sounds as though they're starting to regain consciousness."

"Good," I insisted. "But..."

"What Hope?" His voice was anxious.

"A blind, naked vampire in the middle of the woods?" I shrugged. "You're protecting them not trying to scare the crap out of them."

"Fine," Henry said and then he morphed into his animal form again.

"Better," I uttered eying the fearless deer as he stood vigilantly at the foot of the resurrected humans. All of a sudden Christian took off without me. "Hey!" I hollered rushing after him. "Wait up!"

"God, Hope," he snapped crossly.

"I know you're mad about the residuals."

"Mad?" he snorted. "I'm..."

"I'm sorry."

"I don't care."

I grabbed his arm. "You do care Christian. And I'm sorry for everything I've done."

He shook his head at me and quickened his pace.

"I'll fix this."

"I've heard that before."

"Well this time it's true. You'll help me."

He ran his fingers through his hair and sighed.

"Where are you going?" I asked.

"To get the others. I know where they went."

"You do?"

"Rosa."

"Why would they go to her?"

"Protection."

My eyes widened. "Protection from the beast?"

He shrugged.

"How can you be sure they'll be there?"

"I can't." He halted his stride.

"What's the matter?" I asked stopping.

"Everything Hope. *Everything.*" His voice was hard. He grabbed my arm. "I know you mean well, but the residuals—"

"Enough already! How many times are you going to chastise me for these friggin' residuals? I know I messed up. And the torture of seeing the effects of my actions is killing me." Scarlet tears abruptly welled in my eyes. "But seeing those humans come back to life...out of the ground like that...you've got to admit Christian, it was incredible, practically a miracle!"

"That's no miracle," he uttered running his fingers through his dark hair as usual. "Bravado perhaps, but definitely no miracle."

"Is this about Rosa again?"

"Well the old witch sure knows how to grandstand."

"Christian!"

"The only miracle worthy of discussing is the fact that you managed to kill Reina without getting killed yourself!"

"I did it for you."

"Well it was dangerous."

"Danger doesn't exist if it means protecting you Christian— protecting us."

He smirked. I wasn't expecting him to smirk.

"You're smirking," I said excitedly.

"I'm not."

"You are! Why are you smirking?"

He shrugged. "I guess we're more alike than I realized."

"How so?"

"Danger doesn't exist to me either if it means protecting you."

I pulled him against me and grinned.

"Oh Hope," he sighed. "You're going to give me a heart attack. The things you do. You're fearless." He wrapped his arms around me.

"I hate when you're mad at me."

"I hate being mad at you." He kissed me on the forehead.

I looked up into his eyes. "Why don't you believe in magic Christian?" My voice was soft.

"I do—dark magic even. I don't, however, believe in having the power to heal and refusing to use it."

"This is about Rosa again."

He smirked.

"Let it go Christian. Rise above it. Free yourself from what happened in the past."

"*Free myself from what happened in the past?*" He laughed scornfully. "You're one to talk about the past."

"What's that supposed to mean?" I withdrew.

"Hope, you somehow managed to summon the beast that made me a vampire. And now he's here...in Perish again."

"Residuals again!" I seethed. "I thought you—"

"I'm sorry," he abruptly interrupted. "I'm just a little on edge... knowing that he's here."

"We're gonna get him Christian, one way or another."

"I know."

"But we need all the help we can get, and that means Rosa too."

He nodded reluctantly.

"If the others are with her, under her protection—"

"Fine," he interrupted. "Let's just do this and get it over with."

I grinned. "Now that's more like it."

He smiled at me. I pulled him close again and pressed my lips to his in a kiss. He felt good to touch—practically warm against my mouth.

38. Black Truths

A brisk wind pressed my back as we hustled down the dirt road. The sky was grayer than stone and angry. I could feel the presence of rain in the air. The clouds were heavy and hung like water balloons awaiting an imminent rupture. I felt sick inside. Nausea overwhelmed me again. I stopped dead in my tracks.

"Hope?" Christian uttered. "You okay?"

I shook my head and felt it again—the rock in my belly jabbing me from the inside out.

He put his hand on my back. "You don't look so good."

"I don't feel so good." Just then a rush of blood sprayed from my mouth. With the force of a watering hose the crimson liquid showered the dirt. I doubled over and collapsed on ground.

"You need help."

"I..." but when I opened my mouth to reply blood emerged instead of words.

"Hope," he muttered anxiously. "It's killing you! You need help—help I can't give you." He swept me up in his arms and carried me away with him.

Christian's arms—there was nowhere else in the world I'd rather be. The firmness of his grasp and the sweet smell of his skin made me grin. I was safe in his arms—I'd always been ever since I was a child. Tears welled in my eyes. Crimson droplets seeped through my lashes. I closed them shut. Consciousness was becoming an effort. I surrendered to sleep instead.

My thoughts drifted to another place—another time perhaps. I pictured a city. No city like I'd ever know, but still a city nonetheless. It was gray and tall, familiar and yet utterly foreign as well. Eradan was there. Ever since meeting him his face had been etched into my brain. He was like no one I'd ever met. I could hear his voice too; ranting about the catacombs and the Emerald City. But he was different—more mature, confident and as I looked upon him I realized that he was standing before a legion of glimmer-eyed vampires! A flash of white overwhelmed me. The vision was gone. My stomach throbbed. I felt myself caving with the pain when suddenly the overwhelming smell of apples tweaked my senses. I perked up immediately. The aroma was familiar and strangely desirable. I opened my eyes.

"Thank god!" Christian said. "I thought I'd lost you."

Crusted beads of blood were caked to my lashes. I blinked a few time and cleared my vision. I looked around. I noticed the sparsely decorated walls and religious relics. I was in Rosa's house once again. I recognized it instantly. Christian was standing over me grasping a steaming cup of tea in his hand.

"Apples," I sighed smiling. I pulled myself up against the wooden headboard of the bed and tore the cup from his hand. I downed the drink.

"Thirsty?" he asked.

"Hair of the dog," I uttered swallowing. "It's Marco's concoction. Works every time."

"You've had this before?"

I smiled and finished the last sip.

Christian's expression changed. "You had no heartbeat Hope. I thought you'd—"

"Burst into flames? Not today."

He grinned solemnly. I licked my lips tasting the last of the sweet apple on my mouth when I notice someone hiding in the doorway.

"She made a full recovery," he said stepping aside.

"Maddy," I smiled. She was beautiful, her wild auburn curls sparkling in the dim light of the room. Her face was cherub-like, flush and full of life. The pitter patter of her tiny pulse echoed through my eardrums and I could smell the succulent scent of blood in her veins. "She's human," I uttered pleased.

"She's practically a miracle," he replied sensitively. His voice was soft. He sat on the edge of the bed beside me.

"Did you find B and Eva?"

"Yeah.

"This is Rosa's house isn't it?"

He nodded. "When you collapsed I didn't know what to do. You lost a lot of blood. I didn't know..."

I touched his hand. "You did the right thing." I leaned in to kiss him when suddenly Rosa waddled through the bedroom door.

"You," she said to Christian. "Leave!"

He shot her an unpleasant glare.

"Now!" she ordered. "Hope need rest. Go!"

I grinned and handed him the empty teacup.

"I'll be in the kitchen with B," he whispered kissing the top of my head. "If you need me..."

"She won't," Rosa snapped.

Christian grinned, took Maddy by the hand and left the room with her.

Rosa edged her way toward the bed. "You're feeling better now?"

"Yes. Thank you for helping me."

"I didn't. What you do, you do to yourself." She sat down beside me on the edge of the bed and extracted a strange brown leaf from her pocket. She placed it in the palm of my hand.

"What's this?" I said uneasily.

"Shh," she whispered closing my fist over the leaf. She put her hand on my stomach and took in a deep breath.

"What are you doing?"

"Ah," she said.

"Rosa," I shouted pushing her hand away.

She cackled. "Just like him—strong and stubborn." She smiled. "You so naive."

"What?" I said withdrawing.

"Have the will to love," she shook her head, "only too damn selfish to see it make the power to live!"

I unclenched my fist and dropped the leaf to the ground. "Thanks for doing whatever you did or didn't do. But I've got to go." I moved from beneath the serape.

"We ain't done yet." Her voice was hard. She grabbed my hand and turned my palm over. My skin was tinged with the brown coloring from the leaf.

"Your wooden friend," Rosa uttered dragging her sharp nail across my palm. "Now we free her."

"Thank you. I'm glad you finally decided—"

"I do this," she interrupted, "then you do something for me."

"What?"

"Choice," she said eyeing my palm. "When time comes, you must make choice." She showed me my hand. "Here," she stroked her fingernail across the strange veined leaf stain. "See this fork. Two paths."

I nodded.

"One way lead to light, other to dark." She looked up at me. "When time comes, you must make choice."

My eyes widened and before I could say anything Eva burst through the bedroom door. Rosa freed my hand instantly.

"What are you two doing in here?" Eva's voice was sharp. "I thought we had a beast to fight."

"We do," I uttered.

"I go now," Rosa said getting up. She waddled toward the door.

"Rosa!" I called out.

She turned around.

"What choice?"

She nodded. "When time comes child, you will know." She grinned ominously and left the room.

Eva laughed. "That sounded awfully delicious!" She sat on the bed beside me.

"Just wish I knew what the hell she was talking about."

"Yeah, Rosie's always reminded me of that Yoda guy." She grimaced. "Now she even looks a bit like him too."

"Eva!" I said swatting her in the arm.

"What?"

"What do you want anyway?"

Her smile leveled. "I want you to be honest with me."

"About what?"

"About what is going on with you?"

"Me? Nothing."

She batted her thick bush of eyelashes.

"Don't look at me like that."

"Blondie, you can't lie to a liar. You've been puking blood. Christian told me you've been doing it a lot lately."

"He told you that?" I said mortified.

She nodded. "How've you been feeling?"

"Fine. But I had this weird talk with Rosa and also I had this weird dream—"

"Whatever," she interrupted. "I'm not trying to be your friend here—I just want to know what your symptoms are."

"*Symptoms?* I don't have any symptoms?"

Eva smirked.

"I hate it when you smile. Did Christian put you up to this? Is he trying to get you to lecture me about residuals?"

"Residuals!" she laughed. "I could care less about residuals."

"Then why are you talking to me about symptoms?"

"I know what's wrong with you," she whispered.

"There is nothing wrong with me Eva."

"Nothing other than the fact that you've got a demon bun in the oven like I do!"

"Eva!"

"You're pregnant you idiot."

"No...I can't be."

She grinned. "I always knew you were a skanky little slut!"

"Eva!"

"Nothing to be ashamed of."

"I'm not ashamed. I mean I'm not pregnant!" I swallowed hard, the strange rock in my gut suddenly significant.

"Look," she said calmly. "Remember when I told you how I felt really sick in the beginning like I was hung over only worse?"

I nodded.

"Well that was this."

"But you didn't say anything about puking up blood."

"Well you didn't ask!" She smiled devilishly.

I growled.

"I know y'all sealed the deal in Mexico. I smelled it on you right away. A bit of him coursing through—"

"Eva!"

"It only takes one good shot. And Christian seems like a straight shooter to me."

"Oh my god," I uttered mortified.

"And those brujos in there, they know it too. We're like science projects to them. Give Rosie or that eager-beaver grandson of hers a scalpel and they'd dissect us in a minute!"

Science...dissection...scalpel...I trembled a little when all of a sudden my stomach flip flopped inside of me. I sat up and retched. Blood rushed from my lips coloring the floor with a crimson coating.

"Blondie!" Eva barked. "Get a grip!"

I wiped my lips and glowered. "It's not like I can control it."

"Well you better learn!" She rose to her feet and moved toward the door. "I'm outta here. I don't do BFF very well. I'll send in Christian to deal with your...mess."

"Hey," I said springing up to a sitting position. "Don't tell him about the...*baby*. Okay?"

"Fine." She half-smiled. "But you won't be able to keep it a secret forever."

"I know," I said collapsing back to the bed again. I looked up to the ceiling. *Pregnant?* I moved my hand to my stomach and touched my skin. I started to imagine a love born out of death, so strong that even the bonds of mortality couldn't withhold its vigor and suddenly I felt the rock again. It was small and hard and hiding deep within the walls of my abdomen. My eyes welled with tears. Crimson droplets stained the sheets.

39. Woods

"Hope!" Christian shouted bursting into the bedroom.

I sat up instantly.

"Eva said you'd been sick again."

"It's nothing."

"It's not nothing. I wish you'd stop saying that." He wrapped his arm around my shoulders noticing the fresh stream of tears running down my face. He wiped them away. "Are you getting worse?"

"I'm fine." I leaned my head against his shoulder and nestled my nose to his shirt. Even without purposefully inhaling I could smell his sweet tin-cinnamon scent seeping through his pores.

"Maybe we should leave," he muttered.

"Leave Rosa's?"

"Leave Perish."

"But Perish is our home."

He ran his fingers through his hair which seemed to help him think. "It's dangerous here. Even if we kill him, the beast—and I know we will, it'll never stop. None of it Hope. It will literally never stop."

"Don't say that!"

"There will always be another beast or Reina or Maxim—"

"Christian!" I snapped. "What the hell?"

"What?"

"Where's the fight in you? I thought you've been waiting decades to get revenge on this guy."

He shook his head. "I guess I don't really care about revenge anymore."

"You don't?" I was appalled.

"No." He shook his head. "There's only one thing that matters to me."

"What?"

"You."

My heart sank in my chest.

"Oh Hope," he sighed. "I just want to live a life with you that doesn't involve some kind of bloodshed every minute."

"But bloodshed is who we are."

His expression stiffened. "It shouldn't be."

"Would you rather we live like suckers and just let every wayward vampire that passes through Perish walk right over us?"

"Of course not." He shook his head. "Oh I don't know," he lamented. "This isn't the life I imagined for us."

"Me neither, but things change."

He smirked. "You have no idea." There was a curious poignancy in his voice. He sighed deeply. "I suppose I never thought that he'd really return, you know?"

I kissed his shoulder. "Finish it Christian."

"Yeah but—"

"Finish it." I ran my hand up his arm. "You're not alone in this. I'll be there. We'll all be there. And I think I might even know someone else who can help too. C'mon," I said pulling him off the bed toward the door.

"Where are we going?"

"Ambrose."

"The ship?"

"Not the ship this time—the house."

"Are you sure you're strong enough to fight...I mean with how sick you've been."

I grinned. "I feel better than ever—as though I have the strength of two people within me!"

He smiled, perplexed.

"We'll need Rosa," I said. "I think I might have a way of getting her to finally use her powers to heal."

Christian's eyes widened. "Really?"

"Really."

"This way," he said leading me through the narrow labyrinth of wooden corridors.

We walked for what felt like forever when finally we reached the kitchen. Rosa was sitting at the table in the center of the room. She was hunched over. Her eyes were closed and her breathing was raspy. Baptiste, Eva and Maddy were standing beside her.

"What happened?" I asked.

"She was in some kind of a trance or something," Eva explained.

"A trance?"

She nodded. "Her eyes went all foggy and she wasn't making any sense. She started talking about the woods and people, human people, and some kind of an attack. She went on about a deer getting in the way."

Christian and I exchanged a glance.

"What?" Eva snapped.

"Henry," I replied. "The beast must have found him...in the woods with the humans."

"Henry was out there?" she exclaimed, "with the humans?"

I nodded. "He waited with them after they resurrected." I shook my head. "The beast must have found them."

"So what we waiting for?" Baptiste slammed his fists together.

I grinned when suddenly Marco stormed into the kitchen.

"Abuela!" he shouted rushing toward Rosa.

"She had a vision," I volunteered. "She was in a trance and then she just passed out."

Marco leaned next to Rosa's face and listened to her breathing.

"Is she alright?" I asked.

"Yes," Marco replied. "She's just sleeping now." He was audibly relieved. "I was driving in my car when I felt her weaken. I rushed home immediately."

"You can *feel* her?" I asked intrigued.

"Yes. She is my grandmother. We are witches Hope. We can feel each other's energy." He wrapped his arms around her robust frame and struggled to lift her.

"Let me help you," Baptiste insisted.

The two strong men started lifting Rosa when unexpectedly her eyes flew open. She screamed! They sat her back down on the kitchen chair almost dropping her.

"Abuela!" Marco shouted. "Calm down!"

"Calm down?" she exclaimed. "What were you doing to me?"

"Taking you to your bed," Marco replied. "You were sleeping."

"I wasn't sleeping! I had a vision." She grabbed Baptiste's arm. "Henry, he is hurt—or will be hurt. Find him!"

"Rosa," I exclaimed. "What do you mean *will be* hurt? Are you saying those things you saw in your vision might not have happened yet?"

"Si. That is exactly it. Now go! Find the humans too. Bring them. We can protect them here."

"But Rosa," I insisted, "you promised you'd come to Ambrose—"

"Bring the humans here then I go to Ambrose House."

"We don't have time for all of this. The beast is out there. I need you to do it now!"

"Not until child's parents are safe."

"Damn it Rosa! You really are stubborn," I growled.

She glared at me.

"Fine," I said resolved. "Then you're coming with us." I reached for her arm.

"No!" Marco snapped. "She's an old woman Hope and you are headed for danger."

"Marco!" Rosa barked, offended. "I'm old—not dead!"

"Rosa's vision can easily lead us to the humans," I insisted. "Once they're safe we'll all go back to Ambrose House together." I shifted my eyes to Rosa. "And then you can fulfill your promise to me right?"

"Fine," Rosa agreed rising to her feet.

"Abuela!" Marco shouted. "You cannot go!"

"Marco!" she snapped.

"Abuela, they are young, they are vampires. How do you expect to keep up with them?"

"I be fine," she retorted.

"Abuela!" Marco insisted. "I forbid you—"

Rosa grabbed a cocoon from the shelf beside her, crushed it and flicked it at Marco's face. He stopped speaking immediately. His mouth continued moving, but no noise resounded.

"Good old silence spells Rosie." Eva laughed. "I always hated it when you used them on me."

Rosa grinned. "Let's go."

I nodded.

Rosa waved her hand at Marco's face before leaving and suddenly he could speak again. "Take the child," she instructed. "Guard her until we return."

"Abuela," Marco pleaded. "Please."

"I be fine," she maintained. "And if not, you will feel it. You can come to my rescue." Rosa smirked at him. She sauntered into the hallway and led us toward the front door.

When we got to woods nightfall was quickly approaching. Day was done and darkness was on the brink of prevailing. I liked the night and despite my sudden tolerance to withstand sunlight I was still much stronger in its absence.

"Here," Christian said. "This is where Hope and I left Henry and the humans."

I scanned the clearing. The humans were gone and so was the deer. Only freshly churned dirt remained.

"Hum," Rosa uttered looking around. "They're not far. I saw this clearing in my vision." She moved toward a patch of foliage. "Look." She pointed to a spray of blood on a leaf.

"Was this in your vision too?" I asked concerned. "Does this mean that the attack already happened?"

Rosa shook her head. "Shh." She held a finger to her lips.

The rank scent of death suffused the air and I knew instantly that it was him—the beast! My body kicked into gear. My gums throbbed. My sharp canines shot up into place and my eyes glimmered. I looked over at Baptiste. His eyes were glimmering too. His huge muscles looked as though they were about to burst. Eva stood to his left. She was like a ghost; stealthy and agile. Her eyes radiated as she skulked between the trees. I turned to Christian. He seemed prepared to attack, but there was a strange meekness in his demeanor. I couldn't see his fangs and there was no glimmer in his eyes either. "Christian," I uttered when suddenly the beast leapt through the trees!

"It's him!" Eva shrieked.

Rosa struggled to run, but the beast was upon her in seconds. He swatted her across the face. She bled instantly and dropped to the ground.

"Rosa!" I hollered. I rushed toward her at supersonic speed just as the beast spotted me. We locked eyes; the burning intensity of his stare startled me. I remembered the last time I'd laid eyes upon him. It was aboard the HMS Ambrose. I remembered when he scratched my arm and how desperately he wanted to kill me and had it not been for William, he might have succeeded.

"Hope!" Christian shouted. "Your arm...its glowing!"

I broke eye contact with the beast to look down at my arm. "My god!" I said taken aback. A strange ginger blaze emanated from the scar on my arm. "What the hell?"

"Blondie!" Eva ordered. "He's still watching you."

I looked up again. The beast howled. He flashed his sharp teeth at me before retreating back into the woods. I looked down at my arm. The glowing subsided.

"Your arm," Christian said, "why did it do that?"

"I don't know."

"Where did you get that scar?"

"I...I got it from him," I divulged reluctantly.

"From him?"

I nodded. "On the Ambrose."

Christian's face hardened.

"You are connected to him Hope," Rosa said rising from the ground.

"Rosa," I said leaning in to help her. "What do you mean connected?"

"You and that monster are connected."

"Not me," I said. "It's Christian who is connected to him. That thing is his maker—the one that changed him into a vampire."

"Si, Christian may have history, but you he's connected with." She wiped the blood from her face. I inhaled cautiously. Rosa smelled delicious—different than a human; marvelously mouthwatering.

"Easy there," Christian said inside my thoughts.

"He's led the humans there," Rosa said motioning toward the thicket. "Try to help them before it's too late."

I broadened my gaze. "The memorial grounds are in that direction."

Christian nodded in reply.

"Esperanza," Rosa uttered. "No question the connection you share—use it instead. Use it to find him!"

My face furrowed. "How?"

"When scar smolders he close."

"If you say so," I uttered doubtfully. "Will you be all right out here?"

"Si. I know this woods like the back of my hand."

"Let me help you heal." I moved my teeth to my wrist and began to bite.

"No!" she said recoiling. "Not necessary. Now go!"

"Suit yourself."

"Get the humans."

"And then we'll go to Ambrose House right?"

"Si," she nodded.

Christian and I turned to leave. We started walking. I stroked the scar on my arm and sighed.

"Don't believe Rosa's bullshit," he said.

"I...um...I don't."

"So your scar glows. It's a residual Hope. Not a connection."

"Yeah," I said. "You're probably right."

At that moment the delectable aroma of fresh human blood abruptly flooded my senses.

"Stop," Christian said. He tugged at my shirt and we hid behind some palm fronds together. He inhaled. I watched his muscular chest inflate as he breathed. "Smell that?" he asked. "Fresh human blood."

I nodded and looked around. "I don't see them anywhere."

Christian closed his eyes and breathed in again. "Over there," he said motioning toward the graves.

I perked up and looked ahead.

Christian opened his eyes. "I think he's left them intentionally... for us to find."

"You mean like bait?"

He nodded. "I think he's injured them to weaken us."

"God," I sighed. "What do we do?"

"Outsmart him."

"But those human's will bleed to death if we don't rescue them Christian."

All of a sudden Baptiste pushed through the brush. He was carrying a badly injured deer in his arms.

"No!" I exclaimed rushing toward them.

"B," Christian shouted. "What happened?"

"I found him about a mile or so in that direction." Baptiste laid Henry on the ground.

Christian stroked the animal's fur. "Henry," he said. "Can you hear me?" He pressed his ear to his chest. "He's got a heartbeat. It's faint, but it's still there."

"But he's not healing," I panicked. I ran my hand over a patch of fur and exposed the animal's skin. I watched as the bloody gash struggled to mend itself.

"He's weaker when he's not in his human form," Christian said. "If only I could get him to shift back into a human..."

"We've got to do something," I insisted. "Can we give him our blood?"

"It's not a high he's after Esperanza," Baptiste retorted.

"What about Rosa? Maybe her blood will—"

"No," Christian snapped. "The blood of brujos is dangerous business. The only thing that will help him right now is human blood."

"Human blood?" Baptiste grinned sniffing into the air.

"No!" I barked. "Those are Maddy's parents! We can't."

Christian licked his lips. "Even if it means saving Henry—your very own grandfather?"

"We are not drinking from Maddy's parents, and that's final." My voice was hard. I bit my lip, my mind racing with thoughts. "B," I said. "Do you think you can carry Henry a little further?"

"Yeah."

"Why Hope?" Christian asked. "What have you got in mind?"

"Henry needs blood and we need help." I grinned. "I've got an idea."

40. Cursed

We fled the woods in a hurry. Baptiste carried Henry in his arms, while Christian and I followed behind. It was a long haul back to Ambrose House—even at supersonic, vampire speed. The trees were like an endless smudge of green and the night was alive as we traveled. Crickets chirped and cicadas hissed. Their strange macabre melody filled the air with anticipation.

I stopped instantly. Christian stopped too. The blur of the forest sharpened in a flash. I felt the world falling into place all around us.

"I'm not sure about this," Christian muttered. He grabbed my hand. "He could be waiting for us at the house. It could be a trap."

"It could be."

"He's dangerous Hope."

"I know."

"Do you?"

"He doesn't scare me."

"Well he should."

I looked into Christian's eyes. They were pensive and surprisingly vulnerable. "Does he scare you?" I pried puzzled.

"Don't' be ridiculous!"

I tried helping myself to his thoughts, but they were closed off—tighter than ever.

"Don't try mind-reading me," he warned.

"Then tell me what's scaring you"

275

"It's you. You're the one who is scaring me."

"Me?"

"The thought of losing you to him..." he groaned. "I saw the way he stared at you back there."

"I can handle him Christian. I did it once before."

He ran his fingers through his hair.

"Don't overreact," I insisted.

"You think I'm overreacting? He's after you Hope. I saw it in his eyes. And then Rosa goes and tells us that you're somehow connected to him!"

"I thought you didn't trust Rosa."

"I don't, but how do you explain that scar of yours lighting up when he's near?" He shook his head at me.

"Hey!" Eva shouted as she approached. "You two are incredibly fast."

Christian shook his head at me before marching off.

"What's with him?" Eva asked.

"I don't know."

"Betcha I do."

I grimaced.

"The baby."

"No. It's not that."

"You told him," she grinned. "Didn't you?"

"No. I didn't tell him. He doesn't know and I'd like to keep it that way."

"Fine. Whatever."

I turned my attention toward Christian up ahead. The moonlight radiated upon his skin with the gentle luster of a pearl.

"It's gonna be okay you know." Eva's voice was soft.

"What?" I said startled.

"You and Christian and me—all of us." She stroked her flat abdomen. "We're gonna be okay."

I smiled taken aback. I'd never heard Eva talk with such compassion before.

"What?" she groaned.

"I don't know, I guess I'm just not used to seeing you care."

She looked daggers at me. "Well don't get used to it blondie. It must be the hormones talking."

"Yeah," I smirked. "The hormones."

She licked her lips. "Truth is our family could use some new blood."

I looked at her and grinned. A moment later we both turned our attention toward Christian again.

"You really must have pissed him off," Eva insisted.

"Yeah. I guess I did."

Just then Rosa approached.

"Well finally!" Eva jeered. "What took you so long?"

"Oh Evelyn," she muttered huskily. Her breathing was heavy.

"Are you okay?" I asked, concerned.

"Si," she replied. "Old age is a curse I tell you."

Eva grinned. "So glad I never have to worry about such trivial things."

"Speaking of curses," I pressed, "are you ready Rosa? We're almost at Ambrose House."

"Where are the child's parents?" she asked.

"Still in the forest. We couldn't retrieve them. The beast is using them to bait us."

Rosa sighed. "This is not good."

"Look, I know you wanted the humans safe before you'd undo Alex's curse but—"

"W-w-wait!" Eva interrupted. "What curse? And who is Alex?"

Rosa heaved a sigh.

"And why are we going back to Ambrose House anyway?" Eva snapped. "Don't you think the beast will be waiting for us?"

"Maybe," I replied, "but we have to take that chance."

"I'd feel better in the woods," she insisted. "He doesn't know the woods like we do."

"True, but what we need is in the house."

"Well it better be a friggin' miracle!"

"It's more than a miracle," I divulged. "It's a weapon."

"A weapon?" Her face paled.

The woods suddenly darkened. The moon slid behind a cluster of clouds. The sounds of the night played on my conscience like a funerary march. As we approached Ambrose House a sense of melancholy overwhelmed me. I couldn't deny the fact that Perish had changed. It wasn't the untouched Eden I'd known in childhood any longer. The stream of vampire refugees fleeing the north posed a new and constant danger. Maybe Christian was right. Maybe the danger would never end. Despair entered my thoughts. This was no place to raise a child even if that child wasn't human. But where could we go? Ryan told us of the north; cities overrun with sustenance implant-ridden slaves and Christian and I had seen farther south for ourselves; beaches and towns crawling with feral defectors. No place was safe. Thoughts of Eradan instantly came to mind—his ludicrous talk about the freedom land. If the Emerald City really did exist then perhaps it was worth some serious consideration. Just then the moon emerged from the clouds again.

"Hope," Christian called out.

I perked up and rushed ahead. I pulled him close and kissed him hard; the feeling of his skin was almost warm against me.

"Is your arm glowing?" he asked.

I looked down. "No."

"Good. I suppose that means he isn't inside the house."

My eyes narrowed. "What if Rosa's wrong Christian. You said it yourself—she isn't as powerful as she pretends to be. What if my arm isn't an indicator? What if he is inside waiting for us?"

Christian simply replied, "Then I'll go in first."

"No." I said stopping him.

"It's you he wants Hope, for whatever reason. I can't let you risk—"

"Fine," I interrupted freeing him.

"Wait for my signal," he said. He fluttered his long, beautiful eyelashes and within an instant he was gone.

I stood breathless staring into the darkness awaiting his return. A moment later he reappeared.

"That was fast," I said relieved.

"He isn't in there, but—"

"Is it clear?" Eva interrupted as she made her approach.

"Yeah," Christian replied.

"Good," she said pulling Rosa by the wrist and escorting her inside the house.

"Hope," Christian uttered.

"What? I thought you said it was clear."

"It is."

"Then what are we waiting for?" I said rushing off.

"Wait!" he called out chasing after me.

Ambrose sat like a storybook castle in the distance, moonlight showering each of its unique Victorian details. When we reached the front steps I hurried inside. We needed to resurrect that weapon. It was finally time to put Rosa's power to the test and incarnate the wooden lady from her deep, timber slumber. We opened the front door and slipped inside. The scent of blood nearly suffocated me the instant we entered.

"Dios mio!" Rosa exclaimed. Her old eyes were fixed on the bloodied body of the agile deer lying on the floor in the living room.

"Henry!" I shouted with panic.

"They arrived only minutes before us," Christian surmised.

"He needs more blood," Baptiste piped in. "I've already given him five bottles, but he's still not healing."

"Then get him more!" Eva demanded. "I'll go." She hurried toward the back end of the house and disappeared into the darkness.

"What's wrong with him?" I asked. "Why isn't he healing?"

"I don't know," Baptiste replied.

Just then Eva returned. She was carrying three bottles in her arms. She popped the cork on the first one and started feeding it to the deer as though it were a baby bottle.

"Drink," she encouraged. "C'mon Henry."

"God," Christian said. "He's practically downed the whole bottle already." He moved closer, parted the animal's fur and slid the crusted blood out of the way to inspect the injuries. He shook his head.

"What is it?" I asked.

"His wounds still aren't healing."

"What do we do?"

"Keep trying," Eva said. She pried the cork from the neck of the next bottle and pressed it to the deer's lips.

"C'mon Henry," Christian insisted.

"I'm running out of blood," Eva uttered. "B, go to the vault and get more—as many as you can."

"I haven't got many left."

Her eyes hardened. "What do you mean?"

"I messed up the last two vats and I haven't had any time to cork with all these friggin' interruptions lately!"

"Interruptions?" I scoffed. "Are you really gonna sit there and call all the shit we've been dealing with interruptions?"

"Esperanza!" he raged. "Are you trying to pick a fight with me?"

"Stop!" Christian shouted. "Look." He drew our attention down to Henry. His chest was inert—breath barely left his lips.

"He's not drinking anymore," Eva panicked. "Somebody do something!"

Christian pressed his ear to the deer's chest. "He isn't breathing."

I tried to focus, but the torture of seeing Henry so lifeless was making me sick inside. "Maybe I can go back in time," I suggested. "Maybe I can go back before he got attacked. If I can change it or—"

"Maybe I can help," Rosa interrupted. She waddled closer, knelt down beside Henry and dug her sharp fingernail across her wrist.

"Rosa," I said watching as her fresh, red blood seep from her skin.

"Stop!" Christian shouted. "Do you know what your blood could do to him?"

"Si."

"Then stop."

"He's dying Christian." She held her arm over the animal's insipid lips letting the crimson liquid pool within the opening of his mouth. She closed her eyes and muttered what sounded like prayers.

Silence brought the room to a standstill. I watched anxiously for something to happen. All of a sudden the animal puffed out an immense breath of air!

"He's breathing again!" Christian exclaimed. "And he's starting to heal too."

I smiled with relief. I watched awed as my grandfather swiftly shifted back into his human form again. He licked the last of Rosa's blood from his lips before resuming full consciousness.

"Henry!" I said rushing toward him, but I was distracted by the loud thud of Rosa collapsing to the floor.

"Rosie?" Eva gasped.

I turned to her immediately. "Rosa," I said moving closer. "Wake up!"

She smiled at me, her old eyes slowly closing again.

"Don't sleep. You're not done yet. You promised to help my friend!"

"Oh child," she whispered. "I'm tired. Let me rest."

"No Rosa. I need you!"

"What's going on here?" Eva inquired.

"I need her to help me."

Eva stared at Rosa. "Get up old-timer. You can sleep when you're dead." She grabbed her wrinkly hands and pried her off the floor.

"Evelyn!" Rosa complained.

"Oh shut it you old coot." Eva turned to me. "Where should I put her?"

"The hallway."

Eva hoisted Rosa over her shoulder with ease and carried her into the hallway. She put her down near the front door.

Rosa glowered at Eva and muttered something under her breath.

"Oh knock it off Broomhilda," Eva replied.

"Why *you* care if I break this curse?" Rosa asked.

Eva shrugged. "I don't, but I sure enjoy watching you suffer against your will!"

Rosa kissed her teeth.

"Look," I uttered gently. "I know you're tired Rosa and I swear I'll be forever in your debt after this, but I need you to do as you promised. And you need to do it now."

Rosa frowned.

"Please," I begged.

She shook he head and closed her eyes. She relaxed her shoulders and started rubbing her hands together. A moment later she began mumbling to herself in Spanish. There was a steadiness to her words; it was rhythmic like a chant.

I smiled.

Eva's eyes widened. "What exactly is she doing?"

I turned to Eva and grinned. "She's awakening our weapon!"

41. Awakening

The house was silent, dead silent, except for the sound of Rosa's incantation. It pleased me knowing that she was keeping her end of the bargain. If she could rescind the beast's curse on Alex—the wooden lady, and I was certain that she could, I knew we'd have an invaluable ally on our side.

Watching a witch in action was like nothing else. It was beyond intense. I was fascinated. Every part of her plump, elderly body was involved in the process. Her hands trembled, her legs shuddered, and even her hips swayed. She was working her magic the same way the women worked theirs at the cemetery in Mexico. I remembered it clearly—the concentration and focus they exercised and the metrical repetition of their chant.

"Henry's fine now," Christian said as he drew near.

The sound of his voice distracted me. I turned to him and smiled.

"What's going on in here?" he asked wide-eyed.

"Rosa," I replied. She was moving with a steady calmness now, almost inert.

"What's she doing?"

"Shh," I said. A moment later my eyes began blurring. I rubbed them with my fists in an effort to clear them when suddenly my vision skewed altogether. "Oh no," I expressed. I couldn't see a thing.

"You okay?" Christian asked.

"No. It's my eyes." I blinked a few times and the fogginess

disappeared. I refocused again. "Oh...my...god," I uttered elatedly. I couldn't believe what I was seeing.

"What?" he asked concerned.

"That!" I said pointing ahead.

"What?"

"Don't you see it?"

"See what?"

"The magic! It's all around us." I reached out to touch it. "My god Christian, it's everywhere!"

"What the hell are you talking about?"

At first I didn't reply. I was far too enamored with the presentation unfolding before my eyes. It was beautiful; torrents of magic surging with rainbows of color. It was like a life force of energy flowing from Rosa's body across the hallway toward the wooden lady.

"It's so colossal and vibrant!" I gushed elatedly.

"I don't see anything," he said.

"I don't see anything either," Eva added.

I pulled my eyes away from the conjuring to look at the two of them. "What's wrong with you guys? It's right here in front of us!"

Christian frowned. "Well I only see an old lady standing in our hallway talking to herself."

Eva laughed out loud.

I shook my head at them and returned my eyes to Rosa again, only this time when I looked the magic was gone. "What?" I uttered, panicked. I stared harder to where the beautiful spectrum had flowed only instantly earlier, but there was still nothing.

"Now what's wrong?" Christian asked.

"It's gone. The magic...it was right here."

He slid his arm around my shoulders. "Shh," he soothed.

"Don't *shh* me," I snapped. "I really did see something!"

"Fine."

"Don't you believe me?"

"Of course I do." He tightened his hold on my shoulders.

Eva snorted frustrated. "So where is this weapon of yours?"

"Right there."

"Where?" she pressed.

"There," I said pointing toward the wooden lady.

"That?" Christian scoffed. "That's your weapon?"

I nodded.

"That useless hunk of junk has been hanging on my wall for over two centuries!"

"I know."

"That's not a weapon!"

"It is Christian."

He started walking toward it. "William and I salvaged this rotting tree stump from the bottom of the sea when our ship sank. It's barely even a good example of eighteenth century woodwork let alone a weapon! It's junk."

"It's not junk," I defended. "Believe me."

"I'm with Christian on this blondie." Eva walked across the hall toward it too. "How is this supposed to be a weapon?" She pressed her hand against the wooden lady's body. "It there a bunch of assault artillery hiding inside of it?" Her eyes lit up. "Maybe it turns into a tank like Megaton!" She smirked.

Christian laughed.

"Stop it!" I barked. "There's a person trapped inside there and she's been dormant for over two-hundred years."

"Oh sure honey." Eva wrapped her thin, pale arms around the wooden lady's neck. "This broad's been living with us for as long as I can remember." She leaned in close and planted a kiss on her timber lips. "It ain't nothing but a big hunk of pretty wood!"

"I wouldn't do that if I were you," I warned.

"Why? Afraid Rosa might turn me into a frog or something because I'm toying with her science project?"

"No, but I am afraid of what Alex will do to you once Rosa awakens her."

Eva swallowed hard.

"And when she returns, and believe me she will, do you really want to be the first person standing in her way—a woman with a two hundred year old grudge?"

Eva's face dropped. She stepped away from the wooden lady instantly.

"Are you seriously telling me that she's real?" Christian's voice was stern.

"Yeah."

At that moment a colossal wind swiftly tore through the house. Its force was so tremendous it practically knocked all of us over.

"What's happening?" Baptiste asked moving toward us in the hallway.

"I'm not sure," I replied.

A moment later I spotted Henry staggering closer too. He was back in his human form again, bare-chested and wearing a pair of old sweatpants.

"Where's Rosa?" he hollered.

"Right here," I replied yelling over the sound of the wind. "She's undoing a curse for me."

Henry nodded. "She must be using some form of element manipulation."

Baptiste reached for Henry's arm and held him tightly.

"What's element manipulation?" I asked.

"It's exactly as it sounds," Henry replied. "She's drawing power from the elements."

All of a sudden an incredibly high-pitched buzzing sound resonated.

"My god!" Eva shrieked.

"See," Henry shouted. "She's sourcing the air, using it to invoke the spell. I suggest we all steady ourselves as best as we can."

I pressed my feet against the floor. A moment later I felt Christian's fingers searching to interlock with mine. I grabbed his hand and held it tightly, but I felt the wind picking up pace.

"It's like a tornado in here!" Eva yelled.

Its circular movement was like a cyclone swirling wildly through the entranceway of the house and soon it began encapsulating us within the heart of its spin.

"We're being corralled," Christian shouted.

"Steady yourselves," Henry cautioned.

Slowly the volatile tempest began forcing us toward the center of the room.

"Even I can't fight against its force!" Baptiste raged frustrated.

Just then the ground began trembling beneath our feet.

"Christian," I exclaimed. "Do you feel that?"

"Yeah," he replied.

The trembling increased until it was utterly unstable. My body shifted with the movement and I felt myself slamming against Christian's side.

"Hope!" he shouted catching me.

"Move closer together," Henry insisted. "We can use each other to stabilize." He reached out his hand. I grabbed it instantly and we all fell into place. I tightened my grasp on Christian and watched him reach for Eva's hand. Baptiste was already holding onto Henry's arm and before long he and Eva had also locked fingers too. With our backs together and our hands attached the force of the wind didn't seem so strong anymore.

"It's working!" I said optimistically.

"Hope!" Henry shouted. "What kind of spell is Rosa breaking for you?"

"An old spell. One that was invoked by a vampire."

Just then the antique Persian carpet started flapping. It fluttered like waves in the ocean beneath our feet. I squeezed Christian's hand tighter and fought to steady myself. A moment later the wooden floor boards began jutting up from the ground too.

Smash!

Up and down they cracked; timber shards speckled the air like raindrops. The explosive current shot the splintery debris everywhere. I looked ahead. A line of jagged posts were soaring toward us like a battalion of stakes set to impale.

"Shit!" Eva hollered.

"Brace yourselves!" I insisted.

I closed my eyes and prepared for the impact when suddenly silence reigned. I opened my eyes again. Christian had stopped the moment.

"What's happening?" Eva asked stunned.

"We're frozen in time," I replied.

Henry sighed. "Did you do this Christian?"

"Yeah."

"Why?"

"I don't know. I guess I thought I was helping."

"Well now what?" Baptiste uttered anxiously. "Because I'm figuring we can't stay here forever." He motioned toward the mass of jagged wooden stakes. They hung in mid-air surrounding us on all sides.

"This isn't how I want to die!" Eva panicked.

"You're not dying chica," Baptiste consoled.

"I'm face to face with a thousand daggers!" Her voice was panicked. "This is exactly how I'm going to die!"

"No one is dying!" I shouted.

"Then how the hell do you propose we get outta this?" Her voice was curt.

"On the count of three we hit the floor," I said. "Christian reanimates time and we let the stakes soar over our heads."

"That's your plan?" Eva sneered.

"You got a better one?"

"Girls!" Henry uttered. "It's a fine plan—it's not a great plan, but it will have to do. Ready yourselves."

I dropped to the floor. Christian and the others dropped too.

"On the count of three then," Henry insisted. "*One...two...*"

Then Christian reanimated the world around us. Wooden stakes shot through air at a harrowing speed. I stood paralyzed, a burst of pressure abruptly radiated in my shoulder. I screamed and struggled to steady myself on the floor. Once the ground stopped shaking I looked down at myself and noticed the sharp chunk of wood that protruded through my shoulder.

"Don't move," Christian implored.

"But I have to get it out!"

"I'm hit too!" Eva shrieked.

"Calm down," Baptiste insisted. "They're minor flesh wounds." He started pulling the wooden shards from her legs.

"Christian," I said. "I have to pull it out!"

"No!" he maintained avidly.

He was standing behind me and he wasn't moving. I turned toward him. He turned too. My face flushed. I felt sick inside.

"My god!" I uttered aghast. I could feel his body attached to mine. "We're stuck together aren't we?"

"Yes."

"Take it out!" I demanded. I wasn't afraid—I was revolted. The mere thought of him dislodging the stake was making me cringe.

All of a sudden the most excruciating pain radiated through my upper body. The staked site burned as though every nerve ending within me was on high alert. Each jagged splinter of wood scraped against my fleshy insides as it fled my body. I groaned aloud. "Oh Christian!" I shouted. "It was the count of three! Why did you reanimate on two damn it?"

"I don't know," he said tossing the bloodied piece of wood to the ground.

All of a sudden the wind picked up again. Like an inhale the untamed current abruptly shifted direction.

"Not again!" Eva hollered.

It funneled tightly and before long it was a slim line cyclone spinning before us. I grabbed Christian and sank myself within the cradle of his strong arms.

"Hold on," he urged.

I watched the wind whirl when suddenly it widened in girth.

"Steady yourself!" Henry warned.

Everything not fastened down took flight. Pictures and papers blew through the air. Sculptures and furniture toppled over. Everything was in manic disarray. The hallway was cataclysmic and yet we could have flown over the rainbow for all I cared; deep in the heart of the cyclone I knew I was safe in the arms of my Tin Man.

"I can't take much more of this!" Baptiste raged.

Just then a thunderous strike abruptly echoed. A moment later the cyclone collapsed.

"What happened?" Eva asked. "Where's the wind?"

"Gone," I replied. I looked down. A spread of foggy tendrils suddenly stretched the length of the floor.

"I-I can't move!" she shrieked.

"Me neither," Henry insisted.

Like the tentacles of a translucent sea monster, the colossal sized wafts wrapped themselves around our ankles.

"The fog," I uttered. "It's binding us."

Then another loud noise resounded. It was quick and sharp at first, but soon like the swell of a train whistle, it raged with an ear-splitting shrillness.

"What the hell?" Baptiste hollered.

Yet another fierce wind burst through the house! It shattered windows as it soared. Pieces of glass shot everywhere. Ambrose House was in shambles. The wind tore through the living room and into the hallway before ripping a decent sized opening straight through the ceiling.

"What the…" I uttered appalled.

It blasted through the second story like a flash before tearing a hole through the roof of the house.

"Dios mio!" Baptiste shouted.

All at once it stopped. An eerie silence came to pass in the wake of the wind. I withdrew from Christian and moved toward the damage. I positioned myself beneath the new breach in the roof. Moonlight bathed the interior of Ambrose House. It was surreal, like a window to the heavens had opened within my living room walls. Stars twinkled just within reach and the moon seemed only a breath away.

"Rosa!" Eva shouted.

I pivoted around on my heels, my eyes wide. Rosa was lying on the floor. A stream of blood was trickling from her nose. I went to move toward her when suddenly the heady scent of fire distressed me. I looked over my shoulder, toward the staircase.

"My god!" I uttered astounded.

It was the wooden lady and she was enveloped within a blaze of searing flames!

42. Fire

The fire burned intensely and soon the house was inundated with smoke.

"Fire!" Eva hollered. "We have to get out!"

"No!" I said stopping her. "We can't leave. Rosa must finish this."

"Rosa is unconscious!" she retorted, "and Ambrose House is burning Hope! We need to get out!"

"She's right!" Christian shouted. "Our bodies aren't like humans. We're much more brittle, like twigs in wildfire. We must go!"

Christian's face was vexed. His eyes were harder than usual. I shifted my gaze to Eva; tendrils of smoke were starting to rise from the sides of her neck. I bit my lip, appalled. She was beginning to smolder! I looked at Baptiste. Wisps of smoke rose from his tattooed knuckles. A surge of shock overwhelmed me.

"Your scar!" Christian shouted. "It's glowing!"

I looked down. My scar was inflamed with a ginger blaze.

"He must be close," Christian deduced.

"We can't leave," I insisted.

"We have to. Don't fight me on this."

I shifted my eyes back to the wooden lady again.

"Just leave her Christian," Eva interjected. "If she's stupid enough to want to stay then let her."

He nervously ran his hands through his hair. "Fine," he groaned. "Then I'm not leaving either."

290

"What the hell is wrong with the two of you?" Baptiste's voice was hard.

"Forget them," Eva snapped. "Let Romeo & Juliet commit their suicides if that's what they want!"

All of a sudden a burst of flames exploded. Like fireworks, sparks of light illuminated the hallway. The wooden lady fell from the wall crashing to the floor with a thunderous strike. A cocoon of flames consumed what remained of the wooden tomb.

"The floor!" Eva barked. "It's catching fire. We gotta go now!"

I looked down. Fire had gripped the Persian carpet beneath me. Flames singed the rugged trimming with ease and I knew it wouldn't be long before the entire house went up in flames too.

Christian and I locked fingers when suddenly I felt a searing pain in my palm. I looked down. Smoke rose from my skin and cinders smoldered at the base of my fingernails.

"You're burning!" he exclaimed.

I was burning. "Let go of me," I ordered, "or you'll catch fire too!" But it was already too late. Our skin had begun melding together.

"Pull!" he insisted.

I pulled hard against him and thankfully a quick forcible rip released us! Malleable bits of our flesh whirled through the air like silly putty. I howled with pain!

"The lady!" Baptiste shouted.

I looked ahead. Past the fierce assemblage of writhing flames, the wooden lady's tomb burned with an almost white hot luminescence.

"I'm outta here!" Eva yelled and then she morphed into a smoky darkness and disappeared entirely.

"Eva!" Baptiste bellowed, but the flames had already blocked his only exit and Eva was long gone.

My eyes were glued to the fiery wooden lady. I watched mesmerized as her rotting, lumber limbs slowly began transforming. Wood withered with effortlessness, while fleshy patches of soft, supple skin swiftly assumed its place. Her lumber locks also softened like melted butter and her facial features radiated with an incandescent shine. All of a sudden the blaze ceased! An explosion of water flooded the interior of Ambrose House. Water rushed down the staircase, poured in through the shattered windows, sprayed through the cracks in the walls and rained down in torrents through the gaping hole in the ceiling. A moment later an upsurge of water exhumed the wooden lady's body from her tomb! The tidal wave doused the fire entirely. And when the smoke cleared I knew instantly that the incantation was complete.

There on the charred Persian carpet laid the remains of the wooden lady; a shapely pile of cinder and ash. The well-formed heap sat dormant on the carpet when suddenly it began to stir! Swirling in graceful synchronicity the flakes fell into place and within moments they became an unyielding cyclone spinning mere inches above the ground.

"Not again!" Christian uttered under his breath.

Just then the cinder storm doubled in size and initiated a flash freeze which halted everything! The cinders plummeted to the floor.

"It's a woman!" Baptiste shouted.

It was a woman indeed. Her clothes were old and frayed and her hair was blonde and shaggy, but her skin was soft and her lips rosier than a bright red apple. The wooden lady was alive again and free.

"Alex!" I shouted rushing toward her.

"Alex?" Christian uttered, perplexed.

"Open your eyes," I said. I touched her face. "She's warm. And she's starting to breathe." Her chest heaved. She coughed a puff of dust from her lips.

"Alex?" Christian questioned. His eyes were fixed on her face.

I pressed my ear to her chest. The beat of her heart was strong and steady. I smiled.

Christian knelt down beside me. "I know him," he uttered. "This was William's friend." His eyes were glued to Alex's face.

"Alexandra," I clarified. "And *he's* actually a *she.*"

Christian's eyes bulged. "Impossible."

"The fact that she's a woman or the fact that she's been hanging in our hallway for over two centuries?"

"Both."

I grinned.

"How did you know about her?"

"I was there when it happened."

"On the HMS Ambrose?"

I nodded reluctantly.

"He...I mean *she* looks the same—so incredibly untouched by time."

"Like you," I smiled.

"What happened to her?" Baptiste asked. "I mean how did she get in the tomb?"

"She was cursed."

"Who cursed her?"

"*Him.*"

"Him?" Christian uttered turning toward me. "You mean the beast?"

I nodded.

Christian turned his attention back to Alex again. He leaned closer and reached his hand toward her face to touch her. His long pale fingers hung just above her skin when unexpectedly her eyes flew open. She screamed in terror! Christian withdrew immediately.

"Alex!" I said. "Don't be frightened."

Her short cropped hair was dirty and spiked out at the ends fringing her face like a bushel of straw. Her teeth were yellow and stained terribly and she reeked of embers.

"Who is she?" Baptiste asked.

"Her name is Alexandra," I explained over her whimpers. "She was one of William's friends aboard the Ambrose." I moved my eyes to her. "Alex," I said. "Look at me. Do you remember me?"

The sound of her panic finally dulled. She cocked her head to the side and focused intently on my face.

"Bloody hell!" she snapped. Her accent was thick and airy. "It's you! The siren!"

"Siren?" Baptiste questioned.

"Aye," she uttered alarmed.

I pulled Christian closer. I showed him to Alex. "And him," I said. "Do you recognize him too?"

Her blue eyes widened. "Aye," she retorted. "That be Willy's mate." She blinked her long lashes and scrutinized Christian's face. "He ain't right. He's somewhere between hay and grass, like he ain't grown, but he is changed."

"Are you saying he looks different?" I asked.

"Aye," she snapped offended. "Ain't you understand English lass?"

She struggled to a sitting position. She looked over my shoulder. Her eyes widened, fright overwhelming her sweet scruffy face. "Is this Spaniard a captive?" she panicked.

"Spaniard?" I said confused.

She glowered. "Why ain't he in chains?"

"Is she talking about me?" Baptiste shot back.

"He's not a captive," I explained. "He's a friend."

"Alexandra," Henry interjected. "What is the last thing you remember?"

She drew her eyes away from Baptiste and toward Henry. "And who is you supposed to be?" she asked confused.

"My name is Henry. I'm Hope's grandfather."

"Grandfather?" she blurted. "Ain't you a little young to be a grandfather?"

Henry smiled. He wrapped his arm around Rosa and helped her to her feet. "And this is the woman who brought you back to life. Her name is Rosa."

Alex's eyes narrowed. The expression on her face blanked. She looked as though she was about to faint.

"Alexandra," I said grabbing her. "I know this must be overwhelming for you, but we really need your help."

"Help?" she mumbled, her eyes half-closed.

"What do you remember?"

"Ain't much," she said. "I reckon Willy was there. And you of course. We was hidin' in that hole together before that thing, that monster—"

"Monster?" Baptiste interjected. "What monster?"

"It was even bigger than you Spaniard! Arms burly like an animal and hair long and matted. Even his face wasn't belongin' to a man. He was scarred somethin' dreadful and real angry lookin' and when he pulled me from that hole I thought it was the last of me!" She looked around confused. "Where is I anyway?"

"The Ambrose," Christian said, "well what's left of her."

"You mocking me Sir?"

"No," he replied. "When we hit the reef the ship took on water rather quickly. William and I did our best to salvage all we could."

"We hit a reef?"

He nodded.

Alex eyed the muddled interior of the house. She spotted part of an old rotted bowsprit, wooden pegs wrapped in ropes and other ancient nautical relics scatted about.

"She took on water eh?" Alex said.

"Yes."

"And you and Willy salvaged all you could? Bitts, brails... deadeye?"

Christian nodded.

"And the treasure too?"

His face paled. "How did you know about the treasure?"

"You think I'm fool enough to risk me life without some great reason...I being a lass and all?" Her eyes narrowed.

"Well," Christian said. "I...um..."

"There were whispers of the loot even before we pulled anchor on England. All the crew knew."

"They did? I had no idea."

"Why would ya? You was upper rank. You lads didn't cavort with us scalawags below." Alex snorted. "Where is me mates anyhow? Bathin' in gold or maybe swimmin' in it! Dry land never satisfies the blood of a seafarer after all!"

"No one survived," Christian replied stoically.

"Well *you* did," she countered, "and Willy and that siren sittin' over there too."

"Yes, but..."

"But?"

"It's complicated," he said.

Just then I realized that my scar had suddenly started glowing again! It was bright and singing me with stings. "Christian." I motioned to my arm.

His eyes widened. "He's near again."

"Who?" Alex pried.

"*Him,*" I said. "The beast. The monster that cursed you."

"That ungodly creature survived?" Alex's voice was panicked.

"There's no time for explanations," I uttered. "He's come back to kill us."

"Well if it's death he's after why didn't he kill us on the ship?"

"He tried," I said. "He fed on you the way he fed on the rest of the crew, but when he swallowed your blood he couldn't digest it."

"*He fed on me?*" She grimaced.

"Yeah," I replied. "And your blood did something to him. I think it's because he didn't know that you were a woman."

"And me trickery made him sick?"

"No, but it did weaken him." I smirked. "And I think we can do it again!"

"Heavens no!" she shrieked.

"Please Alex," I begged when suddenly a rush of liquid ash streamed from between her lips.

43. Decision

The transition back to humanity wasn't smooth sailing. As I watched Alexandra cough the last of the gray phlegm from her lungs I couldn't help but contemplate the irony of it all; I was standing in Ambrose House, the former HMS Ambrose, with a two-hundred year old sailor that had been cursed to live in a masthead by the same monster that we were trying to destroy at present. None of it made sense, but then neither did reality. I possessed the ability to travel through time into the past. To me nothing was linear or even logical for that matter. All I knew for certain was that friends were hard to come by and I for one wasn't about to discriminate against where or even when they came from.

"I know this place," Alex said looking around. There was a curious, faraway look in her eyes as though she was recalling bits and pieces of long lost knowledge.

"Well you've been here for as long as I can remember," I admitted. I motioned to the stairs. "You hung on that wall over there."

She turned toward the spot and stared at it.

"Had it not been for Will insisting we drudge you up, you might still have been at the bottom of the sea!" Christian divulged.

I poked him in the arm.

Alexandra sighed. I could practically hear the lingering storm of cinders swirling within her lungs as she released her breath.

"Alex," I said. "We really need you." I looked down at my arm again.

The scar glowed with an even more fiery intensity. "And we haven't got much time."

"What exactly you need me for?" she asked.

"We need you to help us destroy that beast once and for all."

She grinned. "Count me in mates!"

I smiled in reply.

"Let's move then," Baptiste insisted. "If he's close, he won't be hard to find."

"Hand me my cutlass," Alex demanded.

"It's not that simple," I expressed.

"Ain't nothin' simpler than killin' a man."

"But he isn't a man."

"Take it to the woods," Eva uttered appearing from out of nowhere.

"Eva!" Baptiste shouted. He grabbed her by the waist, pulled her against him and kissed her cheek.

She looked around. "What the hell happened in here?"

"A resurrection," I replied.

"And who is that?" Eva asked.

"This is Alex."

Alex nodded.

Eva cringed. "She smells funny...like cinders."

"Beg yer pardon?" Alex's retorted.

"Honestly, if I didn't know better I would have thought you were a little boy!"

"Well I ain't!"

"Relax. Don't get them century old panties of yours in a bunch."

"Hope," Christian said distractingly. "Your arm again!"

I looked down. The scar glowed brightly, but also the skin surrounding the scar as well.

"C'mon," Baptiste barked. "We need to move while we know he's close."

"Lead him to the woods," Eva maintained. "I'm telling you, no one knows the woods like we do."

"But the woods are exactly where he wants us," Christian insisted. "He's baiting us there."

"Then make like we're taking the bait," Baptiste proposed, "and when he comes to catch us we kill him with brute force. An old-fashioned ambush never fails!"

"Now yer talkin'!" Alex cheered. "Ready your sabers mates!"

"Sabers," Eva scoffed, "really?"

"Brute force won't work," Henry articulated. "This creature is very powerful. You need to think of another way."

"I've contemplated this day for centuries," Christian confessed. "When Will and I were on the ship fighting for our lives, we did everything humanly possible to try and kill him."

"*Humanly possible*," I insisted. "Well we aren't humans anymore." My face lit up with optimism. "We might not know how to kill him, but we do know how to weaken him. We know for certain that Alex's blood has done it once before."

"And I ain't doing it again!" she groaned.

"Not you Alex," I looked over at Eva. "Us."

Eva smirked. She was definitely intrigued.

"We know his aversion to a woman's blood." My voice was hard and fast. "What if we trick him again—just the way Alex did on the ship?"

"How stupid do you think he is?" Baptiste pressed.

"Not stupid at all," Eva replied morphing into the likeness of a ginger-haired young man.

"Oh me stars!" Alex gasped. "What on Earth is she doing?"

Eva suddenly transformed back into the likeness of herself again.

"Like watching the hand of god at work!" Alex uttered awestruck.

Eva smiled. "You flatter me Cinderella, although I've always considered myself more like the devil at a day spa."

"Your plan has faults," Rosa interrupted. "You women yes, but vampires first. Your blood not work like hers did."

"*Vampires?*" Alex uttered terrified. "As in blood suckin' parasites?" Her face paled.

"No!" I replied.

Alex trembled. "You tellin' me that you all is no better than that beast out there?"

"God no!" I exclaimed. "We're nothing like him. We're civilized. He's a monster. And he needs to be stopped."

"To stop him you give him what he want," Rosa interjected.

"What he wants we haven't got." I insisted.

"Marco," Rosa said wide-eyed.

"Your grandson?" exclaimed Henry. "No Rosa. Don't intentionally put Marco in danger."

"He's not even human!" Christian added.

"Your beast don't know that," Rosa said.

"Rose," Henry uttered. "This is not your battle to fight. Don't risk getting your grandson involved."

"Tell that to him," she snickered. "He been waiting for a trial. This may be it. The boy has learned all he need. I cannot protect him forever."

Henry tightened his grasp on Rosa. Rosa smiled in reply.

"I'm heading out," barked Baptiste. "I can't stay cooped up in here forever."

"I'm coming too," Eva added.

Baptiste smiled. "Anybody else want to join—"

"Aye!" Alex replied. "I'll join Red and the Spaniard."

"Spaniard!" Eva raged.

"Never mind her," Baptiste uttered.

"Hope," Christian insisted. "Your arm!"

I looked down. The scar and surrounding skin wasn't glowing any longer. "He's gone," I said concerned.

"Doesn't matter," Baptiste insisted. "We'll sniff him out."

He and Eva started walking toward the front door.

"Wait for me," Alex shouted, struggling to move to a standing position.

"God," Eva complained, "what a liability. She can't even stand up so how the hell is she going to fight with us?"

"Just gettin' me land-legs back is all!"

Eva rolled her eyes and opened the front door. A moment later she and Baptiste stepped outside. Alex wasn't too far behind. She staggered through the door toward the porch.

"Lord!" she shouted stepping outside.

"Shut it Cinderella!" Eva's voice was hard. "You want to get yourself killed even before you get into the woods?"

I watched from a distance as Alex reacquainted herself with the world again. The silvery moonlight danced like sparkles upon her mess of pixyish hair. A moment later she staggered down the wooden steps toward Baptiste and Eva.

"We must go now," Rosa insisted.

I drew my eyes back inside the house. Henry and Rosa were standing and ready to leave.

"Them humans won't last much longer." Rosa's voice was hard.

I nodded. "Let's go."

We left the house together. Time wasn't on our side. The beast had put the humans in the woods to bait us, but their wounds were deep and it was only a matter of time before unconsciousness would turn into death. *Tick tock. Tick tock.* The dreaded sound of the clock ticking from within the belly of the fabled crocodile echoed in the back of my mind as I marched across the grass.

"Don't fight today," Christian pleaded.

"Don't be ridiculous."

"I mean it," he said. "This thing—this beast is old and incredibly dangerous."

"I know."

"Then you know better than to fight him."

"Oh Christian," I said looping my long hair up in a knot at the nape of my neck.

"I don't want you near him."

"And I don't want to be near him, but I also know we need to finish this."

Christian sighed. "I don't like this connection you have with him."

"Well I certainly don't like it either."

"It's not too late to leave you know." He grabbed my hand.

"Christian. This is our home. He's not going to take that away from us." I licked my lips. "It ends today."

"But that's just it," he said. "It'll never end." He was clearly frustrated. "Are you prepared to kill every vampire that flees the north and passes through Perish?"

I grimaced.

"It will *never* end Hope."

I swallowed hard. "Well I'm not leaving. This is our home damn it!"

He grabbed my arm and pulled me against him. I could almost feel his heart beating through his chest, pounding with a swiftness I'd never felt before.

"Home isn't a place and you know that. Perish is island and nothing more."

I looked into his eyes. They were green, but not nearly as vibrant as usual.

"Hope," he said. "I don't want to live a life of retaliation and anger." His voice was soft. "That's not the man I want to be."

"But the beast," I said. "He's finally returned. And this is your chance—"

"To what—kill him, finally feel vindicated for what he did to me all those years ago?" He shook his head. "You realize I never would have met you had that monster not done what he did to me."

"Christian," I snapped. "I can't believe my ears!"

"I've lived with anger and rage for a very long time Hope. I refuse to let it ruin our future together."

"Please don't turn that monster into a god!" I begged.

He stroked the side of my face and sighed again. "If killing him is what you want then I'll help you do it. But it won't end with him. There will always be another." He heaved a sigh. "Choosing to stay in Perish is choosing to live the kind of life I don't want to live."

"I don't want to live looking over my shoulder every minute, but I refuse to just give in and leave. Isn't there any middle-ground?"

I looked into his eyes; they were hard and bursting with distress.

"Please don't go into the woods today," he pleaded again.

"This isn't some fairy tale Christian. It's not like I'm Little Red Riding Hood afraid that the big bad wolf will eat me."

"I know," he retorted, "but you are the love of my life and there's a very good chance that the immortal bloodsucking beast *will* eat you."

"Oh Christian," I groaned. "I'm smart and fast and I can shift through time if—"

"I know your capabilities."

"Then why are you so determined to keep me from fighting today?"

"Because," he whispered. "Just because." He leaned in close, pressed his lips to mine and vanished out of sight.

The tick tock of that crocodile started echoing in the back of my mind again. I was standing at the threshold of the forest. The decision to pass through wasn't a difficult one. Despite Christian's reservations I knew we needed to vanquish the beast once and for all. Preserving the sanctity of Perish was paramount—even if we had opened the floodgates to a life filled with retaliation and anger.

I looked down at my arm. It was glowing again. I scanned the perimeter of the woods. I couldn't see the beast, but that didn't mean he wasn't out there. I stepped foot inside the forest. The sounds of cicadas buzzed in my ears. Thoughts of Maddy instantly came to mind and then I remembered her parents; left for dead deep in the woods. Time was running out.

I bolted through the trees at the speed of light. It felt good knowing that I wasn't alone. With the addition of Alex and Marco, our circle of allies was growing steadily. We were a motley pack of proverbial lost boys and we were fearless together, more spirited than even Peter Pan himself and hell-bent on vanquishing the bloodsucking beast one way or another.

44. Butterfly Effect

Nauseas hit me like a hammer. I stopped running instantly. I leaned over a fallen tree stump, parted my lips and let the crimson fluid stream to the ground. The queasiness was coming more frequently now and I had no idea what seemed to trigger it. I wiped my mouth with the back of my hand and looked toward the trees. Dawn loomed; its lemony haze hung upon the horizon in the distance.

"Shh," a familiar voice warned.

I whipped around. No one was there. A sudden rustling in the bushes caught my eye. I edged closer.

"Don't be frightened," the voice continued.

I stopped, perplexed when suddenly and a man appeared from within the brush.

"My god!" I exclaimed.

"Hope. It's me." He was tall and lean, handsome with shiny black hair and strange circular spectacles covering his eyes.

"You!" I said.

"Yeah me—Eradan."

"I know. How could I ever forget someone like you?"

"What's that suppose to mean?"

I eyed him up and down. "You know...your clothes and glasses."

"What's wrong with my clothes?" His voice virtually cracked as he spoke.

"Nothing. Never mind. I like your clothes. They're...different."

He smiled, its warmth radiating intently.

I smiled back. "How did you find me?"

He shrugged.

"Did we cross paths again?"

"No," he laughed.

"Then how?"

"Look it doesn't matter how I found you. All that matters is that I've come to help you."

"Help me?"

He looked around edgily. "This is incredibly dangerous."

"What is incredibly dangerous?"

"*This*—you and me."

I bit my lip, intrigue coursing through my icy veins.

"You understand what I mean right?"

I shook my head.

"Tell me you at least understand why this is dangerous."

I cocked my head to the side and grimaced.

He sighed frustrated. "What do you know about quantum physics?"

I shrugged.

"The time-space continuum?"

I shook my head.

"Damn it," he uttered in frustration. He heaved a sigh, his lean frame inflating like a superhero with the intake of his breath.

"Eradan, why do you care if I know about quantum physics or the time-space thingy?"

"Because then you'd understand the significance of my presence here."

"What significance?"

He pursed his lips. "Let me put in layman's terms."

"Gee thanks."

"What do you know about…what is it you call them…*the lingers… shadows…residuals?*"

"Residuals," I groaned. "Please don't talk to me about residuals."

"So you know what they are right?"

"Of course! They're the outcome of my actions…the butterfly effect…

the thing that Christian's been nagging me about ever since I realized
I could shift through time!"

He smiled.

"Please tell me you aren't here to lecture me too."

He ran his gloved hand through his dark hair and sighed again.
"I'm not here to lecture you."

"Good."

"If you understand residuals then I don't need to explain to you how
dangerous this is for both of us."

My face furrowed. "Dangerous? Why?"

"Because I'm a time-shifter!"

"You are?" I said awed.

"Of course I am. What did you think I was?"

"I…um…I didn't really think about it." I was taken aback. I'd never
met anyone like me before. It was undeniably exhilarating knowing that
others even existed.

"Hope," he said changing the subject, "in the woods today—"

"How do you know about the woods?"

"The same way you knew about the wooden lady on your wall."

My eyes bulged. "Wooden lady…" *How did he know?*

"Shh," he said. "Now listen to me closely. When you're in the
woods—"

At that moment a loud scream interrupted him. I turned toward the
sound. A flock of herons abruptly fled the trees.

"It's already too late," he snarled.

I turned to him instantly, my face vexed with concern. "Too late
for what?" I implored.

"We'll meet again."

"Where?"

"Don't worry," he said retreating back into the bushes.

"How will I find you?"

"I'll find you." And with a strange, inky flash he was gone.

Just then another scream echoed. I turned toward it when suddenly I
realized that my arm was glowing again. I widened my gaze and looked
out among the pines. I could almost feel the beast within range.

Dawn approached like the stroke of midnight and soon the fairy tale
I was living would be over. The light of day would inevitably encumber

my strength and the beast's power would seem unfathomable to fight against. I needed to settle this before daylight materialized.

Tick. Tock. Tick. Tock.

I quickened my pace and flew through the pines. The sharp clanking of rocks shattering flooded my eardrums. All of a sudden a huge boulder whizzed overhead. I ducked down low and hit the ground. The scar on my arm burned with a searing intensity. I perked up and looked around.

"Hope!" Christian shouted approaching out of nowhere. "Stay down," he insisted rushing toward me as another immense rock zoomed overhead!

"What's happening?!" I demanded.

"The fight," he replied. "B, Eva and the others have been trying to defeat him."

"Well let's get in there!" I rose to my feet.

"Hey," he said stopping me. "This is dangerous. *He is dangerous.*"

"I told you," I said as I stood up. "I can handle him."

Christian got up too. "I thought I told you not to come into woods today."

"You did."

"Then why are you here?"

"You know exactly why I'm here."

"Oh Hope," he pleaded. "I don't want you anywhere near that thing!"

All of a sudden a flood of rumbling howls defiled the dawn serenity. I looked at my arm. The scar blazed like flames in a fire!

"Hope," he said. "There's something you need to know."

"What?"

"Rosa's plan worked," he divulged. "The beast came for her grandson's blood."

"Well that's good right?"

He shook his head. "Marco's a witch."

"So?"

"The blood of a witch is powerful."

"I know that. Rosa's blood saved Henry when nothing else would."

"Marco isn't like his grandmother."

"I get that," I scoffed.

"No. His blood isn't like hers."

"I don't understand."

"He works in magica negra."

My face furrowed.

"Black magic Hope. Marco is a dark witch."

My eyes widened.

"Even Rosa doesn't know. She thought Marco's blood would bend the beast to his will, but instead of entrancing him—it invigorated him."

My bottom lip quivered.

"That thing out there...he's even more powerful than he was on the Ambrose."

All at once the earth began trembling beneath our feet!

"What's happening?" I uttered.

"It's him. He's coming!"

I looked ahead. The trees shook like the wing's of a giant cicada.

"Take my hand," Christian insisted.

I reached out for him, but the ground began heaving more tumultuously than storm waves in the ocean. I could hardly keep my balance let alone struggle to reach for his hand.

"Christian!" I shouted.

The scrawny pines undulated overhead. The daunting sound of teetering timber echoed in my ears. This wasn't the work of Mother Nature—it was the devil's way of bending her to his will.

"Hope," Christian exclaimed. "We gotta move!"

I drew my eyes upward. The tall trees bowed tautly. I watched when—*SNAP*, like gunfire, trees cracked all around us. Caving like quicksand, the pines plummeted from above.

"Run!" Christian shouted.

My feet kicked into gear. I sped through the forest at the speed of light. A tunnel of trees exploded in a timber trail closely behind. Slivers of wood showered the air around me. I was merely a breath ahead of being swallowed by the lethal wooden rainfall when all of a sudden I felt myself being pulled away. I closed my eyes and gave in to the swiftness of my speed. Before long the sound of devastation was far behind.

I opened my eyes. Eradan's sweet face filled my gaze. I smiled as he put me down on the ground beside him. "Thanks," I expressed.

"Told ya' I'd find ya'."

"Yeah. You did."

"Looked like you needed a hand."

"No. Not really."

"Is that right," he scoffed, "'cause it looked to me like you did."

I glared. "I was fine on my own."

"That was you fine on your own?" His brows peaked over the rim of his circular glasses. "An instant longer and you would have been impaled."

"And how would you know?"

"Because," he said saucily, "I saw it happen."

At that moment a sudden scar manifested on my shoulder blade. "Oww," I groaned reaching to touch it.

"Told ya'," he scoffed.

The pain radiated with a searing intensity. I glowered at him.

"What?" he defended. "I helped you out."

"Some help," I said wincing.

He planted his hands on his hips, his strange white gloves covering his long fingers. "Would you rather I let you get impaled?"

"No."

"Then don't be so unappreciative."

"Unappreciative!" I raged.

"Don't get all persnickety," he said withdrawing. "I thought you understood residuals?"

"Why do you care anyway?"

"I want to help you."

"Why?" My voice was *take-no-prisoner* hard.

"Because," he said. "You need my help more than you think...and definitely more than you'd ever admit!" His chiseled features stretched as his mouth moved into a wide grin. He laughed.

"How dare you decide for me. I don't want your help and I definitely don't want you needling around in my business!"

"Oh you drive me crazy with your incessant unpredictability."

"*Incessant unpredictability?*"

"Forget it. We're wasting time bickering."

"I'm not bickering. You're the one bickering." I looked daggers at him. "I don't understand why you're even helping me. Are you like some kind of time shifting hero on the lookout for damsels in distress or something?"

"Why? Do you consider yourself a damsel in distress?"

"God no!"

He smirked.

"Thanks for your help," I said stiffening up, "but from here on I can take can take care of myself."

"Are you telling me to leave?"

"No. I'm asking you politely."

He laughed when suddenly I felt him grabbing me by the arms and pulling me to the ground. I landed face first in the dirt.

"Stay down," he whispered. He wrapped his arms around me. The length of his long coat covered us both like a blanket. The sound of trees splintering apart in the distance resonated. "Don't move," he uttered. "Don't react. Don't blink."

Beneath the tent of his brown coat a beaming orange light began gleaming.

"God," he said, "your arm!"

My scar glowed with such a radiant blaze it illuminated Eradan's face in an amber luster.

"Hide it," he instructed. "If the beast sees it he'll—"

"Fine," I replied. I tucked my arm beneath my body. The light diffused instantly.

SNAP! SNAP!

The sound of falling timber grew louder. I knew the beast was close; just outside the shelter of Eradan's coat. A sinister stench suffused the air. The smell of death was ripe. Nausea quickly swelled in the pit of my stomach. My body trembled and my throat burned. I could feel blood in the back of my throat. I bit down on my bottom lip and tried controlling the urge to wretch; I simply wasn't in control of the child within me. A stream of blood rushed from my lips staining the lining of Eradan's coat.

"Crap," he complained.

"What?" I scoffed. "Did I ruin your favorite coat?"

"No," he uttered. "The beast...he'll smell that blood. We have to get you out of here." He wrapped his arms around me and pulled me to a standing position. "Hold on," he whispered. He picked me up and suddenly we were off, zooming through the woods like an inky blot of color.

I hung vulnerably in his arms like a child as he whisked me away to safety. The vomiting, the blood, the danger, the beast, it all paled in comparison to the one thing that was paramount in my thoughts: *Who the hell was Eradan?*

I stared at his face like I was looking upon a guardian angel sent from heaven above to protect me. I smiled. He was fascinating; charming and charismatic and yet incredibly infuriating. He was impulsive and pushy and had no business being in *my* reality, but there was something about him that captivated me. Even with his strange long coat, silly gloves and curious spectacles I was helplessly drawn to him. And despite his overt rudeness and condescension I felt safe in his arms—the same way I felt safe in Christian's arms.

"I think we've finally lost him," he said setting me down.

I looked at my arm. The scar wasn't glowing anymore.

"You'll be safe here," he assured.

"Thanks," I replied when all of a sudden the queasiness returned again. I doubled over and coughed yet another stream of blood from my lips. "My god," I said mortified, "I'm so sorry Eradan." I wiped ·my mouth with the back of my hand and looked up again, but he was gone.

45. Tin Man

I knew I was capable of separating the saving from the savory, but the baby inside me however wasn't quite as shrewd.

When I reached the humans the scent of blood inundated the air with an intoxicating succulence. I could barely contain my urge to feed. My mind was sharp and focused and yet my body panged with hunger. My fangs sliced through my gums, my eyes glimmered and my veins burned, frenzied. It was incredibly difficult pretending as though the scent of fresh human blood didn't invigorate me. I looked ahead. The humans were tied together, sitting back to back on the ground. Their heartbeats were faint, but their blood smelled divine. I watched them like a hawk and when I moved closer I was stopped by the sudden pressure of a hand pressing against my chest. "Christian," I uttered in surprise.

"This is exactly what he wants you to do."

"You're right," I said ashamed.

"Then why are you doing it?"

I looked ahead. The humans were bait and here I was literally about to walk right into the beast's trap. *What the hell was wrong with me?* I was angry with myself for even slightly succumbing to the lure of the blood. I was losing control; as though I'd become some mind-dead host for the growing creature within me and no matter how hard I tried to resist, *it's* cravings were dominating.

"Hope," Christian whispered.

"Yeah," I said quickly. I didn't want him puttering around inside my thoughts—it would be the last way I'd want him finding out about the baby—our baby.

"Are you okay?"

I nodded, feeling the sting of my fangs retracting back within my gums again.

"When those trees started collapsing in on us I thought I'd lost you."

"Me too."

He kissed me on the cheek. "I've been looking for you everywhere. Where'd you go?"

I shrugged, my thoughts moving to Eradan—my time-shifting superman.

"It doesn't matter," he uttered. "I'm just glad to see you're safe." He pulled me against him and squeezed.

"Christian! You're hurting me!" I teased.

He smiled and lessened his grasp. I pressed my head to his chest. The beat of his heart practically shook my ear with the vigor of its thump. I withdrew. "Your heartbeat!" I exclaimed.

"What?"

I pressed my ear to his chest again and listened. "My god Christian!"

"What?"

I listened carefully.

BOOM!

The beat was still sluggish, but far more forceful than usual.

"What is wrong with my heart?" His voice was hard.

"It's strong," I uttered. "Louder than I've ever heard it before." I leaned against him again. I closed my eyes and indulged in the sweet scent of his skin when suddenly *BOOM!* The strike of his heartbeat virtually thrust me away.

"Jeeze," he laughed.

I nodded bemused.

He pressed his hand over his own heart and waited for the thump. *BOOM!* His face lit up instantly. I put my hand next to his on his chest. We waited patiently together for the next beat and there it was— *BOOM!*

"Isn't it wonderful," he gushed.

"Wonderful," my eyes narrowed.

"I'm getting stronger!" he exclaimed. He kissed me on lips and smiled. "Now let's figure out how to rescue these humans shall we?"

He withdrew and walked closer to Maddy's parents. I kept my eyes on him the entire time. There was a renewed confidence in his step as he moved. What was going on with Christian? *Getting stronger*—the strength of his heartbeat suddenly changing should have troubled him not delighted him the way it did.

"Hope," he shouted. "The humans are barely breathing. I'm not sure how we'd get them to safety without killing them at this point."

I pulled my eyes away from Christian to look at the humans again. They were virtually lifeless and riddled with wounds.

"The beast dug right into the man with his teeth," he said, "but he only nicked *her* with his nails."

I nodded. "He wouldn't bite her."

"Why not?"

"Same reason he couldn't bear swallowing Alex's blood—she's a woman." I scrutinized the wounds from a safe distance. "Hum," I uttered. "If female blood weakens him, do you think it could kill him?

"Well..."

"I mean if he drank enough of it...do you think it might work?"

Christian smirked.

Just then the sound of a woman shouting distracted us. My ears perked up instantly. "That sounds like Alex," I uttered.

"Think she's in trouble?"

"Definitely." I started off.

"What about the humans?"

I stopped walking. "Find Alex, kill the beast and then come back for the humans."

"They'll die if we just leave them bleeding like this."

I hesitated for a moment. "Maybe I can fix that." I moved toward them and dug a slit in my wrist with my sharp fingernail.

"What are you doing?"

"Helping them," I said letting a little of my curative blood fall into their lacerations. Their wounds began healing straight away.

Christian smiled.

"What are you smiling about?"

"I'm just impressed."

"With what?"

"How good you are at this."

"At what?"

"Being a vampire."

I grinned, his flattery filling me with self-assurance.

"It took me decades to have the kind of confidence you have already."

I beamed.

Christian's face hardened. "Hey," he said concerned, "your arm. It's glowing again."

I looked down. The scar smoldered dimly.

"He must be getting close. It's not too late to leave you know."

"Christian," I chided. "I'm not leaving. C'mon." A moment later I was speeding through the trees, the sound of Alex's shouts leading the way.

Rays of sunlight stippled the surroundings. Daybreak was close at hand and our race against time was well under way. *Tick. Tock. Tick. Tock.* The crocodile's breath tickled the back of my neck as I soared. I pushed onward. We followed the length of the stream along the edge of the woods until we reached a clearing.

"There," I said noticing Alex immediately. She was standing atop a stretch of low lying candytuft evergreens hollering and singing at the top of her lungs.

"Siren!" she shouted spotting me. She stumbled closer, staggering as she moved.

"Are you okay?" I asked.

"Never better," she giggled. "Shh," she whispered.

"What is it?" I asked looking around.

"Careful the man who digs a grave for he might fall in himself." Her eyes widened terrified and then she started laughing again.

Christian leaned in close to her and sniffed. "She's three sheets to the wind."

"You're drunk?" I snarled.

"I is happy!"

I looked down. She was swinging a flask around in her hand. "Where did you get that?"

"The little cottage," she hiccupped, "in the woods...over that way... or maybe that way..."

"The boathouse?" I asked.

"Ain't no boats in the cottage," she laughed to herself.

Christian nodded. "That's Eva's flask. It's definitely from the boathouse."

Alex staggered toward me tripping over her own feet. She fell to the ground.

"Get up," I insisted angrily. "We've got to get out of the woods."

"Nay I say!" She laughed again.

I started prying her up by her arms.

"Hope," Christian said motioning toward my arm again.

I looked down. The scar was glowing a little more brightly.

"We better get moving," he insiststed.

"Okay." I tugged at Alex's arms. She was limp and uncooperative. "How can we expect her to help us fight like this?"

"We can't," Christian replied.

"Alex!" I shouted angrily. "I didn't summon a witch to undo your curse so that you could get drunk damn it! Get up. We need your help!"

"Alas!" she shouted wearily. "Go on without me Siren. Tell the mates me ship has come ashore."

I slid my hands under her arms and pulled her up like a child. "The beast is coming. And he's coming now! You need to get out of the woods."

"Beast!" she panicked woozily. "Here? Now?"

I nodded. "That's what I've been telling you!"

"Well why didn't you say so Siren?"

I rolled my eyes. "We've got to get out of the clearing." I yanked her to a standing position.

Just then the beast howled. I turned around and scanned the woods. "He's there," I whispered watching his iridescent eyes glimmer through the trees.

"Let me take Alex to safety," Christian said. "You should get away from here—as far away as you can."

The beast howled again, his deep tone echoing like thunder.

"Hope," he insisted edgily.

"What if you distract him?" My eyes lit up. "Lure him away so I can bring Alex to safety. That way I'll be safe too."

He nodded. "Not a half-bad idea."

I propped Alex's arm around my shoulders and held her by the waist.

"I like you Siren," she whispered affectionately.

"I like you too Alex, but right now we're gonna have to make a run for it."

"A run?" she panicked.

"You ready?"

"I ain't barely able to stand let alone run!"

Christian stroked the side of my arm. "Be careful," he warned.

"I will."

He nodded. A moment later he was gone.

"Where'd he go?" Alex asked puzzled.

"To distract the beast."

"Why?"

"To give us a head start so we can get away to safety."

"That was nice," she slurred, "being that he's upper rank."

We started walking when suddenly there was a rustling in the brush behind us.

Alex froze, her body tightening with fear. "What was that?" she panicked.

I peered over my shoulder and scanned the trees. "Don't know. Just keep moving."

The rustling started again. I moved my eyes to the woods behind us when suddenly I spotted the shadow of the beast. He was shifting between the trees, skulking between branches. His long dreadlocks moved like snakes as he prowled. I tightened my grasp on Alex's waist and said, "In three seconds I'm going to tell you to run. Are you ready?" I sighed. "Run!"

I squeezed her tightly and pulled her along with me. We tore off at top speed! Alex kept up pace pretty well for a human. Her strides even synchronized with mine for a few seconds, but before long I felt her falling behind.

"I can't," she uttered breathlessly, her body giving way beneath me.

I peered over my shoulder again. Trees were snapping at their centers and foliage was whirling in the wake of the beast's merciless approach. "C'mon," I insisted.

"Just leave me," she pleaded dragging.

I pulled her close and hoisted her over my shoulder. Her limp body hung like a sack of rocks against me. I started running again.

"Faster Siren! He's right our heels!"

I quickened my pace, but the beast quickened his too and before long he was right behind us.

"Siren!" she hollered. "He's...he's..." And then she screamed.

Silence resounded. The sound of ripping flesh came next as the scent of Alex's blood suffused my senses. My body hungered in response. My fangs shot through my gums and the craving in my belly began dominating again, but I pushed on and continued running. My effort to escape the beast was failing miserably when just then an inky apparition manifested before my eyes. I stopped dead in my tracks.

"C'mon. Jump on my back."

It was Eradan—my own personal time shifting superhero and he was here to save me yet again! I dug my feet into the ground and rushed toward him. He pulled Alex from my shoulder and tucked her tiny body under his arm.

"C'mon," he uttered. "Time's a wasting." He smirked.

I grabbed his shoulders and jumped on his back. "Thank you," I whispered relieved, but Eradan moved with a speed so fast I wasn't sure he'd even heard me at all.

46. Hero

My body fluttered with delight as my secret superman sailed us to safety. How had he found me again? Why had he come? My head flooded with questions as I felt him decelerating to a stop.

"You'll be safe here," he said setting us down within a tangle of tree roots.

"Thank you," I uttered.

He nodded and laid Alex on the ground beside me. "This place is pretty concealed from the rest of the woods."

I looked around. "I know this place!" I said shocked. It was the mangrove estuary where Christian had saved me when I was a child. "I've visited this place hundreds of times in the past, but never actually returned here in the present."

Eradan smiled. "Funny, isn't it?"

"What?"

"How surreal reality actually is when you deconstruct it."

I grimaced. He was way too philosophical for my taste.

He cleared his throat. "Does it bother you that I stepped in to help again?"

I shrugged. "You're a hero. That's what heroes do."

He smirked.

"And this time you got to save not one, but two damsels in distress."

He smiled, but before long his face hardened. "You are aware of the consequences correct?"

"Residuals." I rolled my eyes.

"I can't predict how they'll manifest or even when."

"It's okay. It's worth it."

His brows knit together in the center of his forehead just over the top of his circular spectacles.

"Don't look at me like that," I reproached.

He ran his gloved fingers through his long, dark hair and smiled just as Alex started stirring. "I have to go," he said hastily.

"Just stay with me. I want to talk a little longer."

He grinned, his pretty lips curling up in a gentle smile.

"Please," I pleaded.

"I can't."

"Oh c'mon, we've already ruined reality. What difference does it make now?"

He laughed. "You really are capricious aren't you?"

Just then Alex groaned, her eyes flitting open.

"Eradan," I uttered.

"Till we meet again," he whispered and with an inky blot of color he was gone.

My heart sank in my chest. I was starting to enjoy our brief trysts. I bit my lip wondering when I would see him again.

"Oh me head!" Alex complained.

I looked toward her, the sweet smell of her blood invigorating my senses. "You're bleeding," I said.

"I is?"

"Let me take a look." I moved closer, lowered her tattered coat and examined the wound. "He scratched you with his nails, here across your back."

"Got a dressing for it?"

"I can do better." I brought my wrist to my lips and tore into my flesh with my sharp teeth. Blood emerged instantly. I hung my arm over her shoulder and let my blood drip into her wounds. Her skin began healing right away. "There. You're all fixed now."

"Much obliged," she uttered stretching her arm across her body to feel the newly mended skin.

I nodded at her and noticed something out of the corner of my eye. I turned toward it and extended my gaze. I saw a person—or maybe a line of people running in a row darting through the trees.

"Siren?"

"Shh," I uttered. I swept the forest with my eyes and I saw them again. They were mesmerizing and moved with an inexplicable swiftness. And as I looked closer I realized the startling translucence of their appearance. Brilliant trails of shimmering gold followed behind them as they moved. I skulked closer and widened my eyes. As I looked upon them I felt as though I was looking at phantom, reflections of myself. I edged even closer. Just then a woman, in the flesh, popped up in front of me! I stumbled and fell to the roots underfoot! I hurried to get up again when suddenly I realized that I had been surrounded by women. *Real women*! Young women of all kinds encircled me. I studied them intently, eyeing the peculiar blank expressions on their faces.

"Hope," a familiar female voice beckoned.

I turned toward the sound. "Ryan?" I exclaimed. "Is it really you?"

"Yes," she replied.

She was here in Perish, but why? My thoughts quickly darkened. "What are you doing here?" I asked concerned.

She shrugged. "I don't know." Her face was as bleak as the others.

I moved toward her. "Who are these women with you?"

She shook her head. "Friends."

I looked around again, scrutinizing them.

"This was the last place I remember feeling safe," Ryan uttered. "I had nowhere else to go," she sighed, "and neither did they."

My eyes narrowed. "Where did you all come from?"

"The south. I was looking for a new life—my own piece of paradise remember? I went to Mexico."

And then it hit me. *Reina*. Once I destroyed her, I destroyed her bloodline as well. This was the residual of obliterating her before she became a vampire. These women were her disciples; workers in the Mexican blood trade and now they were here on Perish with virtually no memory of anything that had happened to them.

"I'm sorry," she apologized. "I shouldn't have come."

"Don't apologize," I said embracing her slight frame. "You did the right thing." I eyed the women again. "Are they all vampires?" I asked.

"No," she said withdrawing. "Some are human, but we all feel an inexplicable kindred connection to one another."

"Do you know how you met them?"

Ryan shook her head. "I was on the beach with them in Mexico and something happened."

"What?"

She shrugged. "I don't know. I felt it. We all did. It was like everything changed and suddenly none of us knew why were on the beach in the first place."

I bit my lip.

"Mia, Fiona and Giselle were defectors from the north like me. Some of the other girls have sustenance implant scars on their wrists too. But a few others like Alessandra and Ana..." she shook her head, "no scars. They're humans," she whispered. Ryan's dark eyes glimmered. "Why would we feel so connected to each other? It doesn't make any sense."

I patted her shoulder, guilt cutting through me like ice. A moment later I was startled by a tall girl with dark auburn hair smiling at me. I withdrew from Ryan and moved toward her. "Hello," I greeted extending my hand.

"Hi," she replied. We shook.

"What's your name?"

"Maria."

Maria, I thought to myself and suddenly I recognized her! She was the one with Lobo at the festival in Mexico, the one who gave me the marigold and took us to meet with Ryan. I nearly didn't recognize her; her face was painted like a pretty skeleton the last time I saw her.

"Have I met you before?" she asked, an expression of vague recognition on her face.

I smiled. "My name is Hope."

"Hope," she grinned.

Just then I realized that some of the other women had moved closer too. I turned to my left and shook hands with a short blonde. "Hello," I said.

"I'm Sandra," she introduced.

"And I'm Ana," another girl interrupted.

"Hi," I said shaking her hand too and before long I'd met almost all eleven girls. A swell of emotion stirred within me. Tears welled in my eyes. I felt hugely responsible for these women.

"Hope," Ryan uttered. "We don't want to impose on you, we just didn't know where else to go."

"You're not imposing. Believe me. You've just come at a bad time."

"What do you mean?"

"We've had a much unexpected visit from an old acquaintance on our shores—a very dangerous acquaintance."

"Do I know him?"

"It's Christian's maker," I divulged. "He's very old and incredibly strong."

"And he's after Christian I presume?" Ryan's dark eyes glimmered.

"No. He's after me actually."

"You?"

I nodded. "It's a long story. I don't have time to tell it to you right now. In fact," I said addressing the entire group of women. "I could really use your help. All of you."

"Oh Hope," Ryan said. "I'm not sure they can handle something like this. It was emotional enough travelling all this way to find you." She leaned in close. "Look at them," she whispered. "Some of them are barely even teenagers. They're vulnerable, scared and confused. They aren't fighters Hope. I'm not trying to disappoint you. I just don't think we can help you."

I nodded, the weight of that disappointment sitting heavily in the pit of my stomach.

"You understand right?" Ryan's voice was poignant.

"Of course. What was I thinking?" I grinned. "Your safety should be my chief concern. In fact," I said looking around, "I was in the midst of bringing another young woman to safety when you startled me." I withdrew from Ryan and began looking for Alex. "Alex!" I shouted. She didn't reply "Hey Alex," I called again, but she still didn't reply. I rushed back to where Eradan had left us at the mangrove estuary. She wasn't there. I hurried toward the thicket of trees up ahead. She wasn't there either. She was nowhere.

"What's the matter Hope?" Ryan asked following behind.

"My friend, Alex, I can't find her."

"You know I'd offer to help you, but someone has to stay with them."

"I know," I said. " Look, follow the water's edge west until you reach the boathouse. You and the girls will be safer in there than out here in the woods."

"Thank you," Ryan replied. "Thank you so much Hope."

I nodded in reply and watched her leave when all of a sudden I heard the shrill sound of Alex screaming again. I'd grown quite accustomed to hearing the shrill resonance of her sound. I extended my gaze. I saw tall trees swinging like twigs in the distance once more. I looked down at my arm. My scar glowed with a dim orange tinge. *He was close.* I swallowed hard! The sun shone through trees. God rays of light illuminated the path in front of me in shafts of radiance. Alex screamed again. I dug my heels into the ground and sped through the forest in an effort to save her.

47. Dupe

His big, beastly back swayed as he stomped like King Kong. Alex's slight body hung from his burly arms. I quickened my step and soared like a bird until I was right behind them. When I got close enough I lunged on his back! The force of my body pushed him to the ground. Alex flew from his arms and landed ahead in the bushes. The beast howled! He fell against the ground, hitting his head on the edge of a rock.

"Y-o-u!" he growled. I sprung from his back and spun around to face him. Blood seeped from the wound on his head and trickled down his face. His eyes burned and he was infuriated! He then charged me! I moved instantly, but the beast was fast and before I knew it he was right behind me!

"Y-o-u!" he howled again. There was a bone-chilling ferociousness to his tone that virtually shook the ground beneath me.

I ran like hell until I found shelter within the rotted hollow of an old tree trunk. I ducked inside. A moment later I heard a voice. It was sultry and snarky. *Eva*, I contemplated. I peeked out from inside the tree hollow. The beast was standing merely a few feet in front of me. He shot daggers at me with his dark eyes when suddenly Eva stepped between us.

"Come on!" she said. "I've got what you want!"

My eyes bulged. She had transformed herself into a young, ginger-haired man and she was virtually sacrificing herself to trick the beast in an effort to protect me! My body enlivened with verve.

"Come on!" Eva taunted. The beast lunged at her in compliance! Her body hit the ground instantly. The beast went in close for a taste. He pinned her down, pressing his huge hands upon her slight frame before sinking his teeth into her neck. Eva yelped with the penetration before erupting in a burst of snide laughter. "Drink it!" she snarled. "Drink every damn drop!" her voice was resolute.

I listened to the sound of his sucking. If the beast imbibed enough of Eva's blood he'd be weak. If the beast imbibed more than enough, he'd be dead. I smiled, my eyes glued to them when suddenly I heard my name being called. I peered over my shoulder. "Eradan?" I said perplexed.

"Stop this," he insisted.

"Stop what?"

"Him and her. You must stop it now."

"But why? Everything is working as planned."

"It's not."

"Eradan," I said. "Maybe you don't understand. That's my friend Eva. She can shift in and out of form. She's really a woman."

"But the child she's carrying in her belly is not."

I froze. "How did you know about the—"

"Hope they'll both die if he doesn't stop drinking from her. Do it now!"

My thoughts were like an emotional explosion inside my head.

"Don't think," he said. "Just react."

Eva was quite competent and I had every faith in her ability to deceive the beast. If I left I could make it to the boathouse without the beast following after me and I'd be safe. On the other hand, if Eradan was right about the unborn child in Eva's belly, the beast would drink her dry and end up killing them both.

"Hope!" Eradan shouted. "What are you waiting for? Do it now!"

I nodded in reply. The choice was made. I rushed through the trees in a determined effort to save Eva when suddenly I felt time slowing to a virtual stop. I looked to my right. Christian was standing at my side grasping my hand.

"What do you think you're doing?" he barked.

"Saving Eva. Now let go of me!"

"Eva can take care of herself. If the beast sees you...if he even realizes you're still here..."

"You don't understand Christian." I struggled to free myself from his grasp. "Let go of me!"

"Why?" he said eyeing the way the scar burned on my arm. "So you can get yourself killed? I don't think so."

My blood boiled. I pursed my lips and fluttered my eyelashes and suddenly the world reanimated itself again. I pushed Christian out of my way and stormed toward Eva and the beast. "Hey!" I shouted. The beast stopped sucking. I edged closer. He drew his eyes upward toward me and grinned, blood oozing from the corners of his broad mouth.

"Y-o-u!" he growled frenzied.

"Yeah me," I said tauntingly.

I looked him in the eyes, grinned back and then started running like hell! I tore off into the woods, darting in and out of the trees with swiftness knowing that he would follow. My feet carried me like the wings of a bird and yet somehow the beast was quicker. He moved with a speed I couldn't fathom. He was fast and fierce and closing in on me. I looked ahead. A patch of tall pines stood in the distance. I quickened my pace and hurried toward them just as I felt the beast's rancid breath on the back of my neck! A moment later he swiped at me, swatting hard, knocking me to the ground only a few feet shy of reaching the base of the tree. He howled furiously. I sprang to my feet, looked him in the eyes again and then leapt through the air toward the tree. My body hit the trunk with a thud. I wrapped my arms around its girth and started scaling the slim stalk. Loose bark and moss made my ascent difficult, but within an instant I had reached the top! My vantage point was perfect; I was looking down upon the woods—down upon the beast!

He howled again struggling to make the climb himself, but his huge body was far too heavy and awkward for any branch to hold. He stomped on the ground. The earth heaved with instability. The tall pine I was sitting in swayed like a willow in the wind. I grabbed the trunk a little tighter and tried to steady myself. When the ground settled and everything stopped shaking, I realized that the beast was gone! He wasn't in the tree with me and he wasn't standing at the base of the tree anymore either.

My heart thumped a thunderous strike in my chest. *Where was he?* I climbed down a little further to get a better look. I widened my gaze and froze! He was still there, at the foot of the tree, standing several feet away. He was fuming mad; hissing, snarling and growling like an animal, only he wasn't directing his rage toward me. His dark eyes were fixed on the throng of young woman that had suddenly surrounded him. My body swelled with elation at the sight of their presence. I was beyond grateful that Ryan had convinced her friends to help fight the beast. Now we had strength in numbers. He wasn't going anywhere! Encircled by an army of renegade women, their blood was enough to keep him trapped for as long as it would take me to annihilate him once and for all. He howled into the wind.

"Are you up there Hope?" Ryan shouted.

"Gald to see you made it!" I replied.

"Well you better have a plan honey." Her tone was emphatic.

The beast howled again. Some of the women gasped and screamed while others, the more plucky ones, prodded him with branches.

"We can't hold him off forever," Ryan shouted.

She was right. I had to do something and quickly. "Hey!" I barked. "Y-O-U!" I taunted.

The beast turned around and moved back toward the tree again. He neared the trunk and drew his eyes aloft.

"It's me you want." I smirked. "So come and get me!"

Fury instantly boiled in his dark eyes. A moment later I watched as he tried scaling the stalk again. He wrapped his big burly arms around the trunk and started climbing and this time it was working! I panicked! I ascended even higher until I was nearly at the top again. I swallowed hard and scrutinized my surroundings. I looked up. There was a small knot in the tree just within reach. I pulled myself toward it, but the beast was suddenly right on my heels! I tucked my legs tight to my chest and when I felt him underfoot I struck his head with the soles of my shoes! He growled, but he didn't stop. He reached up, struck me in the thigh, digging his sharp fingernails deep into my muscle!

"God!" I shouted succumbing to the pain. I let go of the branch and let myself slip down the trunk until I was right upon him. I fell against his massive chest. He was huge, covered with hair, scarred and reeked dreadfully and before he could respond I leaned in close and dug my teeth deep into his jugular. He howled stridently, the sound practically deafening me with its intensity, but I didn't falter. I continued draining him. His blood was rank and cold and instantly reminded me of Reina's. It was only a matter of time before I'd slip inside his past and soon discover his weaknesses.

Light and color merged together in a seamless unification. Sounds began to blur into a numbing stream of static. I was going in deep. The trees, the forest and even the beast himself disappeared from my vision. Reality at the moment warped into the wormhole that would lead me to the very heart of the beast's dubious past.

I moved quickly through the torrent of reminiscences until finally I spotted something familiar. I exhaled, breathing out in a single overwhelming burst. The concave time tunnel collapsed, shattering into millions of miniscule pieces. Colorful fragmented particles of the beast's past speckled the air like multihued ashes. Everything went dark and a boom so loud it practically deafened my eardrums cut the silence.

I opened my eyes. A thick haze hung in the air. The sounds of death drowned out the noise of the storm. The cries and whimpers of dying men stung my eardrums. I looked around. I was aboard the HMS Ambrose—again!

I moved through the haze and through the bodies. Stepping over corpses of the crew was like treading the battlefield after a war. I looked down. Their faces were gaunt, pale and virtually indistinguishable. Chunks of flesh had been torn from their throats; evidence of the beast's feeding frenzy. And then I heard something—the sound of sucking! I followed it until it led me to *him*—the beast! He was hunched over in the midst of feeding on someone. His back was to me. He was completely unaware of my presence. I needed a weapon. The corpse at my feet was grasping the hilt of a saber. I crouched beside him and pressed my hand against his sallow body. I slid my hand down his chest until my fingers met with edge of what felt like the saber. I pulled it out. It was lighter than expected and effortless to hold, but it was sharp. I rose to my feet, drew the saber and moved toward the beast.

All of a sudden a man jumped out in front of me! With a steadfast determination he rushed across the deck and charged the beast himself. My eyes widened, awed as I watched the valiant young man sacrifice himself to protect me when suddenly I realized that it wasn't any young man—it was Christian! His hair was long and his skin was flush, but I knew it was him. And for the stolen moments that my eyes fell upon him he was beautiful; full of life and fight. The saber slipped from my hands and fell to the floor of the ship. I was paralyzed; my mind and body in a state of utter distress.

I watched, stunned as Christian leapt on the beast's back. The beast stopped feeding and swatted him away like a fly. Christian flew through the air until smashing against the side of the ship. I could virtually hear his bones breaking inside his body. My eyes welled with wetness. I brought my hand to my face and wiped the stream of blood that had begun descending down my cheeks. I knew exactly what I was watching. It was Christian's last moments as a human and I couldn't bear the sight of watching it and longer. I inhaled.

I began moving instantly. Images flashed before my eyes. I felt sick inside as though possessing the power to shift though time was a curse. Seeing things I was never meant to see and changing things so that they never happened in the first place was more than dangerous—it was like playing god. I didn't deserve to have this kind of power—no one did.

The concave wormhole was long and shrouded in darkness. Images of the beast's past were dismal and drenched in death and yet somehow I felt fine begin trapped inside of it. Seeing Christian moments before he became a vampire affected me profoundly—much more than I would have assumed. It bothered me knowing that it was because of me he stepped in to attack the beast. It angered me knowing that I possessed the power to stop him, but didn't. I felt my heart breaking inside my chest. A breath was on my lips when suddenly I saw something inexplicable: a stunning brightness in the distance. Gleaming with radiance, the curious brightness filled me with a rush of optimism and when I came upon it I exhaled immediately. The wormhole collapsed. Everything went dark and the familiar boom resonated.

I opened my eyes. I was standing in a meadow. The sun was bright and the air was warm. A golden yellow glow tinged the surroundings. I looked across a field of purple lupine toward a large white oak tree in the distance. There were people ahead, two of them, a man and a woman. *The beast?* But when I neared it wasn't the beast at all. It was a young couple sitting together engaged in a picturesque afternoon picnic.

48. Fairchild

They were adorable, in love and utterly enchanting to watch. I couldn't take my eyes off of them. I was inexplicably drawn to them—the paleness of her sweet featured face and the radiance of his dark brown eyes. I edged a little closer and listened in on their conversation.

"Tell me Annabelle," the man flirted.

"Mr. Salazar," she grinned before playing with her long black hair.

"Tell me," he teased. "Sweet Annabelle."

She blushed, her fair cheeks flushing like red apples.

"Anna..." he purred.

"Mr. Salazar it would be impolite for a lady to reveal her deepest secret."

He pulled her toward him. She gasped and grinned all in the same moment. "Oh Anna," he said, "Do tell."

"I am a lady," she smiled. "I will not!"

He smirked. "And if that lady was but *more* than a lady?"

"*More* than a lady?" she giggled.

"A witch," he smirked. "Perhaps then might she divulge her secret to the man she loves?"

She grinned. "In time Robert. In time."

"Sweet Annabelle," he purred pressing his lips to her throat in a kiss. A moment later I heard the distinct sound of his fangs rising from his gums. I exhaled—*accidentally* and started moving again. Not a moment too soon I slowed to a stop. This time that same pretty dark-haired lady, Annabelle, was standing on a porch in mid-conversation with an elderly man.

"We do not mix with them!" the elderly man raged. "It is forbidden."

"Father!" she wailed. "You don't know Robert like I do."

"I don't need to," he said. "I know what he is and that is enough."

"Father, I beg you!"

"It will *never* happen Annabelle!"

"But it already has." She grasped her belly with her hands and stroked it gently.

"What are you saying?" he seethed.

"We are to be a family," she uttered.

"Blasphemer!" her father raged leaning in and slapping her across the face. She fell to the ground.

"How dare you!" a voice growled from the darkness. I looked behind me. It was the young man from the meadow, Robert Salazar. He approached them on the porch. He rushed toward Annabelle and swept her up in his strong arms, but he was different somehow. There was anger in his eyes and fury in his face.

I pushed an exhale from my lungs and started moving forward again until suddenly I was halted by a darkness so ghastly it virtually blocked my travelling altogether. I stopped shifting and when my eyes cleared I realized I was standing in a field surrounded by Pilgrims. It was night and only the blaze of their fiery torches lit up the surrounds. I looked ahead to the big tree at the top of the hill. Three women dressed in black were standing inside a horse-drawn wagon under that very tree. A thick rope was wrapped around each of the women's necks. Suddenly a man slapped the horse and the wagon sped off.

SNAP!

One woman fell to her death instantly, while another lingered, tormented by the noose choking her neck. The third woman looked like Annabelle. She hung in anguish with a little life lingering within her. And then I saw *him* again.

"Annabelle!" he shouted pushing through the crowd toward her.

"D-d-on't," she pleaded wearily.

"I won't let you die because of me!" he said wrapping his burly arms around her midsection and struggling to pry her from the noose.

"Blasphemer!" the Pilgrims hollered. "Witch sympathizer!" they continued and started pelting rocks at him. Their jagged stones scarred his flesh.

"It's...okay," she pleaded breathlessly. "L-let me g-go."

"No!" he shouted when suddenly a sizable stone struck him in the back of the neck! The impact knocked him unconscious. He fell to the ground right away and as he dropped he proceeded to pull Annabelle down with him—killing her instantly.

"Slay him!" the Pilgrims raged, their fiery torches blazing like the breath of a dragon.

I watched as two men in black clothing rushed over and abruptly carried Mr. Salazar away. I followed behind them and listened.

"Eternal damnation is not enough!" one man said.

"Stake him in the heart and cut off his head!" the other man added.

"Bring him to me," an elderly man demanded. It was him—the man from the porch, Annabelle's father. I looked a little closer. A small child no more than three or four years old was standing by his side. She was striking; snow white skin and jet black hair framing her petite features.

"Grandpapa," the girl whispered, frightened. "What has happened to father?"

The elderly man leaned down, cupped the child's chin in his hand and sighed. "Oh child," he lamented, "this creature that lies before you is not your father. He is a demon. A beast! Do you understand me?"

The child nodded obediently. He nodded back before standing up again. He looked down upon Mr. Salazar and groaned. "I condemn you to live eternally as the monster that you are," he said. "You will never feed upon the blood of a woman again. You will live in torment without the privilege of death unless mercy is met by the hand of my daughter's bloodline...the Fairchild bloodline."

I froze instantly. *Fairchild? I was a Fairchild.* My heart thumped in my chest. Just then a blast of energy emitted from the elderly man's hands! The vivid beams stretched the space between the elderly man's finger tips and Mr. Salazar's body. It was magic, the same kind of magic I'd seen flowing from Rosa's hands in Ambrose House. It was strangely beautiful and tremendously powerful. I watched awed, when suddenly all of Mr. Salazar's refining qualities began disappearing. He was transforming—becoming the beast I'd always known him as.

The cracking of his bones resonated like thunder. His back contorted, severing his spine. I watched, appalled as sharp talons crudely extruded from his finger beds and before long his entire body was covered in a dusting of course hair. He then writhed in pain as his skin began stretching and pulling with a disfiguring elasticity. He was mutating entirely. Any shred of his former humanity had vanished altogether!

I exhaled.

I moved with an incredible velocity, my heart in my throat the entire time. I couldn't watch any longer. I closed my eyes and bit my lip.

Fairchild. The name couldn't escape me. My mother was a Fairchild and my grandmother too. *I was a Fairchild!* My mind flooded with questions. I instantly recalled the number of cryptic journal entries I'd read in Moira's diaries. I remembered her calling Fate a dark sorcerer and complaining about my mother refusing to embrace her own potential. I remembered my grandmother's plea as an ambassador of goodwill, imploring that her daughter and her daughter's daughter and those thereafter might finally realize their own truths and thus the power of their birthright. Was *this* revelation that birthright—a maternal bloodline steeped in witchcraft that ran all the way back to colonial Salem?

I couldn't catch my breath. I wanted to die inside. The unraveling of this dark secret—this bizarre eye-opener, left me feeling irrefutably overwhelmed. Knowing that the beast was my forefather changed everything! He wasn't an enemy, he was an ancestor and he had been stalking me for centuries, through time even, with the intention of persuading me to end his life!

Nausea swelled within me. Blood pooled in the pit of my belly while my eyes welled with crimson tears.

I didn't know what to think. All I knew for certain was that I was a time-shifter and that I had been reminded on many occasions of the consequences of my actions. I knew I possessed the power to alter reality—change history even, and I was starting to think that maybe coincidence really didn't exist. William and Christian becoming vampires on that hazy night so long ago aboard the HMS Ambrose was no coincidence—the reason, as deeply as it pained me to admit, was in effect all because of me.

It was *my* presence on the ship that drew the beast there to begin with. He wanted me, not the crew, Christian, William or even Alex for that matter. *He simply wanted me.* The others were nothing more than residual-shrapnel. I felt sick inside knowing that their lives had been compromised all because of me.

My heart sank in my chest. I wanted to crawl up into ball and hide away forever, but I couldn't. I was moving so quickly through the concave time tunnel that I'd arrived back to the present again.

I opened my eyes. I was still on a branch, in the arms of the beast with my teeth lodged deep inside his flesh. I withdrew from him instantly. I bolted sideways to another branch nearby. Perched like a bird, I leaned closer and looked him in the eyes.

"Y-O-U," he groaned pathetically.

"I know why you've been looking for me."

His dark eyes widened.

"It doesn't have to end like this Robert."

He cocked his head to the side. I wondered if he even remembered hearing the sound of his own name.

"You don't have to die," I insisted. "There are other ways."

"N-O!" he grunted, the tree shaking as he spoke.

I struggled to steady myself. "I know someone. She may be able to reverse what they did to you."

"N-O!" he growled again only this time his fierceness shook the tree significantly.

Like a blade of grass in the wind the tree teetered back and forth when suddenly, *SNAP!* Branches broke as the trunk splintered. I slipped from the branch beneath me and began my descent to the ground. Sharp, timber shards grazed my skin as I fell. *THUD!* I hit the dirt with a bang, my bones shattering upon impact. An instant later I felt the weight of the world crashing down upon me. *SQUIISH!*

My body sank into the dirt underneath. I couldn't move! I couldn't breathe! I was trapped beneath the big, burly body of the beast—Mr. Robert Salazar.

A moment later I felt someone trying to pry me out. Face first in the dirt, with my arms extended over my head, I let my rescuer remove me from beneath the beast.

"I've got you," a tender voice soothed.

Christian. He'd come to my rescue. My heart swelled with elation as he liberated me from beneath the body of the beast. I opened my eyes, rolled onto my side and instantly felt myself starting to heal again. Bones cracked back into place while wounds repaired with ease. I propped myself up to a sitting position and looked toward the beast. His big body was splayed on the ground. He was motionless. I stared at him aghast. Hundreds of splintery tree branches had staked his back—a few had even pierced right through. He could have fallen anywhere—but he chose to fall on top of me in an effort to shield me from the blast of the falling tree. Crimson tears welled in my eyes. I rushed toward him instantly.

"Hope!" Christian shouted.

Ryan's women had already surrounded his unmoving body. They were standing in a tight circle prodding him with their rudimentary weapons.

"He's dead," Ryan uttered.

"No," I said shaking my head. "Not yet."

I knelt down beside him on the ground. I leaned in close and tried listening to his heart—or at least what was left of it. And then *BOOM!* He was alive—but just barely.

"Robert," I whispered. "Let me help you. Let me give you back your life."

"N-O," he groaned despairingly.

"You can live again. A *real* life, like the one you used to have."

"N-O."

"Why?"

He fought to lift his head and mustered a smile. "Anna-belle," he uttered emotively.

Sorrow shot through my veins. Robert Salazar didn't want his life back; he wanted death—he wanted to be reunited with his beloved Annabelle again and he'd been trailing me through time to make it happen.

I smiled back. "Are you sure this is what you want?" I looked into his eyes as though I was looking into the last shred of his soul.

"Wah-nt Anna-belle," he groaned.

"Then your Annabelle you shall have. Good luck to you Robert." I continued smiling. I sprang to my feet and grabbed the sharp wooden spear from Ryan's hands.

"Hope," Christian insisted. "He's already dead. What are you doing?"

I turned to him and nodded. "I'm giving him his happily ever after," and with a swift thrust I sank the blade deep within the beast's flesh, bearing down on the hilt with all my weight. The beast howled with the penetration and suddenly a blaze of light enveloped him. I recoiled, and watched in awe as his body started changing. His coarse hair disappeared, the sharp claws on his fingernails receded, his skin smoothed to some extent and his limbs virtually straightened out. After a moment the light dulled and the beast was gone. Only the remains of Robert Salazar were left behind. I rushed toward him.

"Hope!" Christian shouted protectively.

When I reached him I knelt down beside him. I ran my hand through his thick, shiny black hair and noticed that the scar on my arm was still glowing. Crimson tears welled in my eyes. My heart engorged with empathy. I hoped that I had done the right thing. I hoped that he really had been reunited with his Annabelle. A moment later his body burst into flames!

"Hope," Christian said pulling me away.

I watched from a distance as Robert's body burned the same way the vampires in Mexico did when they died. An instant later the flames became little more than a pile of ash on the ground. I looked down at the scar on my arm—it wasn't glowing anymore and I knew that it never would again.

I turned to Christian. I fell against him. He drew me close, into the safe circle of his arm and I began sobbing almost instantly. Overwrought with emotion, blood red tears flowed from my eyes, staining my cheeks and Christian's shirt as well.

"There, there," he consoled.

I squeezed him tighter. I never wanted to let him go.

49. Life

I wanted to tell Christian about everything I'd learned—about the fact that the beast was my ancestor, and that his name was Robert Salazar and that he was under a curse because he fathered a child with a witch named Annabelle, but somehow it didn't seem like the right moment.

The sound of Eva's screams echoed through the trees like another distress signal.

"What's that?" Ryan asked with concern.

"I think its Eva," I replied.

"Never ends," Christian complained withdrawing from me.

"Any more enemies out here that we should know about?" Ryan's voice was hard.

I shook my head.

"C'mon," Christian said. "We'd better check it out."

I nodded when suddenly a gust of wind blew past, disturbing Robert's ashes. I froze for a moment watching his remains dance on the breeze.

"Hope!" Christian shouted distracting me.

"I'm coming," I replied. I rushed toward the ashes and plucked a handful from the air. I stuffed them safely inside my pocket and turned toward the others again. I started to leave when Alex grabbed my hand stopping me.

"She wasn't good."

I looked at her confused. "Who?"

"Eva. I found her in the forest. She was bleedin' and her breathin'... it wasn't good."

"My god!"

"She sent me to find you."

"Okay," I said concerned. "Show me to her."

Alex nodded and all of a sudden we were hurrying through the forest toward the sounds of Eva's screams.

Eva wasn't hard to find. She was near the wide clearing safely tucked beneath a fallen tree trunk at the foot of a mossy knoll. A pool of fresh red blood surrounded her.

"Thank god you're here," Baptiste greeted anxiously.

"What's going on?" I asked.

"I don't know," he said panicked.

At that moment Eva let out another scream. I edged closer watching a rush of fresh blood ooze down her leg. I turned away from her and toward the others. "Christian," I said grabbing his arm. "Get B away from here. Find Rosa for me. Okay?"

"Okay," he agreed grabbing Baptiste by the arm and suddenly they were gone.

"Ryan," I insisted. "You, Alex and the others keep the area safe okay? Set up a perimeter. Can you do that?"

"Of course," Ryan nodded.

"Aye," Alex agreed and they all headed into the woods together.

I knelt down beside Eva on the ground and stroked her fiery, red hair.

"It's bad—isn't it?" she whispered weakly. Her voice was barely audible and her face was tense.

"Want me to lie?"

She struggled to laugh, panic and pain colliding in her single expression. She let out another scream.

"Shh," I consoled running my hand along her arm.

"Shh?" she barked. "Shh is not helping bitch!"

"Fine. Shout then!" I said.

She screamed again, twisting my hand like a corkscrew as she yelled. I looked down at her legs—another wet smearing of blood suddenly oozed.

"What are you looking at?"

"Your legs. I...I think—"

"Baby," Rosa interrupted waddling closer.

"Rosa!" I said relieved.

"Baby?" Eva snarled, "How can I be having—" and then she screamed again, even louder than before.

"She's in labor?" I asked shocked. "She can't be!"

"Why not?" Rosa asked.

"Because," I said. "She's still got six more years to go."

"Say who?"

"My friend Ryan."

Rosa kissed her yellow teeth.

"And her stomach is flat!" I said. "There's no way she's carrying a baby in there."

Eva screamed long and loud. Rosa put her hands on Eva's knees and pried her bloodied legs apart.

"What are you doing?" I asked concerned.

"Helping," Rosa snarled.

"Have you done this before?"

"With human, yes, years ago, but never with your kind."

I released Eva's hand. She grabbed me again and squeezed.

"Don't leave me!" she shouted.

"Okay. I'm not going anywhere."

Eva smiled, but then she screamed yet again only this time her body started vanishing.

"Look!" I shouted. "She's disappearing." I watched intensely as she began flickering like a weak channel on a TV set. "I've seen her do this before. Once when she was weak and she'd lost a lot of blood."

"Evelyn!" Rosa yelled. "Hear me!"

At that moment Eva suddenly appeared again. Her body was present and she wasn't flickering.

"Rosie!" she replied. "Make it stop!"

"I can't make it stop. Only you can finish this."

"NO!" she retorted suddenly flickering again.

"Evelyn," Rosa instructed. "You must do as you are told for once."

"NO!"

"Yes. And soon you must start to push."

"Push?" she snarled. "I can't!"

"C'mon," I added. "You can."

"Don't tell me what to do blondie!" She squeezed my hand even tighter. *CRACK! CRACK!* I felt my bones breaking inside my skin.

"Push or I will cut it out. You choose Evelyn."

"Cut it out!" she begged.

Rosa placed her hand on Eva's stomach and pressed. She shook her head.

"What is it?" I asked.

"It's coming too fast. I can't. She has to push."

"Eva," I said. "You have to push damn it!"

"No freakin' way!" she snarled locking her knees together in a steadfast bind.

"Eva," Rosa barked. "The baby cannot stay inside you anymore." She pried Eva's legs apart again. "Now push."

"No!" she shouted swiftly disappearing again. And as her body faded her skin became somewhat translucent.

"There it is!" I hollered looking within her flesh "The baby—I can see it inside her!"

She grabbed my hand and twisted like it was made of rubber. I winced with the pain as she vanished entirely. "Where'd she go?" I panicked.

"Dios mio!" Rosa uttered.

A moment later she reappeared again.

"Eva! Don't do that!" Rosa scolded.

"I'm not doing it!"

Rosa heaved a sigh. "When the pain comes, you push. Yes?"

"I can't," she said fighting to close her legs once more.

"You can. You will!"

"It's eating me," she wailed, "from the inside!"

"It only feel like that."

"It's got its teeth in me!" she squealed. "It's biting!"

"You are overreacting Evelyn!"

"I'm not! It's trying to gnaw its way out of me damn it! God!" she hollered. "This is torture! Get it out of me now!"

Rosa put her blood stained hands on Eva's knees and pried her legs wide apart this time. "Fine," she said. "This is it Evelyn. When the pain comes push as hard as you can. Okay?"

"Fine!" she roared.

Rosa was in full-on witchdoctor mode as she attentively sought to extract the baby before it devoured Eva entirely. All of a sudden Eva screamed again!

"Now push!" Rosa shouted.

Eva's face intensified and she struggled to push. She grasped my hand tighter than ever.

"Tear it out!" she barked.

"Push harder," Rosa insisted.

"I can't," she wailed, her body flickering like a dimming light bulb.

"Push!" Rosa demanded.

Eva's face tensed as she strained. Another long, loud scream left her lips. She grasped my hand with all her might, pushing my fingers backwards as she squeezed.

"Oh-my-god!" I yelled feeling my bones snapping like twigs beneath my skin.

Eva screamed again. "Get it out. Now!"

Rosa slid her hand deep within Eva's body.

"G-O-D!" Eva howled squeezing me harder. My wrist broke with the force of her grasp! I wanted to crumple with the pain when suddenly Eva freed my hand and collapsed lifelessly upon the ground.

"Eva!" I shouted in an effort to rouse her, but she didn't respond. Her eyes were closed and her face extremely pale. I pressed my head to her chest. *T-h-u-m-p.* Her heart was slow, but still boasting a beat. I moved my eyes up to Rosa. The expression on her face was virtually unreadable. She was holding something in her hand—something frighteningly tiny and covered in blood. I stood up and walked toward her.

"Life," she muttered teary-eyed, "even in death."

I looked down at her hand, at the miniscule fleshy thing squirming in the center of her palm.

"What is it?" I asked appalled.

"Eva's baby."

At that moment Eva stirred. She opened her eyes and struggled to sit up. "Where is it?" she panicked.

"Here," Rosa replied approaching her.

I scrutinized the strange creature in the center of Rosa's palm with fascination. It breathed and moved like a human despite the fact that it looked like a fetus in gestation.

"What is it?" Eva asked.

"Your baby," Rosa replied and it began to change. Right before our very eyes the infinitesimal living thing began growing! Its tiny torso swelled double its size. Its little head inflated like a balloon and its miniscule limbs sprouted long and lean. In a short time it was round and fleshy and looked like any ordinary infant cradled within the crook of Rosa's arms.

The bones beneath my skin began repairing as I drew my hand toward the porcelain skinned child to touch it.

"Don't," Eva snapped stopping me.

I withdrew straight away. It was *her* child—*her* moment and not mine. I watched eagerly as she took the newborn into her own arms and held it against her chest. The baby's eyes glimmered with a radiant silver iridescence. Eva looked down at it and smiled—a real genuine smile. I knew instantly that she would never be the same again. This baby would change her forever.

"A boy," Rosa uttered grinning. She stroked the child's white skin and suddenly the baby disappeared! Like smoke, the infant vanished into nothingness!

"Shit," Eva panicked. "It's a shifter," she uttered looking down at her empty arms. "Find it," she pleaded. "Please."

I nodded and rushed off into the woods. "Baby," I called out in a sing-song voice. "Where are you?" A moment later I heard the distinct sound of cooing in the bushes. "Baby," I hummed tenderly. "Are you hiding behind these big leaves?" I brushed some fronds aside and spotted the child. He was reclined on his back looking up into the sky. "There you are!" I said cheerily. He turned in response to the sound of my voice and giggled or maybe gurgled in reply. "Let's get you back to your mama," I said leaning in to reach for him when suddenly he vanished. "Oh no!" I muttered concerned. A moment later the sharp cackle of Eva's laugher startled me. I hurried back.

"Remind me never to let you babysit," she teased as I approached.

I grinned suddenly realizing that the baby was back in Eva's arms again.

"I called out to him," I said. "And he even responded with a gurgle, but when I went to reach for him he disappeared on me."

Eva froze. "You called out to him and he responded?"

"Yeah. He giggled or gurgled or something."

"Thank god," she said relieved. "I prayed he wouldn't be like me."

I stared at her in confusion. "But he is like you. He's a shifter."

"That's not what I mean." She heaved a sigh.

"What do you mean?"

"When I changed, I lost something."

"We all did," I said, "the ability to taste for Christian, Henry's sight, B's threshold for pain and my sense of fear."

"And me?" she retorted. "What exactly did you think I'd lost?"

I shrugged. "I guess I just assumed it was your tolerance for compassion."

Eva rolled her eyes.

"You don't have to tell her," Rosa interrupted.

"I know," she said, "but I want to." Eva focused her eyes on me. "When I changed," she said. "I lost my hearing."

My eyes widened with her words.

"Henry and I sure got the shit end of the stick didn't we?" She grinned. "Anyhow, I lip-read and I'm damn good at it too." Her eyes narrowed. "Look blondie, don't go treating me like some cripple now just because—"

"Thank you for trusting me," I interrupted.

She nodded in reply. Rosa smiled and I smiled too when suddenly the baby gurgled.

"Did you see that?" Eva said elatedly. "It's like he's listening to us."

"What will you name him?" Rosa asked.

Eva took a long look at the child and grinned. "Stromboli," she said.

"*Stromboli?*" I snickered. "Are you serious?"

"You gotta problem with it?"

"No," I replied. "I like it."

She kissed her baby on the forehead and smiled. "This is the best concoction B and I ever made together. Stromboli." She giggled. "And besides he looks like a Stromboli don't you think?" She ran her pale fingers through the tuft of black curls on the infants head.

I touched his hair too and smiled. "Can I call him Strombo?"

"Not if you want him to answer."

I grinned in reply as a warm wind blew past, sending a strange chill down my spine. A moment later I felt the rock in my belly again. It was hard like a lump, and terribly uncomfortable. Nausea overwhelmed me. Blood rose in my throat. I struggled to suck it back down again. Now wasn't the time for sickness; it was the time for celebration.

50. Magic

A trembling in the trees startled me. I moved toward it to take a look. "Who's there?" I shouted wondering how anyone could have gotten past the army of women I'd instructed to set-up a perimeter in the woods. I heard a voice.

"It's me."

I widened my gaze. "Eradan?" I spotted his long velvet coat behind the bushes. I moved toward him.

"Are you okay?" he asked.

"Yeah. Why?"

"And the beast?"

"Dead."

"So you did what you needed to do?"

"Yeah."

He grinned. "I have to go."

"Already?"

He smiled, his pretty lips curling up in the corners.

"Can't you just stay for—"

"You know the risks," he interrupted. "I really have to go. I just wanted to make sure that you were okay."

"I'm fine." I grinned.

"For now," he uttered ominously.

I raised an eyebrow.

"Till we meet again." He turned away.

"And when will that be?" My voice was more desperate than I would have liked.

He smirked, peering down at me from behind his peculiar circular spectacles. He reached out and stroked the side of my face with his gloved index finger. "You're never satisfied, are you?" he teased.

"What's that supposed to—"

"Just let the future unfold as it may," he interrupted and with an inky flash he was gone.

I touched my cheek and smiled. It was nice having my own time-travelling guardian angel watching over me. I hated his unpredictability and wished that I knew more about him, but for some reason his presence comforted me. I licked my lips and was startled by the soft sound of footfalls approaching.

"Is it safe to come back?" Christian asked timidly.

I rushed through the trees toward him. "Oh Christian," I sighed throwing my arms around him.

"Is Eva okay?" he asked concerned.

"Yeah. She's fine. The labor was dreadful but—"

"She had the baby?"

I nodded and grinned.

Christian gasped. "Wow!" he said taken aback.

"Where's B?" I asked looking around.

"He's waiting with Ryan and Alex. He's...freaking out."

I smiled. "Go and get him. He needs to meet his son."

Christian beamed. A moment later he was gone.

When I reached Eva she was all goo-goo eyed and cutie-voiced gushing over Stromboli.

"Where did you disappear to?" she asked with a snarl in her usual surly tone.

"I was with Christian. I told him to get B. They'll be here any second."

Eva's face lit up instantly. A moment later they approached. Baptiste's eyes widened as he set his sights on the child in Eva's arms. It was incredibly touching to watch.

"Well come on you cowardly lion," Eva barked. "Your son is waiting for you!"

"*Son*," he muttered awed, his face radiant with happiness. He quickened his pace and hurried to their side.

"Stromboli," Eva introduced. "This is your daddy!"

"*Stromboli?*" Baptiste uttered shocked.

"He's the best blend we ever made together B." Her voice was soft and emotive. Baptiste nodded in agreement and beamed in reply. An instant later she handed him the child. He took Stromboli in his big, burly arms and grinned. The love between the three of them was palpable. My eyes welled with tears as I watched. They were a family now—*a real family*. I reached out for Christian's hand. We laced our fingers together.

"That's crazy," he uttered watching.

"What?"

"They have a baby! It's crazy."

"But it's kind of amazing too—right?"

"I didn't even realize that she was ready to have it. I thought she still had like ten more years of pregnancy ahead of her?"

"So did I."

"Well what happened?"

"I'm not sure. All I can figure is that Eva's been keeping herself in one of her shape-shifting modes for a very long time."

Christian's eyes opened widened.

"Maybe she couldn't handle the idea of gaining pregnancy weight so she permanently morphed into the slim version of herself."

"Really? You think she would do that?"

I gave him a hard look. "It's Eva we're talking about here. That woman would do virtually anything to look good."

Christian nodded in agreement.

"See," I said, "I'm not the only one who abuses her ability!"

"Oh Hope," he said brushing his fingers through his hair.

"We can't all be as saintly as you Christian." I grinned.

He leaned in to kiss me when suddenly I felt my body kicking into gear! My fangs shot through my gums and I panged with hunger from deep within.

"Hope?" Christian exclaimed.

"Blood," I said. "I smell blood." I looked at his arm. Several small unhealed cuts oozed.

"Now Hope," he said retreating.

"Why haven't you healed?" My voice was suspicious.

"It's complicated."

I shook my head and gingerly inhaled his blood in the air. It was strong and succulent and different—almost human in scent.

"Please," he said receding. "I never meant to hurt you. Everything I did, I did for us."

"What?" I asked edging closer.

"Now don't overreact," he insisted continuing to walk backward, stepping over sticks and rocks and he moved.

"Christian!" I shouted following him.

"The truth is I didn't even know that there was a cure—at first."

"*A cure?*" I raged.

"And then Marco, when he came into La Fuente that day and wanted the tattoo with the flower—"

"Christian!" I growled. "Why?" when suddenly he stumbled over a rock. His lean body flew backward through the air before smashing down upon the edge of an even larger rock!

I rushed toward him. Blood was everywhere, on his arm, on the ground and even a small stream trickling from the corner of his mouth. I panged for a taste, but resisted diligently. I looked down. Goose bumps blanketed his pinkish colored skin. His face was flush and even his lips were rosy. I was crestfallen. "*Why?*" I sighed through my thoughts, "*why did you do this?*" but he couldn't hear me, and it was clear that he never would again. Our silent connection had been severed the moment he decided to take the cure. Panic overwhelmed me. "ROSA!" I shouted at the top of my lungs. "ROSA!" And within a few short moments she arrived, waddling through the trees toward us.

"What child?" she asked concerned.

"Christian," I said. "Look at him."

Her old eyes narrowed. Slowly she worked her way down to the ground next to him. She closed her eyes and touched his chest.

"Rosa?" I asked impatiently.

She opened her eyes again. "His heart beats," she uttered perplexed. She examined his skin, observing the blatant pinkish hue. "I-I not understand."

"He's human," I said. "Isn't he?"

She nodded shocked.

"It was Marco," I replied. "He's been working magica negra with Christian. I think they've discovered a cure."

"A cure?" Her voice wavered as she spoke.

"I need to speak with Marco. Can you bring him here? Please?"

Rosa sighed. She closed her eyes and called for him via their familial connection. She opened her eyes again, her grey brows knitting together in the center of her forehead.

"What is it?"

She shook her head.

"Rosa. What is it? Tell me."

"Something not right. Marco is...gone."

"What do you mean gone?"

"I cannot feel his presence." She shook her head infuriated.

"Is he okay?"

"There are consequences when working dark magic." Her voice was hard and menacing.

"Will he be back?"

"I not know. He must face the outcome of what he has done."

I sank my head in my hands. "What am I supposed to do now?"

"About what?"

I peered through my fingers at her. "About Christian. He took Marco's cure. He's human now!"

Rosa shrugged. "You are smart and very powerful, like your grandmother was. You will manage."

"You hated my grandmother!"

"Don't believe old stories." She reached out and pried my hands from my face. "There is much power within you child." She grinned. "If only you knew."

"What power?" I said frustrated.

"What power you think?"

I shrugged.

"Magic," she hissed.

My eyes widened with her words.

She laughed and got up again. "Don't look so frightened. I know you feel it inside of you." She grinned. She turned her back to me and started shuffling away.

"Rosa!" I shouted. She stopped walking and peered over her shoulder. "Even if I have felt it, I don't know anything about it. I don't know what to do with it or even how to use it!"

She smiled. "The Fairchild bloodline is rich with history. You come from that history. Trust your instincts." She nodded before turning back around and waddling away.

My heart sank in my chest, my head flooding with questions. A witch?! *How could I be a witch?* I sank my head in my hands again and sighed when suddenly I heard the sweet sound of Christian stirring.

"H-H-ope," he mumbled.

I moved to his side and watched awed as my Tin Man opened his eyes for the first time once more—only this time as a human again.

51. Promise

His eyes were green and bright and different and stared up at me with intensity. I could feel our promise of forever together hastily slipping away.

"Hope," he uttered.

"You scared me," I scolded.

"I'm sorry," he whispered tenderly. He rubbed his forehead and blinked his eyes a few times.

"Are you okay?" I asked.

"I think so."

"Are you human?" I sneered.

He sighed. "I wanted to tell you."

"But you didn't."

He pursed his lips and winced.

"What's wrong?"

"I'm not sure. I think maybe I'm injured."

"Yeah," I laughed, "you are. You hit a rock and you're bleeding. It hurts to be human doesn't it Christian?"

He grinned, stroked his wounds and sighed before struggling to a sitting position.

"My god," I scoffed examining his head wound. "It's barely even a scratch!"

He groaned.

"Big baby," I teased withdrawing.

He inhaled and grinned.

"What?"

"I feel...alive!"

"That's because you are," I groaned grudgingly.

"Can't you just be happy for me?"

My eyes narrowed.

"Please Hope."

I shook my head at him. "You lied to me."

"I didn't lie. I just didn't tell you."

"It's the same damn thing Christian. You took this cure without telling me."

He nodded ruefully. "You're right. I'm so sorry." He struggled to a standing position. "I should have told you."

"Yeah," I agreed, "you really should have." My eyes were fixed on the unexpected splendor of his fragile human frame.

He staggered closer. "How can I ever make it up to you? Tell me what to say to make it better."

I continued staring at him—at the alluring subtle differences in his renewed self. His hair wasn't as black, his eyes weren't as green and his skin wasn't nearly as pale as before.

"Say something," he pleaded.

I shrugged. I was somewhat speechless. Words were lost to me as I continued looking upon him.

"Hope," he uttered tenderly and then he smiled. His face radiated with attractiveness. Standing in the speckles of sunlight his humanity was palpable. I couldn't take my eyes off of him. Butterflies suddenly started trembling in the pit of my stomach. He laughed, the sweet delicateness of his sound shattering me into millions of frazzled pieces. My god, I contemplated, what was happening to me? I was attracted to him; hungry for his human blood, but also intensely attracted to him too!

"Please," he insisted. "Talk to me Hope." He cocked his head to the side and smirked, the expression on his face was volcanic with emotion. Every twitch of his brow and jitter of his lips was fascinating and I was captivated—utterly mesmerized by the novelty of his new precarious self.

He pressed his hand on his hip. I watched eagerly as the veins in his arm throbbed through his skin. Blood coursed through his veins—lots and lots of warm, human blood. I bit my lip again. He ran his fingers through his hair. I watched as each strand fell, but not back into place like before. Instead his dark locks simply dropped in a messy tangle aside his cheeks. It was wonderful. He was wonderful—flawed and real and simply breathtaking. I couldn't repress the urge to grin. I smiled instantly.

"You're smiling!" he exclaimed.

"I'm not."

"You are!"

His lips were like rose petals, but much plumper and more uneven looking. He slipped his hands inside the front pockets of his jeans hiking them down a little. I caught a glimpse of his hips. *Oh his hips*, they were defined and sexy and complete with veins that pulsated as his warm blood coursed through his new body. *Mmm*, I sighed inside my thoughts.

"I'm gonna miss that," he uttered startling me.

"What?"

"Knowing what you're thinking." He grinned.

I returned his grin and gingerly inhaled the curious scent of him. A careful breath was like heaven to my head. His robust tin-cinnamon smell was still effervescent and danced in my nostrils, but there was something more to his smell too. Succulent and mouth-watering his body was redolent of ripened fruit! And like a juicy apple, I wanted to savor in the sweet deliciousness of him. "Oh Christian," I sighed frustrated.

He folded his muscular arms across his chest, the sound of his strong heartbeat suddenly quickening. "I really am sorry," he apologized again, his eyes suddenly changing.

"Why?" I asked.

"You never would have let me take the cure if you knew the risks."

"You're damn right! What if it didn't work?"

"But it *did* work."

I pursed my lips.

"I trusted Marco." He eyed the woods. "Where is he anyway? I know he'll be pleased with the results."

"He's gone."

"Gone? Where?"

"I don't know."

"Will he be back?"

I shrugged. "He used black magic Christian. Rosa said there were consequences he'd have to face."

Christian shook his head, annoyed. "I suppose we both knew the risks we were taking."

I shot him an eye roll.

"What?"

"You really are a hypocrite you know."

He frowned.

"Lecturing me all this time about the *risks* of shifting through time and then you go ahead and take and even bigger risk yourself!"

"Hope..."

"I just can't believe you would do that."

"I know. And like I said, I'm sorry."

He touched my arm. His hand was warm against my skin. I trembled a little. I looked into his pretty green eyes and said, "I couldn't imagine losing you."

"And you'll never have to." He tightened his grasp. The feeling of his fingers against my flesh roused me instantly. He grinned.

"Promise me," I said.

"Promise you what?"

"That I'll never lose you."

He pulled me close. "I promise," he whispered.

I shook my head at him and pulled away. "You can't promise me that anymore."

"Why not?"

"Because you're human you idiot!"

His eyes widened. He pulled me close again. "Just for now," he insisted.

I grinned, intrigued.

"Why are you grinning?"

"Because, you're inviting me to change you back."

His face paled. "But you wouldn't—right?"

I smirked.

"Hope!" he pleaded, "at least have the decency to let me live for a while."

"Why?"

"Because there are so many things I want to experience again!"

"Like what?"

"Well for starters, the sun. I want to stand in the sun without having to endure the burn."

"Okay."

"And sleep. I want to sleep for hours and finally feel rested."

"And that's all?"

"No. Food," he laughed. "I want to eat a little of everything and finally remember what it's like to taste it!"

I nodded. "And nothing else?"

"Well..." he said sliding his hand around my waist. "There is one other thing I want to experience."

The air between us was electric. He was only a breath away.

"Hope," he whispered softly.

"Yes," I replied with bated breath. "Tell me," I sighed. "What else do you want to experience now that you're human?"

His eyes enlivened. "You," he said.

I grinned from ear to ear. He took me into his arms and held me tightly.

"I want you, he said, "more than ever."

"Hum," I replied, "but you're mortal now. I could break you. I could *kill* you."

He grinned. "I'm willing to take that risk." He thrust me against him.

"Christian," I exclaimed; his warm breath falling upon my face in rhythmic swells.

"I want to touch you Hope. I want to warm you with my body."

I beamed.

"I want to kiss your lips and taste the sweetness of your tongue."

I glanced at his face. He was incredibly handsome and somehow much more wholesome looking than before. The scruff on his jaw line was course and uneven and the twinkle in his eyes was vibrant and alive.

"Sweet Hope," he whispered nuzzling his face aside my ear. "I want you to melt under the heat from my hands. Here," he said guiding my fingers to his chest. "Feel my heart."

The steady pounding of my Tin Man's heart roused me eagerly. My eyes glimmered and I could feel my body abruptly kicking into gear again.

"Mmm," he whispered. "I want to make you come alive like never before."

My fangs shot through my gums instantly. The vulnerability of his sweet humanity had undoubtedly heightened my attraction to him. Like fire and ice our mouths came together; his lips on my lips and his tongue tenderly working its way inside my mouth. I slid my hand under his shirt and felt his skin erecting with the onset of my touch. I fluttered my eyelashes and felt the world around us suddenly slowing to a stop. We withdrew from each other right away.

"Hope!" he gasped. "How did you—"

"I don't know," I replied. I was shocked by the sudden acquisition of Christian's former ability to slow-down time.

I was awed and amazed and so was he and together we watched as flecks of dust hung in the god rays of sunlight around us. *BOOM!* My listless heart thumped inside my chest and for that one frozen moment our forever together seemed almost within reach again. I blinked my lashes and the world resumed its normal speed. I touched his arm. His skin shivered. I closed my eyes and let him kiss me again. He ran his warm hand along my back, over my hip and around to my stomach when suddenly I felt a thrust from within. My eyes flew open and I panicked.

52. Leap of Faith

"Hope!" Christian shouted.

"What?"

"Where did you go?"

"Nowhere."

"You disappeared on me."

"I did?"

He nodded and ran his hand across my waist when I felt it again—the thrust, only this time I was conscious of the movement. I bolted forward, through time, just a little. I inhaled and suddenly I was back again.

"What's happening?" Christian snarled.

"I don't know."

"Well stop it," he pleaded. "You're scaring me."

"I can't. I don't even know how I'm doing it."

He sighed and pulled me close again. "Just relax," he whispered and suddenly I felt myself easing under the foreign warmth of his fingers. He ran his hands over my hips and across my stomach again when it happened! *THRUST!* I shot forward—even farther than before. I was still in the forest, but somehow it was different. The trees were taller and much fuller looking. I widened my gaze. Christian was there too, but he looked different. He was older, still human, but a little older. Just then I started moving again and within an instant I was back in the woods—back where I began.

"Hope!" Christian chided. "Stop it!"

"Where was I?"

He shrugged. "You were here and then suddenly you vanished."

"How long was I gone?"

"A couple of seconds maybe."

My face furrowed. "I saw you."

"Me?"

"But you looked different. You looked older."

"Older!" he laughed. "Impossible. You would have had to shift into the future to have seen me older."

The future, I contemplated. I wasn't capable of moving ahead in time, only backward.

"Are you sure it was the future?" His voice was cagy.

I shrugged.

"C'mere," he said wrapping his arms around me. He grabbed my hips and started moving his fingers to my stomach again when suddenly it hit me. It was the touch of his hands to my belly that was triggering my travel.

"Touch me," I ordered.

"What?"

"Touch me," I insisted. "Touch my stomach."

"Why?"

"Just do it."

He ran his hands from my hips across my stomach again. *THRUST.* I moved ahead, only a little, but still ahead in time. I exhaled and returned back to the present again.

"Hope!" he snarled. "Stop playing games."

"I'm not," I replied."

I wasn't playing games, but the baby inside of me however seemed to think otherwise. The fact that our unborn child could be a time-shifter overwhelmed me. I was filled with elation. I beamed. I had to share my secret with him. It was finally time to tell him the truth.

"Oh Christian!" I gushed. I opened my mouth to speak when we were interrupted by the unexpected presence of Ryan and her friends.

"Hope!" Ryan shouted.

I sighed with disappointment and held onto my secret for just a little while longer.

"Your friend, the witch, she told us of the girl's parents. She said that they're still out here somewhere."

"Maddy's parents!" I exclaimed. I'd practically forgotten about them.

"God," Christian said. "I dread to think what condition they might be in by now."

"We need to get to them," I insisted.

"Let us," Ryan interjected. "We want to help."

I smiled at her in reply.

She smiled back, her dark eyes shifting toward Christian. "My god," she said perplexed. "Christian is that you?"

He nodded.

"You look...different." She inhaled the potent scent of his blood in the air. Her eyes widened. "Are you—"

"Human," I interrupted.

Her face paled even more than normal. "How?" she blurted.

"A cure," I said.

"A cure?"

"Yes," I grinned. I put my hand on her shoulder. "Free the girl's parents first. Make your way toward the clearing. If you've reached the water's edge you've gone too far. Take them back to Ambrose House. We can talk more there."

She nodded and grinned. "A cure...seriously?"

I nodded back. A moment later Ryan and her friends disappeared into the woods again.

Christian smiled. "This cure," he said. "It's going to change the world I tell you."

I slipped my hand inside the front pocket of my jeans. My fingers graced the beast's ashes. "You go on ahead of me," I insisted. "I'll meet you back at Ambrose."

"Why?"

"There's something I need to do first."

"Let me help you."

"No," I said. "I need to do this alone."

"Will you be okay...alone?"

"I'll be fine. It's you I should be worried about."

He grinned. "I guess the tables have turned, haven't they?"

"Be careful," I insisted.

"Okay."

I grinned. "Humans don't heal quite so easily."

"I'm starting to remember that," he replied stroking the gash on his head from the rock incident.

I smiled.

"Don't be long," he insisted. He kissed me on the forehead and then he left. He didn't bolt away or zoom off at supersonic speed—he simply walked. There was a carefree spring in his step as he moved as though the simplicity of walking was exciting enough.

I moved my eyes in the opposite direction. I looked toward the trees. I sped off into the pines faster than a rocket and before long I'd already reached my destination—the memorial grounds.

The three stone slabs sat in the distance. My mother, my grandmother and even my biological father William, had all been laid to rest here in this simple cemetery. It felt strange being so close to all of them at once and yet it comforted me deeply too. Even though I'd only just learned of this place, I was glad it existed. I walked toward the stones and smiled. I kicked up a patch of dirt at the foot of the slabs, reached into the front pocket of my jeans and gently pulled out a handful of ashes. I bent down and buried them there.

Robert Salazar might have been a beast and a killer, but he was also a lover, a father and most importantly, my ancestor. It felt right putting him here with the others.

I rose to my feet and kicked some dirt atop the ashes. I sighed. Most of my life I'd lived with half-truths, veils and outright lies. In recent days I learned that even reality was fairly pliable. I didn't know what to believe anymore. The only thing I knew for certain was that having the ability to shift through time was incredibly powerful. Possessing my unborn child's ability to shift through time into the future as well, was even more preeminent. Having that kind of power terrified me to the depths of my soul—and I wasn't afraid of anything. I didn't want to end up here beneath the earth like my ancestors. I wanted to live forever and savor in the glory of seizing eternity, but I needed to be careful. I needed to learn responsibility and find a way to harness the power within me.

I took one last look at the memorial stones before heading home. On my way back I heard voices emanating from the beach. I sped through the trees toward the water's edge. When I reached the sand I saw Ryan and her friends helping Maddy and her parents into the rowboat. I rushed ahead.

"Hey," Ryan greeted. "We found them in the woods. They were almost dead you know."

"God," I lamented a wave of guilt rushing through me. I felt awful for putting their rescue on the back-burner and then forgetting about them altogether!

"They're fine now," Ryan assured. "The girls and I fixed them up as best we could."

"Thanks Ryan. Really."

She grinned. "It feels good helping for a change."

I smiled.

"They're headed back to Cuba," she said. "I *veiled* them. They'll think they were lost at sea. They won't remember anything about what happened here."

"That's good, really good."

"What exactly did happen here anyway?" she pried.

I smirked. "It's a long story."

"I like long stories."

"Good," I said. "Because I've got a feeling we're going to be spending a lot more time together."

"You mean that?" There was a look of surprise on her face.

"Yeah," I said. "I want you to stay—you and your friends. Ambrose is your home too now. We don't have much to offer, but—"

She threw her arms around me and squeezed.

I smiled as she withdrew. "I know it isn't paradise, but the sun is hot, the air is warm, the sky is blue and the grass is always green."

Tears welled in Ryan's star-sapphire eyes. She beamed with bliss.

"Now," I said perking up. "Let's get this family home!" I turned to help the mother inside the boat when I spotted Maddy sitting in the sand sulking. "What's the matter with her?"

Ryan shrugged. "She won't talk. She won't come with any of us."

"Let me try," I said. I treaded through the sand toward her. She was hunched over and crossed-legged fiddling with something. I sat down on the sand beside her and smiled. "Hi," I said. She didn't respond.

"What are ya' doing?" She looked up at me. Her auburn colored eyes were alive and intense. "You family is waiting for you." She looked toward the boat, her tiny features tightening as she stared. "Don't you want to go home?" She shook her head from side to side. "Oh sweetie," I gushed. "You can't stay here. You don't belong here."

"Hope!" Ryan shouted. "C'mon!"

"I'm going to miss you," I whispered rising to my feet. I extended my hand to her. She eyed the scar in the center of my palm. I grinned. "I was about your age when I got that." Her eyes widened. She reached out and placed her tiny hand inside mine. We walked together toward the boat. I helped her inside. I let go of her hand when suddenly I realized that she had given me something. I looked down. Three living earthworms sat twisted in an impeccable braid in the center of my palm. My eyes widened. I looked up again, but the rowboat had already been pushed out to sea. Maddy and her family were gone.

I pursed my lips and drew my eyes to Maddy's worms again. I stared at their wriggling bodies. Maddy had left Perish for now, but not forever. I couldn't help but feel as though I was somehow destined to see her again...

"Hope," Ryan said startling me. "I want to know more about Christian's cure."

I turned to her and grinned. "I don't really know anything other than the fact that it worked."

"So when can I get some for myself!"

My eyes narrowed. "You'd take it? I mean you'd want to be human?"

"Of course!"

"Why?"

"Why not!" she laughed.

"You'd be fragile and weak..."

"Oh honey," she said. "I've been around for a long time. I just want to be normal for once." She smiled.

Normal. My mind swelled with questions again. What was normal anyway? Was humanity normal, or supernatural perhaps? Or maybe normal was a bit of both.

"I must tell the girls!"

"You'd better talk to Christian first. I don't know if he wants everyone knowing about this cure."

"Okay," she agreed. "Oh Hope, you have no idea what this could do for our kind. It could change everything, bring down the hierarchy. Destroy the society! We'd never be forced to live in the shadows of the north again!"

Ryan was talking about the vampire sects that had imprisoned her and so many others for centuries and what she was implying sounded like a revolution! A chill ran down my spine. It was only a cure—Christian never wanted to use it to start a war. *Or did he?* My heart sank in my chest.

"Thank you Hope," Ryan said startling me. "Thank you for trusting me with this."

I nodded. She wrapped her arms around me again and squeezed.

53. Truth

Ambrose House was alive with excitement. I'd never see it this active before. The interior of the house was in utter shambles, but that didn't seem to hinder the lively ambiance any.

I looked to the living room. Eva and Baptiste were doting over baby Stromboli, while Rosa and Henry stood by for moral support. Alex was in the study, cavorting with some of the more spirited women over several bottles of aged rum, while Ryan was in the hallway, preoccupying Christian in an intense conversation about the cure. I didn't belong anywhere.

I pivoted around on my heels and walked back outside. I rushed across the porch and down the wooden steps to the grass and immediately I felt sick to my stomach. Blood-vomit rose in my throat, up through my mouth and out through my lips. I spewed it everywhere. Tears welled in my eyes too and before long crimson droplets rushed down my cheeks. The sun was high in the sky and hot against my skin. Rays of light smoldered against me and I could feel the continual cremation close at hand. I hurried toward the woods.

"Hope!" Christian shouted from behind me.

I stopped walking and turned around, tendrils of smoke swiftly rising from the exposed flesh on my arms.

He grimaced at my bloodied appearance. "What happened to you?" he asked concerned.

I shook my head and cried even harder. I was a mess. Smears of scarlet red blood spilled from my eyes while spots of regurgitated blood stained my clothes and skin.

"Hope!" he exclaimed wrapping his arm around my shoulders. He led me into the shadows.

"Thank you," I sobbed.

"What's that matter? Why are you crying?"

I shrugged and continued to cry.

He scrutinized the speckles of fresh blood on my shirt. "And what's this?" he asked. "Were you sick again?"

I nodded.

"Oh Hope," he said tightening his hold. "Tell me what's wrong?" His face was distressed.

"You want to know?" I sniveled frustrated.

"Yes."

"You really want to know?"

"I do!"

"Well for starters you became human."

"And this is all because of me?" His voice was diffident.

"No. You becoming human was like the cherry on top," I whimpered. I sank my head in my hands. "God Christian. I made so many mistakes."

"Mistakes? What mistakes?"

"You were right all along. The residuals aren't worth it. I never should have shifted through time as much as I did. I never should have gone inside their blood—"

"Whose blood?"

"Yours...Reina's...Robert Salazar's...oh god!" I groaned sniveling.

"Who are you talking about?"

I withdrew from him. "I've been back in time, back through blood, ahead in time and even crossed lines with another shifter. I was connected to the beast and now I know why." My eyes glimmered. "I know the truth about the Fairchild family, Christian. *The maternal side of my family.* I know what I am now."

"You do?"

"It's not hard to figure out when your legacy includes witchcraft and ancestors begin lynched for their power!"

"Hope," he uttered remorsefully.

"Did you know? About the magic in me?"

"I knew about Moira's magic and your mother's too."

I rolled my eyes. "When will you realize that not telling the truth is just as bad as lying?!"

"Oh Hope, I was—"

"Save it," I interrupted. "To be honest the magic isn't even the biggest of my concerns right now."

"It's not?"

I shook my head.

"Then tell me." his voice was desperate.

I looked him in the eyes. "I'm..."

"You're..."

"I'm..."

"Yes..."

"I'm pregnant Christian."

His jaw dropped instantly. He paled like a ghost.

"Christian?" I said concerned.

He was frozen, like a statue, and then suddenly the corners of his mouth curved up into the most radiant smile. "Pregnant?" he uttered.

"Yeah, but after what I just saw Eva go through I wish the hell I wasn't!"

"Hope!" he exclaimed throwing his arms around me and squeezing. "I'm...I'm...speechless!" He beamed with happiness. "When did you know? *How* did you know? Why didn't you tell me right away?"

"I didn't know at first. And then I was sick all the time. Eva and I compared stories and Rosa confirmed it. I didn't tell you right away because I didn't know how you'd react."

He kissed me on the lips. "My god!" he shouted. "I can't believe how happy I am right now!"

"Happy?" I asked perplexed.

"Of course happy!" He leapt toward me and swept me off my feet.

"Christian!" I exclaimed hanging from his arms, "Be careful."

"You're right. I must remember to be more careful with you. Especially now that you're—"

"Actually I meant you!"

"Me?"

"You aren't indestructible anymore. You could pull something or break something."

He laughed easing me back down onto my feet again. He looked me in the eyes and grinned. "Who else knows?"

"Like I said, Rosa and Eva and now you."

"I have to tell Baptiste and Henry." He grinned like a child. "Henry will be ecstatic! He's going to be a great-grandfather!"

I smiled.

"And Eva and Baptiste's son will have a cousin!"

I half-smiled.

"And you and I will—"

"Stop," I interrupted. "I can't do this."

"Do what?"

"Be all happy and gushy."

He stroked my arm. "Why?"

I shrugged. "Because I'm scared, alright."

"Scared," he laughed. "I don't know anyone stronger than you! You have nothing to be scared of—in fact I didn't even think you could be scared anymore!"

"Neither did I. Then I realized I come for a lineage of witches! I'm having a baby and you're a human now! Oh my god Christian I've never been more scared in all my life!"

He wrapped his arms around me again and sighed. "You're not alone in any of this."

I pressed my head to his chest and let the strident thump of his strong heart ease my soul. "Something's about to happen," I uttered.

"Like what?"

"I don't know, but I feel as though we're on the cusp of it. It's something big and it's brewing as we speak."

"Bigger than you and me having a baby!" he teased.

"Yes," I replied stoically, "much bigger. And quite honestly the thought of whatever it could be scares the crap out of me!"

His expression hardened. A moment later I heard the sound of footfalls nearing. I peered over the edge of Christian's body and saw Baptiste approaching.

"Christian," he called.

"B," I he greeted. "How's the baby?"

He beamed instantly. "It's been a hell of a day hasn't it?" Baptiste smiled.

"Yeah," I agreed. "It certainly has."

"What can we do for you?" Christian asked.

"I just got off the phone with Gabe. He needs you at La Fuente tonight."

"*Tonight?*"

Baptiste nodded. "After everything we've all been through it seems hard to believe that we still have a shop to run, but we do. And now that we've got more mouths to feed..."

"One less counting me," Christian smirked.

Baptiste's face furrowed. "So it's true then?"

Christian nodded. "But just because I've changed *what* I am, doesn't mean I've changed *who* I am."

Baptiste shook his head taken aback.

Christian sighed. "I know we need more supply. I'll head over to the shop right away. You get back to Ambrose House. You should be with your family."

"Thanks bro," Baptiste said. "I mean it."

Christian nodded in reply. A moment later Baptiste was headed toward the house again.

"Do you really mean that?" I asked.

"What?"

"That you're still the same?"

He nodded.

I raised an eyebrow at him and glared.

"C'mere," he said tugging me nearer. He pressed his warm lips to my cheek and kissed me. "I'm still the same Christian you fell in love with...only a little more fragile is all."

My expression eased. The heat from his body made me melt against him. "What's it like?" I whispered.

"What?"

"Being human."

He smiled and placed a gentle kiss against my lips. "You've forgotten already?"

I laughed. "No, I just wanted to know what it's like for you..."

He grinned. "It's different."

"How different?"

"Not as easy as I remembered."

I laughed.

"I've already injured myself, bled profusely, chased down the woman I love, nearly had my heart broken and discovered I'm to become a father! This being human thing is highly complicated."

I grinned.

He kissed me on the forehead. "I have to go," he said.

"Oh why," I complained.

"Because my sweet, life keeps on living whether you're human or vampire..."

"Don't be long," I pleaded.

"I won't."

"Be back before sunrise okay?"

"I'll try." He turned away from me and started walking toward the house when suddenly he stopped.

"What's wrong?" I asked, concerned.

He smiled. "I just realized I can't run to work anymore. I guess I'll have to take the bike!"

I put my hands on my hips. "Well I could carry you..."

Christian grinned. He was beautiful. I leaned against a nearby tree and watched him walk across the grass toward his motorcycle. The twilight sun shone against his pinkish colored skin with radiance. Humanity looked good on him. A moment later the sound of him revving his engine resonated. In an instant he was off. I was alone, left with only my thoughts and our unborn child to keep me company.

54. Tattoo

I hated alone time. I needed to be with the man I loved. I needed to be with Christian again.

It was early in the morning in the middle of the night. No one was around. I pushed open the front door to La Fuente and let the sound of silence fill me with bliss. I was delighted when no bells rang. There was nothing left to remind of me of the time that Maxim and Sakura wrecked havoc on Perish. As I stepped foot inside the shop, I realized that everyone, with the exception of me, had lost their memory of Reina. No one would ever know of her deceit and the trouble that she caused when she arrived on our shores. While the beast, however, was still very much a part of our collective memory I was happy knowing that his death absolved him; he was finally free to be with his beloved Annabelle again.

Things felt as though they were somewhat coming together. Our enemies had been vanquished, while or allies had seemingly returned home. Ryan and her friends needed somewhere safe to stay and Ambrose House could be that place for them for now anyway.

"Hope!" Christian shouted noticing me instantly.

"I couldn't be without you," I admitted rushing toward him.

"I'm glad," he said taking me into his arms.

"Is there anyone here?"

He flipped the sign in the window to CLOSED and grinned. "Everyone's gone home. It's just you and me. We're all alone."

"But I thought La Fuente was always open!"

"Not tonight," he insisted seductively. He took my hand and led me toward the black leather couch in the corner of the room. "Sit," he said softly. I sat and looked up at him. He smiled, pulled off his shirt and tossed it to the floor. My eyes widened. He was gorgeous. He dropped to his knees and pressed his hands on my legs. The heat from his touch enlivened me instantly.

"I want you to do something for me," he said.

"What?" I replied eagerly.

"Tattoo me."

"Tattoo you?" I laughed.

"Yeah."

"I don't know how to tattoo."

"I'll teach you." He ran his hands up my thighs and grinned. I practically melted inside. He twisted his fingers around the belt loops on my jeans and tugged. "C'mon," he urged.

I rose to my feet and followed him. "Where are we going?" I asked.

"Over here," he said leading me to the back end of the room. We stopped when we reached his tattooing station.

"Oh Christian. I don't think I can do this."

He eased me into the chair and smiled. "You can do anything," he said.

He pulled out a bottle of black ink and popped open the lid. He stacked a couple of tiny plastic cups on a silver tray and squeezed some ink into each.

"There," he said closing the lid. "You'll only be needing black ink for this."

"Don't make me do this."

He grinned before grabbing hold of his machine. I watched as he inserted a new sharp needle through the barrel. A moment later he pressed on the foot pedal. The machine came alive instantly.

I covered my face with my hands.

"It's fun. You'll see," he uttered. He took his foot off the pedal and the machine suddenly stopped. He grabbed a sheet of paper from the corner of his table.

"What's that?"

"The stencil."

He turned to show it to me. It was a black blossom with drooping bell shaped flowers.

"Flower of Death," I said taken aback. I knew the undeniable power of that particular flower. I'd seen it implemented in a resurrection and now even a full-blown cure.

"Oh C'mon Hope," he urged. "I want you to give it to me."

I bit my lip.

"Please," he insisted. "I'll talk you through it."

"Christian," I groaned.

"Please," he implored grinning.

"Fine. What do I do?"

He smiled. "Put the stencil on me first." He pointed to his right shoulder blade. "Here."

I took the stencil of the flower and pressed it into place. A moment later I peeled off the paper. The outline was perfect. "Do you want to see the stencil?" I asked.

"I trust you."

"You shouldn't."

He smiled. "Now," he said. "Take your machine."

"Should I wear gloves?"

He laughed. I laughed too.

"Take your machine," he continued, "and dip it in ink."

I grasped Christian's cold, hard machine in the palm of my hand and moved it toward the plastic cups.

"Not too much ink or it will spurt everywhere!"

I nodded at him and then slipped the tip of the needle just slightly beneath the surface.

"Good. Now press on the foot pedal."

I pressed my foot against the pedal. The machine buzzed instantly in response. "Now what?"

"Now do it Hope."

I pulled my foot off the peal. The machine silenced. "I can't."

"You can. You've seen me do it a thousand times. You know what to do." His voice was soft. "Just try."

I listened to the steady thump of his human heart. *Ba-boom. Ba-boom.* The intensity of the moment was making me nauseous. *"Do it*

Hope," I told myself inside my thoughts. I swallowed hard and stiffened my spine. If I could travel through time then I could definitely do a tattoo damn it! I pressed my foot down on the pedal. The machine buzzed like a cicada on a hot day. I leaned in close, toward Christian's soft skin and pushed it into him.

"Oww!" he shouted.

I withdrew immediately and took my foot off the pedal.

"It hurts! A lot!"

I laughed.

"It's not funny."

"It's funny to me!"

"Hope," he snarled.

"Let's not do this Christian," I pleaded.

He took a deep breath and refocused. "We're doing this. I'm ready now."

"If you insist." I pressed my foot on the pedal. The machine came alive again. I moved my needle to his shoulder blade and started tracing the stencil on his skin.

"Good," he uttered wincing.

"How do you know if it's good?" I taunted.

"It feels right. I knew you'd been paying attention watching me."

I grinned with pride and eased my hand along the length of the shaft.

"Careful around the stamens," he uttered. "They're tiny and tricky."

I tightened my grasp on the machine and made a conscious effort to exact every minute detail.

"Good," he sighed the moment my hand eased.

I released my foot from the pedal. The buzzing stopped. "I think I'm done," I said surprised.

"Thank friggin' god!" he shouted relieved. "I had no idea tattoos hurt this much! Why do so many humans get these things?"

I laughed, put down the machine and sighed. Small trickles of blood pooled at the tender site of his new tattoo. I gingerly inhaled the scent of his blood in the air and smiled. My body responded instantly. My fangs shot through my gums and I yearned for a taste of him. I leaned in close and licked his sweet skin with my tongue. I moaned.

"Hope!" he said turning around. "What do you think you're doing?"

I pulled away and smirked.

"Don't get any ideas..."

I smiled. "I wanted to seal it with a kiss."

He smiled back.

I ran my icy hands up his warm arms and leaned in close again. I kissed him on the collarbone before working my lips across his neck and toward his shoulder blade.

"Be gentle," he uttered nervously.

I grinned, his tender plea heightening my wanton hunger. I tongued the crimson droplets of blood that surrounded his tattoo and smirked. The taste of him was divine; incredibly pure and unfathomably pleasing. I wanted more. I ran my tongue against the sharp edges of my fangs and readied myself to bite down into him, when suddenly I stopped. I didn't need to ruin this moment. I needed to learn control and now was as good of a time as any to start practicing.

I withdrew from his skin and swallowed my urge to indulge. I reached for my purse and pulled out the cracked antique hand mirror that belonged to my grandmother. "The moment of truth," I uttered handing it to him.

Christian grinned and took the mirror into his hand. He eyed his reflection and laughed.

"What?" I said intrigued.

"Look."

I leaned in close and studied his reflection. "You're so vibrant!" I exclaimed. His reflection was bold and authentic and beautiful.

"And look at you," he uttered eyeing my likeness aside him in the mirror. "A pale princess," he grinned. "My golden-haired snow white."

I beamed in reply. He laid the mirror on the table.

"Don't you even want to see the tattoo?" I insisted.

He laughed. "I'd almost forgotten!" He heaved a sigh. "See Hope, you unhinge me with your beauty." He grabbed the mirror and held it over his head to see the tattoo. "Not bad."

"Not bad?" I retorted defensively. "It's remarkable! There are no jagged lines...no blotches...no—"

He laid the mirror down on the table and pulled me close in a single sweep. He and kissed me on the mouth and sighed. "It's perfect," he whispered. "Thank you my sweet."

"Well you're welcome."

He withdrew from me, picked up his shirt from the floor and pulled it over head. "Hey," he said peering out the window. "It's almost sunrise."

"Oh sunrise," I lamented; the sound of the crocodile's tick tock faintly resonated in the back of my mind.

"Can we watch it?" he asked eagerly.

"Watch what?"

"Sunrise."

I shrugged.

"Please," he pleaded. "I want you to watch the sunrise with me."

I nodded grudgingly.

"C'mon," he said grabbing my hand. He led me through La Fuente and outside the front door.

The air was warm and the sky was alive with pinks and oranges. Color was quickly infusing the world around us. Dawn was breaking and although I hated to admit it—it was beautiful.

"My first sunrise as a human again," he uttered. His smile was bigger than ever and incredibly infectious. I started smiling too. "You look lovely in the sunrise," he whispered. He turned toward me and ran his arm around my shoulders.

"I'll have to leave when it's up you know."

"I know."

"My tolerance has improved, but it's not there yet."

"I know," he grinned kissing me on the cheek. "We'll work on it together."

I grinned.

"I'll support you with whatever you need."

"You will?"

"Yes Hope, whatever you need, whatever you want—'till the end of time!"

"Whatever?" I grinned and stroked my belly.

He looked down at my stomach and smiled. "Whatever," he said reaching out to touch me.

"Don't," I urged stopping him. "I don't want to go anywhere right now. I just want to stay here with you for a while."

"Go anywhere?" he said perplexed.

"When you touch my stomach, *it* moves me through time."

"*It?*"

"*It,*" I nodded smiling. "Our baby Christian."

His face enlivened. "Our baby can time-shift?"

I nodded. "In the woods, when I kept disappearing on you, it wasn't me doing it—it was the baby."

Christian's face flushed, a surge of panic suddenly overwhelming him.

"Don't worry," I insisted. "It's a lot of power I know. I need to learn how to harness it. I'm sick of all these residuals and butterfly effects."

"Good," he said.

I nodded.

"A time-shifter huh?"

I smiled.

"So our baby can already travel into the past."

"Not the past. The future."

His eyes widened.

I stroked my belly and grinned. Christian's face paled instantly. Even though I couldn't read his thoughts any longer it was easy to see that he was already over-analyzing the risks.

"Hey," I said touching his arm. "Don't think. Let's just live in the moment." I reached for his hand. We laced our fingers together.

"I love you," he whispered pulling me against him. His warm breath was like heaven to my skin.

I smiled and wrapped my arms around him. "I love you too," I whispered.

"Hope," he said.

"What?"

"Do that thing again."

"What thing?"

"*My thing.* You know, making time slow to a stop."

I bit my lip.

"Please."

"I'm not even sure I'd know how to do it again."

He smiled, brought my hand to his lips and kissed it. "Just try," he pleaded. He stroked the side of my face. His touch was warm and filled me with delight.

"Okay," I said. "I'll try." I fluttered my eyelashes and suddenly the world slowed to a stop.

"You did it!" he grinned.

I tightened my grasp on his hands. "We did it," I whispered, "together."

He leaned in to kiss me. The touch of his lips to mine assured me that everything was going to be okay. Christian and I were destined for one another. He was the beautiful stranger from my dreams and the one who bestowed my everlasting immortality. He was my Tin Man with a strong beating heart and the soon-to-be father of my unborn child. I loved him more than anything in the world whether human or vampire. I was prepared to stand by him and brave whatever challenges were yet to come. I smiled inside knowing that the future really was ours. The possibilities seemed endless! But most of all I was thrilled that we could still live in our moment of happiness together—happily whatever after.